Never

RESCUE A

Rogue

OTHER BOOKS BY VIRGINIA HEATH

THE MERRIWELL SISTERS
Never Fall for Your Fiancée

The Discerning Gentleman's Guide
Redeeming the Reclusive Earl
Miss Bradshaw's Bought Betrothal
The Scoundrel's Bartered Bride
Her Enemy at the Altar
His Mistletoe Wager
That Despicable Rogue

THE WILD WARRINERS SERIES
A Warriner to Protect Her
A Warriner to Rescue Her
A Warriner to Tempt Her
A Warriner to Seduce Her

THE KING'S ELITE SERIES
The Mysterious Lord Millcroft
The Uncompromising Lord Flint
The Disgraceful Lord Gray
The Determined Lord Hadleigh

THE TALK OF THE BEAU MONDE
The Viscount's Unconventional Lady
The Marquess Next Door
How Not to Chaperon a Lady

Never

RESCUE A

Rogue

MERRIWELL SISTERS BOOK 2

Virginia Heath

ST. MARTIN'S GRIFFIN

NEW YORK

First published in the United States by St. Martin's Griffin, an imprint of St. Martin's Publishing Group

NEVER RESCUE A ROGUE. Copyright © 2022 by Susan Merritt. All rights reserved. Printed in the United States of America. For information, address St. Martin's Publishing Group, 120 Broadway, New York, NY 10271.

www.stmartins.com

Designed by Gabriel Guma

Library of Congress Cataloging-in-Publication Data

Names: Heath, Virginia, 1968– author.
Title: Never rescue a rogue / Virginia Heath.
Description: First Edition. | New York : St. Martin's Griffin, 2022. |
    Series: The Merriwell sisters ; 2
Identifiers: LCCN 2022017197 | ISBN 9781250787781 (trade paperback) |
    ISBN 9781250787798 (ebook)
Subjects: LCGFT: Mystery fiction. | Novels.
Classification: LCC PR6108.E1753 N49 2022 | DDC 823/.92—dc23
LC record available at https://lccn.loc.gov/2022017197

Our books may be purchased in bulk for promotional, educational, or business use. Please contact your local bookseller or the Macmillan Corporate and Premium Sales Department at 1-800-221-7945, extension 5442, or by email at MacmillanSpecialMarkets@macmillan.com.

First Edition: 2022

10 9 8 7 6 5 4 3 2 1

For my tenacious and indomitable daughter Katie
A journalist who is convinced every heroine I write
is based on her
At least this time you share a job title and a way
with words, Pumpkin

Chapter One

Being a thoroughly disappointing son in every aspect of his life was a responsibility Giles Sinclair took seriously. So seriously that if a single week passed without his father's irate censure of his inappropriate behavior, he considered himself a complete failure. After a worryingly quiet few weeks with only one minor skirmish over a reckless wager that had found the Duke of Harpenden's increasingly deaf ears, he was determined to make tonight's expensive party a resounding and scandalous success in time for his weekly audience with his disapproving sire on the morrow.

He sipped his apple juice, strategically disguised in a tall crystal flute so no one would realize he was stone-cold sober, while he watched the eclectic crowd and allowed himself a rare moment of satisfaction. The great and the good, the famous and the infamous, were all crammed into the fashionable Egyptian-themed ballroom of his Bloomsbury town house. Two hours in and it was all going swimmingly, with several of the more outrageous guests already three sheets to the wind. In another hour or so, the majority would be tipsy and that always made for good entertainment. By the time they all poured out onto the pavement in the small hours, it was imperative that a goodly handful had thoroughly disgraced themselves to ensure his latest and most hastily arranged Annual Reprobates Ball was more shocking than the last. Another point of petty principle and, frankly, the only rebellion he had against all the lies his sire had told the world. Lies that had ruined Giles's life the day it started but which his conscience would never allow him to refute.

"I want every champagne glass filled to the brim, Dalton, and not with that cheap stuff you procured from your shady contacts at the docks. Use the Veuve Clicquot with abandon and make no secret of it." Nothing inflamed the duke hotter than reckless spending on frivolous hedonism. Especially if he thought he was funding it all.

Not that he was, of course.

As a point of principle, Giles hadn't spent a single farthing of his allowance in a decade. Instead, like Robin Hood, he covertly put it to work repairing all his father's many misdeeds, anonymously righting wrongs while he lived off his own wits and canny business acumen. And he had done a bloody good job of it, too, enough that he could afford to fill every bathtub in Bloomsbury with the finest French champagne if he wanted and still have change to spare on another shiny new pair of Hoby boots.

Not that the old man knew any of that, either.

Nobody did.

Such restraint, dogged determination, philanthropy, and hard work would only encourage people to reevaluate him, and that wouldn't do at all when being underestimated came in so very handy. And it went without saying that his sordid little secret would thoroughly ruin his already atrocious reputation when his father despaired of that most of all. A two-faced irony that never failed to amuse him.

"The Veuve Clicquot?" His butler-cum-valet rolled his only eye. "Even though half the guests are already so drunk they wouldn't know Veuve Clicquot from horse piss? It's a dreadful waste of good champagne, if you ask me."

"But I didn't ask you, did I, Dalton? I never do, yet you bore me with your unwelcome opinions regardless." Giles grabbed a passing canapé before he waved his wholly unsuitable servant away. "Bubbles for everyone and that is an order."

"Yes, my lord." With his customary insolence, Dalton tugged his forelock then strode off, his intricately carved peg leg clonking loudly on the solid marble floor Giles had had imported at vast expense from Italy.

Both things had sent the duke into a rage.

The marble tiles because they had cost an arm and a leg, and his butler because while Dalton wasn't completely devoid of one arm, alongside the eye and the leg, he had lost a couple of fingers on his left hand.

Dalton had nobly mislaid all those unfortunate body parts as a young sailor at the Battle of Trafalgar but was paid handsomely to solemnly tell anyone who happened to inquire that he didn't like to talk of his former life as a pirate, now that he was trying to be respectable.

As a bevy of liveried footmen distributed freshly filled glasses amongst his guests, Giles sensed her before she spoke, or rather sniffed her. The heady scent of fat summer roses tinged with peach and the merest smidgen of vanilla was as unique a perfume as the unconventional and vexing woman who wore it.

"You will be delighted to learn that Lady Sewell and that awful Russian count you insist on inviting to everything are in the midst of a tryst in your music room."

She had a penchant for bold, fashionable gowns despite her desire to blend into the wall, and tonight's was particularly lovely. The ivory silk skimmed her curves in all the right places while the saucy flashes of red at the hem and the big ribbon that highlighted her trim waist complemented her dark hair to perfection. As was her way, that hair was arranged in a sophisticated but asymmetrical style that went completely against the current fashion for symmetry but suited her regardless, for she wasn't so much a woman who marched to the beat of her own drum but one who made it seem as if everyone else were out of step. She was, as always, stunning—not that he would ever tell her, of course. "I suppose that shocking incident is bound to feature in your newspaper tomorrow, harridan?"

"As usual, I have no earthly idea what you are talking about." Miss Diana Merriwell sipped her champagne with artful nonchalance as she gazed at the sea of twirling silk on the dance floor rather than at him. "But that is hardly a surprise." She always delivered her insults deadpan for maximum effect, and that never failed to make her feline green eyes sparkle. "You rarely make any sense at the best of times, my dear Lord Bellingham, and I confess, I have long given up any hope of you ever doing so. If you weren't so inextricably linked to my brother-in-law, I would have washed my hands of the chore of you last winter—but alas . . ." She sighed as if merely knowing him was a huge inconvenience. "You continue to linger on the periphery of my life like a bad smell."

Giles took no offense at her words. In the last twelve months she had said far worse and so had he, because sparring was what they did.

"Then you flatly deny all of your insightful contributions to *The London Tribune*'s gossip column of late?"

"As if the establishment would ever trust a mere woman to write the news."

"But you are Diana—Goddess of the Hunt and Hunter of the Truth."

She stifled a yawn. "I simply edit some of the stories for spelling and grammar as a way to pass the time. How do you aristocrats stand the monotonous boredom of an inane life of leisure?" Another well-placed barb that made him smile. She loved to put him in his place. Nothing here impressed her.

"And there I was, quietly impressed with your journalistic aplomb, but alas . . ." He stared at the dance floor, too, as if he were bored stiff with it all. "Had I known you had no real press credentials whatsoever and are merely a nitpicking grammarian, I never would have invited you here tonight. And now I am peeved, for if you do not smear all of this evening's shocking scandals over your tawdry paper tomorrow, then who will?"

"A mystery, to be sure—but I am certain you will not have to worry. When one courts scandal like you do, Giles, word inevitably gets around." She slanted him a knowing glance. "And fast, too . . . so your father is bound to be spouting steam from his ears in time for your audience with him tomorrow, exactly as you intended."

Her canny intelligence always grated. "As usual, I have no earthly idea what you are talking about, either, Diana." The more he got to know her, the more he became convinced she read him like a book, and that really galled him. Because Giles liked to think he was always the canniest person in any room and several paces ahead of the crowd—but she was always hot on his heels. Or more often, he trailed on hers. "Hardly a surprise when you rarely make any sense at the best of times, either. You do know I only tolerate you on sufferance because my best friend married your sister, don't you? Although it is still a mystery to me why he aligned himself with such a bunch of lowly commoners." He pulled a face as he sipped his drink, even though his lips were twitching because he loved to put her in her place, too. She wore her common roots like a badge of honor and sometimes wielded them like a shield to ward off unwelcome attention. "We blue bloods must ensure the purity of our species, or civilization as we know it will end and chaos will ensue."

Like him, she wasn't the least bit offended by the insult. "Then you flatly deny going out of your way to annoy your father purely for sport?"

It wasn't for sport. It was necessity. The only avenue available to punish the duplicitous scoundrel for all his many unconscionable sins.

"It is hardly my fault if he finds me disappointing, any more than it is my fault I was born that way." An outright lie and he suspected she knew it, but he would rather die than let her glimpse any of the sorry truth.

While it was true the insufferable Duke of Harpenden had always considered his only son unworthy in every possible sense, Giles had used out-and-out rebellion as a defense mechanism long before he had discovered the *Dirty Secret* and that he really was unworthy in every possible sense. By then, it had been too late to rejoice in that enlightening fact. The dreadful die had been cast, the hand of fate had been dealt, and there really wasn't a damn thing he could do about it apart from the one thing that would blow his entire world to smithereens. A prospect he wouldn't have minded in the slightest if it were just himself it affected. Unfortunately, the awful, unpal-

atable, and toxic truth had dire consequences for a great many innocent people, and more unfortunately, he had failed to inherit his
father's unfeeling, granite heart. If he had, he would have lit the
fuse himself then cheerfully pulled up a chair and enjoyed an entire
plate of biscuits while he watched the illustrious name of Harpenden
implode spectacularly in the full glare of the public gaze.

"I hear rumor that you are about to do something your father
wholeheartedly approves of . . . and that finally, congratulations
are in order." Her sip of champagne was much too nonchalant this
time, as if she were fishing, though for the life of him he couldn't
think what for.

"Congratulations?"

"Does the name Miss Dahlia Regis ring any bells?"

"Doe-eyed Dahlia the dumpy draper's daughter?"

"Surely you mean desirable Dahlia with the newly doubled
dowry?" She stared him dead in the eye. "Or perhaps determined-
to-be-a-duchess Dahlia would be a better description if the rumors
I hear about the pair of you are true?"

He couldn't help but laugh at the preposterousness of her suggestion. "Surely you do not think *I* am romantically linked to Miss
Regis? For she is far too proper for my dissolute tastes." And far
too vapid. Daft Dahlia was her nickname in the gentleman's clubs
because she could not converse without prompts from her pushy
father, but he was too much of a gentleman to repeat that moniker
outside of one.

"Not linked, Giles. *Engaged.*"

"You need more reliable sources, Diana."

Two flummoxed dark eyebrows kissed in consternation. "You
are not engaged?"

"It is not the sort of horror a man forgets. And if I were about to sacrifice my liberty to the fetid prison of the parson's trap, which I absolutely never will, I would not choose a future duchess incapable of even spelling the word *duchess* without assistance. Poor Dahlia is as dim as a pauper's candle, bless her, and where is the challenge in that?"

In truth, Giles had always felt sorry for the girl. Her shameless social-climbing father had touted her about season after season, wafting her ever-increasing dowry under every titled gentleman's nose as bait so unsubtly, he made the poor thing a laughingstock when nobody ever took it. Apparently, even fortune hunters had standards, which the stuttering, sweet-tempered Miss Regis had always failed to meet.

Diana touched his arm. An unusual and sympathetic gesture from a woman who worked hard to mask every emotion except disdain, and a touch he typically felt everywhere because she had always had such an inexplicable and profound effect on him.

"Her father and yours have dined together twice this last week alone." She leaned in to whisper in case anyone overheard. "Once at the Regis house on Bruton Place and once at White's. I also have a reliable source in the legal trade who is convinced the settlements have already been drawn up and signed."

"Signed?" He didn't doubt the validity of the information. Since *The London Tribune* had employed Diana, amongst others, the incendiary quality of their stories had improved. With her spearheading the gossip column and the mysterious Sentinel dominating the news, the paper was a force to be reckoned with to such an extent many ne'er-do-wells, as well as all the other rival newspapers, now feared them. Only last month, one fortune-hunting rake had been forced to flee town on the back of one of *The Tri-bune*'s exposés.

Diana nodded. "I have another lady who claims Mrs. Regis was heard bragging of her daughter's imminent elevation to the highest echelons of society only yesterday at a tea party."

He huffed out a withering sigh as the ridiculous rumor suddenly made perfect sense. "The duke has been trying to marry me off for years. Every month he puts forward another candidate for my consideration." It was his solemn duty apparently, to furnish the Harpenden line with more heirs to continue it in perpetuity, unrepentant that in doing so Giles would be perpetuating his sire's lie. Every well-bred young debutante had been paraded in front of him for a decade. Clearly he was now scraping the barrel if poor Miss Dahlia Regis was the next contender, as she was neither. "They are always presented to me as a fait accompli." Along with the bellowed demand that he do his duty.

The Sinclairs had been obsessed with duty from time immemorial, and choosing not to do it was a cardinal sin, no matter how noble the reasons or how tenuous the legality. Dukes begat heirs who begat heirs without question, and the duke expected Giles to ignore the *Dirty Secret* and do the same without complaint. Although his sire had never had the nerve to have actual settlements drawn up before.

"Madame Devy is making Miss Regis's trousseau." There was something odd swirling in Diana's lovely eyes. Concern perhaps. Regret? Pity? "She has been instructed to embroider every garment with these initials." She rummaged in her tiny, beaded, delightfully frivolous evening bag before she passed him a small square of cloth. On it were the intertwined letters *D*, *G*, and *S*. The

D he presumed was the bride's Christian name; the *S* had to be for Sinclair. Giles couldn't think of another fraudulent future duke with a surname of that letter, and the *G* sealed his fate. "The bride told Madame Devy in a quiet aside that although her parents had said she was always destined for the nobility, she still could not quite believe she was destined to be a duchess. She claimed to be giddy from the excitement of it all."

Giles stared at the embroidered letters, feeling wretched. "Who told you that?"

"Madame Devy herself . . . she owes me a favor . . . I am sorry, Giles, but my sources are reliable. I wouldn't have brought it to you otherwise." There was definitely pity in those vexing green eyes now—although probably more for the bride than him.

Poor Dahlia.

That his father's callous determination to see Giles wed was enough to give that unfortunate, sweet woman such cruel false hope. But how blasted typical of him to leave his disappointing son to be the one to dash it.

"I am not marrying Dahlia Regis!" Or anyone ever, for that matter. Thanks to the *Dirty Secret*, he couldn't—wouldn't—inflict that cruel punishment on anyone.

"My contact at *The Times* says the announcement goes out in two days." She squeezed his arm again, making every nerve ending stand to attention. "I thought you should know."

And with that she disappeared back off into the crowd; part of it but separate, as was her way.

Chapter Two

At ten the next morning, an hour before their regular appointment, and a good three hours before he usually turned up for it, Giles hammered on the duke's front door.

The old man had gone too far this time!

He hadn't slept a wink last night, worrying about how crushed Dahlia would be when all her illusions were shattered and hating the fact she was going to be made a laughingstock all over again. That he would be inadvertently responsible for that weighed heavily on his mind, too. It made no difference that he'd had no hand in the duplicity, had made no promises or even spoken to the girl in at least five years. The unpalatable falsehood had been done in his name; therefore, once he had said his piece to his malicious, lying sire, he would call upon poor Miss Regis himself to break the bad news as gently as he was able.

An onerous task he was dreading.

"Lord Bellingham?" The butler was clearly stunned to see him. "We weren't expecting you for hours."

Giles was all out of silly, flippant comments. "Where is he?"

"In his study, my lord . . ." The butler tried to keep up with him as he stalked down the hallway. "Allow me to announce you . . . please . . . you know how he hates to be interrupted without prior warning." The servant practically threw himself against his master's door as a barricade before Giles could storm in. His expression pleading. "Please, my lord . . . I would urge you to remember that, in your absence, it is the staff who will inevitably suffer his wrath afterward."

Giles knew that better than anyone and would normally do his utmost to mitigate their suffering, but today it couldn't be helped. "Step aside, Carruthers, and make yourself scarce. I daresay this morning will not be pretty for any of us."

Carruthers's face blanched but he nodded in resignation, too used to the noxious family dynamics to doubt that for a second. "I am sorry, my lord."

"Not as sorry as I am."

But much to his astonishment, the duke did not explode in temper when Giles flung open the door. His eyes flicked up coldly, then returned to his ledger and remained there even when Giles shouted as he loomed over his desk.

"Dahlia Regis! Have you no thought for anyone's feelings whatsoever that you would embroil an innocent lady in *our* feud and *your* deception so callously?"

The duke's pen scratched some figures unperturbed. "Close the door, Carruthers." Only when it clicked shut did he deign to look at Giles properly, his expression bland for once rather than furious. "Who told you?"

"That is none of your business."

"Just as this is none of yours." He had the gall to pick up his pen again until Giles tried to snatch it away.

"You have already signed the settlements and placed an engagement notice in *The Times*, but apparently *that* is none of my business also?"

"I have long given up all hope of you ever stepping up to do your duty, runt."

"So you thought if you planned every detail of my nuptials behind my back, I might not notice any of it until after the deed was done? The last time I checked, *Your Grace*"—Giles had never been given leave to call the man Father, nor ever felt that emotional connection with the man to want to—"a groom has to be present at his wedding for the ceremony to be legally binding!"

"The groom will be present!" The duke stood, his mouth curled in the familiar snarl of raw hatred as he slammed his fist onto the desk. "Because the groom is me!"

"What?" Giles could not have been more surprised if the old man had performed a naked dance on the table. "*You* are marrying Dahlia Regis?" He took several steps backward as that unsavory news marinated. "You?"

"The settlements have indeed been signed, the bride is delighted, and the announcement in *The Times* will say as much tomorrow."

"But she is younger than me!" A good few years younger. Poor Dahlia might be considered to be mature by debutante standards, but she was still young enough to be the duke's daughter. "She is less than half your age! That is . . . *obscene!*"

"Obscene?" The duke's eyes bulged. "You think I lack the vigor, runt? Or the stamina? I can assure you, I still have plenty of both!" As his father laughed in his face, an image Giles did not want in his mind materialized regardless. Of poor, hapless Dahlia sprawled under the decrepit duke, wide-eyed and mortified as he panted and heaved above her. "I'll have you know I can still sire an heir!"

A statement that made him want to vomit. "As hideous as that foul prospect is to contemplate, it does beggar the question: Why? Unless you are plotting my demise and need a spare."

"I need an heir—not a damn spare boy! A proper heir as a contingency! Sired in legal, irrefutable wedlock for all the world to see!" While Giles reeled at this new and twisted development in the fetid cesspool that had always been their relationship, his father slumped back in the chair looking older and more tired than he had ever seen him despite the customary flash of anger. "The situation is now too precarious to risk leaving the dukedom solely to you . . ."

"The situation has *always* been precarious." His gut churned at this unforeseen and worrying development. "Yet it has never seemed to bother you enough to rectify your lie before today."

Although it had always bothered Giles.

From the moment he had discovered four years ago that his real mother was his father's mistress instead of his wife, the deception had weighed heavily on his mind. It had also spun his world on its axis. Shifted things, altered everything, and denied him the happy future family of his own that he had always dreamed of. And he had such plans for that, but most especially to do everything for his children that his hostile parents had denied him growing up.

"Things change . . ." The old man couldn't look at him. "Needs must. I can no longer risk leaving sleeping dogs lie." The duke stood and began to pace. Wringing his hands in uncertainty when Giles had never witnessed him uncertain before. "If doubt is cast from any quarter, I must ensure my line is secure—even from beyond the grave."

Doubt? Another shocking deviation from the duke's usual insufferable arrogance on the topic when he had never harbored any doubts about the secret coming out before. Something had to have changed.

Something catastrophic.

Giles's head spun as the ominous dawning of his worst nightmare manifested on the horizon like a conquering army. As much as he feared the weight of perpetuating the *Dirty Secret* for a lifetime, the alternative petrified him more. "What's happened?" He sank into a chair as he contemplated the worst, more panicked than he had ever been in his life. People depended on him. Without his mockery of a title, he couldn't help them at all. "Who knows?"

"Nothing . . ." Distracted, the duke stared sightless at the wall. "Nobody knows the truth . . . I am sure of it . . ." As if he realized he had revealed a chink in his impenetrable armor, his jaw hardened. "I merely want a contingency in case something does." He sat and picked up his pen again as if his ledger were more important than this hideous, frightening conversation. "Read nothing more into it than that." The duke waved him away to return to the numbers he put more stock in than anything. "You are dismissed."

Stubborn, arrogant, and secretive to the bitter end—but Giles knew a lie when he saw one. The duke was suddenly scared of something, and that alone was terrifying.

"So despite nothing whatsoever happening to justify your abrupt change of heart"—not that he believed for one second the duke possessed that sympathetic organ—"and nobody knowing enough of the truth to use it against us as a weapon, you now plan to plant a son in the unfortunate Dahlia's belly with all haste just in case somebody at some indeterminate point in the future might announce to everyone that I am, in fact, not your heir but your bastard?"

"Never use that word!" The duke practically foamed at the mouth as his head snapped up. "Never use that filthy word in my presence!"

Giles threw up his palms. "Then what else am I?"

"You are my heir!"

"Of course I am." The bile stung his throat exactly as it always did when he contemplated the unpalatable reality that had been forced upon him. "Never mind that we both know you have willingly committed intentional fraud for three decades to perpetuate that lie!"

"I did what needed to be done." As always, his father's arrogant, dismissive shrug made his blood boil. "Unlike you, I did what my father ordered and put my duty first!"

"Never mind that what you call duty, the law calls illegal." That was met with stony indifference. "If it comes out, you could face criminal charges!"

And so, too, could Giles. Because in a court of law, what else could his silence be viewed as but complicity? It made no difference that he had held his tongue solely for all the many people who depended on the house of Harpenden for their living. The duke was a skinflint as well as a vicious and vindictive tyrant—but his only brother, the real heir, was worse. His feckless uncle Gervais would spend or whore or gamble those livelihoods away in no time. Bleed the ramshackle Shropshire estate dry. That odious, manip-

ulative monster would be a fate worse than death for all those innocent people when they had suffered enough. Undeniable facts that
had all been used ruthlessly by the duke to ensure Giles's silence.
Nobody wanted to give Gervais Sinclair any excuse to leave wherever it was he had been banished to. Especially Giles. That his
silence had also preserved his selfish sire's hide had been a necessary evil for the greater good. "If the wolves are circling and your
Dirty Secret ever gets out, we could both go to jail."

It was telling that the duke did not deny it could get out. "At
worst, you will be stripped of the title you have never had any respect for and get your name rubbished in the press, but as that is a
daily occurrence anyway, I daresay it will not damage your shocking reputation any more than *you* already have. What concerns me
is the legacy of Harpenden."

It said a great deal about their relationship that the duke
put those things over his only son. And there was no doubting
Giles was his son irrespective of who his mother had been. They
were the spitting image of each other. Both tall, both dark. Both
in possession of the legendary dimpled, square Sinclair chin
that graced every ancestral portrait on the crumbling walls of
Harpenden Hall, going all the way back through the centuries to
time immemorial.

"But *you* could go to jail, Your Grace." A scenario that would
be disastrous to their loyal tenants if Daft Dahlia were left in control of everything while the brand-new legitimate heir grew up on
her watch.

"I could . . ." The duke's hand shook slightly as he picked up
his quill again, and that small, uncharacteristic sign of weakness
set more alarm bells ringing. It was too human an emotion for a

man who had never displayed any beyond anger and disgust. "But for a duke it is unlikely. Besides, if it comes to it . . . *if it comes to it* . . ." He sucked in a wobbly breath. "In the first instance I can blame your mother for the deception. Claim I was cuckolded and only just learned of the truth myself. Everyone knew she lacked moral fiber and took lovers on the side."

"Which one? The duchess or the harlot?"

"Watch your mouth, runt!" The duke eyed him coldly through gritted teeth before he returned his attention to the ledgers. "*If* it comes to it, a good lawyer could argue that I was duped—she did leave this house with my child in her womb—as our physician will indeed testify."

"I daresay there is also another physician or witness somewhere in Shropshire who can attest to the fact that she returned with it empty."

"There isn't—of that I made damn sure."

Which was about as much detail as Giles had ever managed to get from the duke on the dubious subject of his birth. Any mention of his actual mother incurred fury and rigid silence. And hatred. A burning, seething hatred, as if he blamed Giles for the crime of being born.

"Then what the blazes is this wedding all about? Unless it is about the dowry?"

Which was bizarre when the duke had always been fastidious over money. Unless the neglected estate had finally caught up with him and the income had dwindled. "Do you need money?"

Because if he did—or rather if the estate and the people who depended upon it did—then Giles would gladly supply some. "Irrespective of our many differences, if you are in some sort of trouble and I can help in any way, I will. You can trust me on that."

"I wouldn't trust you as far as I could throw you! You have no respect for duty. No respect for tradition or history. No respect whatsoever for our bloodline or the cruel sacrifices I made for our legacy!"

"What sacrifices have you ever made for me?" A laughable comment when he had barely seen either of his parents growing up. "You visited Shropshire twice a year to scrutinize your accounts and spared me five minutes each time!"

Another flagrant truth ignored with a disgusted snarl. "You are flippant and irreverent and see everything about the noble house of Harpenden as one big joke. You care more about the silliness in life than the duty that is required to live it properly. You are just like your m . . ."

"Mother?"

The duke's eyes swirled momentarily with something that, if Giles hadn't known better, looked a lot like pain before they shuttered.

He flicked open his pocket watch, then clicked it closed. The customary signal their time was up.

"The wedding is next Saturday." The usual disgusted resentment returned to the old man's expression, as if he could barely look at Giles without feeling incensed. "It goes without saying, runt, that you are not invited."

Chapter Three

Diana's glass paused midway to her lips as her brother-in-law fiddled with the footstool beneath her sister's feet. "You do realize, Hugh, that women have successfully been having babies since the dawn of time? It doesn't require this much constant *diligence* from the father." The way he carried on, anyone would think Minerva were made of glass.

"Not my woman and not my baby." He grabbed another cushion to ensure her ankles were raised even though there was nothing whatsoever swollen about them while the eldest Merriwell smiled soppily back at him. "Both of whom deserve nothing but my constant diligence." In case she strained herself reaching the six inches for it, he passed Minerva her tea. "Do you need anything else, my love?"

Diana groaned aloud. "She wants you to stop fussing, and if she doesn't, she jolly well should, even if only for the rest of our sakes. It's nauseating to watch."

"Then wear a blindfold," said Hugh, kissing his wife's hand. "Or better still a bag. That way your cynical, embittered eyes will be spared the sight of two people hopelessly in love, and we shall all be spared your constant disdain." He wandered to the sideboard to pour himself a brandy. "All that frowning is giving you wrinkles. I swear I have never seen a young woman of three and twenty look so . . . old."

"Looking old is the least of my worries as I shall likely go mad if I have to endure another four months of this!"

"Then rent yourself that little apartment you keep threatening in Cheapside." Hugh's playful gibe earned him a warning glare from her sister.

"Can you not encourage her, Hugh! She wants an excuse to leave, and I want her here with me." Minerva smiled at her. "For as long as I can keep her."

Diana smiled back despite her discomfort, which was not so much at Hugh's comment but at her situation.

She was here for Minerva, who had begged her to stay at least until she found her feet as a countess in this strange new world they now lived in. She was also here for Vee, who needed the comfort of the familiar while she found her feet in society, too. Both her sisters were happy to adapt to the massive change life had thrown at them. Both welcomed it. That Diana didn't made her the anomaly, but no matter how much she tried to fit in, this luxurious new world wasn't hers. Inside, she would always be the scrappy forger's daughter from Clerkenwell, more comfortable amongst the flotsam and jetsam than she ever would be here in Mayfair.

"I think his fussing is romantic." Beside her, the youngest Merriwell sister, Vee—or Venus as she would rather die than be known—sighed, making Diana roll her eyes. "Well, it is romantic! And we should be so lucky to one day find a husband as devoted as Hugh." For Vee, to have a happy life equaled having a husband to care for her, while for Diana the opposite was the case. She much preferred to care for herself. The moment your life was in somebody else's hands, it ceased to be your life and you ceased to be in control of it.

"That shouldn't be a problem, dear." As Hugh saluted the youngest with his glass, Olivia, his mother and now the self-appointed mother of all three sisters, patted Vee's hand, ignoring Diana's theatrical gagging noises. "With your pretty face and lovely disposition, the gentlemen will flock to you the moment we launch you into society." A momentous event that Olivia had also decreed would happen next season before Vee turned nineteen. The impressionable and dewy-eyed Vee was, of course, delighted by the prospect. But she had always had an unshakable fairy-tale view of things even when there had been nothing about their life to make her believe in them.

Being older, Diana, like Minerva, had not had that luxury. While they did their best to shield their baby sister from the harsh realities of life, they had been left to deal with them. For Diana's first seventeen years that had meant battling both poverty and the relentless chore of their feckless father. Then five more interminable, hopeless years of pitiful wages, hunger, and fear after he had gone. There had been a great deal of fear during those dark days. Rent collectors, usurers, unscrupulous employers, silver-tongued seducers, chancers, perverts, liars, swindlers, and downright scoundrels were all part of her day-to-day existence. All seeking to control her like a marionette because, without fail, all the predators crawled out of the woodwork when a down-at-heel young woman ventured into the streets alone.

If those dreadful experiences made her jaded and tough, then

Diana was grateful for them. The world ate naive young ladies for breakfast and spat out the bones—but a savvy one with claws it left well alone.

Olivia peered at Diana over her sherry, and Diana braced herself for the predictable daily diatribe that, although well meant, was unwelcome. "It is still not too late to launch you *this* year, Diana dear. You could still change your mind." It was a constant source of bafflement to her that Diana had turned the opportunity down flat the moment it was tabled. "The season has barely started and there are still plenty of eligible fish swimming in the sea on the lookout for a beautiful bride. Hardly a surprise when this year's crop of debutantes has been so insipid. There isn't a single diamond amongst the lot of them—but there would be if you tossed your hat into the ring."

"Aside from the inescapable fact that I can think of nothing worse"—because, frankly, she found the whole flimsy concept of the debutante ridiculous and would rather flail her flesh with brambles than parade herself for auction—"I fail to understand how you can believe it is still possible to launch a person into society this season when they have been immersed in it completely since the start of the last. I have accompanied you to every ball, Olivia. Been present at every single tedious soiree you have dragged me to."

Hugh's mother was unfazed by that irrefutable logic. "Because being part of society and being launched into it are two entirely different things, dear. The first is merely a presence—the second a *declaration*."

"Of what?" Too late, Diana realized she had walked into a trap.

"Of marriageability, dear. And if you don't mind me saying, and as much as I disagree with my idiot son's cruel gibe about your nonexistent wrinkles, if you leave it much longer, you are in grave danger of being seen an old maid. Then no decent gentleman will want you."

"And that would be a bad thing because?" It all sounded rather perfect to her. Thanks to Minerva's unexpected but advantageous marriage to the Earl of Fareham, which had moved the Merriwell sisters from their depressing two rooms in Clerkenwell to this palatial house, Diana had more freedom and independence than she had ever had. Hot on the heels of their elevation in status, she had been promoted from a lowly pieceworker and poorly paid copy editor at *The London Tribune* to a fully fledged and permanent salaried reporter. A lifelong dream and a huge personal achievement that far surpassed all the trappings of wealth surrounding her now. With her own income and a blossoming career, she was at last the mistress of her own destiny, did things that truly mattered, and thanked her lucky stars for that precious, hard-won freedom daily. In fact, the only conceivable way she would surrender any of it was if they pried it from her cold, dead fingers. Her cold, dead, resoundingly independent old maid's fingers.

Olivia's instant grin was full of mischief. "Because if the decent gentlemen are swarming around you, it allows the *indecent one* you have always had your eye on to cease dragging his feet indefinitely."

Like traitors, her sisters, Hugh, and even Olivia's sensible American second husband, Jeremiah, who had thus far hidden behind his newspaper, all laughed because like her petite and dogged matchmaker, they all believed she harbored a tendre for Lord Bellingham. Worse, they used every possible opportunity to tell her that the charming rogue harbored one for her right back.

As Diana silently seethed, refusing to dignify that flagrant nonsense with a response, Olivia winked and toasted her with her glass. "Rampant jealousy is a great aphrodisiac . . . not that I suspect the pair of you will need one when you eventually stop fighting the obvious attraction."

The absolute last thing she ever wanted was an aphrodisiac!

If her limited experience of that side of things had taught her anything, it was that she was one of those women who was ambivalent to the appeal of men. "Never mind that I would rather shave my head with a cheese grater." It was Lord Bellingham's flagrant attractiveness that made him so very unattractive. He was handsome and charming and knew it and used both mercilessly to get his wicked way. The list of his conquests was as long as her arm, and it would be a cold day in hell before she counted herself amongst them. Even a blithering idiot understood that future dukes from the highest echelons of society and forger's daughters from the very dregs of it did not even breathe the same air, let alone speak the same language.

"My lord . . ." The butler, Payne, suddenly appeared on the Persian rug as if he had been conjured out of thin air. "Lord Bellingham has arrived and wonders if you are at home?"

"Speak of the devil and he doth appear." Olivia wiggled her eyebrows as Diana shot her daggers. "Of course we are at home, Payne! We are *always* at home to Lord Bellingham."

The butler returned with the man himself in tow, still wearing his greatcoat and clutching his hat, a hopeful sign his visit was to be blissfully fleeting.

"My apologies for interrupting your evening." He smiled at the room in general in his customary laid-back manner, but to Diana there was something off about it. Almost as if the casualness he usually wore like his subtle cologne was forced, which was odd. As, too, was his appearance. The Giles she knew was the picture of sartorial elegance who wouldn't be seen dead in public at this time of the night without a proper tailcoat, daring evening waistcoat, and intricately tied cravat. Not only was he clearly dressed for a morning walk, he was too windswept for Giles, and while he was doing a very good impression of a man comfortable in his own skin, his fingers were too agitated as they twisted the brim of his hat. "I wondered if I could steal Hugh away for a few minutes for a quick word?"

"Of course." His friend was up like a shot and by his expression, Hugh, too, thought something was amiss. "Let's go to my study—"

"Is it a dire emergency? Will everything go to hell in a handcart unless you talk this instant? We are about to go in to dinner," said Olivia, as if any deviation from that plan was entirely unacceptable. "Why don't you join us, Giles? Only Cook has made a cheese soufflé to start and, as I am sure a man of your refinement will know, soufflés can be very temperamental beasts."

"It's not an emergency. It's not even important. In fact, it might never come to anything, which makes it all moot anyway." Yet he still waved the invitation away as he turned back toward the door, which was also odd because he had never once turned down food in the year she had known him. The wretch was constantly eating. "I shall come back later . . ."

"What is the point of that if you are here now?" Olivia was typically relentless. "And if the quick word you seek is unimportant, might come to nothing, and *can* wait till later, I see no reason why you cannot eat first, too, if you clearly aren't busy."

"You make a good point." He smiled again, a little baffled by what had just occurred and a lot awkward. Then his eyes flicked to Diana's briefly, making her wonder if his discomfort was something to do with their conversation last night. The conversation she had been compelled to have with him, rather than reveal in the newspaper first as she should have when it found its way to her desk. As much as Giles vexed her, she wouldn't want to see him trapped in a loveless union with the dim-witted Dahlia, any more than she wanted to see poor Dahlia used that way.

She was tempted to ask outright what the upshot was, but that didn't seem fair with everyone watching. Neither was it prudent when she had kept the true extent of her role at *The Tribune* a secret from everyone.

"Excellent! Then it is settled. Payne, have another place set immediately. Preferably one next to Miss Diana." Olivia beamed at her in triumph. "And tell Cook we are ready the second her soufflé is."

The imminent soufflé proved to be exactly that, and not two minutes later they were all seated in the dining room. Him indeed next to her—but stiffly. Almost as if he was agitated. Worried by something. Which was ridiculous since Giles never worried about anything. Ever.

"I read all about your ball in the newspaper, Giles." Vee hadn't gone to the party because Olivia had deemed her too young for such debauchery. "It sounds as though it was great fun."

"It was rather." Even his smile to the youngest Merriwell appeared false and brittle. At least to Diana it did.

Vee certainly didn't notice as she leaned closer for the gossip. "Was Lord T really so inebriated he had to be carried out?"

Giles grinned at her, leaning in conspiratorially, to all intents and purposes exactly like his incorrigible normal self again. "It wasn't only Lord T but Lady T, too. Neither of them could stand, but for the sake of the lady's reputation we sneaked her out the back door."

"No!" Her sister giggled, still so innocent and cosseted that something like that shocked, which was a miracle really when one considered where she came from. "And was there really an illicit tryst in your orangery?"

"The details I have from the orangery are too sketchy to confirm, Miss Vee, but thankfully Lady Sewell was quite the scandal in the music room." Giles winked at the youngest as he snapped open his napkin. "And with a rather dubious Russian count no less." His eyes locked with Diana's. They seemed troubled behind the usual sparkling mischief. "Or so it says in *The London Tribune*, which seems very informed about the evening for some reason."

"But were there enough scandals to thoroughly incense your father?" These were the first words Diana had uttered since his arrival. "Did steam shoot out of his ears this morning?" They both knew she was alluding to Dahlia and the rumored engagement.

"No . . . at least not for that. However . . ." His handsome face was suddenly perplexed as he leaned closer. Automatically Diana and Vee did, too.

"What are you all whispering about so covertly?" Diana almost groaned aloud at Olivia's interruption.

"The scandalous gossip from last night," said Vee, oblivious to the odd undercurrent. "I am getting it all directly from the horse's mouth seeing as *I* wasn't allowed to go."

Olivia smiled at Vee in maternal sympathy. "I would be derelict in my duty as a chaperone if I allowed an impressionable young lady in my charge to attend a function called the Annual Reprobates Ball."

"But Diana is in your charge and she was allowed to go."

"Your sister is long past the age of majority and I am quite certain that while she does her damndest to be invisible, she has never been impressionable."

"Besides," added Jeremiah with a knowing smile as he tapped the side of his nose, "we all know she was working."

"How many times do I have to tell you all I only edit the punctuation and grammar at the newspaper?"

"About as many as I hear your dulcet, pithy tones written all over that gossip column, missy. We can all always tell when it's been written by you—because you make all that society dirge sound interesting." Being an American, Jeremiah disapproved of the English aristocracy on principle, even though he had married into it. "The piece you wrote about that idiot Lord R's pathetic attempts at love poetry was hilarious. I'd love to know where you found that sonnet. He must have been mortified to have mislaid it."

He hadn't mislaid it and she hadn't found it. She had, instead, been hiding behind a statue and heard it performed to the cringing young debutante on a terrace by the besotted idiot himself and had written it down verbatim. "I have no earthly idea what you are talking about."

"Yet it had your hallmark stamped all over it." Jeremiah waved his fork in her direction. "But if my humble opinion counts for anything—"

"It really doesn't, dear," said Olivia.

". . . You are wasted on the gossip column, Diana. You should write for the other column that *The Tribune* posts from time to time. The one that digs up the real dirt. What's it called?" He snapped his fingers while she did her best to focus on her soufflé and act indifferent, even though her ears had pricked up.

"The Sentinel?"

"Yes, Giles! That's the one!" Jeremiah jabbed the air with his fork this time. "Now, that really is some first-rate journalism. That exposé he wrote last month on Lord Jessop was something else."

He.

How predictable people were.

"It's ruined Jessop as far as society is concerned," said Giles, who seemed to have miraculously found his appetite from somewhere, "although from what I've read he deserved nothing less. To lie about ruining a lady when she rebuffed his proposal just to force her into marriage is abhorrent. I am so glad the unfortunate lady's good name has been restored. Without the Sentinel's timely interference, in another few days she would have been Lady Jessop."

"A fate worse than death, to be sure." Diana addressed nobody in particular. "For the snake has a leering way about him that always makes my flesh crawl." She shivered, picturing another leer from another time from another snake who had wanted more than she was prepared to give.

"Thank goodness the Sentinel found enough evidence to confirm the bounder was lying through his teeth." Giles pulled a face. "Good should always triumph over evil, don't you think?"

It should, but it didn't. Especially where women were concerned. Lord Jessop had targeted the young lady on purpose. Her father was dead, she was young, she had no male relations to refute the accusations made, and although undoubtedly a great beauty, she did not have the important connections necessary to make a selfish predator think twice.

"Thank goodness Lord Jessop isn't as clever as he thinks he is." Discovering he had spent the entire night in question at a notorious gaming hell and brothel rather than ruining the young lady as he had claimed had been a godsend, but it was his drunken signed and dated markers that had hoisted Jessop by his own petard. Those two damning bits of hastily scribbled paper that promised to cover the cost of his intense two days of debauchery had been worth every penny of the ten pounds she had had to pay for them.

"I swear that column is the only thing worth reading nowadays." Jeremiah's comment bolstered her ego. "It relies on hard facts rather than veiled speculations or innuendo."

Giles nodded, waving his own fork now as he tried to muster the energy to be sociable. "And he doesn't beat about the bush with self-indulgent turgid prose like all those other fellows. He gets straight to the point in the first line, making the accusation up front as if courting a libel suit and then backing it completely with evidence. No hearsay, no opinion, but irrefutable, substantiated facts that no court could deny. Look what he said about Jessop." He laid down his cutlery, cleared his throat, and adopted a pose as if he were Hamlet about to launch into his soliloquy. *"Lord Jessop is a blaggard and a blackmailer. A man who waged a war of vicious lies, venom, and vitriol against an innocent to feed his own vile desires."* Serious Hamlet left and a grinning Giles returned. "Aside from the marvelous way it sets the scene, the witty use of alliteration was rather brilliant. It imbued the piece with a cadence one would expect to see in a page-turning novel or a play rather than the newspaper. And he chose such emotive language, too." He counted them off on his fingers. "Vicious . . . vitriol . . . venom . . . *vile*. In four words, the Sentinel has told us how to feel about Jessop's crime even before we know what the scoundrel has done."

Diana dabbed her lips with her napkin to cover her smile. Trust Giles to notice that detail. It made the hours she spent laboring over her opening paragraphs worthwhile.

"Do you know him, Diana?" Jeremiah was always pressing her for information about the paper.

"No . . ." She shook her head blandly as she studied her food. "He's a mystery to all of us at the newspaper office and likes it that way."

Jeremiah nodded. "I can't say I blame him for wanting to remain incognito. The Sentinel has unmasked and upset a lot of nasty people these past few months, and some will want their revenge. If I were him, I'd stay away from dark alleyways."

Diana avoided them already. She knew the worst of the predators lurked in dark alleyways where nobody heard your screams. "You seriously think that bounder Jessop has the time to retaliate on top of all the trouble he is already in?" She scoffed at the extreme overreaction. "He's too busy trying to save his own skin, believe me. He'll end up sloping away with his tail between his legs like that other toad the Sentinel exposed in the autumn—Sir Donald . . ." She snapped her fingers as if she didn't recall a single thing in her bulging file on that investigation. "MacPherson? MacFarlane?"

"McFey." Giles offered her a smug smile at his superior memory. "Sir Donald McFey. The rotter who tried to siphon his ward's trust fund into his own pockets before the girl came of age. Fled across the Channel the day the story broke and before the ink on the arrest warrant was dry."

"You see!" Diana addressed Jeremiah. "My point is proved. When push comes to shove, a villain will always flee rather than seek retribution."

"Perhaps those fools didn't—but others might not think twice about it." Jeremiah's scaremongering was precisely why she hadn't confided her secret to anybody. Her family would all overreact if they knew what she was really doing and then ruin everything she had worked hard for with their well-intentioned mollycoddling.

"Being shunned by society hardly seems a fitting punishment for Lord Jessop's crime. And ruining a lady simply to possess her *is* a crime in my book." Vee's timely comment distracted from the potential danger of her job, but still echoed Diana's own sentiments. "He should be arrested and put on trial for what he did. Had he been a common man rather than a peer, he would have been."

"But Jessop *is* a peer, so as hideous as he is, I doubt his ruined reputation will last forever. The *ton* have short memories where rank and status are concerned." An unfairness that made Diana's blood boil. "Especially as he is as rich as Croesus."

"All the more reason why his behavior was baffling." Hugh frowned at the table. "The man is an earl. That title alone is enough to make him an attractive prospect for many girls on the marriage mart. Especially if the girl's parents are keen to climb the social ladder and can offer an obscene dowry—which he clearly did not need."

"While we are on the subject of the marriage mart, titles, social-climbing parents, and obscene dowries, I have some news myself . . ." Giles shot her a loaded look, and for some inexplicable reason Diana's heart lodged in her throat.

"Don't tell me *you* are getting married?" Hugh's jaw hung slack.

"Thankfully, I am *not*."

She let out the breath she hadn't realized she was holding, and he grinned at her, amused, as if he had heard it.

"But my disagreeable sire is." He paused for dramatic effect, enjoying the way every mouth around the table hung slack. "The announcement of the duke's impending nuptials will be in tomorrow's *Times*."

"*No!*" The word came from everyone in unison.

"Yes indeed. The old curmudgeon informed me of it this morning, and you'll never guess who the unlikely bride is?" He smiled at Diana again, not smugly that she had got it wrong, but in acknowledgment she had helped him to find the truth. "Dahlia Regis!"

"Daft Dahlia the dumpy draper's daughter?" Vee's comment earned her a nudge from Olivia, which made the youngest Merriwell instantly bristle. "Well, she is daft! The poor thing can hardly string a sentence together without her father's assistance."

"Why on earth is he getting married now? And to Dahlia Regis of all people." Hugh's question exactly mirrored the one on the tip of Diana's tongue. "Do you suspect he needs the money?"

"Something certainly smells off about it—but I'd be the last person the duke ever confided in about anything." Giles stared a little too long at his last forkful of soufflé to convince her he was as unfazed by it all as he was trying to appear. "So I have been left with no earthly clue as to his reasoning. All he did tell me is that I am expressly *not* invited to his wedding, which suits me just fine as I can think of better things to do with a day than watch poor, doe-eyed Dahlia shackle herself to the duke."

The duke.

Never Father or Papa. Why had she not noticed that telling distinction before?

"Besides, if I were present, I'd have to object on principle to save the girl and we all know how much I loathe to do the decent thing, no matter how dreadful and dismal her life is destined to be as his duchess." The last fluffy lump of temperamental soufflé disappeared into his mouth. "What if *that* got into the papers? I'd never live it down." He grinned as if he wasn't the least bit bothered by that awful prospect. "And I should like it noted that the Sentinel isn't the only one who can do alliteration well, as in one sentence I managed *decent, dreadful, dismal, destined,* and *duchess*."

Diana shot him a withering look. "Yet your pitiful effort still lacked the cadence of the Sentinel and still resembled the turgid prose of *his* less talented colleagues."

"Poor Dahlia." Vee always felt deeply for others.

"Poor Dahlia indeed, Miss Vee." Giles's over-bright smile fooled no one this time.

Olivia reached for his hand and squeezed. "Your father has always been an odd fruit, Giles dear, and for what it's worth, I never liked him. If we get an invitation, we shall decline in outraged solidarity."

"That's very decent of you, and I appreciate the sentiment, but rather than declining, can you at least send the harridan Miss Diana in your stead? I might not want to witness the event itself, but I would love to read her pithy record of it in *The London Tribune* as that is bound to be a hoot and I do like to laugh." He nudged her playfully with his arm, forcing her to notice how solid it was and sending a waft of his attractive spicy cologne up her left nostril. "Will you do that for me, Miss Diana, Goddess of the Hunt and determined Hunter of the Truth? Even though you hate me as much as the duke does?"

"I really am just a nitpicking grammarian."

"And I, Miss Truth Hunter, am the Queen of Sheba." Giles whispered this much too close to her ear, sending a ripple of awareness everywhere.

Payne chose that moment to approach the table on stealthy feet. "I am sorry to interrupt, but you have a visitor, my lord."

"Another one?" Hugh went to stand but the butler stayed him with a white-gloved hand.

"Not you, my lord, but Lord Bellingham."

Before the perplexed Giles could stand as well, his unconventional butler hobbled in. "Dalton, what the blazes are you doing here?"

The usually insolent one-eyed sailor's expression was subdued behind his black leather eye patch, and something about it raised all of Diana's journalistic hackles. Whatever news his servant had come to deliver, she knew it would be bad for Giles. Without thinking, she groped for his hand beneath the table, and as if he, too, sensed trouble, his fingers laced with hers tight. Very tight. And something odd happened.

Something very odd.

Because it felt as if that was exactly where her hand was always meant to be.

"I am afraid I come as the bearer of grave tidings. Very grave tidings indeed . . . *Your Grace.*"

Chapter Four

"It was his heart."

"He had one then?"

Carruthers winced at the flippant comment, then sighed at the truth of it as he helped Giles out of his coat. "So the physician claims—and an ailing one that he took pills for, although His Grace never let on that secret, either." How typical of the duke to keep them all in the dark till the bitter end. "The doctor said he had been taking them for several years. He had to leave a half an hour ago and said he would be available at home first thing if you have any further questions about your father's condition, but he did tell me to inform you that in his professional opinion, His Grace's heart attack was inevitable. They both knew he was living on borrowed time. That he had lasted this long was apparently a miracle."

"Only the good die young, Carruthers." Relieved of his coat, and with no further excuse to linger in his father's hallway without purpose, Giles stared at the staircase, wincing. "Is he still up there?" Nausea swamped him at the prospect. He wanted to blame the soufflé and the mad dash across Mayfair, but he knew it was fear. He had dreaded this day for four long years, and so much more since the shocking revelations of this morning.

"We thought it best to leave His Grace in situ until Your Grace had paid your final respects. Besides, we did not know Your Grace's wishes for His Grace's remains." The rising bile burned Giles's throat. "Or Your Grace's wishes on everything else, for that matter. Did His Grace inform Your Grace of his final wishes?"

"Stop!"

The butler eyed his raised palm and stared at his feet. "My apologies, Your Grace . . . I am a tad overwhelmed myself, Your Grace."

"Please stop calling me that." Giles rubbed his temple as he tempered his tone. It was hardly the butler's fault that the mere mention of his fraudulent title made him queasy. "I am not ready to be a duke."

"But you are a duke, Your Grace."

"Not in here." He tapped his forehead. "Not yet." And likely never in the eyes of the law. "Please allow me a little leeway to get used to it." He threw out his palms, more overwhelmed than he had ever been in his life, now that all his father's lies had finally come home to roost. Because Your Grace felt wrong—was wrong—in every conceivable way.

"Very well . . . Your . . . um . . ." Carruthers eyed his shoes in discomfort. "What do you want me to do?"

"Fetch me some port." For a man who rarely drank, Giles suddenly needed a stiff one. He stared at the stairs again and steeled his shoulders. "I'll take it in the drawing room once I've seen him."

On leaden feet he climbed the steps slowly while the acid churned and his mind raced. It still failed to comprehend anything but the enormity of the situation. This morning, he had had the rug pulled out from under him, was only just scrambling back up and coming to terms with the possibility of being exposed as an impostor one day, only to have the ground beneath him suddenly crumble, too, now that *one day* had come. Leaving Giles with no clue where he stood or how he was supposed to feel about any of it.

There had been no love lost between him and his father.

Their relationship had always been more toxic than arsenic and more complicated than algebra: the immense chasm between them unbridgeable and ever widening. Yet he still wouldn't have wished him dead. That the duke *was* dead was almost too much to take in on top of everything else. Giles was shocked—dumbfounded, truth be told—but neither sad nor relieved by that incomprehensible fact. Only panicked. Angry.

Queasy.

He took a few moments to calm himself outside the bedchamber door, wishing he had taken up Hugh's offer to accompany him so he didn't have to face this hideous moment alone. He hadn't because he didn't want to drag his friend into a hornet's nest, and he hadn't made any mention of it, either, because he had no earthly idea if it even was a hornet's nest any longer. Had the hornets died with the duke or were they swarming toward Giles with their stings at the ready? Not telling his friend had been either prudent or cowardly, and probably both, when he had gone to Hugh's in the first place expressly to confess it all. Needing someone to know. Needing to know someone cared enough about him to still be there when all the skeletons were revealed.

A moot point now? He had no clue, but knew he needed to find out. Even if the lie seemed doomed to hold, Giles couldn't move forward until he properly understood the past and the full measure of what he was up against. *If* he was up against anything.

He fisted the hand Diana had held as if harnessing her strength, blew out a measured breath, and gingerly pushed open the door. The duke lay on his bed, fully clothed in the evening dress he had died in. Carruthers had left a single lamp burning low on the nightstand, which cast a golden hue over his sire's slack gray face. Giles forced himself to look at it as he edged forward.

The instant wave of grief surprised him.

It wasn't so much for the man or for the end of their relationship, more for what that relationship could have been had things been different. Or had the stranger laid out on the bed been different.

It came as quite a shock to realize he actually knew nothing personal about his father at all. Not what he liked, what he thought, his hopes, his dreams, his memories, his essence. All he knew was that they had never got on and that trying to change that state of affairs was futile because the door had never swung both ways. The duke had always made no secret of the fact that he loathed him. If Giles did not dance his tune, which he could never manage to do, they argued. For as long as he could remember, those arguments were their only conversations. That gulf between them had always been there, although he was buggered if he knew why when the old man had broken the law to make him his heir.

But what a pack of lies he had now inherited. All his now, to manage or expose. Or perhaps the exposure would come from another quarter, and perhaps sooner rather than later, as his sire's panic alluded?

"Why did you suddenly need a spare?"

That was the burning question, but of course, the duke couldn't answer.

"What changed?" His voiced echoed in the silent bedchamber, a dark and gloomy room Giles could not ever recollect setting foot in before. "Was it money? Your sheer disappointment in me?" He had been racking his brains all day and still couldn't fathom it. "Or is there another *Dirty Secret* you neglected to tell me—or more to the one I already know?"

That was more likely the truth.

If the duchess hadn't spewed all her pent-up scorn and hatred for his dubious lineage when he visited her deathbed, he would still be none the wiser. Not that he was much wiser as a result. When he had confronted the duke with that shocking news, still reeling from her venom, he hit an outraged wall. Not *She's lying* or *She's lost her mind* or *It is the laudanum talking*, as he had hoped, but a curt "She shouldn't have told you" before he fell into a stony, disapproving silence. Then she had died within hours and that had been that. Any further questions or mentions of his bastardy sent the duke into a rage and his stubborn Sinclair chin shut his mouth tighter than a clam.

Four years later and Giles still had no idea what his real mother's name had been, or where he had been born, let alone if the woman still existed. It was all none of his business and never to be discussed, and with no trail to follow and no clues left lying around, there had been nothing to find despite the incessant ghostly rattle of the skeletons that had arrived in his cupboard that same day. Clearly the duke had now taken all the answers to his grave, too, content to leave those damn skeletons rattling forever in the background and his bastard son completely in the dark as to who he really was.

Frustration replaced the brief flash of grief. Then anger at the cruelty of it all. Lies, deceit, disappointment, disgust. He had been at war with his parents since the day he was born, yet never knew why or how it would end. Now that it had ended, and he was the last man standing, he still felt as though he had lost. Especially after this morning's argument, which hung in the air like a putrid stench, making those damn elusive skeletons rattle so much louder than they ever had before, looming in the darkness.

"I *will* find it all!" His growl echoed in the void as his gaze moved from the body on the bed to the ceiling and the heavens above it. "Do you hear me?" Then in case the duke really was bound for hell as Giles had always suspected, he addressed the floor, too. Stamped his foot upon it like a petulant child. "I will find the truth—no matter where that path leads!"

He had to.

The last four years had been torture. Spending a whole lifetime in the dark and constantly looking over his shoulder waiting for the ax to fall would drive him mad. Besides, it was the only bit of runt-like rebellion he had left, now the man was gone. That and doing a better job of being the Duke of Harpenden than any of the previous dukes had managed, and he'd start by spending with impunity on their neglected estate while he still legally could. Before he put the duke in the ground, he would begin undoing every wrong the man had done in Shropshire. And then he would modernize it. Spending all the skinflint's money with the same abandon as he had poured the Veuve Clicquot.

That would really send the duke spinning in his grave like a windmill in a gale. He retired to his drawing room.

"Your port, Your Gr . . . um . . ." Carruthers bowed warily as he proffered the glass on a shiny silver tray. Why he had bothered with the tray in the first place when the decanter was not four feet away was a mystery, but he supposed it was one of the formal rituals the duke had insisted upon to prove how much better than a servant he was. "Do you require anything else?"

"Some answers would be good." Giles gestured to the wingback opposite by the fire. A roaring fire he had fueled and stoked himself because this dreadful house had always been as cold as its owner. "Please . . . sit."

"I think I should prefer to stand, as is proper."

"We both know I have never been one for propriety, Carruthers, and I have no desire to get a crick in my neck while we chat, so sit for goodness' sake, as I have lots of questions."

Wide-eyed, the butler perched on the edge of the seat. "I shall do my best to answer them but must warn you His Grace never once confided in me about anything."

Giles toasted him with his glass. "Join the club, old boy. The duke was always as miserly with information as he was with his money. However, servants have both eyes and ears, Carruthers, and they talk to one another, so by my guess you currently know more about things than I do." Because drinking alone felt odd, he went to the sideboard himself and poured a second glass. "For example, did you have any clue he was ill?" He held out the drink and the other man took it, clearly bemused by the informality.

"There were clues, I suppose, but none that I didn't put down to old age."

"Such as?"

"Some weight loss—not extensive but enough to have his trousers altered. Obviously, he blamed the chef."

"*Obviously.*" Giles's wry smile earned him one back, and Carruthers finally began to relax.

"He was not as active; he took fewer walks and used the carriage more." The butler took a tentative sip of his port, then frowned. "Now that I think upon it, he hadn't walked for quite a while. Not for a few months at least, but I put that down to the bad weather. Still, he was out more than was usual. Especially in the last month."

"Do you know where he went?"

"Apart from Parliament and his club, no. I wasn't privy to his comings and goings and knew better than to ask. Perhaps he was courting Miss Regis?"

It was Giles's turn to be bemused. "Now, there's an inconceivable thought." And one that jarred with what Diana had told him. She said he had dined with Mr. Regis at White's before he had dined at their house. That sounded more like the duke. He had never held women in any particular regard and would have preferred to deal with her father. "Did the Regises ever dine here?"

Carruthers shook his head. "We haven't had a dinner guest here since Her Grace died. His Grace never had the patience with idle socializing and always turned down the few invitations that came. To be frank, I am not even sure he had any friends. Acquaintances, certainly, political associates mostly, but the only visitors he accepted were you, weekly, and his estate manager every few months. Occasionally his solicitor." A man who might be of extremely great use. Especially if the duke had changed his will.

"When was the last time he saw Mr. Cribbage?"

"Here? Several months ago. If he met with anyone else outside these walls . . ." The butler shrugged. "Again, I wasn't privy to it. Maybe the answers you seek will be in his papers?"

Giles glanced at the clock on the mantel. It was midnight already and he was exhausted. Certainly, in no fit state to wade through decades' worth of documents searching for goodness knew what to solve a conundrum he couldn't begin to understand. He would need all his wits about him for that gargantuan chore. "What about this last month? Did you notice anything different about his behavior or his demeanor?"

"Other than his constant bad mood?" The butler winced as his face paled. Fear instantly in his eyes. "My apologies . . . it is not my place to speak ill of your father."

"Yes, it is, for I doubt anyone had to suffer the tyrant's wrath more than you did, Carruthers." He smiled at the man who had always been an ally to him on the high days and holidays when he came to London and had saved Giles from that wrath on more occasions than he could remember. "I have always wondered why you stayed with him?"

"Loyalty to the rest of the unfortunate staff who walked in and then out of the door." He shifted awkwardly in his seat. "Might I ask a question about the current staff? They are understandably worried about their futures, now that His Grace is gone—and I cannot imagine you wanting to take up residence here?"

He was right. Hell would have to freeze over before Giles ever called this place home. These dusty old walls held nothing but bad memories of the childhood and adolescence he had worked damn hard to forget. "You can tell them I will see them all right, Carruthers, whatever happens. Unlike the duke, I have never shirked my responsibilities and have always been a man of my word."

The other man's shoulders visibly eased. "Thank you—I told them as much but it is good to hear nevertheless."

"In the meantime, we have a funeral to arrange and doubtless months ahead of us sorting out his affairs, so nothing much will change for everyone in the short term. Apart from the constant threat of tyranny, which ended the moment His Grace's granite heart gave out, I suppose it will be business as usual. I shall certainly be here first thing to start the great sort." Giles drained the last of his glass and unfolded himself from the chair. "But it has been the longest of days and I need my bed, and I suspect you do, too, my old friend."

"I could make up a room."

"Good heavens no!" He shuddered for effect. "Even if the duke's corpse wasn't across the landing, I wouldn't do that!"

"Then I shall have your horse readied." The butler stood, too, and walked him to the front door.

As Carruthers helped him on with his coat, Giles thought of another question. "When did you discover the duke was about to remarry?"

"Only a few days ago. I probably should have sent word to you about that but . . ."

Giles waved that away. "There is no reason to make excuses. I understand. You were reluctant to incur his wrath, and had you told me, we both know he would have dismissed you on the spot. But do you know what compelled him to want to remarry so fast?" Because that was the crux of the matter and the first mystery to be solved.

Carruthers shook his head. "We were all as shocked as you were about the news, and by the speed of it all. It was only Thursday, I believe, that he told me to air out the duchess's room, give it a dust, and change the sheets."

"Air it out and give it a dust?" He shook his own head in disbelief, though bizarrely not surprised that the duke had such little regard for his future bride that he thought it appropriate to put her in the same scruffy room and expect her to sleep on the same mattress his first wife had died upon. Poor Dahlia had no idea what a lucky escape she had just had.

And on the subject of Dahlia . . .

"Has anyone sent word to Miss Regis to inform her of her fiancé's sudden death?"

"Er . . ." The butler pulled a face. "I confess it never occurred to me."

Giles sighed. Midnight. In less than six hours *The Times* would be delivered around the city announcing the engagement. A few hours later, and the rampant society rumor mill would inform everyone the engagement was now emphatically off because her prospective groom was dead. And because dukes didn't die every day, and never without a huge fuss, that news would likely be common knowledge long before *The Times* ever printed it. Especially if *The Tribune* printed it, as he knew it would. A dedicated Hunter of the Truth like Diana would have seen it as her duty to pass that news on.

Just thinking about Diana made the nerves in his hand tingle, so he fisted it again behind his back, wishing he did not wish with every fiber of his being that she were here to hold it tight for the rest of the hideous ordeals that lay ahead.

"I shall send a message to the Regis residence immediately." Carruthers's expression was pained.

"No." Wearily, Giles trudged down the stone steps to the pavement and into the rain. "I shall tell the poor thing myself now."

It would be the first of his sire's many misdeeds he would have to deal with as best he could, but sadly, that awful chore, while unlikely to be the last, would probably prove to be the easiest.

Chapter Five

"Shropshire!" Charlie Palmer, the proprietor and editor in chief of *The London Tribune* gaped at her in disbelief. "You cannot go to Shropshire!"

"I have to." And, more to the point, Diana wanted to. She had decided not to analyze the reasons why in case she came to conclusions she did not want to consider. "The dead duke is being buried there, and because my brother-in-law is the new duke's closest friend, we are all going up to support him in his hour of need. Besides, he's practically part of the family."

Which was another reason she had to be there—because it turned out he had no family beyond them, and nobody should have to bury a relative alone.

"But for two weeks, Diana! Two! When we need you here!" He slapped the haphazard tower of today's *Tribune*s stacked on his messy desk, the headline "The House of Harpenden Mourns" already a day too late.

Charlie had been peeved at that, too, because he had assumed—quite rightly although Diana vehemently denied it—she must have known about the duke's death last night and should have, out of professionalism and loyalty, sent immediate word to the *Tribune* office in Fleet Street so they could be the first to print the story. She hadn't because it was too close to home—it crossed the fine line between her loyalty to the paper and her greater loyalty to her family—and because she couldn't bring herself to add to Giles's woes by unleashing all London's press upon him within hours of receiving the blow.

And it had been a blow, of that she was certain.

She hadn't expected weeping and wailing, or even deep sadness at the unexpected news, because she understood he had an uneasy relationship with his father. Having a diabolical one with her own feckless father, she would never judge Giles for lacking those emotions everyone else expected. Had Diana received word Alfred Merriwell was dead, she was certain the only emotion she would feel was relief.

Yet Giles hadn't been either unmoved or relieved; he had been horrified. Perhaps even terrified by the prospect. She hadn't expected the flash of sheer, blind panic that skittered across his much-too-handsome features before he covered it. And he covered it so well that had she not been sitting directly beside him holding his hand, and seen the way his face bleached and felt how his fingers shook as they gripped hers, she would be none the wiser. But she had, and she had heard the way his breathing became erratic, as if all the wind had suddenly been knocked from his sails.

Moments later, and without looking at her, he yanked his hand away to leave the table with Hugh in tow. Then Hugh had come back. His offer of accompanying his friend categorically rejected and his friend already gone. Thinking of him facing all that alone had kept her awake all night. She had only come to work to stop her acting on the overwhelming impulse to check if he was all right. An act of friendship that went way beyond the strict parameters of their we-only-tolerate-each-other-because-we-have-to relationship. Instead, she had consoled herself that she had spared him the trial of waking up to a sea of reporters and given him a few more hours to digest the tragedy.

As it happened, the news had leaked naturally quite early. Dukes didn't die every day, and it was too big a story to contain. Especially after the announcement of that particular duke's engagement had appeared in *The Times*. Without Diana's help, and to the relief of her conscience, Grosvenor Square had been swarming with reporters by luncheon and the *ton* was abuzz with gossip before it was an acceptable hour for the first nosy visitors to knock on the duke's door to pay their respects. By then, thankfully, Hugh was by Giles's side to assist with the funeral preparations, and Olivia had temporarily appointed herself mistress of Sinclair House to assist with all the day's many callers.

"How can you leave me in the lurch when you are my best bloodhound? Can't you cut your visit short, Diana? Blame your tyrannical employer and tell them you need to return early or risk the sack?"

She offered him a half smile of sympathy. They both knew he wouldn't sack her, because she *was* his best bloodhound and had been since the day he took over six months ago and gave her a chance. "That excuse would only wash in the real world, where mere mortals have to earn their livings. I live in Mayfair now, Charlie, where working at all is frowned upon." A staggering change of fortune she still couldn't quite believe after twenty-two years of abject poverty. "My family—and by that I include the

Earl of Fareham's family—would expect me to put duty to them over my duties here. Besides, our visit to Shropshire proper is only fleeting."

"Two weeks isn't fleeting! Entire wars and revolutions have happened in less!"

"It isn't two weeks—it's barely eleven days."

"Which is closer to two weeks in my book than one, and even one is too many!"

"What do you want me to do? The estate is nearly two hundred miles away and takes at least four days to get to and the same again to get back. We arrive the day before the service and are leaving on the morning after, so it is not as if I am dallying there longer than necessary. And you do have three other reporters working on the gossip column."

"But those idiots don't have your touch, Diana, or your canny eye for scandal." He huffed out a resigned breath that fogged his thick spectacles. "Nor do they dig deep for those shiny golden nuggets that you bring me." It was the gold he most appreciated. "Did you at least find out why the duke was marrying Dahlia Regis?" He had tasked her with that quest yesterday, knowing she would be visiting Grosvenor Square with her family to pay her respects to Giles, and once again her loyalties had been torn.

In the end, she decided that she would pry only if the opportunity presented itself and then decide what to do about it, but by the time they all arrived at the dead duke's house, the drawing room was filled with strangers and poor Giles seemed overwhelmed. Or at least to her he did. To everyone else, he appeared to be bearing it all stoically, but they probably never noticed that the mischievous light in his dark eyes had dimmed or that, despite his usual dashing elegance even in mourning clothes, he seemed uncomfortable in his own skin. So much so that she had worried about him incessantly since and couldn't shake the niggling feeling in her gut that something was very wrong.

"I didn't."

Charlie huffed. "Is the new duke as baffled as the rest of London is, or did he refuse to answer?"

"I didn't ask, Charlie."

"Why not?" He threw his arms up in frustration. "As it is the question of the hour and one my foxhound's nose smells is a juicy story. An exclusive story! One I was relying on my best bloodhound to write. *Today!*"

"And just like that"—she clicked her fingers—"your best bloodhound is neutered. Even the worst hack at the tawdriest scandal sheet will be able to work out who the information came from because my association with the new duke is too close. I'll never be invited to anything again, and my brother-in-law will be furious at the betrayal." She couldn't do that to Hugh after everything he had done for the Merriwell sisters. "The entire family recognizes my style every single time I write a piece for the gossip column, and while they encourage my career and find my stories entertaining, they would be devastated if I turned my privileged insider knowledge on them." She shook her head emphatically. "I cannot and *will not* investigate either the old or the new Duke of Harpenden."

Giles would feel betrayed, too, and as much as he vexed her, she liked him. More than liked him, truth be told, even though she didn't want to. They were friends—after a fashion—as much as a duke from Mayfair and a forger's daughter from Clerkenwell

could be friends. Giles was . . . an affable rogue. A silver-tongued
charmer who dallied with women who were only too happy to dally
back. For all his many faults, he had never hurt a soul as far as she
knew. He was too superficial to be a danger to anybody—female or
otherwise. Although not quite superficial enough that she hadn't
been unnerved by his reaction last night.

"Trust me to hire a reporter with a conscience." Charlie
slumped in his chair. "I'll put someone else on it, although I know
already their piece won't be half as good."

She smiled at her friend, thankful he understood her impossible position and respected her enough not to push. Their relationship had always been like that. From the first day she had begged
him to give her a chance on the gossip column to the day she had
inadvertently become the Sentinel, he had listened to her and respected both her opinion and her instinct. "If it's any consolation,
I'm this close to disclosing a stocks and shares swindle." She held
up her thumb and index finger an inch apart. "For it seems the
Camden Union Canal Company is all a sham, the plans for the over-
due waterway are nonexistent, Lord Tubbs, the owner, is a charlatan,
and the hapless investors are being robbed blind. The list of those
investors is quite impressive and does contain another duke as well
as a goodly few peers of the realm . . ."

"How many peers?" Already he was interested. It warmed
her that Charlie trusted her abilities well enough not to query her
sources or her information.

"Seven that I know of, and one that it'll likely bankrupt. As
soon as I have concrete confirmation of that fact, which I hope
to have by the time I return from Shropshire, the Sentinel's next
column will be ready to go. You could probably have it that same

day, too, if I write it while I am away. It'll likely fill a whole page, perhaps even a double spread, it is so scandalous and convoluted."

"That is *some* consolation." His expression was bland but his eyes were dancing behind his lenses, because they both knew that when a once-in-a-blue-moon Sentinel column made it into *The Tribune*, their circulation tripled. If he realized she chose the deserving and perfidious subjects of the column carefully, he wisely kept it to himself. He also guarded her identity like a state secret. Outside of this office, her alter ego was a ghost. A mystery. Or perhaps a myth. If anyone asked him—no matter how important—Charlie Palmer always said hand on heart that he knew nothing, and that the incendiary stories just arrived as if from nowhere. Like magic or sorcery. A layer of security this devoted father of two daughters had specifically created when one of the leads she followed for the gossip column revealed criminality so hideous, he would only print it if nobody could trace it back to her.

"Two Sentinel exposés in the same month will certainly put the cat amongst the pigeons and make our competitors sit up straighter." He rubbed his hands with glee then pinned her with his gaze. "Who's the damsel in distress?"

Perhaps he did realize how she picked her perfidious subjects after all.

"Lady Melissa Hargreaves is being bullied into mortgaging her house so her brother can buy a stake in the company. She is due to return to town to sign the papers in three weeks; therefore, time is of the essence."

"I'll keep an eye out for her in your absence to make sure she doesn't."

"Thanks, Charlie." She smiled and meant it, because her

friend was one of the rarest of commodities on earth—a truly good man.

"Miss Merriwell." One of the print boys stuck his head around the door. "There's a toff downstairs to see you."

"What toff?" Because as much as she believed Jeremiah's fanciful concerns over the Sentinel's safety were a gross overreaction, she was always cautious and so was Charlie. Her name was never printed in the paper, no matter how innocuous the piece she had written, so it was odd that someone would come here in search of her. "And are you certain he asked specifically for me?"

"He wouldn't give his name, but he's tall and dark and adamant he has to speak to Miss Merriwell and no one else. He told me to tell you he urgently requires the services of a nitpicking grammarian."

Chapter Six

Diana found Giles staring in fascination at the steam presses as they churned out the final copies of today's paper, still emblazoned with the headline announcing his father's death. As he had been yesterday, he was dressed in all black, but with the typical sartorial twist of a white carnation pinned to the lapel of his greatcoat. He didn't hear her approach over the cacophony of the machinery but seemed to sense her anyway because he turned and smiled when she was only a few feet away. That was when the concerned part of Diana, which she always tried to ignore, noticed the shadows under his eyes and the unusual slump in his irritating broad shoulders.

"Look what the cat dragged in." Irrespective of his recent tragedy or his sudden elevation to a dukedom, she knew he wouldn't appreciate being treated any differently. "Or should I be curtsying, *Your Grace*?" She dipped into a deep one with undisguised belligerence, and his lip curled in mock distaste at her effort.

"That's quite enough of that, thank you! There shall be no airs and certainly no *graces* between us, Diana. Besides, and frankly there is no other way of saying this without framing it as a compliment so please do not take it as one, subservience doesn't suit you."

A glimmer of his usual mischief danced in his dark eyes despite the circles beneath them. "You are too rebellious and lack the sincerity we dukes expect from our lowly subjects, so if you cannot commit to doffing your cap with convincing reverence, I would rather you didn't attempt it at all. After all, if a job is worth doing, it is worth doing well."

"For once, you are so right . . . *Giles*. And do not allow that compliment to go to your head, either, as even a stopped clock is right twice a day." Diana folded her arms as she leaned against the only idle printing press. "Aren't you supposed to be on your way to Shropshire already?" As she understood it, the cortege was supposed to have left at dawn. "Or has there been a change of plan?"

"No. The carriages left at a snail's pace as the cock crowed, so I shall easily catch them up. I wanted to meet with the solicitor first to go over the terms of the will. His office is in the city." He flapped his hand in the direction of the door. "As the appointment is not till one, I decided to enjoy the fresh air first."

"And you thought you'd find fresh air on Fleet Street?"

"If one ignores the stench of the fetid River Fleet and the pong of the throng of commoners blocking all the pavements, it's a rather charming place."

"What really brings you to this insalubrious part of town, Giles?"

"I wondered if I could beg a favor?"

"Does it involve spelling and punctuation?"

"Obviously." If she were a betting woman, she would say he was anxious about something but was doing his best to hide it. "Why else would I need the services of the most prickly nitpicker I know?" He gestured to the noisy machines and the hubbub of the print room around them far too casually. "Is there somewhere a bit more private we can go?"

Anticipating listening ears, most notably Charlie's, and in case her wily employer realized who her mystery visitor was and demanded immediate answers to all his questions direct from the horse's mouth, she had donned her pelisse, making ready for a quick escape. "If you're peckish"—which, of course, Giles always was—"Ye Olde Cheshire Cheese around the corner does excellent pies and should be open already. Fleet Street never sleeps, so the ponging throng eat at all hours."

"I can always find room for a pie." They walked the first few yards in a silence that felt more loaded than companionable. "I can always find room for Cheshire cheese, for that matter. Do they serve that, too? And more important, exactly how old is *ye olde*?"

He waggled his arm but clearly wasn't ready to talk yet, and she respected that. For Giles to ask a favor and to have sought her out when they had never had that sort of relationship set alarm bells ringing. For him to have come to the newspaper, too, rather than Hugh's house, when he must have other, more pressing things to do today, meant it had to be personal. For the most closed book she knew apart from herself, that was out of character as well.

"Positively ancient." Diana matched his jokey tone as she slipped her hand around his elbow and tried to ignore how nice it felt to be there. "Rebuilt after the Great Fire, or so the innkeeper brags, with plenty of dark nooks and crannies to discuss punctuation and spelling emergencies in complete and utter privacy."

They stuck to small talk on the short walk to the inn, ignoring all the rival newspaper hawkers shaking their papers in the air and shouting variations on "A Duke Is Dead!" to every hurried pedestrian on Fleet Street. They discussed the weather, the surround-ings, Hugh's besotted fussing over her pregnant sister. Anything that avoided acknowledging the duke was indeed dead, and his re-luctant replacement wasn't anywhere ready for it.

As it was an hour too early for the lunch crowd, the pub was quiet. She found a secluded table in the back while he ordered them drinks and food. When he finally sat down, the mask of the superficial Giles slipped slightly, enough that her sympathy leaked out. "How are you bearing up?"

"Oh, you know me. Giles Sinclair is always stoic." He shrugged, doing his best impression of a shallow man unaffected by the blow he had been dealt, but he looked tired. There was a tightness about his dark eyes she had never seen before. "It is no secret there was no love lost between the duke and me, but I didn't wish him dead."

"Which doesn't answer my question at all."

"No . . . I suppose it doesn't." He had sought her out specif-ically, yet still seemed unsure about whether to trust her with whatever it was that had brought him. Unless he simply needed someone to talk to who understood his situation?

"You do not need to pretend with me, Giles. I am the last per-son on earth who would judge you for being unable to grieve a father who didn't deserve it. I doubt I'd shed a single tear for mine. In fact, I am convinced I shan't. He would have betrayed us all to save his own slippery skin—no matter how low and despicable it was. He was the worst father in the world, and I have always loathed him."

An understatement. She hated him with every fiber of her being, especially as she got older. As Alfred Merriwell had sunk further into moral oblivion and his life of crime, he threw his daughters into danger. Sometimes out of sheer carelessness and neglect, and sometimes on purpose.

"I see we finally have something in common." He smiled without humor, clearly awkward at being vulnerable but more uncomfortable with seeming callous or unfeeling. "The duke was a difficult man to like."

"Then how do you feel about his demise, beyond guilty that your heart isn't affected in quite the way you think it should be?" If her journalistic experience had taught her anything, it was that sometimes the best questions to ask were the ones that went straight to the point.

His wry expression confirmed she had hit the nail on the head.

"I cannot deny I am still in the baffled and bewildered stage. It was all so unexpected after all, and still so fresh, I've had precious little time to contemplate the gravitas of the situation or what the blazes to do about it beyond arranging the funeral. The duke neglected to leave instructions for anything despite apparently knowing he was knocking on death's door. Hence I am burying him in the family plot in Shropshire next to the duchess whether he likes it or not." By his frown, he was obviously in two minds about that decision, reminding her he was decent to his core. Or at least she had always suspected he was. "It's most likely the latter, to be honest, as there was no love lost between the duke and duchess. They loathed each other, too."

First, she had noticed the distinction of "the duke" and now "the duchess." Clearly he never mentioned his mother with any affection, either, a snippet that was both telling and sad. It plucked at her toughened, cynical heartstrings. There was a story there, she was certain, of a difficult, lonely childhood that had shaped the fraught relationship he'd had with his father and likely the man he was today. A story he was determined to keep intensely private.

Something that they also had in common. Thanks to her own father, there were things in her own past—unpleasant and best-forgotten things—that Diana had never shared with another soul. Not even her beloved sisters knew about the most awful memories from their final year with Alfred Merriwell. They were just too personal. Too painful. The barely healed wounds too deep to ever seal completely no matter how much she tried to leave everything in the past where it belonged.

"If the duke did not want to spend eternity rotting beside her, he should have had the decency to tell you as much. It was most inconsiderate that he didn't. If I were you, I wouldn't give it a second thought." He smiled at that. "You have quite enough on your plate without trying to read his twisted mind from beyond the grave."

"Do you ever mince your words, Diana?"

"Do you want me to?"

He shook his head, his eyes amused now instead of burdened, and that pleased her. "Good heavens, no! One of the *only* things I like about you is your honesty."

He took a tentative sniff of his ale. He wanted to talk, she could sense it, just as she sensed trusting didn't come easily to him, so she made no attempt to fill the silence that stretched until he had no choice but to give in. He had sought her out, after all, not the other way around.

After an age, he sighed. "He's barely been dead two days and already I feel as though I've been dealing with the aftermath for months. Since yesterday, the Grosvenor Square house has been more like Piccadilly Circus than the dour mausoleum the duke lived in. I've had to have meetings with the physician and the undertaker. This afternoon it's his crusty old solicitor and the uncertainty of the will."

"I hardly think his will is uncertain. You are his only heir, after all."

An odd emotion passed quickly across his face before he shrugged. "I suppose so . . . but with the duke one never knows. I wouldn't put it past him to do one last thing to punish me for existing." He waved that strange comment away. "But that joy is for later. Besides, it gave me a good excuse to escape this morning, and like the lazy chap I am, I left the last dribs and drabs of callers to Olivia because I'd had quite enough of them." Irritation dripped into his tone, and she couldn't blame him. The majority of those visitors politeness forced him to receive were only there as voyeurs. Olivia and Jeremiah had had to watch them like hawks to stop the intrepid from wandering off and snooping about the house.

"She mentioned there were a lot of them yesterday."

"'A lot' is putting it mildly. There was a huge influx of enthusiastic mourners who were insistent they all had to pay their respects to the duke now that he's dead, when they all avoided the old curmudgeon like the plague while he was alive." His nose wrinkled in disgust. "Which baffles me completely, as staring at the corpse of a distant acquaintance is not my idea of a pleasant way to spend an afternoon."

"Humans are macabre and inquisitive beings."

"They are indeed." He slanted her a brief glance. "And poor Carruthers and Hugh have been fielding the hordes of journalists who demand all the gory details—and still loiter outside even though they have them." Giles paused and stared into his tankard for a moment. "Thank you for not tipping the press off sooner, by the way. Your thoughtfulness on my behalf was much appreciated. It gave me the chance to break the news to Dahlia before anybody else did."

"How did she take it?"

His brown eyes clouded as he gripped his drink tighter. His hands giving him away again as they hinted at an ordeal he would never admit to. "She was distraught. Genuinely distraught, the poor thing. I felt wretched for the girl. After all these years waiting for a fiancé willing to bite at her father's well-baited hook, her decrepit betrothed up and snuffs it before she's reeled him in. The only solace I took from delivering the bad tidings was that I knew, once she was over the initial shock, she was going to be much better off in the long run. His advanced age aside, the duke would have made the poor thing's life a misery."

Giles looked a little lost for a moment, until he covered it with feigned excitement as the pies arrived, making her wonder what miseries the duke had caused him over the years to warrant such a statement.

"I invited her to the funeral, though. Despite the inevitable awkwardness, it seemed the right thing to do. Thankfully, the Regises declined as Mr. Regis did not feel he could leave his business for so long—which I cannot deny is a huge relief. The man made no secret of the fact that he is still keen for his daughter to become the Duchess of Harpenden, and clearly believed I owed him the courtesy of stepping up seeing as the previous duke had so grievously inconvenienced his plans." His eyes widened in mock

horror. "He was even prepared to renegotiate the terms of the marriage settlements while poor Dahlia was still weeping inconsolably
in her nightgown! Can you believe that?"

"Do you suspect your father was marrying Regis's daughter
for his money?" She wasn't asking for Charlie or *The Tribune*,
because she already knew she wouldn't share Giles's answer with
anyone, but the unlikely alliance between a pompous and snobbish
peer of the realm and a brash cloth merchant's daughter was a puzzle that made no sense.

He cut into his pie and watched the escaping steam dance. "I
genuinely haven't the faintest idea. If it wasn't for the money, then I
am at a loss as to why he was shackling himself to Dahlia. Because
it certainly wasn't love. The duke didn't know the meaning of that
word."

Yet another sad and telling comment that made her want to
squeeze his hand again. In case she did, she sat on one of her own
and sipped her drink with the other.

The pastry disappeared into Giles's mouth and he chewed
thoughtfully. "I am hoping the crusty solicitor can shed some light
on his motives, because it was all very out of character."

"Perhaps the duke simply wanted some companionship in his
dotage?"

He looked at her as if she had gone stark staring mad. "The
duke wasn't enamored of people in general and always preferred
his own company. All I know is he was—" He stopped abruptly,
and something about the way he tried to appear nonchalant told
her he chose his next words carefully. "Not himself . . . Something was amiss." His dark eyes were troubled for a moment before he shrugged. "He was also in a dreadful hurry to get the deed

done—he had procured a special license, and the wedding was planned for Saturday."

"Saturday? *This* Saturday?" All her journalistic hackles rose in unison, suggesting something was indeed amiss. "As in tomorrow?" Something wasn't right.

He nodded, then exhaled a slow breath as if steeling himself. "Which brings me neatly to the favor I need to ask . . ." He was staring at his pie again, rather than at her. Definitely uncomfortable while pretending not to be. "Only I was hoping you could put a little something in that tawdry gossip column you don't write?"

For once, she didn't deny it. "What sort of something?"

"The deceased Duke of Harpenden's poignant final words of love for his fiancée."

"Last words?" She folded her arms and stared at him across the table. "But Hugh told me he died alone. By the time the butler found him, he was already cold."

"An annoying little detail that I would prefer you omit from the article as it would rather spoil the sentiment of what the duke choked out with his tragic last breath."

Diana didn't try to mask her suspicion. He was asking her to lie—in print—and that jarred with all her principles. "And what, pray tell, did he say during those 'poignant' last moments that a devout Hunter of the Truth would consider printing in her tawdry rag?"

He smiled, looking sheepish, boyish, and utterly, sinfully, annoyingly handsome all at the same time.

"Whatever words you think Miss Dahlia would take the greatest comfort in reading on the morning of what should have been her wedding."

And in an instant all her principles were shot to smithereens.

Because that lovely, thoughtful gesture amid everything else Giles had had to deal with over the last two days did more than pluck at Diana's toughened heartstrings—it also broke through the impenetrable wall she had built around that jaded organ.

Chapter Seven

"It is all rather straightforward." Mr. Cribbage, the duke's crusty old solicitor peered at the will through his precariously balanced spectacles. "As his heir, as well as his only offspring, you inherit everything, whether it be entailed or not. There are no other beneficiaries, so it is all a simple transfer of deeds, titles, and funds that shouldn't take too long."

Giles hadn't expected that and couldn't stop his face from showing it. "Are you sure?"

"Did you anticipate something different, Your Grace?"

Only the sky to fall down and everything to go to hell in a handcart. "Are there any caveats or stipulations? Any letters or documents attached that might . . . affect things in any way?"

"None at all."

"No pensions or private *personal* agreements I need to honor?"

"His Grace had a talent for avoiding such responsibilities, Your Grace." The solicitor's face was bland but with that single, disapproving sentence, he went up several notches in Giles's estimation. He slid the ornate wax-sealed parchment across his desk. "As you can see, the helm of the good ship Harpenden is now yours entirely—to chart whichever course you see fit."

Because he couldn't believe it, Giles took several minutes to read the duke's last will and testament, which was indeed as straightforward as Mr. Cribbage had promised. All his sire's worldly goods were now his, lock, stock, and barrel. He was even mentioned specifically by name—and his was the only name on the document apart from the duke's. He stared at the precise signature for the longest time until he noticed the date beneath it.

"This will is four years old."

"Life is a transient thing, Your Grace, and none of us know when we shall be called to meet our maker; therefore, it is important to have one's affairs in order." Mr. Cribbage's smile was a tad patronizing, as lawyers' smiles were prone to be. "As your father's legal counsel, I insisted he was properly prepared from the moment he inherited the dukedom. As I am now your legal counsel, presuming you would like me to continue to represent the house of Harpenden, I shall insist you do the same and with all speed to ensure the smooth transition of the line of succession—should the worst happen."

Not something Giles had the energy to think about when it was the current line of succession and all the responsibilities that hung in the balance. "But this is four years old, Mr. Cribbage. Isn't there a more recent will that now supersedes this?" One that laid bare the *Dirty Secret* and prevented Giles from fixing everything his sire had broken.

"His Grace and I reviewed the document annually, and as there were no changes to be made after the duchess died and all provision for her was removed, there was no reason to replace the existing will with another document that would only say the same as this one."

"Can I ask when it was last reviewed?"

Mr. Cribbage consulted his notes. "On the first of September this year."

Recent enough to ensure the *Dirty Secret* apparently remained intact in the eyes of the law, but not quite recent enough to give him any peace of mind that it would remain so. "And you last met with him?"

"The first of this month as was usual. Just a few days before he died." That certainly constituted recent enough, yet still did not alleviate the overwhelming feeling that Giles was also living on borrowed time—as a duke at least.

"During that meeting, or any subsequent meetings, did His Grace intimate that he was considering changing his will . . . in view of his declining health or impending marriage perhaps?"

"I am afraid I was never privy to the state of your father's health, and when I drew up the marriage settlements there was no request to alter the will accordingly—although I did raise the matter of making suitable provision for his new bride. In view of the vast age difference and the likelihood he would die long before her, I thought that prudent. However, His Grace was in no mood to consider my advice on that particular occasion." He tapped his papers. "I made a note to revisit it at our next audience postmarriage in the hope he would be in a more agreeable frame of mind."

"I take it you knew he was marrying in haste, Mr. Cribbage?"

The solicitor stared at him levelly. "I did, Your Grace, and you should also know I cautioned him against it for the exact same reasons as I mentioned before. Miss Regis was half his age. In my vast legal experience, such marriages rarely stand the test of time and fall apart long before the older spouse passes."

"But let me guess, he was in no mood to consider that sound advice on that particular occasion, either?"

The solicitor acknowledged that with the merest raise of his brow before he returned to rifling through the documents piled before him.

Giles was impressed. Fair play to Cribbage for standing up to the duke. Few did and his sire never took it well. The only opinion the duke ever cared about was his own.

"In view of the suddenness of His Grace's passing so soon before his wedding day, I think it sensible to show you the marriage settlement in case there are any repercussions. I cannot envisage any, as the dowry had not yet changed hands so there is nothing that needs to be repaid, but you never know and forewarned is forearmed." He slid another sheet of parchment across the table and waited patiently for Giles to read it.

"But this is only for ten thousand pounds?" Not quite the king's ransom the gossip columns had led everyone to believe Mr. Regis had invested in Dahlia, and nowhere near enough for a duke when even a decrepit and curmudgeonly one could command a dowry at least double, perhaps even triple this. "Assuming he needed the funds in a hurry, why did he take her for so little?" Unless his speedy engagement to Dahlia had more to do with the need for a contingency heir than the duke had let on.

"I am afraid I have no clue, Your Grace, except to say he really didn't need the funds at all." Another sheet of paper was placed on top of the settlement. "As the state of his accounts is testament."

Giles scanned the meticulous columns of large numbers in astonishment. "He wasn't on the cusp of bankruptcy, then?" Far from it, in fact, as there seemed to be tens of thousands squirreled here, there, and everywhere. The annual income from the Shropshire estate alone was staggering. Obscenely staggering when one considered the way the duke had systematically bled his poor tenants there dry. It took several seconds for his slack jaw to work; several more for his mouth to be able to formulate a word.

"Unbelievable." He had come here for answers and was doomed to leave with even more questions.

The solicitor shrugged, perplexed by Giles's panicked reaction. "He has left you a very wealthy man, Your Grace. A very wealthy man indeed, so there is really nothing to worry about on that score."

"So I see." He blinked at the columns again, still not quite believing what was written in black and white. Still none the wiser as to what any of it all meant.

"As I said, all his affairs were in good order." Mr. Cribbage passed him another sheet, clearly oblivious to the mother of all messes that his former client had left his son alongside the money. "There are also some stocks and shares, and some properties here in town that command a healthy rent, but His Grace was more about saving his money than speculating it." Or spending it, either, if the paltry outgoings were any gauge. Giles spent more a year on boot polish than the skinflint duke did on pensions. Shock rapidly turned to anger. Outraged fury for all the misery the duke's greedy behavior had caused so many over the years.

"He was sitting on a bloody fortune!"

"He was indeed."

"Yet he still allowed the Shropshire estate to decline unforgivably. Refused to modernize. Evicted tenants the moment they hit hard times. Found all manner of unreasonable excuses to avoid paying pensions, or tradesmen or merchants. Scrimped on wages. Heating. Dismissed servant after servant without either just cause or impediment. Ruined countless livelihoods and lives simply to hoard it all in the bank?" The injustice of the duke's steward-ship had always jarred with Giles's strong sense of what was right and wrong. He had always assumed the man counted the pennies so carefully because there was a finite number of pennies to be counted. But now he knew all this, the injustice of it all left him reeling. "How the blazes did he sleep at night?"

"It always baffled me." Mr. Cribbage smiled, and in that mo-ment Giles realized he had climbed several notches in this man's estimation, too. "But a new broom sweeps clean, or so the old prov-erb says, and there is no legal impediment forcing you to follow in his footsteps if the path he trod veers in a different direction from your own."

"I am not sure the duke and I were ever on the same path, Mr. Cribbage, so I can guarantee you mine will veer a different way. In fact, if he was headed north, I would prefer to march south."

The lawyer smiled, impressed. "I always found the north a tri-fle chilly, Your Grace, so south will make a refreshing change."

"Then let's begin with the pensions. All of those that should have been paid need to be paid as soon as possible. I have a list." A long one. There were so many amends to make for the sins of his father, he had to prioritize the worst travesties first before he forged ahead with the rest of his long-awaited plans. "And I should like them backdated."

It was foggy by the time Giles arrived in Shropshire a few days later; the chilly twilight mist hung heavy, like the ominous weight of all the lies of the past. The angry sky above mirrored the exact shade of the slate roof of Harpenden Hall and ladled gloom onto his impending sense of doom, and a real sense of foreboding added to all his confusion.

This was the first time he had set a foot this close to his childhood home in a decade—yet despite his joy at seeing his familiar Tudor-beamed sanctuary again and the small arc of unfamiliar faces who had gathered outside to greet him, he had never felt quite so alone anywhere in his life.

A woman of middle to late years, petite stature, and a substantial bosom dipped into a curtsy. "Welcome to Harpenden Hall, Your Grace. I am Mrs. Townsend, your housekeeper."

"It is a pleasure to meet you, Mrs. Townsend."

"I am only sorry it is under such sad circumstances, Your Grace. And at such short notice. We have barely had time to ready the place. It has been a few years since your esteemed father visited."

She was being polite because according to Carruthers, the duke hadn't made the trip to Shropshire at all since the duchess's funeral. Before that he rarely visited—and when he did, he was always in such an odd and testy mood everyone sighed in blessed relief when he left. This place had always been his income, not his home, which was likely why Giles had always loved it. Always considered it home, even though he had known for years that it really wasn't.

One by one the housekeeper introduced the tiny band of resident staff. One cook, one maid, a footman, one young groom who looked to be barely out of leading strings, two gardeners, and the gamekeeper. He recognized none of them. "Mr. Bryant, the steward, sends his apologies as he has been unexpectedly detained but will try to be here tomorrow."

Unfortunately, Mr. Bryant was a name he recognized only too

well. That bully had been the steward of the estate for over a decade and was the man, alongside his hired band of bullies, who had diligently refused Giles entry to the grounds for the last ten years upon his cruel sire's instruction. He had always loathed him, although probably nowhere near as much as the estate's tenants did.

"That is a shame, Mrs. Townsend." But probably just as well. He was too exhausted to pull his punches with the duke's right-hand man tonight, and in the immediate short term—because that was all that nasty piece of work had left in *his* employ—Bryant might well be a valuable source of answers to all the questions Giles now had. He certainly hoped so. Otherwise, he was well and truly scuppered where to search next, as all he had hit so far were brick walls. A thorough search of the duke's ordered study and his meeting with the solicitor hadn't offered him any answers, and he didn't dare hire a Bow Street Runner to investigate the mystery of his birth.

Until Giles was certain this estate was running as it should, with everyone who worked the land thriving as they should, the fewer people who knew about the *Dirty Secret*, the better. After that . . . well, frankly, he had no plan. How on earth did one plan for the unknown? All he could do was take things one day at a time and hope for the best while expecting the absolute worst to happen at any given moment.

As out of the blue as the duke's engagement had been.

As unexpected as the duchess's last words to him had been.

An interminable prison sentence and a lonely curse he could never share with anyone.

While the acid in his stomach churned a little more at that hideous reality, he covered it to beam at his eight new employees. "Is this the entire complement of staff, Mrs. Townsend?"

"It is, Your Grace. Up until now we have had little need for more. Though I daresay we shall be run ragged over the next few days when your guests arrive on the morrow."

Instantly, his addled, overworked brain pictured Diana, and a wave of unexpected longing hit him hard before he ruthlessly pushed the image away.

What the devil was the matter with him?

Ever since she had grabbed his hand beneath the table, his mind had been consumed by the vixen. To such an extent he was tempted to consult his pocket watch again to count how many hours it would be until she arrived in Shropshire!

What the blazes was that about?

Hoping his new uncharacteristic and inappropriate longing was caused by tiredness brought about by the fraught circumstances and too many hours on horseback, Giles inhaled a lungful of frigid air and stood straighter to get the blood flowing back to his head. "Then it is a good job I thought to bring a reinforcement for this trip."

Right on cue, Dalton limped up beside him. "Where do you want me to shove the coffin?"

Giles smiled at his new housekeeper, whose eyes had widened at his contrary servant's crudely worded question, and decided not to apologize for him. Dalton was always uniquely Dalton, God love him, and the sooner she realized that the easier it would be for all of them. "Have you prepared a suitable place for His Grace to lie in repose, Mrs. Townsend?"

"I did, Your Grace. I thought the private chapel would be best, especially if the locals want to pay their respects as I doubt you'd want them traipsing through the house at all hours with their muddy boots." She ushered the young groom forward. "Could you please escort Mr. . . . er . . ."

"This is Dalton, Mrs. Townsend. Just Dalton. We don't bother with the mister."

"I run His Grace's household." The reprobate straightened his shoulders, peering at the woman down his nose with his good eye as he marked his territory like an alley cat.

"Perhaps back in town you do, Mr. Dalton." She offered him a tight smile in defiant retaliation. "Although I am sure I can find something for you to do here. Once I have met privately with His Grace and overseen serving his dinner in the formal dining room, I would be delighted to show you around Harpenden Hall and discuss what your particular duties might be here."

Both servants glared at Giles, expecting him to take sides, but he didn't have the energy. His timepiece burned in his waistcoat pocket, reminding him of *her* again. "Dalton, if you wouldn't mind seeing to His Grace. Mrs. Townsend, I could murder a cup of tea and a plate of something sweet and biscuit-shaped."

Mrs. Townsend bristled. "Wouldn't you like a personal tour of the hall first, Your Grace, to familiarize yourself with the surroundings and work up an appetite for your dinner?"

He smiled to cover his gritted teeth. "No need, as I know every nook and cranny well." She might well have been the custodian of the place for the last few years and think herself in charge, but this house was more his than anybody's. Or least it was for now and had been since the day Giles had been deposited to the drafty nursery on the third floor. "I lived here for my first twenty years, Mrs. Townsend." Just him and his succession of nannies and tutors until he was sent away to Cambridge kicking and screaming and, shortly afterward, banned from ever returning and forcibly removed each time he tried.

Without thinking, he reached for his watch and glanced at the dial. "It's getting late. I'll have the tea and biscuits in my bedchamber as I am all done with today, Mrs. Townsend." With everything and everyone. "It's been a long week and tonight, all I need is some sustenance, a hot bath, and some fresh sheets to sink my weary bones into."

Thwarted, she replied with a curt nod as she curtsied. "If that pleases Your Grace."

"And before you have any ideas to the contrary, I'll be the one seeing to his bath!" After issuing that parting shot to his new rival, Dalton stalked off in the direction of the laden carriages muttering under his breath.

Giles didn't wait to be invited in and strode through the front door, leaving everyone else standing outside. He shrugged off his soggy greatcoat and tossed it on the banister, then took the ancient, creaking stairs two at a time in his haste to get away. He needed to be alone with his jumbled, racing thoughts, fraught nerves, and conflicting emotions or he would end up exploding in public. And that wouldn't do when nobody here had done anything except the jobs they were paid poorly to do.

Instinctively, Giles headed to his old bedchamber in the east wing despite knowing Mrs. Townsend would have prepared the duke's room in the west wing for him as befitted his new station. Amid all the chaos, he had neglected to inform her he didn't want it, but he did not have the current capacity to care. Once inside, he threw himself on the bed to stare at the ceiling. The familiar cracked plaster was like an old friend, and he sighed aloud in relief that at least something else beyond blasted Diana felt solid and constant while everything else seemed so uncertain and up in the air.

There was so much to do.

So much to take in.

So much unexplained.

So much at stake.

So much still out of the sphere of his control, the weight of it all was suffocating him.

There was only one thing he understood fully and without a shadow of a doubt tonight: that was he too damn tired and overwhelmed to consider anything logically. So instead, he closed his eyes and gave in to the exhaustion, attempting to block out everything for the sake of his own sanity.

Except as he drifted off, exactly as it had every single night for the last dreadful week, his addled and overwhelmed brain decided to wander down a path it had no right wandering when his whole world was a lie that could implode at any moment.

Toward a vexatious dark-haired vixen who never minced her words or pulled her punches. To the woman who had been the constant pithy, prickly bane of his life all the time he had known her. The woman who could expose his lies to the world in a heartbeat if she uncovered them, but also the woman whose reassuring hand and presence had stopped him falling into the abyss when the worst had happened.

The woman his wary, frightened, lonely heart missed more than waking Giles was prepared to acknowledge. The woman who was now, reassuringly, only eighteen hours away.

Chapter Eight

"Can you move your legs, Jeremiah! They are taking up far too much space and crushing my skirts."

Jeremiah glared at Olivia over the top of his newspaper and gestured to his knees, which were drawn up about as far as he could in the confined space. "And where would you have me move them to, woman?"

"To your half of the carriage, Mr. Peabody, if you please, as is fair and reasonable." They had been bickering continually since they left the inn at Ludlow several hours ago, and after three and a half relentless days of travel, it was grating on Diana's last nerve.

"Fair! Reasonable! How, pray tell, *Mrs*. Peabody, is it reasonable for a woman of barely five feet to command additional inches of empty space because she doesn't want her stupid dress creased when a man of over six feet is scrunched up and restricted opposite her getting everything creased in the process? My joints are so damn stiff, I'll have to be lifted out of this goddamn carriage if we ever get to our destination!"

"There is no need to resort to coarse language, Jeremiah. Have some consideration for the girls' tender ears and stop being so self-ish."

Before Diana's temper exploded, it was the usually diplomatic Vee who groaned aloud first. "Please stop! And if you cannot stop, kindly stop the carriage so I can get out as I'd rather walk the last few miles than listen to any more nonsense from the pair of you!" She wagged a finger, her pretty face stern behind her spectacles. "You have both been intolerable all morning and that isn't fair on those of us crammed in here with you."

While the outburst impressed Diana, who had always thought the youngest Merriwell needed to grow a backbone, it stunned Olivia. Before she could counter with some outrage, her sister surprised them all again. "It was you who insisted the four of us share a carriage for the entire journey, Olivia; therefore, you of all people should make the best of it."

"Amen to that!"

Jeremiah's quip earned him a glare from Vee until, like his wife, he looked chagrined. There were a few seconds of blissful but tense silence until Olivia broke it.

"I don't know about you, Jeremiah, but I feel like a naughty child who has just been admonished by a stern schoolteacher."

"Well, it is funny you should say that," said Vee, grinning as if that were a compliment and the atmosphere wasn't as brittle as glass, "because the Reverend Smythe from the orphanage has asked me if I would consider taking over some of the lessons once we get back. He says I have a way with the children and am especially good at teaching them their letters." She had been volunteering at the small but progressive Covent Garden Asylum for Orphans since it opened to great philanthropic fanfare in the spring.

"Oh, that is wonderful, dear! I can see you as a teacher." Unlike Diana's, Olivia's bad mood could always evaporate in an instant. "But why did you not tell us before? When we could have all done with some good news as a distraction."

"To be honest, with poor Giles's loss and the funeral, it completely slipped my mind." Vee's sunny smile also evaporated. "I do so hope he is all right. He seemed to have taken his father's death badly—and by that, I mean much worse than I would have expected. He looked . . . so lost and overwhelmed when I last saw him."

Lost and terrified, more like, but Diana didn't say that.

"I should imagine the shock of taking on the dukedom has a lot to do with that." Jeremiah's ill temper of moments ago had also disappeared. "And be in no doubt, it's a lot to take on. You only have to consider the work Hugh puts into his estate to realize Giles has a mountain to climb, as his is apparently triple the size. Actually . . ." He frowned and snapped open his pocket watch. "As we've made good time, we're probably driving through it now. He's inherited over seventy-five thousand acres."

Diana gazed out of her window at the soaring hills all around them, stretching as far as the eye could see. Even on this gray day it was stunning. Narrow roads and rivers ran in the valley between them. Quaint villages, tiny hamlets, farmers' fields, and dense woodland peppered the vast expanse of green. For a girl who hadn't left the cramped confines of London until very recently, and only had the gently rolling land of Hugh's estate in Hampshire to compare it to, Shropshire seemed wild, untamed, noble, and majestic all at once, and quite unlike any scenery she had ever experienced before. Winters would be hard here, she realized; bitter and isolated.

The summers a glorious display of all the beauty nature had to offer. The pace and challenges of life so different from what she knew and understood, it was like another world. A world that a forger's daughter from Clerkenwell would have no concept of.

To think the erudite, flippant lover of leisure and quintessential bachelor-about-town Giles owned all this? Came from all this? It beggared belief.

Their carriage wound its way upward around a hill, meandered down the other side, and as it did she saw a pretty manor house from another era nestled on the side of the next hill along. Whitewashed walls with age-blackened Tudor beams crisscrossing them warred with a dense blanket of ivy that covered one corner. Despite the lack of sunshine, the diamond lead-light windows twinkled in their frames while a profusion of dainty but ornate twisted chimney pots sprouted from the slate-tiled roof, puffing welcoming smoke into the dull midmorning sky.

She sensed he was there before the driver announced their destination and experienced a sudden rush of relief and excitement, which she decided to put down to the end of the long journey rather than the thought of being reunited with him. Like the rest of the family, she had worried incessantly about him all week, as any sort-of-friend-who-only-tolerated-the-other would after his recent bereavement. Yet bizarrely, she had also missed him.

So much so that a worrying ache beneath her rib cage had bothered her for the duration. She refused to link it to the odd moment she had experienced during their last meeting, when she had wanted to hug him close and tell him everything would be all right. That had merely been her sympathy and compassion coming to the fore, a basic human response to a sad situation and nothing more. A friendly gesture because they were friends—of sorts. Giles viewed the world through the same cynical, jaded lens as she did, adored the ridiculous, was fluent in sarcasm, and didn't take himself too seriously. Appreciating that did not make her blind to all his flaws, and those flaws were manifold. Certainly, enough that she was as immune to his effusive charm, sinful good looks, and broad shoulders as she was to all men. Noticing those things, appreciating the aesthetics of them, and having your head turned by them were two very different things.

Two *very* different things.

And it was also perfectly normal to *feel* certain things for the opposite sex from time to time in an overtly physical way even though she wasn't predisposed to that sort of nonsense. Such reactions were natural in all the creatures of the earth after all, and being aware of those unconscious, lustful impulses was a long way from acting on them. Diana had always been curious and inquisitive, and now Minerva had found a man whose touch she obviously enjoyed, it was entirely normal to wonder, hypothetically, if one might have a similar effect on her. Not that she had any plans to turn that hypothesis into a reality, and even if she did, it wouldn't be with Giles. Dukes and forger's daughters were a laughable combination. Ridiculous, in fact. Why on earth would she want to kiss him when he vexed her so? But of their own accord, her lips tingled at the idea . . .

"What are you smiling so wistfully at?" Vee's question startled her. The fact that she was indeed smiling wistfully about a man startled her more.

"The scenery—of course." The "of course" an unnecessary clarification that earned her a disbelieving look from her sister and

Olivia, which she ignored as the carriage turned abruptly into a driveway. "Who knew the delights of Shropshire were so charming?"

"And speaking of charming delights of Shropshire . . ." Jeremiah nudged her and winked as he pointed out the window. Like an idiot, she looked and blushed like a beetroot. Because to make her misery complete, Giles was bounding down the steps to greet them.

As Jeremiah assisted his wife, Giles came to her side of the carriage and opened the door with a mile-wide grin. "You're early!" He seemed delighted by that. "I did not think I would see you till this evening."

"We made good time yesterday and overnighted in Ludlow instead of Worcester." She smiled back, a little overcome at the sight of him and a lot unsettled. He reached for her hand to help her down, and as every nerve ending rejoiced at the innocent contact, her stupid lips tingled all over again.

Chapter Nine

"And this is the Great Room."

Giles led them all into a vast oak-paneled room with a high vaulted ceiling supported by beams so thick that each one had to have been carved out of a single giant tree. After hours of traveling they had all needed some time to unwind and untangle before they took tea, so a much-too-rested Minerva, who hadn't been crushed in the same carriage with Diana, Vee, and the warring Peabodys, had suggested they stretch their aching legs with a tour of the house.

Harpenden Hall was a fascinating place and as charming as its owner, with wonky wattle-and-daub walls, creaking wooden floors, and a plethora of strategically placed suits of armor. There were two guarding the door of this impressive room, both clutching pikes, which added to the air of gravitas. One wall was dominated by a roaring fireplace so large Diana could have stood upright inside it without needing to bend, and it could easily accommodate Olivia, Vee, and Minerva beside her. The longest table she had ever seen occupied the middle, surrounded by heavy chairs with worn tapestry seats.

"In days of yore, this would have been where the Dukes of Harpenden held their feasts." Giles ran his fingers on the polished tabletop like a lover, clearly more attached to this house and everything in it than he had ever let on before.

"How many ancient dukes are there?" Minerva spun a slow circle, taking in all the portraits lining the walls.

"Excluding me, twenty-six. We Sinclairs can trace our lineage back to the Norman Conquest when Guillaume Saint Clair was given the first dukedom by William the Conqueror himself. Apparently, they were childhood friends, or so the unwieldy family histories state." Guessing bluestocking Vee's obvious question, he smiled at her. "The earliest volumes are on rolled parchment scrolls in the library, which I shall take you to see next." He pointed to a very crude, flaking portrait of a dark-haired man in armor with an unflattering bowl-shaped haircut. "That's Guillaume. You can separate out all the dukes from the non-dukes by the unsubtle family crests they had chiseled into their frames in case anyone confused them with the less worthy portraits gracing the walls. They all took being a duke much too seriously."

Vee peered at the Latin inscription on the molded gilt shield. "*Officium Supra Omnia?*"

"Duty Over Everything." Giles rolled his eyes at the portrait. "Words old Guillaume, and every duke since for that matter, lived by. He built the first Harpenden Hall on this site. It was a motte-and-bailey castle, more fortress than house, but necessary to suppress all the revolting locals who apparently did not take too kindly to being subjugated by the rampaging French."

He wandered to the next portrait and folded his arms, clearly enjoying being a knowledgeable guide. "Construction of the stone castle was begun by Guy Saint Clair around 1080."

"You have a castle?" Jeremiah was as impressed by this achievement as only an American could be. "Where's that?"

"What's left of it is at the top of the hill. It was destroyed during the latter stages of the Wars of the Roses, which incidentally also killed the tenth duke, Gerard. Then this chap . . ." Their host marched several yards down the room to a long picture of a dashing ancestor who looked a lot like Giles, but in doublet and hose, an impressive ruff and a scandalous amount of well-turned leg on show. "Godfrey *Sinclair*—we'd completely anglicized by then—built this house in the early 1500s."

"Guillaume, Guy, Gerard, Godfrey . . . *Giles.*" Diana couldn't help but laugh. "Don't tell me that all the Dukes of Harpenden have Christian names beginning with a *G.*"

"Of course they do." He pretended not to find that amusing. "For the aristocracy, my dear Miss Diana, our traditions are almost as sacrosanct as our noble blue-blooded line. We cannot risk tainting it with another random letter of the alphabet, or the bedrock of British society might crumble. It is also likely where my lifelong love of alliteration comes from. It's in the blood just like my superior nobility and inbred sense of duty." He winked at her and it did odd things to her insides. "My sire was a Gerald. An ugly, staid, and harsh name I am grateful I wasn't saddled with—though it suited him down to the ground. There have been several Georges, which I think lacks originality. Two Gilberts, a Granville, a Godwin, a Grégoire, a Gregor, *and* a Gregory. As you would expect, the Grégoire was one of the more flamboyant dukes while the Gregor was as dull as his flat consonants suggest. The Gregory hovered somewhere in between, and was more average than exceptional at anything, as Gregorys are prone to be."

"Which duke was the naughtiest?" Vee adored history and the worst of it most of all.

Giles pondered the question then shrugged. "I suppose that depends on your definition of *naughty*. If we are talking blood-thirsty, then hands down it's the original duke Guillaume, who never thought twice about burning a village or hanging a peasant in the name of duty. My grandfather—who was one of the Georges—allegedly killed a man during a duel that had something to do with his wife, or so the local gossip says."

Hugh stared at the paintings then at his friend. "It's not just the letter *G* you all have in common. You all look similar, too."

He was right. They did. In fact, apart from the outfits, there was a startling family resemblance going all the way back to the conquering Guillaume.

Giles nodded and pointed to his jaw. "It's the legendary square Sinclair chin. We were all cursed with dashing, dark good looks, impressive stature, and this saucy dimple that drives *all* the ladies wild." He wiggled his eyebrows suggestively at the ladies present. "I come from a long line of perfect physical specimens, so any swooning you might feel in my presence is perfectly understand-able. I wouldn't judge you for it."

Diana rolled her eyes. "I would. I disapprove of swooning."

"And I heartily approve of it." Her eldest sister smiled at her husband as if the sun rose and set with him. "Or at least nowadays I do." A comment that set Diana's eyes rolling all over again.

"Your father was a handsome fellow in his day, too, Giles." At Giles's staggered look, Hugh's outraged one, and Jeremiah's jealous one, Olivia became defensive. "Well, he was handsome! Any woman would have had to be blind not to notice Gerald Sinclair in his prime, but even his dashing dimple and legendary square Sinclair chin did not compensate for his dour personality. I never once saw him smile."

"I don't think he knew how." Giles gestured to a large group painting of a man, woman, and two boys, then tapped the foot of the taller of the sons who wore the sternest of the four dour expressions. "Even as a child he was a sourpuss."

"So apparently was his daddy." Jeremiah frowned at the picture and the twin expressions of pompous disdain on the twenty-fifth duke and the dark-haired boy who would become the twenty-sixth. "Who is that?"

They all stared at the pretty blond curly-haired cherub dressed in a profusion of lace.

"That's my uncle Gervais."

"Since when did you have an uncle?" Hugh's hands had gone to his hips.

"Since always, dear boy—but I've never met him so don't look so hurt that I neglected to mention him."

"Gervais . . . Gervais Sinclair . . . why does that name ring a bell? Oh . . . *Oh!*" Olivia's eyes widened as her hand covered her mouth. "Now I remember!" She shook her head as if she couldn't quite believe whatever it was she had just remembered and gazed at Giles in pity. "What a dreadful family you come from, Giles."

When neither elaborated, Diana asked, "What was wrong with Gervais?"

"It's finding what was right about him that would take less time to answer." Olivia was now frowning at the cherub. "He was a man of many faults and vices with the coldest eyes I have ever seen." She shuddered at the memory. A genuine shudder rather than a feigned one and so out of place on Olivia, it unsettled them all.

"What she is politely trying to say is that Gervais Sinclair was—*is* if he is still alive—a thoroughly nasty piece of work by all accounts." Giles was unoffended by Olivia's visceral reaction. "A debauched libertine, liar, and larcenist who left a trail of destruction, debt, and scandal wherever he went and who did something so heinous, evil, and atrocious he became persona non grata in society. However, as I was still in leading strings when he was banished in disgrace and the duke couldn't speak of him without turning purple, I was denied all the goriest details of the scandal."

"Lady Caroline Derbyshire." Olivia was still shaking her head. "The poor thing. Gervais Sinclair went out of his way to woo her after Giles's grandfather disowned him and eloped with her to Gretna Green."

"Eloping isn't a criminal offense."

"Not usually, Diana, you are quite correct. But when the bride gets taken there bound, gagged, and drugged it is."

Their host nodded. "Indeed—dear old Uncle Gervais was a kidnapper." It was Giles's turn to frown at the cherub. "Before that, by all accounts, he was in and out of debtors' prison and gambled away every coin that crossed his palm." He turned to Vee with a matter-of-fact expression. "Gervais is undoubtedly the naughtiest Sinclair in recent years. His infamy puts my scandalous reputation to shame."

"And why have I never heard of this, either?" Hugh was put out by his best friend's blatant secrecy and his mother's poor memory.

"After all these years, suddenly all of these skeletons are jumping out of your cupboard."

An odd look skittered across Giles's features, which he covered with a mischievous smile. "And this is coming from a man who hid the fact he possessed a sister from me for a decade!" Hugh had had plenty of those skeletons himself before he fell in love with Minerva. "People in glass houses really shouldn't throw stones, old boy, and in my defense I never mentioned Gervais because nobody ever mentions Gervais after what he did."

"The Derbyshire elopement was a dreadful scandal at the time, dear." Olivia patted Hugh's arm. "Thankfully, the law caught up with him before they crossed the border and Gervais was arrested and charged, but he absconded on the journey back to London and fled the country. Many suspected your grandmother aided his escape, Giles. She never made any secret that Gervais was the apple of her eye, and she wouldn't have been able to bear it if he were convicted and perhaps executed for the crime. Her husband—"

"Dueling George," said Giles helpfully while pointing to his portrait.

"The very one . . . yes, he was a truly disagreeable man, too . . . was dead by then but your father sent her away on the back of it and we never saw her in society again. I suppose he didn't want the scandal rehashed after he had worked so hard to bury it."

"I never met her so I couldn't comment with any authority on the state of their relationship." Giles stared at her portrait and shrugged. "Though I do recall being told she had died when I was ten or so. I have no idea if my father attended her funeral. Such knowledge would require a conversation rather than a lecture, and we never had one of those, either." He was making light of it, but the lonely tales of his childhood tugged some more on Diana's heartstrings.

"And Lady Caroline?" Vee's eyes were wide.

"Disappeared from society, too, the poor dear, we never saw her again. All very sad and tragic, and all thanks to the vile Gervais." She stared at the portrait as if the mere likeness in oils offended all her sensibilities. "Do you know where the scoundrel is now, Giles?"

"I haven't the vaguest idea. He could be long dead for all I know, and by the sounds of things, good riddance if he is." He stared at the portrait for the longest time, then sighed as if all his immediate ancestors were a mystery to him. "Shall we continue exposing the Sinclair skeletons over some tea?" He gestured to another door flanked by suits of armor. "I've asked for it to be taken to the library as that has always been my favorite vestibule and is much cozier than the drafty drawing room."

He opened the door with a great flourish for Vee, who was first in line, and beamed at her awed expression. "It's quite a library, isn't it, Miss Vee?"

Her sister nodded. "One I could lose myself in for hours. Weeks even!"

Like the Great Room, this one also had high vaulted ceilings, but instead of oak paneling it was thousands upon thousands of books that covered the walls.

"Godfrey Sinclair was a scholarly fellow and insisted on a space with some gravitas for all his books. I adore the smell of this room." Giles inhaled and so did Vee, then they grinned at each other.

"Beeswax and knowledge, my favorite combination."

"I am glad you approve, Miss Vee, for I am declaring this space yours for the duration of this visit."

Vee sighed. "In that case, I might never leave."

One by one they all filed past him to explore the space, but Diana held back. Once everyone was out of earshot, he regarded her quizzically as she rummaged in her reticule for the precious cargo she had had to get up at the crack of dawn to collect before the Standish carriages left for Shropshire. "I brought you a present."

"*You* brought *me* a present, harridan? Has the world gone mad?"

"Don't get too excited, it is only—"

"Your tea, Your Grace." Out of nowhere, Dalton rushed toward them holding a cup and saucer, the clonk of his wooden leg reverberating around the cavernous space, the beverage sloshing over the sides in his haste to get to his master. "Brewed to perfection for precisely four minutes and, as you can see, is the exact burnt umber shade you favor."

Hot on his heels was a small, plump woman who seemed extremely put out by Dalton and elbowed him as she barged past. "Your biscuits, Your Grace." She proffered a plate of shortbread at him as if it were as precious as the Holy Grail. "Fresh from the oven and sprinkled with sugar exactly as you like them. I saw to the sugar myself."

Diana turned to Giles, perplexed. "What is going on?"

He leaned toward her and whispered, his warm breath against her ear playing havoc with her senses, "The War of the Servants. Shropshire versus London. Dalton versus Townsend. Both feel threatened so are fighting for my affections by trying to outdo each other."

"Shouldn't you put a stop to it?" It seemed appropriate to whisper in his ear, too, but Diana instantly regretted it because it felt too intimate when only mere inches separated them and he smelled divine.

She could sense his smile against her hair. "I should. And I had every intention of doing so—but it is just too entertaining." He straightened, transforming into a commanding creature she had never seen before. One who looked every splendid inch the Duke of Harpenden as he glared at his warring servants with haughty disdain. "Are you aware that you are neglecting my guests?"

Dalton and Mrs. Townsend scurried away like ants to do his bidding, glaring at each other as they did.

"You are incorrigible." But Diana couldn't help laughing.

"I am—but this week has been light on levity." The duke dissolved and Giles returned to stare pointedly at her closed fist. "It has also been light on gifts, so hand yours over this instant." He held out his palm.

She passed him the clipping of *The Tribune*, making sure her fingers made absolutely no contact with his, for safety's sake. "I thought you might wish to read last Saturday's gossip column seeing as you missed it."

She waited while he scanned it until Giles smiled, obviously touched at the piece she had written for Dahlia's benefit but slaved over for hours for his sake.

"Tell her she brought the sunshine to my twilight."

The intensity of his gaze unnerved her and made Diana self-conscious about writing something so romantic when she prided herself on not possessing a single sentimental bone in her body.

She shrugged, irritated that her cheeks had begun to heat. "I couldn't imagine the duke waxing lyrical about love, so I told the writer to make it short and sweet but believable." A brief interlude with the duke clutching the lapels of a trusted servant, knowing he was about to die and giving one final redeeming instruction before he went with a bittersweet smile on his face. "I think they did a good job."

"The writer?" He wasn't fooled for a second. "Then kindly tell *the writer* it is perfect. Thank you."

Lost in his gaze and before she had the presence of mind to step away, he reached for her hand, laced his fingers with hers, and she felt the soft kiss he bestowed upon them everywhere.

Chapter Ten

An hour ago, at a little past midnight, gathering every box, ledger, letter, folio, and scroll into the center of the disorganized estate office at the back of the house had seemed like the most sensible way of tackling it. Now, as he stared at the utter chaos scattered around him, Giles sincerely wished he had been more methodical. But he had been angry. In a foul mood that not even Diana's or Hugh's presence could shift, he had suppressed it during dinner and that somehow made it worse now. Clearly, alongside everything else, he was more unsettled by the looming funeral on the morrow than he had realized, and still uneasy about riding out and dismissing Mr. Bryant, the steward, on his own doorstep when the snake had failed for the second day in a row to make an appearance at the house.

He wasn't so much unsettled because the bully hadn't had it coming, or even because Bryant hadn't had any helpful answers to his questions of the past, but more because being so ruthless and curt did not come easily to Giles. He had always worked hard to be different from the duke in the way he treated those who worked for him, choosing understanding and benevolence rather than wielding his power like an executioner's ax. Especially an employee who had served Harpenden for such a long time.

For the entirety of Giles's life, the duke's staff had changed with more frequency than the king's guard. Aside from Carruthers, only Bryant and Agatha, the duchess's former lady's maid, had lasted longer than a decade, and even Agatha and her fifteen years of loyal service had been sent packing within hours of her mistress's death. On that particular day, he had been too busy reeling from the news of his parentage to give poor Agatha much thought. But he had thought of her quite often in the four years since and worried about what had become of her. He would not give Bryant the same consideration. The man could rot in hell with the duke as far as he was concerned. Which was all well and good on a moral front, but on the practical it left him steward-less and drowning in a sea of papers he had to digest and understand fast in order to take full charge of the reins. Yet thanks to his need to blow off steam in private, what had been disorganized clutter was now a homogeneous mess and he had no earthly clue where to start.

But start he must, not just for the sake of Harpenden's abused tenants but also to search for the truth of his past, so he bent for one of the rent books that had been tossed on a pile in a large wooden chest and flicked through it. Like the state of this office, there was no rhyme or reason to the contents, which were more a hastily scribbled set of jottings than an actual account of a tenant's hard-earned rent. Apparently, as in everything he touched, the steward's definition of record keeping left a lot to be desired. Finding the answers he sought in this shambles would be nigh on impossible.

Disgusted, Giles threw the useless notebook across the room

and growled, then for good measure kicked the chest as well, imagining it was Bryant's slithering viper's head.

"What on earth are you doing?" He spun around at her amused voice, and his breath caught in his throat at the sight of her leaning, arms crossed against the doorframe as if she had been there for quite some time.

"Trying to understand how the estate has been run this past decade." A blatant lie when he knew the answer to that already. Badly.

"At half past two in the morning? You should be in bed, Giles. You have a tough day tomorrow."

Despite her concern, Diana clearly hadn't been to bed, either. Still fully dressed in the formfitting long-sleeved burgundy gown she had worn at dinner, she had a casual, rumpled, languid look about her that was very becoming. Poking beneath her hem were bedroom slippers rather than shoes; feminine, embroidered silk confections that would have been at odds with her no-nonsense character if he hadn't known she had a particular penchant for fine things. Her hair was unbound. He had never seen her hair down before, and it fell almost to her waist. Wayward dark tendrils flecked with copper framed her face and shimmered in the lamplight, begging to be touched.

"So should you." His words came out croaky, but he didn't dare clear his throat in case she realized it was strangled because of her. "If anyone needs the benefit of some beauty sleep, it is you."

"You need significantly more beauty sleep than me. Although, to be frank, even if you slept for a week you'd still look a fright." It was a blunt barb, said with little enthusiasm, and she smiled as she sighed it away. "I knew I wouldn't sleep straightaway, so didn't bother. I never can on the first night in a strange bed—no matter how comfortable and grand the bed is. And mine is so grand it needs steps to get into it and has a curtained canopy sprouting ostrich plumes."

He had put her in the old-fashioned Queen's Room on purpose because he knew its grandiose ridiculousness would amuse her. The green theme also matched her eyes—not that that had a bearing on his choice. Not that he would admit to, at any rate.

"I'll have you know ostrich plumes were de rigueur in olden times. No self-respecting lady-of-the-manor would dare sleep under anything not sprouting feathers." What the blazes had made him say "lady-of-the-manor"? Especially as this manor was his and he certainly couldn't risk it having a lady. Not without ruining the poor thing's life.

"What do the lords-of-the-manor sleep under?"

"Bearskin, of course, or wolfskin or even lion skin if they traveled. Something ferocious that they wrestled into submission with their manly bare hands."

"Complete with their heads, fangs, and dull, staring glass eyes, I suppose? Very restful." She pushed herself from the frame and walked toward him, the soft wool of her dress molding to her curves and her long, shapely legs like a second skin, as if she had discarded the petticoats and stays that usually went beneath exactly as she had her hairpins. The unwanted image sent a bolt of lust directly to his groin. "Which of those terrifying beasts did you wrestle to their deaths?"

"Giles Sinclair is a lover not a fighter." What the blazes had made him say that? And why were his features attempting to smolder as he said it?

Typically, she was unimpressed with his flirting. "What a hideous thought." She stopped on the periphery of the mess he had made and eyed it with curiosity, completely unaware that she stood basking in the light from the fire, which made those copper flecks in her hair crackle. "I came down to make myself some hot milk to see if that would make me drowsy."

"If you had rung your bell, someone would have brought you some."

She shrugged as if the concept never occurred to her. "Insomnia is depressing enough without inflicting it upon somebody else, and unlike some overprivileged folk"—she gave him a withering glance—"I am used to doing everything myself. Even after a year of being waited on, I doubt I shall ever get used to having servants." She gestured behind in the direction of the kitchen with a flick of her head, which made her pert breasts jiggle a little, confirming she had indeed discarded her stays, and he almost groaned aloud. "Would you like some?"

"Yes." Giles barely recognized the high-pitched squeak that had apparently replaced his deep, dulcet tones. "That would be lovely." He would choke back a vat of hot milk happily if sending her to warm it gave him a few private moments to give his body a stern talking-to!

She swished away toward the quiet kitchen and Giles sagged against the desk.

What was all that about?

He had always found the minx attractive. He'd have to be blind and half dead not to, but the attraction had never knocked him sideways before. It had always been something he had acknowledged then put away in a neat box marked DO NOT TOUCH because

Diana was off limits for so many reasons. The main ones being she was the prickly sister-in-law of his best friend—that was number one—and she also wasn't the sort he usually dallied with. The safe sort who enjoyed transient relations and came with no strings attached. That certainly wasn't Diana. Just like her sister had been to Hugh, Diana was a forever kind of woman. The sort a man would need to spend eternity with because accepting anything less would be pure, unmitigated torture.

Bloody hell.

Bloody.

Hell.

Where the blazes had that dangerous thought come from?

After all the yearning he had done this past week, alongside the unmistakable utter joy at seeing her again, the rampant, insistent lust and errant thoughts of forever were a new and worrying development a man in his precarious predicament could not afford.

"How do you feel about tomorrow?" While he was still reeling, Diana had returned and was back to leaning on the doorframe. Thankfully, she assumed his widened eyes were to do with the milk she had set warming, so she rolled hers. "I've used a saucepan before, Giles, and I can see it from here so don't panic. I won't burn your lovely house down."

He offered her what he hoped was a wry smile despite his suddenly racing heartbeat. "As well as can be expected, I suppose."

"We'll all be there beside you. Even me and Vee are breaking with tradition to stand shoulder to shoulder with you at the graveside in your hour of need, so you won't be alone." Yet the only person he cared was there was her, heaven help him, because clearly all the stress of the last week had now sent him mad. Stark, staring mad if he was entertaining impossible thoughts like that!

"Even so, I cannot deny I shall be glad to get tomorrow over with." Then, because his mind was so addled and before he was able to stop it, some of his real concerns leaked out. "It is distracting me from all the work that has to be done. Work I have desperately wanted to do for years . . ." He clamped his leaking jaw shut to stare at the chaos of the office, then realized a determined Hunter of the Truth like Diana wouldn't leave it there. Nor did he want her to. Not tonight at least. Tonight he needed to unburden himself of some of it with someone who cared. He hoped that was her.

"The duke neglected this estate for years and left a bully in charge in his stead. It has been grossly mismanaged for the last decade and run entirely for profit—to the detriment of the tenants. I had been told about the evictions and warned about the state of the farms, but I had no idea how bad things had got until I was allowed back here yesterday."

She frowned. "Yesterday?"

"It has been a while." He shrugged to cover the grief of that cruel punishment. "I made the mistake of criticizing the duke's flagrant neglect of his tenants the day I turned twenty-one. I offered—actually I demanded, and such forthrightness never went down well—to leave university and replace Bryant as the steward, because I knew I could manage it all better than that unsympathetic good-for-nothing. I grew up here. I knew the people and the land like the back of my hand and had spent all my formative years learning everything I could about estate management from the library, had so many plans to modernize and expand but . . ."

Giles ran an agitated hand through his hair at the sudden flash of pity in her expressive green eyes. "Typically, I got banished for opening my mouth. I regularly went behind their backs to visit the farms over the years, and tried to help where I could, but this is the first time I have been allowed to pass through the gates in a decade. It's practically impossible to do anything meaningful with no access to the accounts or the power to change things."

"The more I hear of your father, the more I dislike him. Did he have any decent qualities?"

"If he did, he kept them hidden from me." An unexpected flash of grief hit him, again for all the things a father and son should be to each other rather than what they were. "I have been racking my brains all week trying to recall one single poignant memory for his eulogy and I've drawn a blank. The man hated me. Resented me, though heaven only knows what for, and as I refuse to perjure myself in church, what I have written is now very dry and quite impersonal. Perhaps I should hand it over to a nitpicking grammarian to pretty up?"

"I wouldn't worry about prettying anything, Giles, as I am sure, no matter how dry it is, what you have written is fitting. More often than not, people get the funeral they deserve. At least yours will get a eulogy, a few mourners there on sufferance, a fancy family crypt to lie in, and his name carved in marble. Mine will probably get tossed into an unmarked pit in a prison somewhere. Don't get me wrong, he deserves nothing less, but it makes one think about one's own legacy doesn't it?"

Legacy. Oh! How he loathed that word.

"How do you want to be remembered?" A more personal question than he usually asked her, but one that deviated from the rutted path of his tenuous legacy. "Let me guess—'Here lies Diana, a troublesome wife to her poor nagged husband, devoted mother to her battalion of fearsome warrior daughters, and determined Hunter of the Truth till her final breath'?"

"I shall settle only for the latter as I have no desire for the former, thank you very much."

"Whyever not?" She had said as much before to anyone who happened to mention it, but he suddenly needed to understand her reasons. Thinking of Diana spending a lifetime alone seemed so sad because she deserved everything. Almost as sad as the fact he had to spend his alone, too, when he didn't deserve it either. He had always avoided serious monogamy out of necessity—not choice. "Don't you want a family?"

"You met my father." He had. Alfred Merriwell was an odious crook with no redeeming qualities whatsoever. A man who had abandoned his own daughters simply to avoid the responsibility of them before returning like a bad penny to try to blackmail his eldest. "He was enough to put me off men for life."

A legacy she didn't deserve, either. "It strikes me as grossly unfair to tar all men with the same filthy brush. We are not all like our fathers. I would certainly hope I am nothing like mine." Now he sounded as though he was putting himself forward as a candidate. "Perhaps you might give one a try one day and they might surprise you?"

Whoever that lucky fellow was, Giles knew already he would despise him on principle.

Her eyes clouded for a moment, then she pulled a face. "I am too suspicious to be surprised and too happily wedded to my freedoms to be bothered to try. As his daughter I suffered seventeen years as a powerless chattel. It did not suit me."

"Therefore, you think marriage a prison and all husbands the jailers?"

"Not always. Some couples seem to thrive together, and I realize many more rub along quite content, but I have always chafed against the confines of other people's expectations; I am too selfish to compromise any of what I fought hard to achieve. I much prefer to make my own decisions, even if they are flawed sometimes. I loathe being at the mercy of others and beholden to comply with their rules." Her dark brows furrowed as if her own stark honesty surprised her before she disguised it with a smile.

"So much so that even being the middle sister annoys me. I plan to grow old disgracefully in my own little apartment somewhere, doing exactly as I please, when I please. And before you say I shall be lonely, as everybody always does whenever a woman dares break the accepted mold we are all supposed to fit in, I shan't. I have two sisters who seem determined to fill the world with offspring, so I shall lead my nieces and nephews astray whenever I feel the transient urge for the hearth and home of family." Before he could respond, she turned on her heel. "And talking of hearths, I'd best fetch our milk. I don't want to face the wrath of Mrs. Townsend if it boils over and burns on the range."

When she came back a few minutes later clutching the handles of two steaming mugs in one hand and a plate of biscuits in the other, she seemed so determined to change the subject to something less personal, she did so while walking. "These, I take it"—she pointed to the anarchy on the floor with the biscuit plate—"are the estate accounts?"

"Sadly, for the last four years at least, yes. Alongside everything else unfiled from contracts to correspondence."

"Oh dear. That really is an unholy mess to unravel."

He nodded as he stared at the carnage. "It appears once my father stopped his fleeting annual duty visit, his dreadful steward stopped organizing. I don't know where to start, really wish I hadn't, and fear it will take the best part of forever to get into the heart of it all."

She blew out a slow breath then smiled. "But a journey of a thousand miles always begins with a single step, Giles, and many hands make light work. I propose we fortify ourselves with this hot milk, and then, seeing as apparently neither of us is in any mood to sleep, I suggest we get cracking on it."

Chapter Eleven

In her haste to finish it before they left in the morning, Diana was in grave danger of making a hash of her promised article. Not all of that was her fault. Today had been consumed by the funeral. There had been few opportunities to write much of it on the way to Shropshire, because she had shared a room with Vee at every inn they stopped at, and she could hardly work on it in the carriage in full view of everyone.

The first real chance she'd had to make some headway on it was last night, but she had allowed herself to become distracted by Giles and had helped him organize a fraction of the mountain of papers amassed in his steward's office instead of writing until she was done as she intended.

She bitterly regretted that now for two reasons.

The first being she was now so behind with her Camden Union Canal swindle story it was unlikely she would get the thing finished for the day she got back, as she had faithfully assured Charlie she would. And second, she had enjoyed those few uninterrupted, unwatched hours with Giles far more than she was comfortable admitting.

Especially to herself.

Even as they both started yawning, she had lingered in his company longer than she should have simply because she had wanted to—as her current wandering mind and severe lack of concentration were testament. No human could function properly on three hours' sleep. Diana always needed at least seven.

Yet she had still chosen listening to all his plans over counting sheep, impressed more than she had been prepared to acknowledge aloud at the altruism he had been plotting for at least a decade. A rent amnesty for six months to make up for his father's overcharging, urgent cottage repairs, new roads to help his tenants get their produce to market easier, interest-free loans to help them purchase modern farm equipment or to improve their herds, a school and apprenticeships. He wanted the younger generation to have more choices in the world than their parents had had and the opportunity not to work the land if they wanted a different path. All admirable goals, which he intended to fund out of his now uncomfortably deep pockets—just as soon as he could make head or tail of Mr. Bryant's atrocious record keeping.

They had talked nonstop for hours and that had been . . . nice.

There had been an easiness between them since he had sought her out at the newspaper office, which added a new dimension to their sparring relationship. Giles was confiding in her, and apparently her alone, and that was both humbling and rather lovely. Last night, as he had poured out all his worries about the state of his estate, he seemed to want her advice as well as her help. He had certainly allowed her carte blanche to organize the mess he had made of his steward's office in the way she saw fit, teasing her about her nitpicking skills coming in handy in his hour of need while lugging ledgers and boxes to her designated piles uncomplaining.

More than once she had caught herself watching as he did that. The way the muscles bunched in his arms beneath the soft linen of his rolled-up shirtsleeves as he lifted and the way the fabric of his breeches pulled taut over his tight behind each time he bent over were most distracting. Enough that her mind had wandered to them plenty of times since, just as it wanted to do now.

Good grief, she'd never get this story written at this rate!

She wasn't usually prone to daydreaming, and if her cynical mind wandered, it was usually to the dark or tragic circumstances of something rather than musing on the components of a gentleman's physique.

Diana huffed and gave herself a good telling-off for that uncharacteristic weakness, then dipped her quill in the ink again and forced herself to write:

According to my source at the Stock Exchange, Lord Jonathan Tubbs is still selling shares for £150 apiece, and has already sold . . .

She doubled-checked her notes for accuracy.

. . . a staggering 800 fake certificates at that extortionate price. Where those funds have gone is unclear. Lord Tubbs claims they are being used to purchase materials and to pay the wages of the battalion of Irish navvies he has hired to dig the canal, but a year after the plans were approved not a single spade of earth has been dug yet anywhere along the proposed route; nor is there any sign of those navvies in the lodging houses nearby. Lord Tubbs, however,

*is lording it up all over the capital and spending his
pocket money as if it is going out of fashion—which
is ironic when one considers Lord Tubbs isn't actually a lord at all. He was born Hubert Greengage, a
humble miner's son from Cornwall. After a misspent
youth, young Hubert was transported to ten years'
hard labor in the Antipodes . . .*

"I see you are in the midst of writing a piece for that tawdry
rag you *don't* write for?"

Diana squealed at the interruption. Then promptly knocked
over the inkwell as she tried to cover her damning article with
one of the books she had grabbed as a prop to hide what she was
really doing if anyone happened to wander into the library. Thick
blue ink oozed over the desk, forcing her to gather up her precious
notes and hug them close to her chest while she attempted to mop
up the spillage one-handed with a fresh piece of paper.

"You frightened the life out of me! What do you think you are
about, Giles Sinclair, sneaking up on me like that?"

"I certainly did not sneak." He frowned in mock offense as
he saved the books from the ink. "Giles Sinclair never sneaks. Or
creeps or shuffles or prances, for that matter. He either strides in
a manly fashion that makes all the ladies swoon, or he moves with
deadly stealth." He passed her a pristine handkerchief to finish
off her mopping. "I *strode* in here to tell you dinner is about to be
served. Or at least it will be in fifteen minutes." Then he seemed
awkward to be there. "Olivia sent me."

Of course she had. Olivia had been bending over backward
since their arrival to thrust the pair of them together at every opportunity. She had even used some unsubtle maneuvering to sit Diana

beside Giles in the chapel earlier, as if she assumed all that thrusting would suddenly bear fruit. As if they weren't apples and oranges and the charming duke from Mayfair who could trace his lineage back a thousand years and the cynical forger's daughter from Clerkenwell who did not even know her own grandparents might suddenly forget all those stark differences to make an unlikely jam.

"How was your ride?" Hugh had insisted they gallop across the fields together the moment the funeral was done so Giles could clear his head.

"It certainly blew the cobwebs out. And before you ask, yes, I do feel better for it." He shrugged, the tight, pinched expression he had worn since this morning finally gone now that his father was in the ground. "One onerous task is done. Only another nine hundred and ninety-nine to go." He began to rearrange the stack of books on the desk into a neat tower rather than look at her. "Is Jeremiah still wedded to leaving at the crack of dawn? Only you have barely been here five minutes and it is such a long way to come for a fleeting visit."

"It cannot be helped. He has business that cannot wait and must be home by Monday."

"But you and Vee could stay on with Hugh and Minerva . . . Have a bit of a holiday . . . See a bit of Shropshire . . ." The books had ruler-straight edges now but he still refused to meet her gaze. "Use your nitpicking talents to help me finish organizing my paperwork . . ."

"Ahh—you just want a minion because you don't want to deal with all that mess yourself." But she was sorely tempted to stay without the need for any incentive beyond spending more time with him, and that was a worry. More concerning was the strange desire to witness the same need mirrored in Giles's eyes, but they were resolutely rooted to the books still. Deflection again? Her silly heart warmed at the prospect. "But alas, that minion cannot be me. I have to be back at the newspaper by Monday, too."

"Why? Don't they have other nitpicking grammarians they can call upon?" He gestured to the crumpled pile of papers still clenched against her bosom. "Or are you writing something scandalous for them that cannot wait?" Two dark brows wiggled as his arms folded again because flippant Giles had replaced the vulnerable one. "Is that why you have squirreled yourself away in the farthest corner of my library?" He reached for the corner of the most precarious sheet to take a peek and she instantly tugged it out of the way, making him smile in the most sinful fashion. "I see I have hit the nail on the head! The nitpicker isn't a nitpicker after all, it seems, but a shameless peddler of gossip exactly as we all suspected. What is it about this time? A tryst? A new mistress? A juicy gambling debt from a dubious establishment?"

She feared her laughter sounded hollow. "Oh, you know me . . . I am tenacious, and I figure if I keep bombarding *The Tribune* with stories, by the law of averages, one of these days they will have to print one."

Giles yawned. "That pathetic lie is getting very old when we all know that you, Diana, Goddess of the Hunt and dedicated Hunter of the Truth, always write their most scintillating snippets of gossip." He pouted. "I've confided all sorts to you this last week. I was even beginning to consider you a friend—in the loosest possible sense of the word—but now I see the heartfelt confidences only go one way, I shall have to revert to secrecy again to even things up."

For a moment, she was tempted to capitulate until she remembered the stakes. Maintaining the translucent lie of the gossip column within their close-knit family group ensured that while they were teasing her about it, they were also distracted from the whole truth. If her sisters discovered what else she did, they would worry about her, and rightly so, because there was no denying ruining the lives of powerful people came with an element of risk.

"How many times do I have to tell you that I merely correct spelling and gr—"

"Liar!" Giles lunged to grab one of her papers and in her panic to snatch it back she sent half of them scattering across the floor. As she scrabbled to gather them up he started to read the sheet he had nabbed, so she caught the hem of his coat, praying he hadn't grabbed anything important.

"Give that back!"

"*Investors beware! As the Camden Union Canal Company is merely the latest moneymaking façade of an infamous serial fraudster . . .*" He paused to grin, swapping the page to his other hand as she wrestled his arm. "It starts well. The first line is catchy, and it certainly hooks the reader." He pivoted as her fingers grazed the page, stretching his arm way out of her grasp, and started to walk as he read to better dodge her, swatting her flailing hand away like a fly while his long legs ate up the ground.

"*The swindle, and be in no doubt the Camden Union Canal Company is a swindle of gargantuan proportions, has already relieved unsuspecting speculators of £120,000 since its inception earlier this summer.*" Feeling sick, she watched his suddenly narrowed eyes quickly scan the damning words she had labored far too long over.

"I mean it, Giles! That is private! Give it back now!" He continued reading silently to himself, totally immersed and oblivious

to her protestations until he stopped dead and she almost crashed
into the back of him as she lunged again.

This time he didn't fight her and instead, after she had retrieved the page from his suddenly limp fingers, simply stared at
her, the cogs of his clever mind turning so fast she could practically hear them whirring. Panic made her babble.

"It's really nothing. Nothing beyond a silly idea I have been
tossing around to while away all the hours in the carriage and—"

"Ahem . . ." Neither of them had heard Mrs. Townsend approach, and they both jumped in surprise to see her stood in the
middle of the library. "I am sorry to interrupt—but dinner is
ready. Everyone is already seated and waiting for you."

"Yes, of course . . ." Diana nodded like a woodpecker, grateful
for the excuse to escape even though the last thing she was now
capable of doing was choking down food at a family meal.

She bolted for the door, hugging her notes close while her racing mind scrabbled for an explanation that would sound plausible,
trying to ignore the rapid approach of his boots behind her and
praying he would keep his suspicions to himself. She had almost
made it into the dining room when his big hand caught her elbow
on the threshold.

Giles tugged her to face him and blinked at her in shock.
"Bloody hell, Diana!"

He blew out a breath, raking a hand through his dark hair
as he stared straight into her soul, his expression a cross between
sheer disbelief and dismay. "No wonder you are so cagey about
what you do at *The Tribune*—" Thankfully, he lowered his initial
growl to a ragged whisper. "You're the bloody Sentinel!"

Chapter Twelve

Diana had paced her bedchamber like a caged tiger for hours after dinner, her head spinning and her heart beating nineteen to the dozen.

He knew!

Giles was in no doubt she was the Sentinel and she had no earthly idea what to do about that or, worse, what *he* intended to do about it.

She'd denied it, of course. Even managed a brittle laugh as she pitied him for his vivid imagination before Olivia had bustled out to fetch them. Yet she knew he wasn't fooled for a second. Thank goodness, Giles had kept his own counsel in front of the others throughout dinner and had remained uncharacteristically subdued as they all sat in the drawing room afterward. Her guarding the book she had hastily folded her incendiary notes into because his gaze kept wandering to it.

The others put his lack of conversation down to the dreadful few days he had had and made allowances. After all, he had sacked his steward then buried his father in quick succession. Two ordeals that would take their toll on anyone. Those things still undoubtedly played on his mind, but the intense glances he kept sending her way when nobody else was looking told her she had added to his burdens, and the guilt from that weighed heavy despite his knowing not being her fault.

When Olivia had begun to play the piano, and Vee volunteered to turn the music pages, he had moved beside her on the sofa and waited until everyone was immersed in the tune before whispering in her ear.

"Meet me here at midnight."

"I hardly think that would be proper . . ." Like a coward she had tried to stall, even though she knew her excuse was a pathetic one in view of the hours they had spent all alone in his steward's office the previous night.

"Propriety be damned, Diana! You have never cared one jot about it before." Even as his soft murmur sent ripples of unwanted awareness down her spine, she heard his anger loud and clear. "We either talk down here or I come to your bedchamber. You choose."

The last thing she wanted was Giles in her bedchamber, so she agreed. Facing him on the back foot, her secret hovering in the air above her head like an ax waiting to fall, in a room she had dreamed about him in again last night would be unsettling in the extreme.

So the drawing room it was.

She sucked in a calming breath before she pushed the door open, wishing that same breath didn't catch in her throat the second she saw him basked in the firelight, on the exact spot on the sofa where they had sat too close earlier. The swirling emotion in his stormy eyes like liquid amber as he stared at her wordlessly over his shoulder. In deference to the late hour, the servants had turned all the lamps down low, casting most of the room and the perfect angles of his face in shadows.

The overall effect of his presence and blatant intimacy of the setting unnerved her more than she had bargained for, so she used the excuse of quietly closing the door to compose herself before she turned back, feigning bravado as she walked toward him.

"Should I stand for your blistering lecture or would you prefer us to swap positions while you loom over me wagging your finger."

"What good would either of those things do? I am not your lord and master, Diana, and you are a grown woman who will do as she pleases irrespective of what I have to say on the subject."

He patted the seat beside him. The same seat where the seductive timbre of his deep voice had sent tingles ricocheting to each nerve ending mere hours ago. "But I should still like to have the discussion in order to know how to proceed with the burdensome new knowledge I wish, with every fiber of my being, that I did not possess."

Closer, she could see myriad other emotions in his irises beneath the obvious anger. Frustration. Indecision.

Concern.

That one shone brightest and left her off kilter as she perched on the edge of the cushion next to him. She didn't want him to care, had never wanted any man to care about her nor care about him in return, but now that she knew he did, it ran riot with her emotions. More guilt layered thick—because he really did not need this now, too—while her silly heart basked in the revelation that he did care. A lot.

"What the hell were you thinking?"

She stared at her hands as she smoothed her skirts, trying not to feel wretched about something she had absolutely nothing to feel guilty about. "About what specifically?"

"You know exactly what, Diana!" He threw his hands up in the air. "Let us not play games when I know you are the Sentinel and you have been playing fast and loose with your own safety for months!" He blew out a ragged breath. "Have you any idea what danger you've put yourself in?"

"I am in no danger whatsoever." She kept her own tone reasonable even though such diplomacy went against the grain. She needed to keep Giles on her side if she was going to keep her most closely guarded secret intact. "Believe me, I have always been exceedingly careful and discreet. I never do anything to put myself in harm's way. That is why, after all this time, nobody apart from the newspaper proprietor, and now you, knows the Sentinel's true identity. And to be fair, if you had been a gentleman earlier and not stolen my private property in such a childish way, you would still be none the wiser."

"But I am wiser and now I am worried sick!"

"While your concern is lovely, Giles"—really lovely for some inexplicable reason—"I can assure you it is entirely unnecessary. I have been careful to cover my tracks and I am quite capable of looking after myself. In fact, I have been doing so for many years."

"Really?" He looked her up and down. "You think a slip of thing, like you, is a match for a burly brute baying for blood?"

She had bested more than one burly brute in her time and all before she wrote for the newspaper, but she wouldn't tell him that. "Nobody is after my blood, Giles."

"Yet! But it is only a matter of time."

"Only if my identity gets revealed—which hopefully it won't."

She stared straight at him, hoping he would see sense and praying she could be diplomatic enough to make him see it. "There are three people on the planet who know I am the Sentinel. Not even my own sisters have worked it out, and they know me better than anyone." She gazed deep into his eyes unflinching, trying to ignore the odd effect his had on hers and failing miserably. "I should very much like to keep it that way."

"Hugh is my best friend, Diana. I cannot, in all conscience, keep it from him. You are now the most feared columnist in the capital. What if something were to happen to you? How would I explain away my silence? He would never forgive me and, frankly, I wouldn't blame him as I would never forgive myself, either."

"Giles . . ." She leaned closer and stroked his arm, touched by his obvious concern, then wished she hadn't when her wayward palms begged to go wandering up his biceps and over his broad shoulders. In case they did, she sat back and fastened her hands together in her lap like a nun.

"Why on earth would anything happen to me? For who would ever believe the most feared columnist in the capital was a woman? And such an unimportant one at that? You have to concede, being me is the perfect disguise for that endeavor. Most people in society do not even know my name, and if they do they look down on me. To all intents and purposes, at best I exist on the periphery. A fish out of water. Too educated to be common and too common to be one of them. The Earl of Fareham's sister-in-law, a charity case with the most dubious connections and no money whatsoever. Unremarkable, unimpressive, and so inconsequential, I blend into the paneling."

He frowned at that. "Have you never looked in a mirror, Diana?

Because believe me, you are far too beautiful to blend into anything."
Despite being backhanded, his unexpected compliment excited her.
He flapped his hand in the vicinity of her body, looking uncomfortable to be talking about it. "One cannot blend in if one is cursed with being temptation incarnate."

Did that mean he was tempted by her, too? And why did that possibility make her pulse quicken with anticipation instead of revulsion?

Before she allowed her mind to meander down that unfamiliar and unsettling path, Diana forced a laugh that said he was being ridiculous and his compliments were water off a jaded duck's back. "If I am, Giles, that is surely all the more reason why I will be forever underestimated. Men only ever see the face and the figure—especially of a woman of no consequence—never the canny woman beneath. Even if somebody came sniffing around the newspaper looking for the Sentinel, I have worked there as an overlooked nitpicking grammarian for three years. I was correcting the shocking spelling of my peers long before the Sentinel came along and usurped them, and they all still think I am so desperate to become one of them, even my contributions to the gossip column are shrouded in the utmost secrecy. Apart from Charlie, all the men I work with see me as a joke. A silly girl trying to compete in a man's world."

"You are the least silly girl I have ever met." An even better compliment than being called beautiful but not quite as thrilling as being described as temptation incarnate. "And only a blithering idiot wouldn't see that."

"People only see what they want to see. You know that better than anyone, Giles. Outside of our circle, who else knows you are far more than the irreverent gentleman of leisure that you want them to see?" She had him there. She could tell by the way he couldn't meet her eye.

"And if a man can so easily fool his fellow men, I can assure you it is much simpler to do so as a woman. Most men are brought up to believe the fairer sex are weaker in every way, especially intellectually, so they do not question it. They'll laugh at us for trying to be more or dismiss our efforts because they feel threatened. If they begin to view us as equals, they will have to treat us as equals, and they are unlikely to do that unless they really have no other choice and a bloody revolution is imminent. For now, the whole world is a man's world and the suitable, acceptable roles of women very clearly defined."

"That's as may be, but—" She didn't let him finish. The stakes were too high to allow him to shut her down with maybes.

"You claim to be the Sentinel's biggest fan, and you believe good should always triumph over evil—and that is exactly what my column is for! So I am begging you, Giles, please don't go to Hugh. If my family finds out, you know they will try to make me stop and—"

"Of course they will make you stop! You are putting yourself in danger."

"Not yet, I haven't and . . . well . . ." Emotion choked her throat. "I have worked so hard to get where I am. Do you have any idea how difficult it is for an insignificant woman from my lowly background to get to where I have? To be able to make a difference? To matter? That is everything to me. Please don't take it away."

"You are asking me to lie to the same family who have welcomed me into their fold with open arms. Who traveled two hundred miles to stand beside me at a graveside this morning out of nothing but solidarity so I didn't have to face the ordeal alone."

"Not lie, Giles, I would never ask that of you." At least not yet. "They harbor no suspicions beyond my contributions to the gossip column and have no problem with that aspect of my career—that is the bulk of what I do, I swear it. All I am asking you to do is keep the rest of my work a secret. Just until I can prove to you that all your fears are ungrounded because I am good at my job and even better at hiding it from the world."

His silence was deafening.

He stared into the crackling fire as if that might hold the answer, his fingers gripping his thigh. His hands again, the only visible sign he was at war with himself. After an age he exhaled and turned to face her, his gaze more intense than she had ever seen it. "For now, Diana, I will hold my tongue—but I reserve the right to tell him the moment I feel the situation warrants it or your safety is in peril."

She wasn't capable of hiding her relief. "Thank you." She reached out and squeezed his hand with both of hers, then dropped it like a hot potato when she heard footsteps outside a split second before the doorknob turned.

Chapter Thirteen

Dalton came in grinning, taking in their close proximity and her flushed cheeks with a knowing smirk. "I couldn't help but notice you were both still up *again* tonight, so I took the liberty of bringing you a nightcap." He deposited a silver tray on the side table. "A bit of brandy to warm your cockles on this cold night, to banish all the stresses from your minds and help you *relax*." The word "relax" dripped with innuendo. "It's the good stuff, too, for you deserve the best, Your Grace, especially after the day you've had. Proper cognac and not that smuggled rubbish that's piled in the cellar gathering dust." He removed the stopper from the decanter, sniffed it sighing, then poured two generous glasses almost to the brim and held them up to the firelight for inspection. The liquid glowed copper red within the crystal.

"I know you aren't much of a drinker, Your Grace, but this is a real treat, trust me. It's very smooth." He winked at Giles with his good eye as he pressed the glass into his hand as if winking were something butlers did to dukes all the time. "I had a little nip of it myself to be sure after I liberated it from Mrs. Townsend's cupboard." He passed the second glass to Diana and winked again.

"Not only will it help you sleep, miss—when the time finally comes for sleeping—but it'll also put hairs on your chest."

"Because surely every young woman is desirous of a thick pelt of hair protruding from her bodice." Giles rolled his eyes at her. "It is a mystery to me that you remain single, Dalton, for you have such a poetic way with the ladies."

"Like you, Your Grace, it would take a very special lady indeed for me to give up my wild bachelor ways." Dalton tugged his forelock as his eye flicked to Diana before he grinned again solely for his master. "Alas . . . I haven't found mine yet." He wiggled his eyebrows some more. "But if you want my opinion—"

"I really don't, Dalton."

The servant grinned at Giles's narrowed stare. "Then I shall leave you both in peace to continue whatever it is that you are doing all alone while the rest of the house sleeps, and if anyone asks"—he tapped his nose—"be assured I saw nothing."

As usual, neither of them chose to acknowledge the blatant insinuation, and instead sat awkwardly while they waited for the butler to limp away. Only when he was gone did Diana speak. "Well . . . that was embarrassing." Her cheeks were on fire.

Giles frowned as if he hadn't heard her or anything his matchmaking manservant had said. "What am I thinking?" He slapped his forehead. "I cannot leave here yet, even for you . . . I have too much to do." He stared at her pained. "I am going to have to send Dalton to protect you in my stead."

"What?" He was being preposterous. "I don't need protecting!"

"But what if something happens while I am here? It'll take a week for your message to get to me and several days before I can get back to town—even if I ride through the night I will still arrive too late to help you. I am afraid it is settled. Dalton will accompany you home."

"Settled!" Outrage dripped from every pore. "I do not answer to you, Giles Sinclair, or anyone for that matter, and I have managed well enough for six months without a bodyguard!"

"More by luck than judgment!"

Her temper snapped. "How is that keeping my secret? I shall stick out like a sore thumb traipsing around everywhere with a one-eyed, one-legged, tactless pirate glued to my side! Let alone how I shall explain his presence to my fam—" His finger shushed her lips and they seemed to blossom to life beneath his touch.

"I am not an idiot, Diana. And despite all outward appearances to the contrary, neither is Dalton. I wasn't suggesting that he follow you around like a bad smell, more that he be close to hand if you need him. An extra pair of eyes and ears for both our sakes—at my house in Tavistock Square. A ten-minute ride to Fleet Street rather than a week and two hundred miles away." He seemed to notice where his finger was and gently removed it, unconsciously fisting his hand as it withdrew. "Those are my conditions, Diana. My decision is made and I will not be swayed. You accept Dalton in exchange for my silence . . . at least until I can return and stand guard over the Sentinel myself."

"When will that be?" Something else had replaced her outrage. Diana couldn't quite explain what beyond a deep-seated disappointment because his sad expression said he would not be returning anytime soon.

"Who knows . . . three months . . . four . . . perhaps five. There is much to do and only me to do it."

"Five months." Her heart plummeted at the prospect. "I shall miss you." The truth escaped her still-tingling lips before she could stop it. To cover her mortification, she sipped her drink. To her complete surprise, the taste was pleasant. The tawny liquid as smooth as Dalton had promised as it warmed her throat and gave her the perfect excuse to change the subject. "My father used to drink brandy—whiskey, rum, and gin, too—horrid stuff that made your eyes water just from sniffing the fumes. But this is nice." She was holding out an olive branch. One he hesitated before taking.

"It was the duke's one extravagance—he'd palm off the cheap stuff on everybody else, but he only ever drank the finest cognac. I've never tried it because of that. Never wanted to appreciate anything he did or have anything in common with him." He sniffed it as if it were something noxious before taking a tentative sip. "You're right, though. It's not bad."

He sipped some more and she did, too. Her because her head told her to bolt now that they had reached an accord, but her heart wanted her to stay. To soak up every moment of these last hours before they had to say goodbye. Giles seemed in no hurry to leave, either, and settled back cradling his glass while looking into the fire lost in thought. After an age he sighed.

"They shape us, don't they? Fathers? Even when we wish they didn't."

"They do indeed." Alfred Merriwell had certainly shaped the woman she was now. "Mine would betray you as soon as look at you if he benefited in some way."

Diana sipped more brandy to take away the sudden bitter taste of all those countless disappointments and betrayals—but always one in particular. The fateful occasion when he had offered her to a creditor for the night as payment for a gambling debt.

She still recoiled at the memory of that brute pressing his foul lips against hers in that alleyway as his fists pinned her wrists to the wall. A dark alleyway her father had duped her into entering. He had denied it afterward, of course, acting all incensed and suitably relieved that she had escaped, but it had been the final nail in his coffin. And perhaps the final nail in hers, too. She had certainly never been quite the same afterward. Any residual naïveté died that night in that alleyway, and a very different woman had stalked out of it.

One who no longer took a person's word for granted and never trusted anything. Yet one who grabbed hold of the reins of her own destiny with both hands that same night. Who charted her own course and did everything possible to make sure she was never at anyone else's mercy again.

Bile burned in her throat at that unwanted memory, but she masked it with a matter-of-fact shrug in case the canny Giles saw her discomfort and asked what was wrong.

"Is that why you are so hell-bent on hunting out the truth and holding the villains accountable?"

"Probably . . . I suppose I know what it is to feel powerless and voiceless and at the mercy of others." Why did she keep trusting him with the truth? "But I also know those things can change in an instant if you know how to fight your enemy." With that brute in the alleyway, only some quick thinking and a well-placed knee had given her the briefest opportunity of escape. "If you are brave enough to wield it, the truth is always the most powerful weapon against evil."

With Alfred Merriwell, that truth had been his own duplicity. His lies, which had freed her wrists from his shackles. An irony she had always thought fitting.

Even at seventeen, Diana had realized that if he would betray his own flesh and blood without blinking an eye, he wouldn't think twice about doing it to anyone else. Once she started digging around that suspicion, she discovered that he had not only betrayed someone else but also snitched on some real villains—and to Bow Street, no less—for the reward. The cardinal sin as far as his criminal associates were concerned and one that would end with his garroted body washing up on the banks of the Thames if it were ever disclosed.

She had enjoyed spelling it all out to him behind her sisters' backs.

Enjoyed watching the fear in his eyes as the tables turned and he realized that her threat to expose him if he ever risked one of his daughters again was as real as that foul brute in the alleyway. Within days he had abandoned them all and she had rejoiced in that, too, proud it had been her foot that kicked him out the door even though it had plunged the Merriwell sisters into worse poverty as a result. Even with that, she had never regretted her decision. Dirt-poor and vulnerable was infinitely better than being dirt-poor, vulnerable, and at the mercy of him.

"You wield that sword well." He smiled for the first time. "And to think we all underestimated you as a mere gossip columnist."

"I am that, too, but for different reasons. Society gossip amuses me and entertains the masses. What I put in that column is always harmless. A bit of light titillation. Others might print different, but I prefer to avoid the malicious in favor of the ludicrous. I never want to hurt good people." She slanted him a begrudging glance. "Blue-blooded or otherwise. I prefer to store up all my self-righteous indignation for the ones who really deserve it."

"Like your canal swindler rather than Dahlia Regis." Giles regarded her as if he were seeing her in a whole new light. "How the devil did you find that dreadful story?"

"Much the same way as I find all of them. I keep my eye on the news and an ear to the ground. Because I am suspicious by nature and always think the worst of someone first with no benefit of the doubt whatsoever." He smiled. "And I have a vivid, cynical imagination, refuse to believe in coincidences, and have the memory of an elephant. If something sparks a question in my mind, I'll dig until I find the answer. More often than not, once the answer has been found, there really is nothing else of interest there—but sometimes you kick a hornet's nest. With the canal company it was overhearing a snippet at a ball a few months ago. Just one gentleman waxing lyrical to another about his lucrative new investment and the enormous dividends he had been promised, which sounded too good to be true. So I did some digging on the company and its owner and suddenly there were hornets everywhere."

For some reason, she told him everything about that investigation from start to finish. What she had found, how she had found it, the peers involved, even the damsel in distress who had ultimately created the sense of urgency to uncover all the truth so swiftly. By the time she finished, they had both drained their glasses.

"A Hunter of Truth and a fearless Kicker of Hornets." The soothing effect of the cognac had lowered his voice to a deep, silky rumble, his eyes sleepy and his body relaxed. "Do I need to worry about all the rattling Sinclair skeletons making an appearance in your column?"

"Of course not. I would never write a story that close to home. Besides, the Sentinel isn't interested in the past. Why would *he* waste *his* valuable time on old news when the present is more damning?"

"Care to make a bet on that?"

"Apart from Gervais the dastardly kidnapper, what other scandalous rattling skeletons are there in the Sinclair cupboard?" Her tongue tripped over "rattling" and "skeletons," and she realized that the enormous glass of cognac Dalton had poured had gone straight to her head. Somewhere during their conversation, she had scooted closer and was now propped against the cushion so close to him she could smell his subtle cologne. So close she should probably move, but didn't. Sitting here, chatting amiably to him was currently the only thing she wanted to do.

"Too many to count." As he said it, he winced slightly, his fingers tightening around his glass as he stared into it rather than look at her. He frowned and attempted a smile, which did not banish the flash of panic in his eyes. "Dalton was right—this stuff is smooth. A bit too smooth and definitely too potent. My head is spinning." He glanced at the clock as he deposited his glass on the side table. "It's late and you have to leave at the crack of dawn."

"And you are doing your utmost to avoid my question all of a sudden." She nudged him playfully—perhaps flirtatiously. The brandy lowering her usual inhibitions as well as her guard. Enough to make Diana forget that she was still a forger's daughter from the crowded streets of dingy Clerkenwell, and he was a duke who owned all the infinite hills outside.

"I have just bared my soul to you, Giles, and confessed my darkest secret. Don't you think you owe me the same courtesy? I leave tomorrow and I won't see you for months." Of their own accord, her fingers traced his sleeve until she noticed him watching their path and let them fall away. "Fair's fair. An eye for an eye and a tooth for a tooth and all that. Therefore, surely it is also one deep, dark secret for another? If only for insurance purposes, I should be granted one rattle of those intriguing skeletons." Was she flirting? It felt like she was. She had grabbed his arm again to anchor him in place.

"I am not sure I want anyone to kick that hornet's nest. Especially not the Sentinel."

Something about his posture suddenly cut through the brandy to raise all her journalistic hackles. "Is your secret that bad?"

He nodded.

"And you don't trust me not to keep it when I have proved to you already that I can?" She pursed her lips as if annoyed. "I am offended." Which was rich when she was predisposed not to trust anyone beyond her two sisters, and even then she still held back. Her role at the newspaper was a case in point, as was what had happened in the alley and after. Neither of them knew how she had ruthlessly purged their father from their lives. Nobody did.

"Don't be. I don't trust anyone not to keep it. The risk is too great." His lazy, wry smile was tinged with sadness, and something about his expression set loud, clanging alarm bells ringing.

"Are you in trouble, Giles?"

"I have absolutely no idea."

"A very cryptic answer."

He shrugged, resigned, all the light gone from his face. "Yet the only one I have—even for myself."

She took his hand and he stared transfixed at their interlaced fingers. "If ever you are tempted to trust someone, I would like to help. I owe you—I also have a proven track record of rescuing people who deserve rescuing."

"Alas, not even the Sentinel can rescue me from this. In fact, I don't wish to be rescued. I never made the bed I have been forced to lie in, but I am determined to cling to the mattress for as long as I can before I am kicked out of it."

"Kicked out of it?" With every sentence her intuitive gut clenched in fear. "Who could do that?"

He shook his head, staring lost into his empty glass. "Who knows?"

Why wouldn't he let her help him? He looked so troubled and alone. So sad she couldn't bear it. "Surely another pair of eyes and ears could help protect you from whatever it is you fear."

"I see you are quoting me back to myself again." He laughed without humor.

"Are you going to make me dig for it, Giles? I will if you try to keep me in the dark, because I am the one now worried sick for your safety and digging is what I do best."

"You don't give up, do you?" His thumb idly stroked her palm, but there was indecision in his eyes now.

"Never."

"Even if I beg you to for your own sake?"

"Especially if you beg me to." She squeezed his hand tighter. "You are my friend. I care about you."

He stared at their joined hands for an eternity, indecision warring with the obvious temptation to waver until he swallowed. Hard. Then stared deeply into her eyes as if he needed to see inside her soul.

"If I tell you my dreadful *Dirty Secret*—do you promise to

suffer Dalton without complaint for as long as needs be?" She nodded. "And do I have your word you will never tell anyone what I am about to tell you, even if it releases buzzing hornets everywhere and your silence is technically breaking the law of the land?"

Dread settled in her stomach. Not for herself but for him. He was scared of something. Something huge. Diana could sense it. "I swear on my life your secret is safe with me." She drew a cross over her heart, and he smiled as he shook his head.

"All right . . ." He inhaled deeply then blew out a labored breath, his fingers suddenly gripping hers as if he needed her strength simply to get the words out. "Good grief . . . I cannot believe I am about to do this but . . ." Instinctively she held his hand for all she was worth. "The duchess wasn't really my mother and I am, in fact, the Duke of Harpenden's bastard."

"*What?*" Of all the dreadful things her vivid imagination had conjured, it certainly wasn't that. Her eyes blinked dumbstruck yet she didn't doubt the validity of his revelation. The weight and anguish of the truth were evident in every nuance, plane, and sinew of his body.

"He needed an heir and when she couldn't provide him with one, he foisted another woman's child upon her. Which means, in the eyes of the law, I have no legal claim to the title I now hold. The duke covered his tracks well, so well I was none the wiser until a few years ago, but I suspect not well enough that it is quite as secret as he thought. In fact, during our last conversation he alluded to as much. He said he needed a legal heir as a contingency, sired in irrefutable wedlock for all the world to see to ensure his legacy remained in his line."

"That was why he was marrying Dahlia Regis."

He nodded. "He was scared of someone, Diana. Scared of the truth coming out. So I fear I am living on borrowed time as the master of Harpenden, and all this will be snatched away before I can repair the mess he made of it."

"Hence your haste to get it all fixed so quickly."

He nodded. "I have no idea how long I've got."

"Do you know who your real mother is?"

"I haven't a clue—but there is clearly someone out there who does. Biding their time, waiting for the chance to destroy me now that the duke's intended fraud is actual. When the duchess spat the truth at me on her deathbed, she called her my father's harlot, so I do, at least, know who he really was." He pointed to his chin, attempting irony. When she didn't smile back his wry one slipped and she saw his pain. "You see—I did warn you it was a deep, dark, dirty, and dangerous secret." He lifted their interlinked hands, studying them in the dim light before he sighed.

"And seeing as the cognac has decreed this is a night for sharing deep and dangerous secrets, here's another one I shouldn't confess to you but apparently I am going to anyway though heaven only knows why." He traced the pad of his index finger down her cheek and across her lips, looking so lost and defeated it broke her heart. "I am going to miss you, too, Diana. Undeniably so much more than a man in my precarious and untenable position should."

"Oh, Giles . . ." Without thinking it through, and before talking herself out of it, her hand cupped his cheek and he leaned into it. Then he sighed against her mouth as he pressed his lips to hers.

It was a brief kiss. Over before it had started because he pulled away. "I'm sorry."

"Don't be." And because she meant that, Diana closed the distance again to kiss him back.

She wasn't entirely sure what sort of kiss she had intended because she had never voluntarily kissed a man in her life, but his surprised her more than the pleasant taste of the cognac that lingered on his lips.

It wasn't passionate; nor was it chaste. It was soft but intense. Gentle but powerful. Honest and filled with longing. So lovely that it was Diana who deepened it and who was the first to wrap her arms around his neck. When he pulled her into his arms, she went willingly, savoring the moment and every delicious but alien sensation he elicited.

She ran her hands over his face, his shoulders, his chest, arching against him when his palms explored the curve of her waist and hip, smoothed down her thigh, and settled possessively on her bottom. Even then his touch was light and not intrusive, as if he understood she needed to feel in control. Needed a route of escape even though she wasn't the least bit inclined to take it anytime soon.

As their tongues tangled, a passionate fire within her sparked then kindled for the very first time. The most unexpected surprise, and she reveled in it. Her hungry body rendered her powerless to do anything else. It came alive beneath his hands. Wanted things it had never wanted before and that want possessed her, making her bolder and more insistent as the kiss stretched. Deepened. Introducing her to a sensual, open, trusting, passionate version of herself she had never met before. Never knew existed.

She moaned when his lips found her ear and traced a lazy path down her neck, plunging her fingers in his hair when they finally returned to her mouth where they belonged.

She would have allowed him more liberties if he had not been the one to end the kiss again too soon. But he did, wrenching first his hands and then his mouth away and staring deep into her eyes breathless and stunned. His own darkened with the desire that she knew burned just as intense in hers.

He reached for her hand, then after the longest pause kissed the back of it. "I read somewhere you should never drink anything stronger or older than you are, and I suspect that potent cognac predates us both and evidently neither of us is a match for it." He smiled with regret as he tugged her to stand. "It's bedtime, my fierce Truth-Hunting Hornet-Kicker. You in yours and me, sadly, in mine. I want no regrets on my already overburdened and over-wrought conscience tomorrow." He kissed her fingers one last time before severing the contact completely. "Especially not yours, Diana. I could not bear that."

Chapter Fourteen

"The company currently calls itself Edward Davis Ottoman Imports. Before that . . ." Dalton squinted at his pocket notebook as he sat on Diana's desk. As thoroughly at home in the newspaper office in just two months as she had been after two years. "It was the Byzantine Trading Company and the Limehouse Persian Import Export Consortium. It changes names more often than I change my shirt, but in all cases, a Mr. Coleridge was the major shareholder and certainly the man raking in all the profits." Profits he was currently using to buy up more unsafe and unsanitary slum tenements in the notorious Westminster rookery of Devil's Acre so he could demand extortionate rent from the voiceless masses who lived there. If they couldn't pay, he took their ramshackle hovels away that same day, not caring that with each callous eviction he left poor, defenseless people to the mercy of the unforgiving streets."

"And the imports?"

"Cheap rugs and knickknacks for household decoration—or so the excise men are told. But I found this." He pulled out a handkerchief and unwrapped it to show her the broken halves of a chalky statuette of a miniature Venus de Milo. "They seem to dispose of a lot of breakages because there was a mountain of these outside. But look at the break and the construction . . ." As she picked it up Diana could see that the figurine was broken across the middle rather than at the weaker points of the arms and the legs; the inside was hollow and crusted brown, but not all the way through. "Back in my sailing days the easiest way to smuggle stuff was inside of something. The brandy runners across the Channel often hollowed out the masts of the ships to carry their booty. Others used special containers or barrels with false bottoms." Dalton was a wealth of shady and dubious information—most of it useful.

"They wouldn't carry much brandy in this." Diana slotted the eight-inch statue together. "Barely a glass, in fact."

"Brandy don't come from the Ottoman Empire, Miss Diana—but opium does, and with opium powder a little goes a long way." He retrieved a small bottle from his coat pocket and placed it on her desk between them in her tiny back office at *The Tribune*. The innocuous brown label announced it as Smith's Herbal Restorative. "It's laudanum—but that stuff is three parts poppy to seven parts alcohol and not the one to ten you'd buy over the counter at the apothecary. It's brewed strong, and probably at his warehouse, specifically for the opium eaters, and deadly as a result."

Diana picked it up and examined it, then removed the stopper to take a sniff. A waft of sweet cinnamon enticed her nostrils; the sugary tincture stuck to the cork like honey. "Where did you get this?" The deeper she dug into Mr. Coleridge's shady affairs, the worse his crimes became.

"I noticed one of the warehouse men liked his gin, never seemed to run out of money, and seemed to be very popular with the ne'er-do-wells at his local pub who come there expressly to seek him out. As I suspected, he's pocketing some of the product and selling it on the sly. I can't say he's careful about it, either, as he didn't know me from Adam yet happily let me ply him with a good pint of mother's ruin before he sold me this for tuppence."

"Would he recognize you?"

Dalton laughed. "Not a chance. He was so pie-eyed when I left him, I doubt he'd know me again if I walked right up to him. He was already three sheets gone before I topped up his glass and face-down by the time I left."

"Good work, Dalton."

Diana couldn't quite put her finger exactly on when and how Dalton became her assistant, because his role had evolved over those initial weeks after Shropshire.

She started sending him on errands to give her some peace when his constant loitering presence in her life had become annoying. Miraculously, he had proved to be more of a help than a hindrance—especially after he had worked out exactly what she did for the paper. Giles had been right on that score. There were no flies on Dalton. He had put two and two together with lightning speed, but unlike Giles, he came from her world, respected that she could look after herself, and didn't rush in like a gun half-cocked whenever there was a whiff of danger. Instead, he watched and waited, and while he did both, he helped her dig.

Even so, his rough-and-ready appearance, surly countenance, wooden leg, and leather eye patch blended better with the flotsam and jetsam of the shadiest parts of the capital than she ever could. Even dressed in her old, patched clothes from the Merriwells' hand-to-mouth Clerkenwell years, Diana had always attracted unwanted attention from the male of the species, whereas those same men did their level best to scurry past Dalton without making eye contact at all. Therefore, it made sense to entrust him with such aspects of an investigation to see if a story had more legs than he did. With him beside her, nobody bothered her as she probed deeper, and she could dig in blessed peace without the constant need to look over her shoulder because her intimidating new shadow took his role as her protector as seriously as he did that of her assistant.

"What's next, Miss Diana?"

"Nothing for tonight or tomorrow. This evening I have to attend a dreary yuletide soiree at Lady Bulphan's with my family. A night of badly sung carols, childish parlor games, and forced festive gaiety stretches before me, and tomorrow has been decreed a family day by Olivia. Apparently, working on Christmas Day is frowned upon by the aristocracy. Not that any of them work or give their servants those days off, but such is the glaring double standard they all live by."

Dalton grinned. "It's not our place to question our betters, Miss Diana, no matter how daft they all might be. Hopefully, somebody will disgrace themselves for you at Lady Bulphan's so you at least get a decent story out of the ordeal, while I enjoy a lovely day off. Might even squeeze in a little courting time." He wiggled his eyebrows.

"Is courting a euphemism for carousing?"

"I'm a reformed character since I met the woman of my dreams." He had been waxing lyrical about this mystery woman on and off for weeks but remained annoyingly tight-lipped as to her identity. All she had managed to prize out of him was the tantalizing titbit that the woman of Dalton's dreams was a lady and that because of the huge gap in their stations their relations had to remain clandestine. This was always accompanied with some nose tapping as if he were leaking a state secret and would be dragged away in irons if he revealed any more. All so ridiculously and typically Dalton it never failed to make her smile. "My carousing days are done. Or at least I suspect they are as I've been thinking the unthinkable for a little while now."

"The unthinkable?"

Dalton wiggled what was left of his ring finger and blushed when she gasped. "I know. I've surprised myself with my flowery musings. But if you want my opinion, when you meet the one, there ain't much you can do about it, is there, beyond make things official?" He winked at her. "You can't choose what the heart wants—no matter how much you try to tell it that it doesn't want a charming duke with a twinkle in his eye."

"You are as subtle as Olivia and both my sisters combined." Nothing ever got by her older sister: Minerva had been like a dog with a bone. Probing, suggesting, and nudging her regarding Giles since she returned from Shropshire a week after Diana had. She was convinced she sensed a change in the wind in the both of them and claimed Giles had been "wistful" and "a little lost" from the moment he had waved her carriage off. While that description of him did odd things to Diana's insides, the same accusations raised her hackles. Probably because there was a grain of truth in them.

"We can't all be wrong, now, can we?" Dalton tugged his forelock with mock insolence. "Merry Christmas, miss."

"And to you, too, Dalton." She retrieved the expensive bottle of cognac she had bought him at Fortnum's from beneath the desk and handed it to him with a smile. "I got you a little something as a thank-you for all you have done. I hear it puts hairs on your chest." Amongst other memories best not revisited—although she did with alarming regularity anyway beyond all the unsubtle, long-distance matchmaking she was subjected to on a daily basis.

Two months had done nothing to dim her memory of that kiss, and with every passing day she missed Giles's irritating presence in her life a little bit more. As much as she didn't want to make Dalton right, she didn't want to miss him, no matter how many times she tried to explain away her uncharacteristic behavior that night, or her strange feelings for a man she certainly didn't want to have such feelings for. The implausible and disconcerting fact remained— that kiss had affected her exponentially, and something had shifted within her. Something she had not realized was there in the first place to shift.

Thankfully, with Giles two hundred miles away in Shropshire and unlikely to return for the foreseeable, there was still time to shift it all back to where it belonged before it did any long-term harm.

When she next faced him, she was determined to be completely over it. Her feet firmly planted back on stable ground and her usually sensible, independent, and level head no longer taking random and unwelcome flights of romantic fancy in the clouds. She would leave that nonsense to Vee, for pity's sake, or Minerva, or now even Dalton apparently, because it wasn't for her.

As if she really wanted a man! Or needed the burdensome complication of a man in her life, when her career was going so well and she was finally happy with her lot. Finally free to make all her own decisions without the threat of disappointment, danger, or poverty forcing her hand elsewhere. Most men were unreliable and selfish creatures who almost always took more than they gave. One delightful, surprising, but drunken kiss didn't change that. Stone-cold sober and it likely wouldn't have felt delightful at all, hence she had vowed never to allow another drop of brandy to cross her wayward lips again. Especially around Giles. Flippant, philandering Giles. The only rogue she knew whose scandalous behavior didn't just feature occasionally in the gossip columns—it was a weekly fixture!

Or had been before he left for Shropshire. Before she had discovered there was so much more to the charming wretch than met her jaded eyes. Before he had plucked at her toughened heartstrings. Before he had mined under her defenses and entrusted her with his deepest, darkest secret. Before she had learned he wasn't a duke at all.

Before *she* had kissed *him*.

"You bought me the good stuff." Dalton smiled at her gift. "It wasn't necessary, miss, but is most appreciated."

"You deserve it. Much to my chagrin, you have proved to be a useful bane to my existence."

"I suppose I shall see you the day after Christmas?"

There was no point in telling him to take more time off from his sentry duty, because he wouldn't. "Yes indeed, Dalton. Bright and early on Tuesday please. Coleridge isn't going to catch himself, and thanks to this"—she tapped the top of the toxic Smith's Herbal Restorative—"the pair of us now need to do some serious digging in the filthiest part of the docks with all haste to finally see him brought to justice."

"I shall be sure to bring my shovel, miss. Alongside my pistol."

He winked, looking as disreputable as any ne'er-do-well, and limped away, leaving Diana to ponder.

Except it wasn't the dangerous little bottle that occupied her mind, or the investigation into Coleridge; it was Giles again. All alone for Christmas with only the portraits of his ancestors, his estate burdens, and his rattling skeletons for company.

Giles paused on the top of High Holborn, still unsure of his next destination after three interminable days of travel. The sensible option was his bachelor house on Tavistock Square because it was dark, he was disheveled and starving, and after too many hours on horseback, he was frozen solid. His greatcoat hung heavy with the frigid night mist, and his cheeks burned with the cold. But instead, it was Berkeley Square that called to his heart like a siren's song. Or rather it was the minx that lived there who called to his soul.

To himself he knew his early return to town had absolutely nothing to do with Olivia's posted invitation demanding he spend Christmas with them. No matter how convenient that excuse was, his return had everything to do with his visceral need to see Diana. The last nine weeks had felt an eternity, but he had tried to ignore that to focus on the enormous task at hand, reminding himself hourly he owed it to Harpenden's tenants to fix the estate before it was taken away from him.

To that end, he had sent his apologies a fortnight ago after deciding a visit wasn't wise. He was still trying to sort out his former steward's chaotic papers, urgent works had barely begun on the most dilapidated tenant cottages, and overall, despite excruciatingly long days of work, he felt as if he had barely scratched the surface of his ever-growing list of things to do. Christmas in London with Diana was an indulgence he could not afford. At the time he declined the invitation, he had also reasoned their kiss was still too fresh in his mind and he needed a bit longer to get over it before he dared face her again. He was in no position to kiss her, no matter how much he wanted her. A week later, after he had reasoned that he likely would never get over that kiss and reminded himself he had hired good people who would continue doing what he paid them for whether he was there or not, he changed his mind and left Shropshire that same day in case he changed it again.

He tried not to contemplate why.

Self-indulgent introspection served no purpose and changed nothing about his situation. Whatever his intense feelings for Diana, he had no right feeling them when he could offer her nothing beyond uncertainty, scandal, and ruination.

That depressing fact hadn't deterred him from coming, though, and his lack of resolve and willpower shamed him almost as much as the prospect of seeing her again excited him. The proverbial rock and a hard place: entirely selfish and completely impossible. The situation so blasted unfair it made his blood boil.

As misery swamped him, he turned his horse toward Bloomsbury and not Mayfair.

Better to face her in the morning. To retire for the night to regroup, recharge, reset his usually pragmatic head, and resist what his exhausted heart desperately wanted but knew it couldn't have. Besides, if he turned up in the crumpled clothes he had worn for days, they would all know why, and he might just as well carry a placard announcing he had feelings for her. Feelings it wouldn't be fair to indulge even if she was open to indulging them—which knowing the pithy, determined-to-remain-a-spinster-forever-because-I-am-wedded-to-my-freedoms Diana, she wasn't. She hadn't been able to look at him as he waved them all off on his driveway the morning after their kiss. He still had no clue whether that had been because of embarrassment, uncertainty, or downright mortification at what they had done. But it did not bode well for her reciprocating his feelings.

Which, all things considered, was categorically for the best.

Giles knew that without a shadow of a doubt, and accepted it, but still it made him sad. So sad and depressed, he trudged his weary horse home to Bloomsbury with as much enthusiasm as Atlas with the entire world on his shoulders.

His quiet house did nothing to improve his mood. As the staff weren't expecting him, the lamps and fires in the main rooms weren't lit, and because Dalton was apparently missing in action and gone who knew where, the panicked young maid who had opened the door to him organized a tray of cold cuts to be brought to his bedchamber while he waited for another maid and a footman to draw his bath. To depress him further, there were no biscuits to be had for love or money as it was the cook's afternoon off so there wouldn't be any till tomorrow. The entire tray was savory.

Even so, Giles made short work of it in silence and was in the process of stripping off his shirt when his truanting butler-cum-valet finally reappeared.

"Where the blazes have you been, you slacker? And more importantly, why weren't you here as a good butler should greet his weary master after he's endured a long and arduous journey half-way down the country?" If one discounted the vixen who had consumed him for months, he had missed his irascible mangled right hand, too. "It is what I pay you for, after all."

"I would have been here if you'd have told me you were coming." Entirely unrepentant, Dalton shrugged as he gathered up Giles's discarded clothes. "I do have better things to do with my time than hang around the front door on the off chance you might walk through it."

"An outrageous deflection to cover up for your shirking."

"I've been working, not shirking."

"A likely story." Giles lowered himself into the tub and sighed as he was enveloped in hot water before pinning the malingerer with his glare. "While the cat's away, the mice will always play."

"If that's the case, then I've been *playing* on Fleet Street these past two months upon your orders." Dalton paused his tidying long enough to glare back. "That woman of yours works some unsociable hours at that newspaper. This morning she started at seven and was still working when I left her not a half hour ago."

He decided to tactfully ignore the "woman of yours" comment even though it did odd things to his heart. "You left her! Unsupervised and unprotected this late at night! When I expressly instructed you to guard the wench!"

"I left her about to get into her brother-in-law's fancy carriage, which always takes her home. A carriage that had been waiting outside for her for a good hour beforehand, too, so she is neither unsupervised nor unprotected. Not that she needs much protecting, if you want my opinion, as she's as wily as a fox."

"I never want your bloody opinion and people hunt foxes!"

"They do, but that one gives as good as she gets—worse

actually—and I wouldn't fancy my chances against her in a fist-fight." Dalton chuckled with what looked a lot like affection. "Miss Diana would fight dirty." In case Giles missed his drift, he covered his genital area with his ruined hand.

"How is she?"

"Diana's a firecracker. Always busy. Takes no nonsense. I like her."

"I didn't ask for your opinion of *Miss Merriwell*, I asked how she is—in herself. Is she in fine fettle? Is she happy?" *Is she as miserable as me?*

"She is as fit as a butcher's dog and seems as happy as a pig in—" Giles held up his palm to stay the inevitable expletive and Dalton grinned. "But that wasn't what you were really asking, was it? You wanted to know if she is pining away for you."

Giles did and was disappointed to hear it sounded like she wasn't. "I meant nothing of the sort. Perish the thought!" He shuddered for effect. "I was merely checking the prickly minx hadn't got herself into any trouble in my absence."

"Of course she hasn't—because she's too smart to get caught and I've been glued to her side. Just as you asked."

"Thank you for finally following an order to the letter, Dalton." Giles made no attempt not to sound begrudging. "It makes a pleasant change."

"That you *ordered* me to watch over her, however, is telling in itself as I've never known you to be so diligent about a lady's welfare—and a *nice* young lady's welfare to boot. You're usually the love-them-and-leave-them sort. The sort who chases game girls who've been around the park many times before because they enjoy the ride." He waggled his eyebrows. "But this one has got under your skin, hasn't she? You are interested in her—in the *romantic* sense."

Giles decided not to dignify that futile truth with a response. "Go fetch my favorite soap, you feckless wretch. This stuff the maid brought doesn't lather as well."

Dalton grinned as he pointed. "I knew it! You fancy her! Though I can't say I blame you. Miss Diana is a fine bit of skirt. Wherever we go, she draws male eyes like flies to a dung heap."

Jealousy burned swift and hot, both at the faceless men who dared admire her and at his insubordinate butler who had enjoyed two months with her while Giles yearned, but he covered it with boredom. "My soap, Dalton?" For good measure he clicked his fingers. "I would like it before my bath chills—if it's not too much trouble."

The rascal tugged his forelock before disappearing into the dressing room, then returned unwrapping a fresh bar from Giles's favorite barbershop. "Your Floris, Your Grace, for heaven forbid Your Grace should have to suffer that fancy French milled soap the well-meaning maid brought when you turned up unexpected. What was the girl thinking to bring you something so fine and expensive?" Dalton slapped the soap into his hand. "And on the subject of the staff—downstairs are in uproar, by the way, and thank you for asking. They, like me, were under the impression you wouldn't be gracing Tavistock Square with your presence for Christmas and now they are going to have to rush around on Christmas morning like headless chickens trying to ready the house for a celebration and fill the larder for the selfish master who couldn't be bothered to tell them to expect him. They do have the post in Shropshire, don't they?"

In his haste to get to her, Giles hadn't given a second thought to anybody else. Knowing how devoted to him his diligent staff were, he now felt guilty for that oversight. Turning up out of the blue at Christmas wasn't fair, and they deserved better. "That sounds an awful lot like a chastisement, Dalton."

"A chastisement, Your Grace? *Noooo* . . . Heaven forbid someone as lowly as me should pull up someone as important as you on their behavior. I know my place, *Your Grace*. Why should you care if they have to sacrifice their hard-earned Christmas goose to your table instead? Or change all their own plans at a moment's notice when they thought they could risk some time off during your prolonged absence? So long as you're all right, *Your Grace*, that is all that matters, for we live to serve." Dalton daintily lifted the corners of his coat as he curtsied, his smile as false as Giles's claims to his dukedom.

"Well, haven't you developed some revolutionary opinions in my absence? Clearly you have been spending far too much time with Miss Diana." Giles made a great show of lathering up the Floris on a flannel unperturbed. "But for the record, and because I respect *all* my other servants with the stark exception of *you*, you can inform them they need go to no trouble on my account for I shall barely be home over Christmas. I have been invited to spend it at Standish House with Lord Fareham and his family. All anyone here needs to worry about tomorrow is my breakfast and my biscuits. In fact, if Cook bakes a few decent-sized batches of shortbread and leaves them laid out on the sideboard, I shall help myself to biscuits for breakfast as a Christmas gift to myself. Then they can all still enjoy the day off with my blessing, free to spend the generous Christmas bonus I shall also give them with impunity on their own

Christmas gooses." He frowned. "Or should that be geese?" His nitpicking grammarian would know.

"I shall tell them that good news just as soon as I have laid out your clean clothes, Your Grace."

"As I am apparently filled with festive spirit this evening, I have decided to spare you that task, too. Consider that *your* Christmas bonus, Dalton." Giles soaped his head then lay back to enjoy the spicy scent of Mr. Floris's superior bubbles as they popped on his scalp. "Tonight I intend to sink into my crisp cotton sheets, curl up on my decadent duck-down mattress, and snuggle under my extravagant Welsh woolen blankets for at least the next ten hours, and not even a team of unbroken wild horses laden with saddlebags bulging with freshly baked shortbread could drag me from my bed sooner."

"Really?" His butler rolled his insolent eye and disappeared into the dressing room again to rummage. "Do you want your crimson silk waistcoat or the green brocade? Both are suitably festive, but if you want my opinion, I think you cut more of a dash in the scarlet."

"Are you going deaf in your dotage, Dalton?" Giles chuckled at his own brilliant but unintentional bit of alliteration. The grammarian would like that, too, even though she always did it better. "I said I am going straight to bed just as soon as I finish this bath, and absolutely nothing can dissuade me from that splendid plan of action."

"But it is Christmas Eve, Your Grace. Christmas. *Eve.*" His servant reappeared clutching both waistcoats and with a full set of evening clothes draped over his arm. He wiggled the waistcoats, beaming. "And that means it is Lady Bulphan's annual yuletide soiree tonight and I know how much you adore the out-of-tune carol concert she always puts on. You were sent an invitation." He pulled the embossed linen card from his pocket and flapped it like a fan, which he peered coquettishly over. "I fetched it specifically from your enormous pile of social correspondence the second I returned, as I suspected you would need it."

"Why on earth would I need it after two hundred miles of muddy road?" Perhaps Dalton was going deaf. Or he was over-compensating in his eagerness to please after Mrs. Townsend had served Giles in his stead in Shropshire. "Toss it on the fire, Dalton, I insist." He closed his eyes and flapped his hand in the general vicinity of the roaring fire that had only just been laid. "Christmas Eve, Lady Bulphan, and her out-of-tune carolers will have to get by without me this year as I have an unbreakable appointment with the arms of Morpheus." And the inevitable nightly dreams involving the same dark-haired temptress who had haunted them for two whole months. A green-eyed, no-nonsense vixen who smelled of fat summer roses tinged with peach and whose unschooled lips set his body ablaze with desire and made his heart contemplate the impossible.

"That is a shame, Your Grace." Dalton made a show of gathering up the clothes and trudging back toward the dressing room with them, his gruff voice muffling as he disappeared inside. "Because I have it on the highest authority that a certain prickly minx whom you have absolutely no romantic interest in whatsoever, and whom you did not just ride two hundred muddy miles expressly to see, is also heading to that same soiree . . ."

Chapter Fifteen

Lady Bulphan's was a seething crush by the time Giles arrived, with cheery revelers spilling into the hallway from the ballroom, the drawing room, and the dining room, making it impossible to navigate with any speed. As it was the nearest, he headed for the drawing room first, then spent an eternity shaking hands and swapping inane pleasantries with every person who clamored to greet him.

And clamor they did.

In their droves and with their marriageable daughters in tow, circling around him and forming another unwelcome barricade between him and his intended destination. With every forced smile and insincere "Merry Christmas" he scanned the room but saw neither Diana nor any of her family.

"Your Grace." While searching the sea of faces, he failed to notice Mr. Regis and Dahlia until it was too late. "We have called at your house several times these past weeks and despaired of you ever coming back from Shropshire. I'm sure your man told you?" The businessman had a determined glint in his eyes as he pushed his daughter forward. "Dahlia, especially, was eager to speak to you."

Dahlia looked nothing of the sort but nodded, forcing a polite smile as brittle as his. "Seeing as we were unable to be there, I wanted to . . . er . . ." She shot a panicked glance at her father.

"You wanted to inquire about the funeral service."

"Yes. I did . . . um . . . was it a lovely service?"

"I should have written, Miss Regis, and now feel bad that I didn't." With everything else that had happened, poor Dahlia had completely slipped Giles's mind. "It was a lovely service." As lovely as a sparsely attended and impersonal funeral could have been when one considered the duke's objectionable character and fiscal abuse of his tenants. But as Diana had wisely said, it was undoubtedly the funeral he had deserved. There hadn't been anything but dry eyes in the chapel, or at the graveside, but this gentle creature did not need to know that. "As per your instructions, Miss Regis, I laid some flowers in your name."

"Thank you, Your Grace. That is most thoughtful." She curtsied again, clearly ill at ease as she gestured to her gown. It was too bright for her delicate coloring and too tight for her generous figure and it was obvious from her wince that she knew it, too. "I . . . um . . . apologize for my lack of proper mourning attire, only I . . . um . . . we . . ." Her gaze flicked again to her father, who only glared at her inarticulateness and discomfort. "We were unsure of the proper protocols pertaining to the . . . um . . . unusual situation. Your father and I were never officially engaged, you see, so . . ." Her rounded cheeks blushed scarlet.

"Please do not trouble yourself with any concerns, Miss Regis." When the rules of propriety dictated he probably shouldn't be here at all, let alone resplendent in his scarlet silk waistcoat, Giles was in no position to judge. "It is Christmas Eve. A day for celebration. His Grace would have wanted you to move on and enjoy the yuletide, not waste it in grief." At least he would have if he'd possessed an ounce of humanity.

"I see you are celebrating the yuletide as well." Mr. Regis scanned him up and down, taking in the jaunty waistcoat and the sprig of mistletoe Giles had pinned to his lapel in his trademark mischievous homage to the season. At least that was how he justified it to Dalton, who had referred to it, with a knowing wink, as his "emergency mistletoe" in case an opportunity with the "prickly minx" presented itself. "I presume it wouldn't be seen in any way as inappropriate if we invited you to dine with us this week?" Regis took a step closer, practically pinning Giles to the wall. "Which evening would suit?"

"Alas—I already have plans for Christmas Day. Then Tuesday I have urgent business meetings all day and intend to return to Shropshire first thing on Wednesday." He threw that lie in, preempting Dahlia's pushy father but smiling at the girl to soften the blow, noticing she looked relieved he was busy. "Sadly, this is a fleeting visit."

Her father, on the other hand, was annoyed to be thwarted. "And when do you return, sir?"

"Not until the spring at least." A vague enough date to spare him any further invitations, or so he hoped. Until Mr. Regis scuppered things.

"Perhaps we could visit you there next month then?" Giles kicked himself for his own lack of forethought. He hadn't anticipated Regis would invite himself, yet realized too late that he should have. The man was like a hungry dog outside a butcher's window. "I have business in the north in January and I am sure my Dahlia would love to finally see the estate she should have been mistress of."

"That would be delightful." About as delightful as having pins hammered beneath his fingernails.

"Shall we agree on a date?"

Not in a million years. "Let us not be that formal, Mr. Regis."

"We shall call at our convenience then once my business is concluded."

"A splendid idea." So long as Giles remembered not to be in.

After her father nudged her, poor Dahlia blushed again. "Thank you, Your Grace. I . . . um . . . hear Shropshire is . . . um . . . lovely but . . . um . . . have sadly never been."

"My business takes us frequently north . . ." As Mr. Regis droned on, Giles sensed her before he saw her dark, lopsided tresses striding purposefully around the edge of the room toward the door.

Straightaway his fatigue and anxious mood disappeared. Even the relentless Mr. Regis receded into the background. Diana was the most splendid sight for sore eyes. The sense of elation at seeing her after so long sent warmth radiating beneath his skin and lightened his aching limbs. Transfixed, he drank her in, instantly amused by her no-nonsense manner even when she was unaware she was being watched.

As always, Diana portrayed with every inch a woman on a mission to avoid joining in. He had never once seen her dance or socialize outside of their circle, and she gave short shrift to any of the gentlemen foolish enough to attempt to engage her. She was always either unsociable or unnoticed. The latter had always baffled him because he had always noticed her, but knowing what she did for the newspaper her behavior all made sense now.

Tonight, her brow was furrowed as she rummaged in her reticule while her heavy shawl dragged along the floor. She avoided making eye contact with anyone and did her best impression of an irritated woman on the cusp of anger, and as a result the crowd parted like the Red Sea to allow her to pass. Then, just like that, she was gone again. Swallowed by the crush in the hallway and instantly leaving him bereft.

Not caring if it would be construed as rude, he made the snap decision to take a leaf out of her book and emulate her tactics to escape.

"If you will excuse me." Regis bristled as Giles interrupted him midflow. "But I have just spied someone I urgently need to talk to." He started walking away before he finished the sentence, and in the absence of a reticule patted down his coat the moment his feet hit the hallway, as if he had mislaid something important as an excuse not to meet anyone else's eyes. It worked a treat and he managed to march his way across the entire hall and, when he spotted her hair again, half the ballroom in hot pursuit unencumbered.

"Giles Sinclair! As I live and breathe!" An acquaintance from White's stepped into his path and forced him to stop as Diana darted into an alcove. "I haven't seen you in forever! How are you, old boy?"

"It's Your Grace now." Another acquaintance slapped him on the back as he blocked his view. "My condolences. I heard the news. Just terrible. Allow me to introduce you to my sister . . ."

It was a conspiracy. Fate doing everything in its power to thwart him. Before he could excuse himself, Diana glanced furtively around before she slipped out of the French doors onto the terrace. Then Vee rushed toward him from nowhere and grabbed both his hands.

"You are late, Giles!" Like his knight in shining armor she dragged him away. "Do excuse us—but His Grace asked us to save him a chair for the carols and they are about to start." She tugged him several feet away before she grinned. "They are like vultures, aren't they? There is nothing like an unattached duke to put the cat amongst the pigeons—and just look at all the pigeons."

She inclined her head toward the determined ring of chaperoned debutantes eyeing him like a juicy steak. "You've suddenly become eligible instead of scandalous." That wouldn't last long. "Typically, all the single ladies are convinced, since your elevation to the dukedom, that you are obviously in dire need of a duchess as soon as possible. Speculation is rife as to whom you are going to pick. There's even a page in the betting book at White's dedicated to it, or so Jeremiah says, filled with all manner of names, though not mine." She pouted. "I am quite put out by that." Then she laughed aloud at his shocked expression. "That was a joke, Giles! So don't look so panicked. You are far too old for me, I think of you as a brother, and we all know you are besotted by my sister."

Before he could argue she grinned. "We got your note but never expected to see you here tonight. We are all over there." She pointed to the rows of chairs lined in front of a makeshift stage then waved, and several pairs of hands waved back. "Hugh has been sent to fetch you some champagne and Jeremiah some dessert because Minerva thinks you look as though you need both."

She meant well. They all meant well, but despite all his efforts to get here, he still hadn't had a moment with Diana and he couldn't go another minute without having one. Preferably alone. "Champagne sounds splendid, Miss Vee, as does the dessert and the superior company well away from the vultures, but first I must . . ." In the absence of a better excuse, he pulled an awkward face.

"Ah." Ever helpful, Vee nodded in understanding and pointed to an open doorway to their left. "The retiring rooms are over there. Do you need an escort in case you are ambushed again?"

"Hopefully not—but if I am not sipping that champers beside you in ten minutes, strap on some armor and come and rescue me again."

Even though it was in the opposite direction to the one he wanted, he headed to the open door in case Vee or the others were watching, then hugged the wall as he dashed toward the alcove before he fled through the closest French door into the night.

The terrace was empty. Hardly a surprise when it was as cold as ice outside. Giles squinted at every shadow yet saw no sign of her.

"Diana?" He didn't bother whispering as there wasn't another soul about to hear.

"Giles?" He heard her before she emerged from a topiary Buxus bush. He couldn't suppress his smile or his joy to see her, and she offered him a somewhat begrudging but shy smile back. "My family said you were home—but I didn't expect you would turn up here after such a long and tiring journey."

He had come for her. He knew it, and in all likelihood now that he had clearly followed her outside, she knew it, too.

"Rest is overrated and besides, it is Christmas Eve." He gestured back toward to the party in full swing behind. "How could I resist Lady Bulphan's legendary concert of badly sung carols? I also heard rumors of some amateur theatrics. The Nativity I believe, set to music and written by Lady Bulphan herself. How

could I not come?" He shrugged with awkwardness as he sauntered toward her, cursing himself for having no clue how to behave
now he was finally here. With all his incessant pondering these
past two months, why the blazes hadn't he rehearsed something to
say? Something erudite, flippant, and funny that broke the ice and
put them both back on familiar territory.

"Are you in trouble?" Her instant concern touched him.

"No more than I was when I last saw you. So far nobody has
crawled out of the woodwork to call me an impostor."

"That's good." She glanced at her hands and that was that conversation done.

"How have you been?"

"Busy." She was struggling to meet his gaze. "Everyone is apparently back in town for Christmas so there has been plenty of
gossip to write."

"Is that why you are out here now?" He gestured to the thick
shawl she was swaddled in. It was more blanket than evening wear,
no doubt brought intentionally in case her covert work brought her
outside. "You are on the hunt for a story?"

"I needed to do something to pass the time before the concert
starts, and nothing induces scandal more than Lady Bulphan's potent wassail." She gathered her ugly shawl tighter. "The outrageous
Lady Sewell and her fake Russian count have already partaken of
more than their fair share . . . so that should be entertaining. I
know how much you adore them."

"They certainly liven up even the dullest affairs. Have you
ever noticed that when he is inebriated, the count quite forgets he
is supposed to be Russian and some cockney slips out?"

She shot him an of-course-I-noticed look. "That is because

Count Alexi Nikolaev is really plain old Mr. Alec Nicholls, a shop-keeper from Stepney. I checked. Months ago."

"Of course you did. And you kept that to yourself because . . . ?"

"He isn't hurting anybody and her husband is a beast. It cannot be easy being married to that man." He liked that she was rescuing Lady Sewell, too. Clearly the fearsome Sentinel kept more secrets than she ever exposed—which was reassuring seeing as she now knew his.

Giles still wasn't sure how he felt about that.

He swung between remorse and relief that he had told her the *Dirty Secret*, panic-inducing fear of imminent exposure in the press and the reassuring certainty that, no matter what, he had her on his side.

"Well done on that canal story, by the way." Why was this so hard? Giles was as awkward as a green youth at his first ball. So desperate to impress a pretty lady but with no practical clue how. He blamed the kiss. It hovered between them unresolved. "Dalton has been sending me *The Tribune* and I followed those reports with interest. It blew up quickly once you printed it . . . buzzing hornets everywhere."

She nodded as her teeth worried her bottom lip, dragging his eyes to it and reminding him of her taste. "There is a warrant out for the swindler's arrest but—typically—he absconded as soon as his duplicity came to light." Her fingers played with the tassels on the shawl.

"Another vile villain vanquished by the Sentinel's slashing sword of truth."

She rolled her eyes at his shocking, overworked attempt at alliteration. "How are things progressing on your estate?"

"I took your sage advice and visited every tenant to ask their opinions of my plans."

"How did they react to the lord-of-the-manor knocking on their door?"

"With relief. It has certainly gone some way toward regaining their trust—although I still have a long way to go with that as you would expect after years of rule by fear."

Oh, how he wished his evening trousers or coat had pockets so he could shove his fidgeting hands in them. Instead, he clamped them behind his back and resisted the urge to rock on his heels like an admiral inspecting the fleet. They were barely three feet apart now, yet it still felt like miles and he loathed it. Giles wanted the easiness back. The sparring. The sarcasm. The connection. But thanks to the cognac, they had ruined that relationship by shifting the dynamic between them until neither of them knew quite where they stood. They weren't enemies. Yet they weren't friends anymore, either, because they had crossed that boundary, and tragically, they could never be lovers, no matter how much she tempted him. An affair with Diana would never be enough, and thanks to the *Dirty Secret*, forever was impossible. At least it was if she wasn't interested . . .

"Do you think we should discuss what happened between us? Do I need to apologize?" He held his breath as he watched her reaction, silently hoping he would see hurt at the suggestion despite knowing his precarious situation dictated they should never repeat it.

"No . . . *No!*" She waved her initial indecision away with a flick of her wrist and an over-bright smile. "A definitive no to both. All water under the bridge, Giles. Probably best forgotten."

"All done and dusted." He should have been relieved but wasn't. "A moment of madness in a fraught situation."

"Absolutely! I cannot think what came over us. What were we thinking?" She held up her palm. "Don't answer that. Because we weren't thinking, were we?" Her tinkling laughter almost sounded convincing. Almost—but not quite. Something in her eyes gave her away, making him wonder if she was as disappointed as he was that they were both prepared to leave it at that. "Emotions were high, neither of us had slept properly in days, and we were both pickled by Dalton's potent nightcap."

She wanted to blame the brandy. The coward's way out but he was too scared of the alternative to call it. The cowardly route was certainly easier than the I-wonder-if-you-might-consider-breaking-the-law-by-becoming-my-duchess route that his addled mind and yearning heart were currently seriously contemplating and to hell with the consequences. "I found out later it was fifty years old."

"That explains it." She pulled a face as if the mere memory of their indiscretion horrified her. "That cognac was almost as old as both of us combined."

"Indeed." Something inside him was dying. Probably hope. "No wonder we lost our heads. As if you and I . . ." He pulled a face of disgust that she instantly copied.

"Heaven forbid."

"Even if I wasn't in such a precarious position and I was able to offer something—which obviously I cannot—I'd have to be a fool to have a romantic entanglement with a headstrong and opinionated harpy like you. Talk about incompatible."

"We come from different worlds." She nodded, playing with the tassels of her shawl for all she was worth. "Not that I have any interest in a romantic entanglement, either, but if I did suddenly feel the urge, it wouldn't be with a privileged idiot such as you. I barely like you."

"And I barely like you, too, harridan." The forced chuckle grated like rusty nails in his throat. "Thank goodness you feel the same! It will be a relief to get things between us back to normal. We've been much too polite and cordial of late and that is unsettling."

"Agreed . . . I felt compelled to be nice to you after what happened to your father, but I much prefer tolerating you on sufferance." She nibbled her bottom lip again then offered him another fake smile. "Thank goodness we finally agree on something. I was dreading you coming here and plighting your troth, then having to turn you down and breaking your heart in the process. That would have made things so awkward."

Because this wasn't? Giles nodded anyway. "I was terrified my superior skill at kissing might have turned your head and that you'd been swooning away for me for months. I was convinced I'd have to fight a duel with Hugh because I had broken your heart and shattered all your girlish hopes of a Valentine's wedding."

She laughed. A loud, brittle sound that echoed around the empty terrace. "My heart is as detached as it always was, I have never swooned in my life and I still loathe weddings. St. Valentine's Day, too, for that matter. But I am glad we had this conversation. After two months of worrying about it, I feel as though we have finally cleared the air." If that was the case, why did it still hang heavy between them like a shroud? "Vee is delighted you are home." The abrupt change of subject came out too fast, making him hope against hope she was lying through her teeth just like he was. "She has really missed you, though goodness knows why, and bored me silly about it on the carriage ride here. As has Hugh. They are both thrilled you've returned. He lamented your absence daily."

He should have left it at that. Brushed it all under the carpet where it belonged and set things back on an even, if awkward, keel, but irrespective of what his sensible head and prudence cautioned, his mouth decided to disobey. "And what about you, Diana? Did you miss me, too?"

Chapter Sixteen

"I—I . . ." As she floundered at his unexpected and forthright question, Diana almost—almost—confessed the unpalatable truth. That not only had she missed him, but not a day passed that she hadn't worried about his welfare or recalled his kiss. Fortunately, a sound behind them saved her from herself. She grabbed his sleeve and yanked him behind the topiary then pressed a finger to her lips. "Shhhh!"

"We are hiding now because . . . ?" Giles mimicked her covert stance despite being bewildered by it.

"Because I just overheard Lady Pamela Beckett and Lieutenant Rory Fitzherbert arrange to meet out here." Admitting she was working was better than admitting she cared about him.

"That is hardly worthy gossip, Diana, let alone anything scandalous enough for *The Tribune*, when everyone knows Rory Fitzherbert has been head over heels in love with that girl for the last year."

"Or so we all thought—but while you were gone, Lady Pamela became engaged to Lord Stifford. They are due to marry tomorrow—on Christmas morning." An unlikely and hasty turn of events that not even Diana had foreseen.

He frowned, perplexed. "Why on earth is she marrying him?" Why did Giles always smell so . . . alluring, drat him? And why did his whispered, deep voice still send distracting shivers down her spine when she was determined to double her efforts not to be distracted by him? "Stifford's an odious little boor who I am convinced wears a corset under his coat as I am sure I have heard it creak a time or two when we've played billiards. He cheats at that, too, which is another reason I don't like him."

"That's as may be but he is her choice and clearly the lieutenant is unhappy with it because he was fuming when I heard him, and demanded she meet him outside immediately to discuss it." It had been a nasty, hissed conversation as he had accosted her outside the retiring room. Diana hadn't heard the actual words, but the tone raised her bloodhound's hackles. "He made her cry, Giles."

"So you are here more to protect Lady Pamela than write a story, aren't you?" She was. She had been that frightened woman in the presence of a bigger, stronger man, but her upbringing in a very different sort of environment from Mayfair meant she knew how to fight back. The genteel Lady Pamela wouldn't have a clue.

Giles studied her with interest. "I am starting to think that my Goddess of the Hunt is as much a rescuer as she is a Kicker of Hornets." He prodded her arm as if she were a strange, mystery substance rather than a woman. "I also suspect there lurks a soft center beneath your hard-as-nails exterior. That you are more a rose cream than a nut brittle." He peered at her face, his mere inches from hers thanks to the limited space behind the Buxus, and her stupid pulse ratcheted up beneath his gaze. "How do you plead?"

She didn't deny it. "She was crying, Giles. Frightened. I couldn't ignore that."

"Why on earth would she be frightened of Rory? I've known him for years and he wouldn't hurt a fly, let alone the woman he adores." As two male boots approached, Diana pressed her finger to her mouth again and glared before she mouthed *Be quiet!* The feet did not stop at the edge of the terrace but instead jogged down the steps into the garden and disappeared down the path.

When her companion failed to see the urgency of the situation, she tugged at his sleeve. "We *need* to keep an eye on them, Giles. For her sake."

"We really don't." He regarded her with exasperation tinged with pity. "And I should just like it noted now for the record so you will be in no doubt that you are wrong once this fool's errand is over. Mark my words, they are having a final tryst before she marries her creaking, corset-wearing cheat in the morning."

"Remind me again—which of us uncovers the truth that nobody else can find and which of us cannot even organize his own paperwork?" She glared down her nose for good measure to let him know she thought him a cretin, wishing the mention of the paperwork in Shropshire didn't remind her of the kiss they had shared there.

Clearly amused by her suspicions, he gestured for her to lead the way, so hunched like thieves they went in the same direction of the boots, taking a convoluted route to avoid the path where her prey might see them. He followed her lead as they darted from hiding place to hiding place, chuckling softly as they crouched behind the assorted flower beds and shrubberies, until they spied Lieutenant Fitzherbert pacing to the left of a small ivy-covered pergola that resembled a birdcage.

Diana motioned for him to crouch down further, mouthed *Over there* as she pointed to a solitary clump of bushes butting the right side of the pergola.

Giles shook his head. "It's too exposed and much too close. We'll be stuck there for the duration, which likely won't be wise if they *are* having a tryst."

"We need to be close else we won't hear anything useful."

"What the blazes do we need to hear? If they are having a tryst—which they *are*, by the way—we certainly don't want to hear that!"

"He made her cry, Giles! If he has dragged her out here to continue his onslaught, or worse attempts to bully her into changing her mind, we shall need to hear it to know when to step in!"

As Rory turned his back to stare at the sky, Diana darted across the twenty feet of open lawn before he could stop her. Giles followed and threw himself behind the bush, too, before the fellow suddenly turned and resumed his pacing—this time right in front of the pergola and completely blocking their exit just as he had cautioned.

While Diana pressed her nose against the leaves to watch, Giles nudged her with his elbow. "Do you do this sort of thing often?" He was squatting on the soggy grass and huddling as best he could in the insubstantial fabric of his evening coat. "Because freezing to death in a Mayfair back garden isn't my idea of a fun way to celebrate Christmas Eve. I hope *The Tribune* pays you well for this nonsense. For the record, I should also like it noted this is a ludicrous way to make a living."

"Will you stop distracting me while I am trying to concentrate!"

"Well, it is."

She shushed him again, the whites of his eyes the only brightness in the shrubbery they were now trapped in as they waited in silence for several minutes. The only sounds were the lone hoot of an owl in the distance, the soldier's boots stamping on the floor while he tried to keep warm, and Diana's racing heartbeat, which to her disgust was racing more because of the proximity of her vexing companion than the situation.

Suddenly, the boots stilled.

"Pamela!" Rory rushed forward as she hurried up the path and much too close to their bush for comfort. As they ducked to the ground for cover, two bodies collided amid the unmistakable sounds of fevered kissing.

"See!" Giles couldn't resist hissing in Diana's ear. "I did tell you she was in no danger." She narrowed her eyes in response but continued to watch them like a hawk.

When the star-crossed young lovers finally prized their lips apart, it became obvious that Giles, the gloating wretch, was right.

Rory's anger wasn't directed at Lady Pamela but at her father, who disapproved of the soldier and was forcing her to marry Stifford. Rory begged her to run away with him—tonight—to Gretna Green and to hell with her father. She initially refused because she was a dutiful daughter, then she capitulated because she loved him and they clung to each other in joy.

It was all very heartfelt and very private, leaving her feeling like a voyeur when the kissing started again in earnest. That was when she finally gave up her eavesdropping and huffed.

"It seems you were right, and the lady doesn't currently require rescuing." Oh, how that concession hurt!

"Apparently so and now we are stuck—just as I said we would be." He shivered and burrowed deeper into his coat, his tone more peeved than self-congratulatory. "Freezing to death and listening to two people in the grip of passion."

"Should we try to make a run for it?"

Giles assessed their position and shook his head. "They are bound to see us." To prove that point and make her misery complete, the moon decided to peep from a crack in the dense clouds overhead, illuminating not only the two entwined star-crossed lovers at the entrance to the pergola but the twenty feet of open lawn they would have to navigate to escape back to the terrace unseen. "I say we be brazen about it and announce our presence. Make out we are just having a stroll and enjoying the moonlight exactly as they are."

"Because that wouldn't be improper at all, would it?" Diana gestured to their surroundings. "Us emerging from a bush as if we've been having a tryst, too!" She was snarling as if their predicament were suddenly his fault, and he grinned at that irony. "I'd be ruined!"

"Why would you care?" He had the gall to laugh. "You are not after a husband and your complete ruination would ensure you were spared any unwelcome proposals. Thoroughly ruined, you can live your life in that blissful freedom you claim to adore so much."

Sometimes men were so stupid. "If I am ruined, so is my career! One cannot write society gossip, Giles, if one has been shunned by society and isn't invited to any of their functions!"

"You are overreacting." She ignored that comment, aware she was indeed overreacting but being huddled next to Giles was scrambling her wits.

"And I should like it noted for the record that I told you so."

She ignored that, too, fuming that he had the audacity to be right and she would likely never hear the end of it—Giles enjoyed nothing better than saying *I told you so.* "We are simply going to have to stay here and sit it out until their business is concluded!" Diana winced as she glanced at the embracing couple and contemplated the full extent of the business they could engage in. "Which hopefully won't be long . . ." *Please God!* "Seeing as they are apparently on the cusp of eloping and they only have a few hours to get away or she'll be walking up a different aisle with a groom who wears a corset."

"Then the least you could do is share that ugly shawl with me until they pry their blasted lips apart and run away to Gretna." He tugged the edge of it and she yanked it away glaring.

"Absolutely not!"

"But it's big enough for two and I am freezing!"

Diana clutched the shawl tighter. "I am not sharing a shawl with you under any circumstances, Giles Sinclair! That really wouldn't be proper!" Crouching next to him was playing havoc with all her senses. Sharing her shawl with him was almost as intimate as sharing a kiss with him and would undoubtedly be just as distracting.

"Because this is proper?" He glanced around the tangled branches they were crouched behind, dumbstruck. "Much longer out here and I will likely catch a chill!" He tugged at the shawl again. "Do you want my death from exposure on your conscience?"

Diana stared down her nose at him. "I never asked you to follow me."

"Au contraire, madam!" He did the best impression of her feminine tone in a hushed whisper while mimicking all her exaggerated hand gestures that had got them here. "*We* need to keep an eye on them, Giles! *We* need to be close else we won't hear anything useful! *We* need to know when to step in! What was all that if not clear and concise instructions for me to follow?"

"Will you stop saying *I told you so*!" She huffed a cloud of frustrated, misty air into the night. "I didn't realize *we* would be stuck out here for the duration."

"Well, we are—thanks entirely to you—and I'm freezing, so stop being so stingy and inhumane and share your ugly shawl, witch, or my chattering teeth will give us away and you'll be ruined anyway."

A weak and wayward part of her instantly welcomed that prospect . . .

Pamela did not give her the opportunity to contemplate that unwelcome, errant thought for long, though, because she suddenly peeled herself from her man with a squeal.

"Somebody is there, Rory!" Through the veil of leaves they watched Lady Pamela gesture in their general direction. Like the fierce soldier he was, Rory started toward the lawn, ready to defend his lady's honor. "I heard something. I know I did. What if it's Lord Stifford? Come to claim me? Or my father?" Pamela was crying again because apparently she did that a great deal and at the slightest provocation. Diana was seriously tempted to go shake the girl by the shoulders and tell her not to be such a pathetic victim all the time.

"Who's there?"

For Giles, surrender seemed the most prudent option, but before he rose and waved the white flag for them both without her consent, Diana grabbed his hand and dragged him around the back of the shrubbery a split second before Rory came into view.

"There is nobody here, my darling." With their bodies pressed side by side and their backs pressed into the leaves, Giles and Diana stood as still as statues holding their breath. "Perhaps you heard a fox or a badger." Rory's voice receded. "But let us not tempt fate. If we leave now, it will be hours before anyone realizes we are gone, and we could be well on our way down the Great North Road by then and married before they can stop us."

Together they exhaled as they watched the couple scurry hand in hand back down the garden.

"That was close." Giles's sentiment echoed her own.

"I hope they make it. I wouldn't wish Stifford on my worst enemy."

"Because you are a rescuer to your core." Giles slanted her an amused glance. "But I am sure they'll make it. Love is supposed to conquer all, isn't it? At least in fairy tales." He began to unfold his limbs only to still again when he heard another feminine giggle approaching from the other side of the garden. One glance at Giles's annoyed face confirmed she wasn't imagining it before two pairs of new feet crunched down the path in their direction. "Good grief, this garden is like Piccadilly Circus!"

Diana simultaneously shushed him and rolled her eyes, then hunkered back down in her shawl. As he crouched beside her she unraveled some of it and draped it around his shoulders, making no secret that she was sharing it only under duress. He burrowed into the warmth, and as she had predicted she instantly regretted her charitable gesture because it felt too intimate. Just the heat from his annoying long body gave hers ideas.

"We shall have to be quick, Alec . . ." Of all the people for Fate to send Diana next, it had to be Lady Sewell and her fake Russian count. Two people most definitely outside for a tryst. "Before we are missed." Their feet came closer then disappeared inside the pergola right next to Giles and Diana's hiding place.

A male voice laced with broad cockney came out in a silky murmur. "Nobody will find us here, Gertrude. This is the perfect dark place to do dark deeds."

Dark deeds!

Oh no!

There was the ominous squeak of metal as they lowered themselves onto the seat inside and then a giggle laced with innuendo, which was smothered by a noisy kiss.

Beside her Giles groaned in despair. Moments later, Diana did, too, for it turned out Lady Sewell was every bit the game old girl she had always suspected: She was only too happy to immerse herself in those dark deeds with rampant enthusiasm.

"Oh, how I have missed you, my darling. How I have missed your kisses . . ."

Diana winced at Lady Sewell's lusty moan, her toes cringing inside her slippers that she had to hear it beside Giles of all people, while her vivid imagination decided to analyze it against her will.

What on earth was the fake count doing to make the woman lose her head so?

Giles obviously knew because he was wincing, too—but at her in an apologetic way as if he expected the sounds from the pergola to get much worse before they got better. Thanks to his nearness, she did not need to see his expression to know what he was thinking; she could feel it the tension in his muscles. So close she could feel the alluring heat from his skin beneath all the layers of his clothes. So close every nerve ending she possessed fizzed at the intimacy of the situation, and with mortifying curiosity, too. As if they suddenly were eager to know if they might work in the same way as Lady Sewell's with the right encouragement. The sort of encouragement who was currently sniggering beside her and whose seductive kisses had woken her stupid nerve endings in the first place!

Annoyed, she nudged Giles hard in the ribs to shut him up. That only made the wretch laugh more.

"Oh, Alec . . . my darling." Lady Sewell made a scandalous sound as her lover did something to her that involved much rustling of petticoats until the greedy kissing resumed with a vengeance. "Oh yes, Alec . . . touch me there . . . right *there* . . ."

What was that all about?

And more important, where on the female body was *right there*?

One foolish side glance at her amused companion confirmed he knew exactly where *right there* was. Sensing she didn't, he winked. "It shouldn't be long now, rose cream." He collapsed in another fit of the giggles at her outraged expression while Lady Sewell moaned some more fevered directions to improve her experience.

Then the fake count groaned as his lady clearly returned the favor, a carnal, guttural sound that hinted she was teasing more than just the fellow's lips. Deciding to ignore Giles at all costs, Diana stared at the heavens instead, praying for a miracle and for time to speed up, and when her prayers were ignored she clenched her eyes shut and slapped her palms over her ears while nature took the rest of its course.

"Oooohhhh, Alec . . ." A bubble of mirth escaped from Giles's mouth, and with her eyes still screwed closed, Diana whacked his arm, praying this time for either the ground to swallow her up or the Almighty to smite him with a thunderbolt to spare her from ever having to face the smug wretch again.

"Oooohhh, Gertie . . ."

After what felt an eternity of grunting, thrusting, illuminating murmured encouragement, and quivering leaves, and while Giles had to bite his hand to stop his laughter echoing around the garden, Lady Sewell reached her exuberant and noisy crescendo. A few more seconds and one final, decisive quiver of the pergola later and her lover followed suit. Or at least she assumed that was what his repetitive benediction of "I'm coming, Gertie!" meant.

There were a few blessed moments of silence before the pair hastily repaired their clothing and slunk off into the night murmuring sweet-but-salty nothings about the dark deed they had just done. Throughout it all, Diana remained rigid with mortification. Her entire head, and as much of her body as she could squeeze under it, were now covered by her shawl in the forlorn hope it might, miraculously, render her invisible if she wished for it hard enough.

It didn't work.

"So . . ." Giles nudged her with his elbow, the same second the coast was clear. "If we ignore the glaring fact that we would have been spared that abhorrent ordeal if you had listened to me in the first place, and that I told you so at least three times and was ignored, the obvious question that now begs to be asked, Diana, is—did you at least manage to hear anything useful?"

Diana emerged from the cocoon of the shawl like a firework. "You are insufferable!"

In the absence of the prayed-for thunderbolt, she whacked him over his irritating head with her reticule. "Insufferable, incorrigible, and irritating in the extreme!"

"But right!" he said, still laughing at her. "You have to concede that."

She snarled, wanting to strangle him until his smug, amused, annoyingly handsome face turned purple but settling for another thwack with her flimsy embroidered silk reticule instead. "Be in no doubt, Giles Sinclair, as you congratulate yourself for being right for the first time in your entire useless life, that I haven't missed you at all!"

As his hysterical laughter finally let rip, and with as much dignity as she could muster despite her face being on fire and her bodily urges all over the place, she stormed off down the lawn.

Chapter Seventeen

"And a good morning to you, too, old chap. Merry Christmas."
Giles lowered the covers on his old chap, ignoring the fact it was as
stiff as a board and standing proudly to attention ready for action.
Instead, he stretched his arms behind his head on the pillow to
stare at his ceiling. Even if he saw to it—again—he knew it would
make no difference because the moment he saw Diana, his frisky,
opportunistic appendage would be up again like a shot.

At least today, he could blame last night for his discomfort and
he chuckled at the memory of it.

Their little interlude in Lady Bulphan's garden had been pure
torture. Both before they ventured off the terrace and after. The after, in particular, was responsible for his current state. If snuggling
next to the minx beneath her shawl behind a bush wasn't temptation
enough, he had been subjected to the flustered sight of her blushing while another couple copulated mere feet away. It had been apparent throughout that her curious mind tried to figure out exactly
what was going on. The overwhelming urge to enlighten her with a
practical demonstration had almost killed him and had tested every
speck of willpower he possessed until he saw the glorious irony of his

predicament. Then he had chosen to laugh rather than cry at Fate's
warped and twisted sense of humor.

In a strange sort of way, it proved to be just the tonic he had
needed. One that instantly lightened his mood for the first time in
weeks. Months even. Yes, his situation was still dire, his estate still
desperate for modernization and his feelings for Diana futile and
his future as uncertain as a roll of the dice in a game of chance.
But those painful twenty minutes trapped behind that bush had
reminded him that it was good to be alive and that something unexpected, ridiculous, and spontaneous in otherwise dreadful circumstances could still bring a smile to his face, no matter how
hopeless he felt inside. Such was life's rich tapestry.

Today would bring more unexpected smiles, as would the
day after, and as time moved on perhaps the crushing sense of
despondency and uncertainty would fade and so, too, would his
inappropriate feelings for Diana. And then perhaps Giles would
find some real joy in his life. If last night had taught him anything
alongside the reminder that he still possessed his characteristic
joie de vivre, it was that he could always make the best of things.

It wasn't as if he had a choice.

He stared at the ceiling some more while he waited for Dalton
to make an appearance, and when his useless servant failed to turn
up after half an hour of staring he hauled himself up, then tried to
find some joy in the cold wash he had to have as a result.

Clean and unashamedly naked, Giles took his time contemplating his wardrobe. It was Christmas after all and he was spending it with his favorite friends, so he chose a bold gold waistcoat as
a jaunty nod to the season and even tied a fussy cravat—the sort
Diana would find dandified and frivolous—purely to vex her revo-

lutionary sensibilities. Suitably attired for a day of celebration, he bounded down the stairs with a welcome spring in his step.

Dalton met him in the hallway.

"I had your healthy biscuit breakfast laid out in the dining room as you requested." He jerked the thumb of his mangled hand in that general vicinity. "I suppose you'll also be expecting tea despite it being my day off." In honor of that day off, Dalton being Dalton, he, too, was dressed for the occasion, except in his case it was as if he were sunning himself on the deck of a ship sailing in the Mediterranean rather than in a peer of the realm's residence in bohemian Bloomsbury. To that end he hadn't bothered with a coat or buttoning his floppy linen waistcoat, his shirtsleeves were rolled up to his elbows, and the least said about the scruffy shoe on his hairy stockingless only foot, the better.

"As it will be only the second cup of tea you have brought me in two months, you work-shy insubordinate, yes, I do. I shall need something to dip my shortbread in." Giles shooed him away. "Step lively."

Dalton's one eye rolled as he tugged at his forelock, then he clonked down the hallway on purpose at half his usual pace while Giles rubbed his hands together at the thought of his impending sugary repast.

His lovely cook hadn't let him down, bless her, and had baked an array of crumbly sweet treats for him to graze upon, and graze he did for the next half an hour, savoring each sublime bite. Determined to view the world again through the rose-tinted spectacles he had made a conscious decision to put back on. From this day forward, positive thoughts would replace the negative, because all the negativity was wearing him down.

"You've got visitors." Dalton frowned as he marched back in. "Two of them. Shall I let them in?"

"That entirely depends on who they are and how long they intend to stay." The only people who called on Christmas Day were either family, which he did not have, or do-gooders rattling the collection plate for charity. Or carol singers, he supposed as he bit into a sublime square of shortbread, which he wouldn't mind at all. Especially if they were atrocious.

"They wouldn't give their names nor state their business neither, but said it was a matter of grave import that they had to deliver to you in person."

Then they were definitely do-gooders. "Grab my purse and I'll allow them to rinse me of all my coin before I depart." This was the season of goodwill, after all. "As they are bound to be after money."

"They're after something, that's for certain, but my instincts tell me it'll be more than a few shiny coins these fellas want. If you want my opinion . . ."

Giles stayed him with his hand. "I really don't."

"They're a pair of ne'er-do-wells. That's why I left them stood on the doorstep and locked the door behind me."

"I sincerely doubt ne'er-do-wells work at Christmas, Dalton, any more than you do. You've clearly been spending too much time with Miss Diana if you are suspicious enough of a couple of gentlemen callers to batten down the hatches on a day like today."

"I never said they were gentlemen neither, Your Grace, and I'll fetch my pistol alongside your purse, if you don't mind, just as a precaution. One of them, the younger one, talks with the same funny twang as Lord Fareham's father-in-law, Mr. Peabody." He pulled a ferocious face that warned he expected skulduggery just for that.

"Last time I checked, being an American wasn't a crime, Dalton."

"Says the man who didn't have to fight the blighters in 1812!"

"Of course I didn't have to fight them in 1812!" Sometimes his manservant's strange logic made absolutely no sense. "Because I was only . . ." Giles did a quick sum on his fingers. "Seventeen and still growing up in Shropshire! And you didn't fight them, either, because I know for a fact the navy pensioned you off after Trafalgar." He pointed to Dalton's scrimshaw leg. "You're unfit for service—naval or otherwise."

"Shows what you know because I was a merchant seaman for the East India Company during that war, and part of the crew of the *Nautilus* when those damn Yankees on the *Peacock* captured us. They locked us in the brig, even though the blasted war had been over for six months. Killed a couple of my shipmates in the skirmish. I'll never forgive them for it. But that was in 1815, not '12. Same war, though—technically."

"And one of my visitors was on the *Peacock* and murdered one of your friends?" Thanks to his late night, Giles was struggling to follow.

"I couldn't say, but I recognize the older one from somewhere. I might forget where I put my leg each night but never forget a face." A fascinating insight into his butler's strange mind, which frankly boggled his.

"Right, then . . ." Giles huffed as he frowned, completely confused and bemused by all the kerfuffle. "Why don't I go speak to them and find out for certain before you shoot someone on my doorstep?" Perhaps then he could enjoy his biscuits and what was left of the morning in peace.

He marched out of the dining room with Dalton limping behind him, flung open his front door expecting to confront a couple of plate-rattling do-gooders, then froze.

Because he recognized one of the faces, too—but only in paint.

"Well, if it isn't my long-lost nephew."

The face was older than the one in the portrait, quite a bit fatter, and the once golden hair dulled by time. But the likeness was unmistakable.

"Uncle Gervais?"

Olivia had been right. They were the coldest eyes Giles had ever seen. Bright blue but flat. Like the dead eyes of a corpse or the menacing stare of a shark. His gaze flicked to the younger man. He couldn't be more than twenty, but his golden hair and good looks matched those of the portrait hanging in Harpenden Hall, branding him as this man's son despite the green eyes. Intense green eyes that swirled with enough emotion for the both of them.

"I am indeed, Giles, and this is your cousin Galahad." Another *G* for the Sinclair family tree. Diana would find that amusing. "We came to visit your father at Christmastide, but alas, it seems we were too late . . . my sincere condolences." There was nothing sincere or condoling in his scathing tone.

Without being asked, Gervais Sinclair stepped over the threshold and swept his gaze up and down over Giles. "You're the spit of him. A mirror image of dour old Gerald in his prime—you even have his height." Stood too close, he craned his neck up to smile at him while he scrutinized his face. "Yet I see nothing of your mother in you. Nothing at all. Odd that, don't you think?" And just like that, Giles knew why the man was here.

"Is it?" He feigned nonchalance even though his mind was racing. "Don't all children favor one parent over another?" He made a point of staring at the cousin he had not known he possessed. "Young Galahad here is the spit of you in your youth. Or at least he is the spit of the only portrait of you we have at Harpenden Hall." He was being too jovial. Too defensive. So he held his ground, pulled himself to his full height and folded his arms. Became the duke this unwelcome visitor apparently knew he wasn't. "I believe my father had all the others destroyed after you absconded from justice because he couldn't bear to look at you. Kidnap, wasn't it? Of an heiress, too, which I believe is a capital offense? Has that outstanding warrant been canceled?"

Gervais's expression hardened. "All scurrilous lies and falsehoods that would have been dismissed had your father intervened as he should have and defended my good name."

"Perhaps he knew he could not defend the indefensible?"

"More like he was too tightfisted to hire me a lawyer and wanted an excuse to cut me off without a farthing."

"From what I have heard, you were disowned by my grandfather long before that."

"For youthful high spirits? For sowing my wild oats?" Gervais smiled as if butter wouldn't melt in his mouth. "From what I've read about you, you've done much the same. So did Gerald, of that I can attest. But he was hard like that, your grandfather. Cruel, callous, and unforgiving. Even my pompous brother struggled to meet his ridiculous expectations of how a Sinclair should behave." Which beggared belief when the duke had clearly been a chip off the old block.

"Neither I nor my sire spent time in jail, Gervais. My oats have certainly never been that wild."

"Shall we air all our dirty linen here or in private?" Two emotionless blue eyes stared at Dalton for a moment, who had mirrored Giles's combative stance and was glaring out of his one good eye for all he was worth. "But be in no doubt, nephew, air it we must."

Giles gestured to the drawing room. "You have me intrigued, so I shall spare you five minutes before I send Dalton for the authorities."

Gervais wandered into the room as if he owned the place, running his hands along the expensive striped silk damask that covered the settee. While Galahad sat, he waited until Giles had closed the door before he spoke again.

"A nice place you have here. Clearly you enjoy spending the Sinclair fortune."

"This house and everything in it came from my pocket." At least Gervais couldn't take that away. "I have always had a talent for speculation."

"I'll bet your father loved that." Bitterness laced the other man's tone. "Back when I knew him he disapproved of the stock market. It was always too risky for his staid tastes." Because his uncle seemed determined to remain standing, and because Giles did not want to appear the least bit intimidated, he sat and crossed one leg over the other in a relaxed pose.

"The duke never changed that opinion."

"I'm not surprised. He never liked spending money. He was too much like our father in that respect. Sour-faced, straitlaced, and tight-fisted, the pair of them. Both much preferred to leave it all to gather dust while they congratulated themselves for the impressive numbers scratched in their precious ledgers. It is such a shame my brother lacked the backbone to be his own man, as

I'll admit he showed some promise for a while in his youth. Even cut himself off from the old man for a whole winter in outraged rebellion at his unreasonable demands." Had he? This was all news to Giles when his sire had always claimed to have put duty over everything, exactly as the family motto stated. "Still married the bride the old man had picked out despite his short-lived stint in Wales. Duty over everything and all that. Even if you cannot stand the wench who stood next to you at the altar." Gervais picked up a silver box and turned it over to peer at the maker's mark. "But clearly you are cut from different cloth." He smiled again as he put the box down. "A very different cloth indeed."

Diana would ask the most direct question, so he did, even though he feared the answer. "What do you want, Gervais?"

"What I am due." He glanced around the room then pinned him with his glassy stare. "Your fortune and your title."

He forced a laugh. "Have you imbibed of too much Christmas spirit?"

"I am the legal heir."

He tried to remain amused. "I suppose you are, presently, *my* legal heir. If I happen to die without issue . . . but as you see I am hale and hearty and quite robust so have no immediate plans to follow my father into the ground. Unless your plan is to murder me? If it is, you probably shouldn't have forewarned me of your dastardly plans as now I am on my guard."

Gervais offered him a smug smile. "I am my brother's legal heir. The second son of the twenty-fifth Duke and Duchess of Harpenden."

"But I am the only son of the twenty-sixth."

"You are his bastard, Giles, and I have proof."

Dread settled like lead in his stomach, but he made sure his expression remained amused. "Then I should be intrigued to see it, as it is news to me."

"Your mother was a harlot." Galahad decided to open his mouth for the first time. "And we have a letter that confirms it."

Gervais shot his son a warning look, and the boy seemed to shrink under his glare.

"Oh, a letter . . ." Giles's voice dripped sarcasm. "From the alleged harlot herself, I imagine. Because that is all the proof any-one needs of your outlandish accusation. I might as well hand it all over now, I suppose? Lock, stock, and barrel, as clearly the scrib-bled words of a random prostitute trump the official records of my birth, my patents of nobility, and my father's will." He shook his head laughing. "I wish you luck with that, gentlemen. I suppose I shall soon see you and your damning letter in court." He frowned. "Oh . . . wait. Wouldn't that mean also alerting the courts of your return, Uncle Gervais? And there I assumed that was the last thing you would ever do when there is a noose somewhere that still has your name on it."

"They don't hang dukes." Gervais was unperturbed, a wor-rying sign he had something both damning *and* conclusive in his pocket. "And we both know that I shall soon be one. And there can be no trial without witnesses, and thankfully everyone who could bear false witness against me is dead."

Giles sighed and slowly unfolded himself from his chair, mak-ing a great show of examining his cuffs as if bored with all Ger-vais's nonsense. "What I know, without a shadow of a doubt, is that our five minutes are up, gentlemen. While your little visit has been entertaining if nothing else, alas, it is Christmas Day and I have better things to do than indulging in your fanciful whimsy any longer." He swept his palms in the direction of the door. "Knowing my officious and suspicious butler, he's already called the constable and the watch, so I shall bid you a fond adieu as I am sure you are equally eager to be gone before they arrive."

Gervais smiled as he sauntered to the door. "I shall keep in touch, Giles."

"It is *Your Grace*, Gervais." Suddenly, the title he had always dreaded owning mattered.

"For now it is." The older man laughed as he clicked his fingers at his son, then sailed through the door to where Dalton hovered in the hallway, a scowl on his face and a well-used pistol now slotted into the thick leather belt now wrapped around his waist. "But be in no doubt those days are numbered—*Your Grace*."

Obviously feeling empowered by his father's threats, Galahad prodded Giles's chest with his finger as he walked past. "You just better pray, cousin, that you find your father's harlot before we do." A telling sentence that briefly narrowed Gervais's soulless eyes before he covered it with an oily smile.

"Until next time, nephew . . ." He made a great show of glancing around the hallway and smoothing his hand over the frame of Giles's favorite Canaletto. "Enjoy your good fortune . . . while it lasts."

They left, and left Giles reeling. As soon as Dalton slammed the door he limped back toward him with a grim expression. "Bet you wish I'd shot him on the doorstep now."

"Exactly how much of that private conversation did you eavesdrop on from the keyhole?"

"Enough to know we're in a lot of trouble."

"'We,' Dalton?"

"Duke or bastard, I'll not desert you." His butler searched his face then sighed. "I take it you knew about the harlot before that devil told you?"

Giles nodded. "I found out when the duchess died. It certainly explained why she never liked me."

"And your real mother?"

"Is a mystery, Dalton. I've been hunting through all the duke's papers for weeks trying to find her, and there isn't a trace."

"Well, clearly there is, and dear old Uncle Gervais knows it."

"It would appear he does and, pardon my pun, Dalton, but if he can prove it, I won't have a leg to stand on. Legally, Harpenden is his."

"Then we'd best make sure he can't prove it, hadn't we?"

"I am not going to ask anyone to help me break the law, Dalton—even someone as disreputable as you."

"Well, if you want my opinion on the law . . ."

"I'm almost sure I don't, Dalton."

"There's only one kind of justice—what's right and what's wrong. While you've only ever tried to do right by the good folks on your estate for the decade I've known you, he's as malevolent a wrong 'un as any I've ever met and I wouldn't trust him with my name let alone your dukedom."

"I'm actually rather touched, Dalton." And he was. Giles was certainly overwhelmed enough that a few tears pricked his eyes. Of course, they might well be grief at losing Harpenden before he had fixed it. Or self-pity because he was destined for Newgate.

"I'll cancel my plans with my ladylove and we'll set to work straightaway. And if I could be so bold as to offer another opinion, Your Grace . . ."

"As if I could stop you."

"If I heard the son correctly, and we need to find your mother with all haste before your uncle does, we're going to need the services of the Sentinel. For nobody is better at digging up dirt and stopping wrong 'uns doing wrong and seeking proper justice for the wronged than Miss Diana Merriwell."

Chapter Eighteen

As Diana returned from her walk, Payne staggered past laden with greenery, closely followed by Olivia clutching a reel of scarlet ribbon and a pair of scissors. At least she assumed the bush with legs was Payne.

"What on earth is going on?"

"The house needs to look more festive." The older woman smiled too sweetly as she bustled past. "It feels like Christmas in some rooms and not in others." Then she directed Payne. "We shall do the music room next. Then Hugh's study."

"Will Hugh be working in his study on Christmas Day?" Her question fell on deaf ears, so she huffed instead. "I thought working today was frowned upon." She had certainly had to lie after breakfast to escape for long enough to write the exclusive truth of why Lord Stifford had been jilted—or would be sometime in the next half an hour. Thank goodness she had found a hackney, and the story she had written while shivering on a bench in the middle of Hyde Park, as the maid she had been forced to take fed the ducks, was now winging its way to Fleet Street. Hopefully with the same haste Lady Pamela and her lieutenant were racing to Gretna.

Vee emerged from the drawing room, clutching a book to her chest and grinning. "Olivia wants to ensure no stone is left unturned." She pointed to the ceiling in the hallway, which was now festooned with hanging bunches of mistletoe everywhere. "It is bad luck *not* to kiss under mistletoe, so she is keen that you and Giles are presented with plenty of opportunities to succumb. Especially after last night . . ."

"Last night?" Diana swallowed as she tried to appear confused.

"Olivia is convinced she saw you sneaking back into the party from the terrace, closely followed by Giles. He apparently looked very pleased with himself."

"Doesn't he always?" Convinced she could lie about it without spontaneously combusting in a blush, Diana decided to brazen it out. "But then again Lady Bulphan's carol concert and the musical Nativity were atrocious, and he does find humor in the most bizarre things."

"Then you do not deny the pair of you shared a moment on the terrace?" Vee's eyes widened in a knowing fashion.

"We shared a hello on the terrace. A *quick* hello as I recall."

Which was sort of true. The actual greeting had been quick. The mortification of what happened after had lasted an eternity. To her horror, it hadn't ended in the garden, either, as Lady Sewell's lusty but fake Russian count had sat in the vacant chair beside Diana for the musical massacre of the Nativity.

Giles, the wretch, had enjoyed her discomfort immensely from his seat three chairs away and made no attempt to hide it. In fact, he had laughed so much he had barely been upright by the time the three wise men sung about their offerings to the baby Lord Jesus.

Thankfully, after an out-of-tune Balthasar sang the immortal line *Allow me to dispense some frankincense*, neither was Hugh, and she was supremely grateful for Lady Bulphan's dreadful lyrics for hiding the true source of Giles's amusement and her embarrassment from everyone else.

"Well, Olivia is convinced she sensed a frisson between you, and she is determined to encourage that. She also thinks the only reason Giles turned up last night was because of you . . ."

Had he? That was intriguing . . . "Oh, for pity's sake!" The admonishment was as much for Diana's own foolish romantic musings as her sister's theory. "When are you all going to get it through your thick heads that I have no interest in Giles?" She glared at the mistletoe. All so strategically placed it would be near impossible to avoid it. "Help me rip this down, Vee!"

"Absolutely not." Her baby sister beamed. "Two footmen were dispatched to Covent Garden this morning to fetch it all, and poor Payne has been hanging it for an hour. It would be disrespectful to undo all their hard work."

Diana narrowed her eyes at the Judas. "You are in cahoots with Olivia. You are betraying your own flesh and blood for that meddlesome woman! Your own sister!"

Vee grinned again, unrepentant. "So is Minerva. She is supervising Hugh and Jeremiah while they decorate the dining room. Olivia wants it all done before Giles arrives."

"Oh, I see." Her hands went to her hips. "This is a family-wide conspiracy."

"It's just a bit of mistletoe, Diana."

"It is not just a bit of mistletoe!" It was coercion. Manipulation. Temptation at every turn to succumb to another one of Giles's much-too-potent kisses when she still wasn't over the last. "If you will not help, I shall do it myself!"

Diana marched into the drawing room and was about to drag a chair into the hallway to do just that when the bell rang and Giles arrived.

"Giles!" Vee's delight as she welcomed him sealed her fate, because everyone else suddenly came running. Hands were shook, cheeks were kissed, and they all lingered in the stupid hallway so long they made it awkward that she hadn't gone to greet him, so with gritted teeth, she did, ensuring she kept him at least six feet away with one eye on the ceiling at all times.

"Merry Christmas, Giles."

"Diana . . ." He seemed so relieved to see her that everyone else smiled with mischievous delight. "Merry Christmas."

Because nobody else spoke, she had to. "Perfect timing, as always, for luncheon is about to be served. Anyone would think you smelled it all the way from Bloomsbury."

At Diana's instigation they all filed behind her toward the dining room where a mountain of cold cuts and tasty treats had already been piled on the sideboard for people to help themselves. Olivia's idea, to make this meal more convivial and casual than the formal Christmas dinner they would all eat later. Typically, despite the informality, she was somehow placed next to Giles at the table under a ball of mistletoe so large it was a wonder it hadn't already fallen and taken some of the plaster with it.

As he sat, he whispered in her ear. "I need to talk to you. *Alone.*"

She snapped open her napkin and tried to hide her response with a smile. "Well, that won't be happening today! Olivia has it in her head we need a matchmaker." In case he had missed the glaring evidence of that, she raised her gaze skyward. "She has set traps everywhere."

"What are you two whispering about this time and so *covertly*?" Olivia's question drew everyone else's gaze. "Or should I not ask."

"We weren't whispering at all, Olivia." Giles smiled as he flicked open his own napkin, sending a waft of his spicy cologne her way. The same fragrance he had worn last night when they were huddled beneath her shawl, which had scrambled all her wits. "I was merely commenting on what a lovely spread you have put on."

"Oh, that is a shame." Olivia could barely contain her evil smile as she watched them over the rim of her glass. "As I was hoping it was a continuation of whatever the pair of you took half an hour to discuss last night on Lady Bulphan's terrace. Or were you just enjoying the moonlight?"

As Diana's cheeks threatened to heat again, Giles's quick thinking saved them. "I cannot speak for Miss Diana, but I was on the terrace avoiding Dahlia Regis and her father. The latter seems to be laboring under the misapprehension I will take the duke's place next to her at the altar and decided to thrust her at me at every given opportunity. She didn't seem so keen, though, which is a relief for me, albeit an unflattering one. For who wouldn't want this?" He pointed to his dimpled chin. "Giles Sinclair makes all the ladies swoon. I am famously irresistible."

"And yet some of us can still resist you with little effort at all." Her droll comment garnered a few chuckles and thankfully, the conversation shifted direction. Soon the table was filled with laughter and conversation.

For the next hour Giles remained in the thick of it, as jovial and entertaining as always, but she sensed something was off. There was a stiffness to his posture and a jerkiness to his movements that gave it away. Or at least they did to her. Nobody else seemed aware anything was amiss.

As the plates were cleared he leaned toward her. "I really do need to talk to you." His hand reached for hers under the table, setting her nerve endings fizzing. "I am in trouble, Diana."

"What sort?" But she already knew.

"The worst sort and I need your help."

"Who fancies a proper game of cards?" Jeremiah rubbed his hands together at the prospect, because for him "proper" meant playing for money rather than points.

"I'm game," said Vee, rising. "I shall fetch my purse."

"Noooo!" said both Minerva and Hugh in unison.

"You cannot allow her to play." Hugh grabbed Jeremiah's arm. "Vee always wins. That girl has the luck of the Irish."

"Even Vee has to lose sometimes." Jeremiah narrowed his eyes at the youngest Merriwell because he knew Hugh spoke the truth. "By the law of averages she has to lose one day and I have everything crossed that it is today."

As they all rose and lamented Vee's uncanny talent for gambling and fleecing them for every coin no matter what the card game, Diana took her time leaving the table while Giles insisted all the other ladies leave before he did. Within seconds he had returned, patting down his coat as if he had left something behind and closed the door.

"I had a couple of visitors this morning." Straightaway he began to pace, raking an agitated hand through his dark hair as his cheerful, flippant, festive mask dissolved. "Gervais and his son."

"Your uncle Gervais? The kidnapper?"

"The very one and guess what? He knows. He has a letter that proves my mother wasn't the duchess, and he intends to use it to claim the dukedom and everything that goes with it."

"What did the letter say?"

He stopped pacing only long enough to shrug. "Who knows? I didn't see it."

"Who is it from?"

"I don't know that, either. All I do know is that I am convinced they don't know who or where my mother is." He told her everything about his morning. What was said, how it was said, how it was left. All the while his boots ate up the floor like a man possessed, his expression so devastated it broke her heart. Once his tale was told he finally stopped and his whole body slumped in defeat.

"I just wanted more time. Was that too much to ask? I assumed if I fixed things at Harpenden, then I could hand it over and wish my successor well, safe in the knowledge that I had seen everyone right first, but now . . ." He huffed and sagged against the wall. "Now I am more frightened for the estate and its tenants than I ever was when the duke was at the helm. Gervais will run it into the ground. Rinse it for all it is worth. Dalton called him malevolent, and he is right. The badness shimmered off him, Diana. It was so tangible a presence it felt solid. Even his own son is terrified of him."

"Then we need to stop him."

"Dalton said that, too. Said I owed it to my people to protect them from that lying lobcock." He shook his head. Laughed without humor. "How pathetic is my situation that I have resorted to taking Dalton's advice all of a sudden?"

She smiled a little, too, as her hand brushed his arm in sympathy. "What's a lobcock?"

"Despite my scandalous, illegitimate, un-aristocratic roots, I am still too much of a gentleman to tell you." Bleak despondency replaced the familiar but brief mischief in his eyes. "What am I going to do?"

"We beat Gervais to your mother."

"We?" He closed his eyes for a moment as if she had said something profound. "And how do *we* find her? I've searched everything both in Shropshire and at the duke's house here, and I cannot find a thing."

"That's because you do not know what you are looking for."

"And I suppose you do?"

"Not yet, but I will—I promise." Her mind was whirring now. "I'll need to start my search in your father's things before I rattle all the Sinclair skeletons. But there is every chance you might not like what I find, Giles." Such an investigation was too close to home for her not to be nervous of the outcome. "I feel I need to prepare you for that. When you kick hornets, some sting."

"I am doomed already, Diana, and I would much rather a friend rattled the truth from those damn bones than a foe."

If she could rescue him she would. Right now if she were able— but thanks to Christmas, she couldn't. At least not without arousing suspicion. "Tomorrow? First thing? I could meet you in the duke's house in Grosvenor Square."

"Thank you." He reached for her hand. It was a friendly gesture.

Yet seemed so much more because neither of them severed the potent contact and just stared.

"Didn't I tell you they were having another moment?" At the sound of Olivia's voice they jumped apart to find both the older woman and Vee grinning at them from the doorway.

"I dropped my favorite stickpin and Diana found it." Giles tried to brazen it out, but her guilty blush gave them away. "I couldn't see it for looking. Perhaps I need spectacles like you, Vee? Do you think they would suit me?" He wafted a hand in the air near his face. "I suspect they would give me an air of gravitas that will make all the ladies swoon even more than they do now."

"What do you think, Diana?" With a butter-wouldn't-melt-in-the-mouth expression, Olivia deftly turned the tables. "Would you swoon more over Giles in spectacles, or would they make no difference?"

"It would make no difference to me either way, as neither would induce me to swoon over him."

"Then perhaps a kiss would." Her wily blue eyes were triumphant as they glanced up at another looming ball of mistletoe hanging above their heads. "It's dreadful bad luck not to kiss under the mistletoe—unless you have already . . . in which case you can ignore it."

The gauntlet was down, because they both knew she was caught between the devil and the deep-blue sea, as either answer would result in a day full of ribbing. Trapped, she picked the lesser of two evils and pulled a face as she nudged Giles and pointed to her cheek. "Get it over with or we'll be hounded all day with this nonsense."

"Be still my beating heart." He rolled his eyes at Olivia and her sister. "What hot-blooded male could refuse such an enthusiastic invitation?" He turned to her, the usual mischief suddenly dancing in his dark eyes. "But Giles Sinclair never shrinks away from a challenge. Prepare to swoon, Diana." Before she could argue, he tugged her into his arms, dipped her backward, and kissed her like he meant it.

Chapter Nineteen

She arrived at the duke's silent house the next morning with Dalton, cloaked and smuggled through the servants' entrance for propriety's sake. Giles had never been more relieved to see anyone in his life.

"Thank you for coming and I am sorry about yesterday." He was and he wasn't, because despite its brevity, he had thoroughly enjoyed the feel of her in his arms, and her outraged blush afterward had been quite delightful.

Being a gentleman, he acted chagrined at her subsequent, outraged chastisement and didn't mention that during the few moments before she remembered to be outraged by his impertinence, she had melted against him and kissed him right back.

"In my defense, it seemed like a good idea at the time." He winced recalling how she had been teased mercilessly afterward, especially by Vee who had taken great pleasure in telling everyone she was certain she had miraculously seen Diana swoon. "Let's face it, it is the sort of thing I would do with little provocation and I figured a lackluster peck on the cheek wouldn't have stopped Olivia in the long run."

She waved that away with a tight frown, taking in the musty study and the shelves of ledgers and neat wooden file boxes lined beneath them rather than talk about the kiss a moment longer. Perhaps she hadn't dissected it with the same focus as he had afterward? Or even thought about it at all. There was every chance their quick, five-second smacker hadn't made her body sizzle in quite the same way as his had. A depressing thought but undeniably for the best now that his world was about to implode.

"Is this everything?"

"I scoured the house and the attic after he died and found no more of the duke's papers. He was quite meticulous." Giles tapped one of the ledgers as he forced his mind to focus on the task at hand. "There is a separate book for each year, and they are all in chronological order. Every bill, receipt, and contract detailed in each of these ledgers is also in date order in its corresponding box."

"And his private correspondence?"

Giles shook his head. "There isn't any."

"Not even in his bedchamber?"

"There were no papers in either the one here or in Shropshire— unless they are sequestered and stitched inside his mattresses. I'll confess my searches weren't that thorough, but then he wasn't a sentimental man. He never even kept the letters and pictures I sent him as a child, so I suppose once he had read one, he tossed it away."

"Don't you think it's odd that he kept nothing personal?"

Giles tried not to stare as she undid her cloak and tossed it onto one of the old leather wingbacks. Tried not to notice how the fine wool of her green dress draped her pert figure to perfection, or how the shade of it brought out the emerald in her clever, feline eyes. "Of course I think it odd. It is beyond suspicious but he was a man with a deep, dark secret, so I suppose such caution was par for the course. Did your forger father keep any private correspondence?"

She smiled a little as she shrugged, drawing his gaze to her lips briefly and reminding his of their potency. "A fair point, but important clues come in many guises and we should start with his most personal effects first." She pointed upward. "Which way is his bedchamber?"

"Believe me, there is nothing to find there. That room is as spartan as a monk's and as soulless as . . . well . . . my unsentimental sire."

"I shall be the judge of that. In my experience, even when tracks have been covered thoroughly, something gets left behind."

"He buried his hornet's nest under thirty-one years of compacted dirt, Diana. There is nothing there."

"Vesuvius buried Pompeii nearly two thousand years ago under tons of molten lava, but with some shovels and some dedicated, *obedient* diggers who listened to instructions from their wise leader, humankind still found it. As you have put me in charge—"

"Did I?"

She pretended he hadn't spoken. "We shall do things my way."

Giles led her upstairs to the room he had last entered on the day they removed the duke's body. Despite the natural frigid chill in the room after months of no fire in the grate, there was another underlying it. The remnants of the essence of the man and his cold heart.

Aside from the stripped bed, everything had been left as it had been on that day. His old, dented pocket watch lay on the nightstand beside a solitary candlestick. His slippers side by side on the floor. His hairbrushes, comb, and razor were lined ruler-straight on the dressing table. All personal things yet impersonal at the same time. To test that theory, Giles picked up the watch. Turned it over in his hands and still felt no sentimentality toward the object even though he had seen it a thousand times attached to the duke's waistcoat.

"That looks old."

"It is. He owned it for as long as I remember." Giles traced one of the dents in the battered silver case with the pad of his finger. He clicked it open, shook his head at the scratched glass and rust-spotted face. "It is as ugly as it is tatty, but it worked, so it never would have crossed his mind to replace it." He snapped it shut, the familiar sound reminding him that his allotted time with his sire was up. An intrinsic part of the duke yet he still felt no connection to it or the man who had owned it at all. Because that frustrated him, he discarded it. "What exactly are we looking for?"

"I have no idea until we find it."

"Or not, as is most likely going to be the case. I've already been through this room with a fine-tooth comb."

"Well done you—but now we are both going to do it properly."

Diana left him to search through the nightstand while she rummaged through the dressing table. When all they had found were the everyday items one would expect, like matches or hair pomade, they both moved to the adjoining dressing table. That proved to be just as fruitless.

Being suspicious by nature, Diana insisted they move the

furniture, remove drawers, and check beneath and behind things. Still there was nothing beyond the dust and fluff the maids had neglected to find, no doubt because it was all too much trouble for a master who did not appreciate them.

"I did tell you there was nothing here."

She skewered him with her glare. "If you are going to start telling me you told me so again, Giles Sinclair, then you can solve your own mystery and I shall go. I did have other plans for today. Urgent newspaper work I have postponed to help you."

He pretended to sulk even though she had a point. "You are no fun."

"When I work on any investigation, I am thorough and never leave a stone unturned. Not to put too fine a point on it, you need me, Giles, or you're done for." She followed him to the door, and he opened it then stepped back to allow her to pass first, which she did before she paused. "Did you check inside the watch case for an inscription?"

As if she knew he hadn't, she marched back to the nightstand. With nimble fingers she clicked it open and scanned inside the lid, then shook the mechanism out. He could tell the way her brows kissed and her lush lips pursed that she had found something.

"Is this the duchess?" She held up the case, and Giles was staggered to see an enamel inset in the back.

He took the watch and stared at the picture of the woman. Despite the crudity of the execution, he could see she was pretty. Dark curls, dark eyes. Mouth slightly curved in an enigmatic smile as if something amused her. "No. I have no idea who she is." But all at once he felt a connection with her. Was that wishful thinking? Desperation?

Probably both.

"Interesting . . ." She couldn't resist a smile. "Clearly the duke wasn't quite as unsentimental as you thought, Giles."

"Clearly." But staggering regardless. He now had more questions about the past, and the man who had fathered him, than he'd had five minutes ago. More questions but not a single answer. "Who is she and why is she in this watch?"

"Can you hear that?" She cupped her ear with her hand and grinned into the silence. "The first distant buzz of a long-buried hornet."

"Is that your unsubtle way of telling me that you told me so?"

"One room down—another fifteen to go."

"Fifteen?" He pretended to whine like a petulant child. "Then we are going to need more biscuits."

She rolled her eyes as she sailed out, expecting him to follow, and he did. But not before he pocketed the watch, suddenly needing to have it with him even though he had no idea why.

Chapter Twenty

It was late evening by the time Diana got home. After the better part of the day searching the upper floors of the duke's house, she had gone to the newspaper to delve into the printed history of the Sinclair family, and then completely lost track of the time.

"And what time do you call this?" Olivia's voice came from the drawing room. "Dinner is in less than fifteen minutes, young lady." Family meals were sacrosanct as far as the new matriarch was concerned. Diana forgave it because Olivia was so lax and understanding about everything else.

"I can change and be presentable in five."

She hurried up the stairs, grateful to find the maid had already laid out her clothes on the bed and filled the washbowl with fresh water. A quick swish confirmed that while it was no longer hot, it was tepid enough to do. She had stripped to her undergarments when her door opened.

"Can you help me with my hair, Tabetha?"

"Tabetha has a nasty sniffle so I sent her to bed with a toddy." Instead of the maid, it was Olivia who wandered in. "And as Vee is doing Minerva's I thought I'd come to do your hair instead."

"There's really no need. I can manage myself." Just as Diana always had before life had diverted her from the path she had always known.

"I know, dear, but indulge me. I am still not happy about abandoning you for Hampshire." Persuasive blue eyes locked with hers in the mirror's reflection. "You could still change your mind and spend New Year's with us and travel back the week after?"

Diana shot her an exasperated look, and the other woman smiled her resignation. They had been over this at least fifty times in different guises in the past few weeks so Olivia knew she wouldn't budge. As usual, she had pleaded her work at the newspaper as the excuse to stay in Mayfair, because if she discounted Giles's predicament it was almost true. With everyone back in town for Christmas, Charlie needed all hands on deck at *The Tribune*—especially Diana's.

While extended breaks were the norm for the well-to-do, those who worked for a living did not have the luxury of disappearing willy-nilly for a month at a time to rusticate in the countryside. While she technically no longer needed to work for a living, it was inconceivable to her that she wouldn't. Earning her own money was something two decades of poverty had taught her went hand in hand with independence. She also wouldn't leave Charlie in the lurch at one of the busiest times of the year, any more than she would entrust leaving the important work she did for him to one of the less diligent reporters. And then there was the Coleridge story. She was so close to unmasking that scoundrel, she could taste it.

"I know . . . the newspaper cannot spare you and none of them can spell for toffee, and I also know that I am not your mother or your guardian or officially your anything and that you are long past the age of majority and free to do as you please. But it still doesn't sit right with me to leave you alone here with nobody to watch over you."

"All alone bar the housekeeper, the three footmen, four maids, the cook, the scullery maid, the stable master, two grooms, the stable boy, and the coachman who you insist takes me everywhere . . ." Diana ticked off Hugh's Berkeley Square staff on her fingers. "How on earth will I cope in all this secure luxury?" She gestured around her sumptuous bedchamber. "And for only three weeks, too?"

"If you are going to make fun of me, then at least let me fuss over you a little bit to ease my overprotective conscience." The older woman smiled at her. "Even though you hate it."

"I don't hate it, I just . . ." She sighed, uncomfortable with the over-familiarity and unnecessary concern while being touched by it at the same time. "I am not used to it, that is all." Diana had been nine when her mother died, and she had little memory of being mothered by the woman before then. Minerva had tried to fill that void for Vee but they were too similar in age for her to do that for Diana, so she had learned to be self-sufficient long before she had had to be.

"It has only ever been the three of you. I understand. And all this is still so new, it takes a bit of getting used to. In your shoes, I, too, would probably be wary of it. You are here only because your sister decided to marry my son, and knowing you as well as I already do, you would have managed just as well if she hadn't. I would also resent any curtailing of my hard-won freedoms, no matter how well meant. But this is just hair, Diana—not an offer of adoption or a new set of restrictive rules."

Olivia grinned as she picked up the hairbrush and motioned for her to sit. "I am not trying to become your mother or curtail your lifestyle or even try to stop you writing for that gossip column." Before Diana could deny it, she wagged the brush to stop her. "In fact, I am rather proud that at such a young age, you are your own woman and have found your own path. Why do you think I have never tried to stop you working there?"

To be fair to her, even when at her most meddlesome, Olivia hadn't. Right from the outset she had sensed interfering in her career would be the catalyst that pushed Diana away and had cleverly constructed a compromise that had suited them both without the need to ever discuss it. So long as Diana traveled to and from the newspaper in one of the Standish carriages, what she did in the long hours in between was tactfully ignored for the sake of family harmony. In return, Diana kept her work private when in Olivia's world. It was never mentioned outside of their close-knit family circle, not even hinted at, which also worked in her favor because it gave her the anonymity she needed to do her job properly. In short, they had created an unspoken status quo that worked for everyone.

Of course, that would change in a heartbeat if any of the family learned she often left the safety of those offices to investigate the Sentinel's controversial stories.

Diana flapped a hand at her hair. "Please don't do anything too rigid or use the curling iron."

Olivia beamed as she ran the brush through her tangled locks. "I wouldn't dream of it. Those tight, constrained ringleted styles all the young gals favor wouldn't suit you at all. You are too unique and mature for all that. How about something like this?" She twisted her hair up so loose curls dangled a little to one side exactly how Diana liked it. "Something seemingly artless and simple—but with a bit of panache?"

"That's perfect."

"Good. Because we want you to look pretty for *you*—and not because Giles is coming to dinner, too."

Diana pulled the expected face. "Again? Wasn't his tiresome company all day yesterday and Christmas Eve enough? At this rate he'll be moving in."

"He is on his own, Diana, and I worry about him." Olivia spoke around a mouthful of pins. "He wasn't quite himself yesterday, did you notice? Not during that delicious moment when he swept you off your feet, of course, because that was the pure, unadulterated, naughty Giles we all know and love—" Her eyes widened with mischief. "But before that magnificent effort under the mistletoe, and after, he seemed distracted. Troubled even."

Diana schooled her features as if she were considering it. "Perhaps he is still a little preoccupied with the burdens of being a duke? From what he told us about his planned modernizations and renovations, he is swamped with work in Shropshire, so a little preoccupation is hardly a surprise. Let's face it, such responsibilities and decisions must have come as quite a shock to a man who had nothing to worry about beyond deciding which garish waistcoat to wear or what food to put in his bottomless stomach next."

"I do not believe that shallow version of Giles for a second and neither do you. A great depth of character hides behind that polished veneer, alongside a forward-thinking business mind. A man with fluff for brains doesn't amass a stock portfolio like his by chance. According to Jeremiah, our favorite, flippant duke has fingers in all sorts of lucrative pies from shipping to steel and steam engines and was independently rich before he inherited." A fascinating snippet of information that begged some more serious digging. "He's philanthropic, too." Diana knew that already from his plans for the estate. "The Reverend Smythe from Vee's orphanage let slip over too much sherry last summer that Giles gave him a thousand pounds toward building it on the strict proviso his donation remained between them." Olivia poked a pin into her creation. "He's a good person, Diana—but a private one. The sort whose world could be falling apart and he would still ruthlessly hide it behind a smile."

More proof, if proof were needed, that Lady Olivia Peabody was as sharp as an ax. "Did he mention anything concerning when the pair of you were alone?"

"Irrespective of what you might believe to the contrary, Giles and I do not have that sort of relationship. I daresay I would be the last person he ever confided in." Lying when the older woman was brushing her hair, her canny blue eyes staring intently at her reflection, didn't come quite as easily as it usually did. "Did he say anything to Hugh?"

"No—but we both noticed he was unusually quiet. Not quite so . . ."

"Glib? Irritating? Exasperating?"

"I was going to say entertaining." Olivia smiled. "But your adjectives sound much more *promising*. There is more frisson to be had in exasperating than there is in entertaining—and the frisson between the pair of you since his return has been palpable." She wafted an imaginary fan in front of her face. "It is a mystery to me why you both fight it when we all think you go together very well."

"Do you ever stop matchmaking?"

"Somebody needs to nudge the pair of you in the right direction, and I am starting to see obvious glimmers of partiality in both of you after your prolonged separation. But then absence always does make the heart grow fonder. Giles, certainly, could barely take his eyes off you yesterday. Especially after that kiss . . ."

Diana huffed heavenward even though that knowledge warmed her. "I have no control over *his* eyes and no interest in them, either." And if he was staring, that was probably down to his dire situation and the urgent need for her help rather than anything else.

"Yours wandered to his a time or two, as well."

Only because Diana was worried about him.

Obviously.

Mostly.

They were looks of concern. At least a great many of them were. There may have been the odd stray, improper glance that fell outside those strict, acceptable parameters, fueled by the brief kiss which had thrown her wildly off kilter, but the second she caught one, it was nipped in the bud. Every time her stupid lips tingled with awareness, she repeated the same mantra she always had, even though it seemed less and less effective. She didn't need a man, had never desired that sort of restriction in her life, and especially didn't desire him.

She didn't.

Even if parts of her—like her wayward lips—were beginning to question that resolve.

"My eyes wandered to his no more than they wandered to anyone else's in the room. How many times must I reiterate I have absolutely no romantic interest in Giles? You said it yourself, I am fiercely independent and would resent anything that curtailed that. A man in my life would ruin everything I have worked for."

"If you say so, dear."

"The last thing I need is a husband laying the law down and telling me what to do."

"Does Jeremiah tell me what to do? Does Hugh tell Minerva? Of course not! They wouldn't dare."

"That is because they are exceptions."

"No, my dear, they are *exceptional*. Neither I nor your sister would have settled for anything less than men who love us for what we are. I cannot tell you how liberating and empowering that heady feeling is. To share your life with someone who understands you. Who shares all your hopes and your dreams and strives for them beside you. Who is there through thick and thin, no matter what, just because you are you." Olivia sighed in a dreamy fashion. "I have a feeling Giles might be exceptional, too, because for some inexplicable reason he seems to enjoy your sharp tongue and suspicious nature and I cannot imagine him wanting to change either for the earth. And you have a soft spot for that rapscallion. He's a challenge who makes your eyes sparkle."

"He's a challenge, all right. An insufferable one." Before Olivia could insinuate further, Diana decided to use the awkward topic to her benefit. "Although I must confess, since Shropshire, I have been intrigued by his background. Despite the physical resemblance, he doesn't seem to fit with the rest of his ancestors, does he? I mean, he is nothing like his father in character at all."

"Thank goodness. I couldn't stand his father. The Sinclairs always looked down their noses at everyone else and strode around as if they owned the place. Even when we were younger and attended all the same soirees, I did my best to avoid him and his awful brother."

And there was her way in. "I had a rummage in the *Tribune* archive for the Derbyshire scandal. You were right, it was shocking. The disowned, dissolute second son of a duke abducting a woman for her dowry must have made for compulsive reading. But I suppose you lived and breathed it, didn't you?"

Solemnity instantly replaced the dreaminess in her eyes. "I remember it well, dear. I was a young bride at the time and had just found out I was expecting Hugh." Always one for telling a good yarn, Olivia happily took the bait and settled in for the duration.

"I'd only met Gerald a handful of times before my marriage, as he tended to stay in Shropshire, learning the ropes I suppose, with his father. He was such a serious soul. Handsome, like Giles, but without any of his charm or effervescence. Even as a young man Gerald Sinclair was dour and pompous and obsessed with his status. We barely exchanged ten words in ten years growing up. But I knew Gervais well. He lived here in town with the duchess and because we were a similar age, and both were the offspring of dukes, we moved in the same circles. In fact, his mother and mine often took tea together before the scandal happened. Gervais was always a little wild, even as a boy. Spoiled rotten, my mother would often say when his tantrums raised a few eyebrows. His every whim indulged by the old duchess who could never see any fault in her flaxen-haired little angel."

"You saw them, though?"

"We all did, dear. Right from the nursery Gervais's many faults were glaringly obvious. He could be charming and there was no doubting he was handsome, but there was always an air about him that made me feel uncomfortable. And oh my goodness, did he have a temper! If he didn't get his way, he lashed out with venom as both a boy and a man. I seem to recall there was a particularly nasty incident involving a maid at Sinclair House. I was only sixteen or so at the time and not yet out, so I was shielded from the worst of the gossip, but I did overhear my mother tell a friend that Gervais had allegedly been violent toward the poor girl."

"He forced himself upon her?"

Olivia shrugged as she slotted a pin in the tumbled chignon she was creating. "One can only assume it was that, because my friends and I were supervised more vigilantly whenever Gervais was around afterward. Then, for whatever reason, he was no longer around and none of us saw him for years."

"Where did he go?"

"Officially? Nobody ever said. The Sinclair family have always been a secretive lot." Olivia was right on that score. "But rumors were rife of gambling debts and debaucheries, and of the duke cutting him off."

"How old was he then?"

"He couldn't have been more than three and twenty because it happened during my first season. After that, I do know he spent at least one stint in Fleet when his father refused to pay his creditors because that made the papers, but I doubt it was a one-off. He relied on his mother after that, or so we all assumed, and I know she and her husband fell out over it. Theirs had never been a happy marriage, but it deteriorated after Gervais's disownment to such an extent she set up a separate household in a rented house on Curzon Street. I don't think Giles's grandparents ever exchanged another word again before he turned up his toes a few years later. They certainly always ignored each other at any public engagements they happened to collide at, which made things quite awkward for the unfortunate hostesses. They even sat on opposite sides of the church when Gerald married."

"And when Gerald inherited—did the tide change for his brother?"

"They were never close but I believe Gervais was tolerated initially when his brother became the duke, largely because the new duke remained in Shropshire even when his wife preferred to stay in town." Olivia shook her head. "That was another unhappy Sinclair union, but as I can vouch, arranged marriages are rarely blissful. I was lucky with Hugh's father, as he was a decent man through and through—but as you know, we had our ups and downs and it took us years to find some common ground."

In case the conversation wandered farther down that meandering path, Diana pulled it back. "How did Gervais behave then?"

"Ah yes . . ." Olivia grinned at her reflection. "We were talking about Giles."

"Actually, we were talking about Gervais."

"Of course we were, dear, and I shall endeavor to maintain my focus, as it is perfectly understandable that you would wish to know what sort of family you will be marrying into." She ignored Diana's stony glare to laugh. "But I digress again . . . Gervais remained a scandal for the next few years. Enough to be excluded from all the good houses, though some of the lesser ones still tolerated him. He was the heir, after all, and a handsome and sometimes charming one at that. After Giles was born—and to much fanfare in the newspapers, I might add—Gerald Sinclair moved permanently to London, and once the *ton* realized Gervais was never going to inherit his dukedom he was pushed to the periphery again. It was his shocking reputation, of course, but he wouldn't have seen it like that. He bad-mouthed his brother everywhere and constantly complained about his allowance. Knowing his penchant for reckless spending way beyond his means, Gervais must have been up to his neck in debt and trouble by then. Enough that even his blinkered mother's handouts could not sustain him, especially after she fell out with her other son."

"Over what?"

Olivia shrugged. "Who knows? Gervais probably. Around the same time he tried to court Lady Caroline Derbyshire. When she would have none of him, he abducted the poor thing. You already know the rest. Suffice to say, the spare Sinclair packed quite a lot of scandal in his first thirty years, I can tell you. Thankfully, his nephew, although a rapscallion, is nothing like him so you can rest easy on that score."

"What became of Lady Caroline?"

"Another mystery. I did hear she went to a nunnery in Kent to recuperate from her ordeal, but then her father died and she didn't return. My mother, who adored gossip—"

"The apple didn't fall far from that tree."

Olivia grinned but didn't deny it. "My mother once said she believed poor Caroline remained in the sanctuary of that nunnery and took Holy Orders, but I have no idea if that was just her theory. She did like to speculate with little evidence to support it."

"Like mother, like daughter."

"We shall see." She popped the final pin into Diana's hair and stepped back to admire her creation. "You look ravishing, darling. Giles won't be able to resist you—but for propriety's sake, you should probably put on your gown before you go downstairs. No matter how charming the suitor is, a lady only sheds that on her wedding night . . . or thereabouts." She winked as Diana rolled her eyes and bustled toward the bed to eye the dress critically. "This pink is lovely, but your turquoise is more seductive." She cocked her eyebrow. "What say you I fetch that, as the mistletoe still works till Twelfth Night if you are tempted to loiter with him under it again?"

In answer, Diana snatched up the pink and shimmied into it. "It will be a cold day in hell before I kiss Giles Sinclair again!"

Olivia chuckled as she did up the laces. "If you say so, dear."

Chapter Twenty-One

"Receipts, bills, and more boring receipts!" Giles tossed the papers back into their labeled box and pushed it to one side beside him on the ballroom floor with its predecessor before he reached for another biscuit from the tea tray Dalton had only just topped up. As they had finished searching the duke's house and the place gave him the shivers, Giles had had the entire contents of his sire's study transported to his house yesterday instead. It was certainly warmer here in Tavistock Square, as well as less oppressive. It also made smuggling Diana in and out easier because her family did not live on the doorstep.

"This is torture. Futile torture. And we are going to need more biscuits."

"Will you stop distracting me while I am trying to concentrate." Her eyes never rose from the book she was studying.

"Well, it is torture. We've gone back thirty-one years and there's nothing out of the ordinary." They had spent the best part of ten hours hunting through the duke's papers and found nothing else of any significance since the enamel, but while he was tearing his hair out at their lack of progress, Diana remained as calm as a swan.

"I am almost done with my ledger, too. Fetch me 1794, would you? I can at least make a start on that before I have to leave."

"I wasn't alive in 1794. I was barely alive in 1795 so I wouldn't bother."

She glanced up from the ledger only long enough to give him a withering look. "A seed sprouts roots before shoots, Giles."

"And now you are talking in riddles, Diana."

"Oh for pity's sake!" She finally sat up from her cross-legged puddle of petticoats and folded her arms, giving him her full attention. "Stop being so shortsighted. Do you think you just appeared out of thin air thirty-one years ago? Babies take nine months to gestate and then there is the time before, which must be factored into our investigation."

"Before what?"

"Before your conception, idiot!"

"I really do not want to have to contemplate my conception." Giles pulled a face at the unsavory image of the duke huffing and puffing that skittered across his mind. "Please don't make me. I am still not over the trauma of Lady Sewell and her fake Russian count."

"I wasn't so much referring to that . . ." She flapped her hand as the beguiling hint of a blush stained her cheeks. "More the courting period that came before it."

"Men don't tend to court harlots, Diana. It's more a spur-of-the-moment financial transaction than a study in wooing."

"The woman in the watch doesn't look like a harlot."

It was the first time either of them had vocalized his growing suspicion. "You think she is my mother?"

"I think she might be." Diana waved a finger around her own

face. "There is something about her eyes and her expression that reminds me of you. An irreverence . . ."

"As if she sees everything as one big joke."

She winced as if she had hurt his feelings. "I didn't say that."

"You didn't—but the duke did. During our final conversation when I swore blind he was on the cusp of comparing me to my mother." Giles retrieved the watch from his waistcoat, opened it, and stared again at the woman in the enamel. "You are right . . . she doesn't look like a harlot." But she looked like someone he understood.

"If I am right, Giles, then it also stands to reason that whatever she and your father shared was more than a spur-of-the-moment financial transaction. She meant something to him. Why else would he have carried her around on his person till the day he died?"

"It is hard to contemplate the duke with a soft side. He was always . . . so . . . terse and ducal."

"How old was he when he inherited?"

"Much younger than me. Five and twenty? Give or take a year. But he had been trained for it from birth by my grandfather, so he was likely much better prepared for the responsibility. Back in old George the Dueler's day, the Sinclairs stayed at Harpenden Hall and Gerald accompanied him everywhere, learning at his knee, whereas Gerald, my crotchety old sire, did his level best to avoid the place while I was growing up in it and much preferred to stay in London. I had to train myself."

"I wonder why?" Her gaze flicked to the open watch still in his hands. "Olivia said he was wedded to Harpenden in his youth. Barely left the place. Yet after you were born, we have proof he avoided it at all costs. Painful memories perhaps, of a love lost or a love denied?"

Giles scoffed at that fanciful nonsense. "The duke's heart only pumped blood, Diana. It wasn't capable of love. But if Gervais was correct, I am not sure the duke spent all those years at Harpenden." He mimicked his uncle's menacing tones. "He cut himself off for a whole winter in outraged rebellion but still married the bride the old man had picked out in the end despite his short-lived stint in Wales."

"Perhaps that stint in Wales coincided with . . . um . . ." Diana blushed again as she avoided his gaze.

"My parents getting passionate? Sadly, I doubt it, as for the duke to have cut himself off from his father, his father would have needed to be alive, and he died when sour old Gerald was in his middle twenties. He was the same age as me when he brought me home—one and thirty—and George the Dueler had been dead for years by then. Gervais also said it occurred before he married the duchess, so I fear the short-lived stint in Wales is a red herring. Another frustrating, pointless dead end."

Her nose wrinkled in the most charming way. "Still, it is worth investigating."

"Why?" At this rate, they'd be searching all the way back to conquering Guillaume for blasted clues.

"Because it feels significant, Giles. Anything out of character or vastly different from the norm is always significant—and your cold father falling in love is about as vastly different from his norm as it was possible to be. Besides, you put me in charge, and I say it is."

"I really didn't." But he still leaned to retrieve the ledger she'd requested and passed it over. She frowned at the slim size of it.

"Is this part of a set?"

Giles checked and shook his head. "By the looks of things, going backward from '94 they are all much smaller. They used a different stationer perhaps?"

Diana did a quick flick through it and huffed as she slammed it shut. "This is apparently just the Grosvenor Square accounts. There has to be another for everything else." She glared at him as if he were a half-wit who had given her the wrong book, so he slid the whole pile over to her.

"This is everything going back to 1788 when the twenty-fifth duke died. I left all the older ledgers back in Grosvenor Square but I can assure you they all look like this."

She went from book to book discarding each with growing impatience until she decided to have one of her eureka moments. "Your father lived predominantly in Shropshire before you were born! It's all there! It has to be there!"

"Which is all well and good, but we are here."

"Then you must race to Shropshire to dig there, Giles."

"I don't have your eye, Diana." Would it be too much to ask her to accompany him? Presumptuous, certainly. Improper, definitely, so he forced a smile. "But if you give me some pointers, I shall try my best." And if he failed—when he failed—at least he could say he tried.

"Giles, I . . ." She chewed her lip and he saw the guilt war with indecision. He shook his head.

"I know. You cannot come. It's all right. Really it is."

"Sorry to interrupt, Your Grace." Dalton's head poked around the door. "But Lord Fareham is here to see you."

"Hugh is here?" His surprised gaze locked with Diana's mortified one. "And you let him in?"

"He is your best friend. I could hardly leave him stood on the doorstep like Gervais, now, could I? But I had the good sense to put him in the drawing room out of harm's way."

"He cannot see me here!" Diana stood then started to twitch and flap. "They think I'm at the newspaper! They are sending the carriage to the newspaper!"

"He cannot possibly see you in here, so calm down. Hugh is miles away in the drawing room." To call him a liar, Dalton winced from his lookout point at the door as Hugh's boots clicked toward them.

Diana's eyes widened as she snatched up her shawl and reticule, then dashed toward the French doors. But instead of escaping out of one of them like any sensible person would, she hid herself behind one of the curtains. Quite badly, in Giles's humble opinion, because the toes of her turquoise slippers clashed as they poked beneath the heavy red velvet drapes.

"What the blazes are you doing in here?" Hugh wandered in and surveyed the organized chaos on the floor.

"Still trying to fathom the duke's accounting system." Realizing there was nothing to be done about Diana and her slippers, Giles circled the mess so his friend had to have his back to her to face him. "But I think I have finally cracked it. At least here I have. The shambles in Shropshire is another matter."

His friend pointed to the two steaming cups of tea on the tray. "Have I called at a bad time? Were you expecting company? Or do you have company?" Hugh sniffed the air where Diana's peachy fragrance still lingered and grinned. "Have I interrupted a romantic tête-à-tête with one of your game ladies?"

"Not at all, old chap." His toes began to curl in his own boots as the curtains fidgeted. "One of those teas is for drinking and the other is for dunking." To prove that, he picked up a shortbread finger and plunged it into Diana's cup. "That way, all the dunking sludge remains in this cup while the other is sludge-free. Don't you just hate a chewy beverage? And speaking of beverages—Dalton, you slacker, go and make a fresh pot. Hugh and I will take it in the drawing room, where we are going to need more biscuits."

"One for drinking and one for dunking, ay? In a strange sort of way that makes sense." Hugh shrugged, picked up the spare cup, and took a sip, and because he had clearly decided to remain here in the ballroom for the duration rather than out the door where Giles was gesturing, plonked his behind on the tallest pile of thick ledgers. "I thought I'd stop by and say cheerio as we all leave for Hampshire in the morning. We could have postponed it if you had told us you were coming home for Christmas—but alas, you came too late and my mother had already made countless dreary plans. You still have an open invitation, of course, if you fancy a jaunt south."

"Sadly, Shropshire calls and I'll be leaving tomorrow myself." Maybe. Maybe not. There was every chance he could be taking a one-way jaunt to Newgate instead if Gervais had beaten him to the truth. Shackled in chains and stripped of everything, his *Dirty Secret* and rattling skeletons daubed over every newspaper. Despite the acid that very real prospect churned, he smiled at his friend. "I suppose I shall see you for the christening?"

"Yes . . . Yes . . . All a bit daunting. I keep waking up in the night in a cold sweat at the thought of impending fatherhood. Who'd have thought it? Me? As a role model. I pray the child is born with Minerva's good sense because if the poor thing is like me . . ." Hugh blew out a slow breath. "But I suppose it's the way of things. We all have to grow up and eventually settle down. I mean look at you. You're a sensible duke now and . . ." It was his uncomfortable smile that set alarm bells ringing.

"What's wrong?" Because something clearly was.

"I also wanted to talk to you about Diana." The teacup clattered in its saucer and Hugh stood, cringing. "I was sent to talk to you about Diana. About your intentions toward her."

"My intentions?" The turquoise toes shuffled awkwardly, and Giles forced himself to ignore them.

"We're both men of the world. Have both sown more than our share of wild oats and . . . well." Hugh groaned and he ran his hand over his face. "Normally I wouldn't interfere in your affairs, but Diana is family and Minerva wants to be reassured that if you have any intentions toward her sister, they are noble. Especially after what apparently happened under the mistletoe the other day."

"I was playing to the gallery, old boy. Having a bit of fun at Diana's expense—and your mother's." Which was sort of true.

Initially.

Hugh, and the vixen hidden behind his ballroom curtains, did not need to know that what had begun as a bit of humorous deflection in an incriminating situation had become so much more the moment his lips fused with hers and decided that was exactly where they wanted to be. "I genuinely have no intentions toward your harridan of a sister-in-law—noble or otherwise."

"Excellent." Hugh rocked on his heels. "Excellent . . . Because I would hate to have to challenge you to a duel over Diana's virtue."

"Her virtue is perfectly safe with me." More was the pity.

"But if you did, say, have a slip, you would do the right thing, wouldn't you? I mean, we've all seen the way you look at her and the kiss under the mistletoe was apparently quite passionate according to Vee and my meddling mother and . . . well . . . what with us going to Hampshire for a few weeks and her staying here in London . . ."

"And my imminent departure back to Shropshire as soon as the first cockerel crows."

"Yes. Yes, of course." Hugh sagged in relief. "You being in Shropshire is certainly a weight off my mind. You'll both be well out of temptation's way." His friend eyed him levelly. Man to man. Friend to friend. Sworn protector to potential despoiler. A stark warning in his gaze. "As much as I am loath to make my mother right about anything, old boy, there is an undeniable frisson and now that I am a married man, my first loyalty has to be to Minerva."

Giles raised his palm in oath. "You have my solemn pledge Miss Diana Merriwell's person is persona non grata as far as my carnal urges are concerned. In fact, perish the thought." He executed a comical shudder. "A fellow wants a bit of warmth to snuggle up to, not an arctic chill."

"Excellent." Hugh smiled reassured. "*Excellent*. Glad we got that sorted." He shook Giles's hand and slapped him on the back looking like a man who had just been reprieved by the hangman. "I shall leave you to your account fathoming and biscuit dunking with a clear conscience and no need for pistols at dawn—and shall see you at the christening."

Diana waited until Dalton shouted the all clear before emerging from her curtain cocoon. "That was close."

"It was but thanks to my superior acting skills he was none the wiser. Not that I had to act some of that, of course. Frissons and carnal urges indeed. *Us*."

"Indeed." Her voice was clipped. "Perish the thought." Giles watched her wrap her shawl around her and tie it as tight as her smile. "Thank goodness he didn't stay long, as Olivia would kill me if I was late for dinner again." Dalton clonked back in and she hurried toward him as if he were the prodigal son returning from years in the wilderness. "Is the carriage ready?"

He nodded and she smiled at the reprobate. Almost as an afterthought she turned back to smile at Giles. Except this was her strained smile again. The one she reserved for people she was miffed at, yet he had no idea what he had done wrong beyond playing to the gallery again. "Same time, same place tomorrow? I shall school you in everything I can think of to help you dig alone."

He nodded and selected another biscuit to cover his overwhelming sense of despondency as he watched her leave. But as he dunked it in his tea, he heard her whisper intimately in his irascible and recently head-over-heels-in-love butler's ear that obliterated all the self-pity and stood his hair on end.

"And I'll see you in our usual spot at midnight, Dalton. Don't be late."

Chapter Twenty-Two

Thanks to another last-ditch plea from the family for her to change her mind about Hampshire, it was closer to half past midnight when Diana was finally able to sneak out of the back door. She pulled the ratty collar of her sad, patched coat from her Clerkenwell days up against the chilly air, then crept around the edges of the garden wall until she reached the back gate to the mews. With both Vee's bedchamber and Olivia and Jeremiah's backing on to the garden, she never took any chances when necessity dragged her out into the night.

As usual, Dalton's unmistakable silhouette stood at the corner. However, this time he was joined by another unmistakable male shape. A very tense-looking outline of Giles.

"What is he doing here?" She addressed Dalton rather than the man who was glaring at her through hooded eyes. Trying not to notice how attractive Giles Sinclair was in one of Dalton's scruffy old naval coats. Without his trademark impeccable tailoring and neatly styled hair he looked too rumpled and crumpled. As if he had just tumbled out of bed. Too accessible and sinful and not an image of him that her vivid, and of late fanciful, imagination needed.

"*He* is here because *he* is livid." Giles jabbed the air between them with his finger. "You promised me faithfully, madam, that you never put yourself in harm's way and yet here we are! It's the middle of the night and you are apparently headed to the docks! A place filled with cutthroats and scoundrels! If that isn't harm's way, then I don't know what is!" He jabbed the air some more. "And if I hadn't just happened to overhear the dangerous plans you and my feckless butler made behind my back, I would be none the wiser! Why is that, Diana? When we have spent near every waking moment in each other's company since Lady Sewell shuddered beside us in the shrubbery?"

"I am working, Giles." And it was none of his business. Especially as he harbored no intentions toward her, noble or otherwise.

She had no idea why she had taken such umbrage to those particular words of his when he had undoubtedly said much worse and she wasn't interested in either of those intentions. But she had. "I work for the newspaper, remember, and have responsibilities outside of my charitable favor to you."

"I've tried to explain to him that this trip is the last piece of the puzzle on a long investigation." Dalton jerked his thumb at their new spare wheel. "And that you are in no danger because you have me to protect you, but he was adamant he was coming, too. If you want my opinion, Miss Diana—"

"She really doesn't, Dalton, and neither do I!" Giles was still fuming and in no mood to see reason.

"I think he was more jealous than he was angry because he thought you were my ladylove and the pair of us were having a midnight tryst." Dalton winked his only eye, grinning, unaware that the thought of Giles being jealous went some way toward making her feel less aggrieved about his lack of intentions. "And he's here to stop us from having one."

"I am here to make sure the minx doesn't get herself killed because it appears, Dalton, you lying, deceitful, traitorous wretch, that you cannot be trusted as far as I can throw you!" Giles stomped off in the direction of their waiting hackney, leaving Diana blinking at his broad back.

"I think he likes you, miss."

"Oh, do shut up, Dalton."

"And if you want my opinion—"

"I really don't, Dalton."

"I think you like him, too."

They rode to the docks in tense silence. Giles sulking, Dalton grinning, and Diana pretending to check her notebook because every time she glanced at rumpled Giles and his swirling, brooding dark eyes as he glared at her, it played havoc with her pulse. So, too, did Dalton's ridiculous suggestion that Giles was being jealous and possessive. He had been much easier to resist when he was a duke in her mind. Dukes and forger's daughters from Clerkenwell were a million miles apart. A forger's daughter and a harlot's son felt like natural bedfellows.

Not that she wanted him in her bed.

Of course she didn't.

She had never been tempted by all that nonsense. Her mind had only wandered there because Giles, the wretch, had brought up Lady Sewell and the shrubbery again.

Tonight at least.

All the other times it had wandered toward him and the carnal in the last two months she wouldn't think about. In case she did, and because a bump in the road made his knee brush hers, Diana shuffled as far as she could across the seat away from him and his wit-scrambling lips. Needing those pitiful inches of space suddenly, more than she needed air.

When they pulled up, and before she could escape the intimate confines of the carriage, he grabbed her hand. As always, it sent ripples of awareness ricocheting throughout her body.

"What is the plan?"

"We just need to confirm that this"—Diana pulled out the little vial of Smith's Herbal Restorative—"is being made here. Then I can send that information to the authorities tomorrow evening and hopefully, if I can convince them to seize the warehouse and arrest its owner, get the perfect final paragraph of the Sentinel's story to newspaper before it goes to print. Charlie is banking on me."

"And who is Charlie?" Something that looked suspiciously like jealously now burned in his eyes as his fingers tightened around hers.

"The proprietor of *The Tribune* and my employer. Nothing more." Diana wasn't entirely sure why she clarified that last bit when he had referred to her as an arctic chill, so she gave herself a stern talking-to as she tugged her hand away.

She didn't want a man. Didn't want the restrictions of one or the trials and tribulations that one would inevitably cause. Didn't want to have to compromise on anything, now that her life was exactly as she had always wanted it. Ever.

She especially didn't want Giles.

She didn't!

"Any evidence you spot that suggests that the Edward Davis Ottoman Imports company does more than ship in trinkets, you make sure to pass on to me." She leaned to open the door and he beat her to it, insisted on helping her down, which set her nerves bouncing some more. "Hopefully, we'll be able to find what I need without having to break in." She could have kicked herself for that comment because Giles almost exploded. Before he did, she offered him a weak smile. "That was a joke, Giles."

"It had better be."

In a scene much too reminiscent of the ill-fated one that had happened in Lady Bulphan's garden, Diana crouched in the shadows as the three of them approached the windowless warehouse. Giles much too close to her person for comfort and Dalton limping behind with his good hand clamped around the handle of the pistol he always tucked in his belt.

The building was a great spot for wrongdoing. The banks of the River Thames lapped along the back wall, providing easy access both to and from it by small boats that would not be easy for the excise patrols to detect at night. All around it were more warehouses in various states of dilapidation, except in deference to the hour, they all sat silent and would until dawn when the workers returned. But as this run-down wharf was one of the original Elizabethan moorings and the bulk of the trade had long since moved to the newer, modern docks along the river, it had the air of the forgotten about it. Another perfect place to do dark deeds.

A slice of light bled into the night from beneath the big double doors. They moved as close as they could, huddling behind a tower of empty packing crates several yards away. Without waiting for any instruction, Dalton dashed forward and pressed his ear against the wall. As they waited for his assessment, Diana tried and failed to put enough distance between her and her new protector to make her feel less aware of him. He might be dressed like a nobody, but he was still all Giles, drat him, from his unique spicy scent to the peculiar effect he always had on her.

"There's at least ten of them in there, maybe more." Dalton darted back behind the crates to join them. "But they are busy. Lots of clattering and banging."

"Could they be making something?" If the drug wasn't made here, she would have to find out where it was made before she could close this investigation. To stop Coleridge exploiting people for his own greed, the case against him had to be watertight.

"Hard to tell." Diana followed Dalton's gaze to the busy dark shadows that punctuated the line of light beneath the door.

"It looks to me like they are cooking something." When they turned to him, Giles wasn't looking at the front door at all—but the steep sloping roof closest to the river's edge. More specifically at a vent of steam spouting into the air from beneath the eaves. "Unless that is a chimney, in which case that's the oddest position of a chimney I have ever seen." He said it as a flippant aside, not realizing it was significant, and seemed surprised when they left him behind to scurry toward it.

The tiny blackened window was barely a foot square and at least seven feet from the ground but it was cracked open. "Fetch some crates for me to climb up." Diana needed to see inside.

"From where?" Giles searched the immediate vicinity then frowned at the tower they had originally hidden behind. "Fetching them from there is bit risky, don't you think? If somebody hears, we're done for, and if they wander out and see them moved, then we're also done for."

"Do you only ever see the problems and not the solutions,

Giles!" As she hissed at the Vexing Voice of Doom who hadn't been invited, Dalton interrupted.

"If you want my opinion—"

"We really don't, Dalton." Giles scowled but his servant ignored it.

"I could probably lift Diana high enough to look through that window. She could sit on my shoulders . . ."

A suggestion that sent Giles into an apoplexy. "If anybody will be lifting *Miss Merriwell*, it will be me! You can keep your filthy hands to yourself!"

She almost intervened in favor of Dalton because the thought of Giles's hands on her body instantly reminded her of the last time they had been there, and she did not trust it to behave at the contact. Thankfully, she found another solution. The metal remnants of an old crane hoist protruded from the brickwork a few feet away from the window that she could perch herself upon while she peered inside. She pointed at it in relief. "Could somebody give me a boost?"

It was Giles who cupped his hands together, forcing her to have to brace hers on his distracting shoulders before he hoisted her into the air.

Of all the views Giles did not need in his current mood, the greatest was the sight of Diana's delectable bottom hovering above his head. He also did not need to feel the womanly turn of her long legs. As she lunged sideways, to lock one foot on another rusty piece of tangled metalwork, Providence decided to send a different view to torture him thanks to the way her skirts simultaneously

ruched up and billowed. Now, where there had once been the reassuring barrier of unflattering, patched wool and petticoats between her calves and his eyeballs, there was instead the tantalizing
column of her silk-clad leg.

Trust bloody Diana to dress like a washerwoman and still insist on the luxury of silk against her skin. Worse, if indeed his
predicament could be worse, if he moved those eyeballs an inch,
he would see a lot more than her seductive stockings and the saucy
rosebud garters beneath her knees. He would see flesh.

Thigh flesh.

Creamy thigh flesh that joined with smooth, pert bottom flesh.
Bottom flesh that his greedy hands had only experienced over her
clothes, and just that had been enough to fuel his wildest fantasies
ever since.

Sorely tempted and ashamed of the direction his wayward
thoughts were going, he did the gentlemanly thing and closed his
eyes while he held her ankles to stop her plunging to the floor and
sending dangerous smugglers spilling into the yard.

"See anything interesting?" Dalton's whispered question
made him want to groan because while he wasn't looking with his
eyes, his imagination was keen to fill in the blanks.

"Yes!" Diana sounded excited. He could hear her smile. Picture the way her green eyes sparkled. The almost naked leg flexed
some more, and the silk whispered against his fingertips like a siren's song. "We've got him, Dalton!"

Being naturally difficult, the woman on the ledge wasn't satis-
fied with that victory. She needed to watch the goings-on for several more minutes before she concluded she had seen enough. All
the while Giles gritted his teeth and tried to think of all manner of

unpleasant things to stop his mind wandering to the carnal. None worked and it wandered there with impunity, and that, inevitably, made his body behave with equal inappropriateness. Before he surrendered for the sake of the tenuous grip he still had on his sanity and left her bewitching ankles to Dalton to secure, she finally hauled herself vertical and began to dismount.

A task that proved infinitely more complicated than the climbing up because she couldn't turn around—but at least her skirts had returned to their proper place. The same could not be said for his vivid imagination.

After half a minute of painful fumbling for a suitable foothold, Giles had had enough. "Just fall backward and I'll catch you."

"Don't be ridiculous!"

"Trust me, I will catch you and then we can be gone!"

The suspicious minx narrowed her eyes before she ignored him, then proceeded to twist herself awkwardly on the crane bracket. Her triumph at facing outward was short-lived as she now had to let go of the metalwork behind her to climb down. Left with no other option, Giles held out his arms and she eyed them warily until she, too, concluded there was no other way.

With obvious reluctance she took his hands, wobbled, then lunged for his shoulders. The obtuse angle pushed him backward so that she toppled against him, leaving Giles smothered by her bosom because she had wrapped her flailing arms tight around his neck as she fell the last foot.

What happened next was destined to haunt his dreams for days, possibly months, maybe even years to come as he stared glumly through the bars of his tiny cell in Newgate.

The slow, firm press of her lush body plastered against his as she, and her magnificent curves, slithered to the floor in the cage of his arms and left nothing to his imagination. His hands on her waist. Her flattened breasts trailing down his face, neck, and chest until they were abdomen to abdomen. Thigh to thigh. Her womanhood to his manhood. The old chap only too delighted to be enticed into action. Much too intimately entwined for comfort, they blinked at each other for a split second until her feet touched the earth and she briskly stepped away. Thankfully, a mere moment before his randy friend stood to full attention against her person.

"Let's go before somebody sees us!"

They made a run for it but only got a few feet before they heard voices. Giles grabbed Diana and yanked her behind a haphazard mountain of ropes and tarpaulin, causing her to slam against him again before they dropped to the muddy ground out of sight. More exposed in the center of the alleyway and the stark whites of his eye wide, Dalton pivoted and dived behind a stinking pile of rubbish, somehow dislodging his leg in the process. The pale scrimshaw appendage seemed to glow in the weak moonlight as the back door to the warehouse creaked open.

Two men emerged, lighting pipes. One pulled up a nearby box to sit upon while the other seemed content to stand. A dim lamp dangled from his hand. Thankfully, both stared toward the river.

"I bet they are waiting for a boat." He could tell by the way her neck craned that she was keen to spy some more despite the obvious danger and the fetid, chilled water that was seeping between all their seams thanks to the puddle they were sat in. "That must be how they distribute the opium."

"Why else would they have a warehouse by the river? It doesn't take a genius to work that out, so the authorities will, too, without the need for us to witness it."

That earned him a stern glare. "Will you stop distracting me while I am trying to concentrate!"

Giles bit his tongue for all of five seconds then nudged Diana and gestured to the yard. "We've seen enough. If you keep your back to the wall, you should be able to sneak out to safety while they are occupied."

"You expect me to leave a job half done to save myself!" Her outraged hiss tickled his earlobe. "Never mind that I will not abandon Dalton to those ruffians!"

"Dalton is a big boy and can save himself." Giles suspected that, even legless, his wily servant had emerged unscathed from worse scrapes with less. "And as a drunken sailor facedown in the docks is a nightly occurrence, I doubt our two new friends would blink an eye if they saw him. You, on the other hand, stick out like a sore thumb. Once you are clear, wait for me beyond the yard and I will escort you home."

"I knew bringing you was a mistake." But she darted across the alleyway and flattened her back to the wall of the warehouse anyway. However, being ornery and stubborn in the extreme, she began to edge not toward the yard as he had instructed but toward the ruffians on the riverbank.

Incensed, he followed suit and tried to tug her the correct way. She snatched her wet sleeve from his slippery, muddy fingers and elbowed him in the ribs. "I do not answer to you, Giles Sinclair! You run away like a rat if you are not up to the challenge, but I still have work to do!" And she was off again, shuffling a few inches at a time toward the Thames.

Vowing to strangle the minx the second it was safe to do so, and while Dalton slithered from his hiding place on his belly in the direction of his glowing leg, Giles had no choice but to follow her.

A couple of feet later, Diana crouched behind the large, rotting husk of a barrel that had the beginnings of a bush sprouting out the top, then pointed at the hazy outline of a blackened barge edging toward the shore. "No lamps aboard means they are avoiding the river police, and by the size of that boat I'd say they only travel local as it's narrow enough to navigate the canals rather than the river."

"Is your plan that we wait for it to sail off again then dive in and swim after it?" That he could still be sarcastic surprised him because Giles was cold and he was scared. Muddy water had penetrated all his crevices and his heart was hammering so loudly it was drowning out the sound of everything else—yet oddly he had never felt so exhilarated.

"I just want to see if the boat has a name so the excise men can track it." She bent to lean from behind the barrel, her delectable bottom inches from his face again. "But by the looks of things, the paint is purposefully worn."

"Splendid."

"There are three men on deck . . . no, wait . . . four . . ." As she placed her full weight against the barrel to get a better view, the decayed base of it shifted and screeched ominously against the flagstones.

"Who's there?" The man with the lamp raised it to the alleyway, the soft glow bathing the barrel they were now crouched behind in light.

Two hobnailed boots crunched closer, paused, then the unmistakable click of a pistol hammer being cocked turned Giles's blood to ice.

The feet came closer and he weighed his options. Perhaps if he lunged at the ruffian he could buy Diana enough time to run away? Their eyes locked in the darkness and he gestured to the exit with a flick of his head as he mouthed, *Run.*

She frowned and mouthed back, *But he has a gun.*

Giles nodded and shrugged. Oddly at peace with his fate.

This was it.

As he braced himself for the impact of the bullet and likely his impending death, Diana transformed unfazed before his eyes. The headstrong, waspish, intrepid Goddess of the Hunt dissolved into a giggling, simpering, flirting tease the moment the lamplight picked them out through the veil of twigs sprouting from the barrel top.

"Follow my lead." She whispered that without moving her lips a split second before she dragged him against her body. She giggled again as her hands fumbled under his coat. Hooked one of her long legs around his as she fisted his shirt and yanked him hard against her until their faces were inches apart, then pushed him playfully back as she wagged her finger.

"Naughty—I told you kissin' is extra no matter how handsome a fella you are." Her accent was suddenly laced with the essence of the gutter. Beneath her breathy giggle it switched again in a heartbeat, and she whispered, "Pretend you want me."

Giles didn't have to pretend.

All his wildest nightly fantasies involved the woman whose heart currently hammered against his own. As she had commanded it, and as they apparently did not have a better plan that didn't involve him being aerated by a bullet, he slid his hands possessively around her waist and pretended to nuzzle her neck.

"It's another bleedin' lightskirt," the closest ruffian groaned back to his armed companion before he hollered at them and the pistol, thank the Lord, disappeared from view. "Oi! Clear off! This is private property not a bloody brothel! Didn't you read the bleedin' signs, strumpet?"

Still holding Giles in place, Diana's expression went from eager to disinterested in a second as she shifted to glare at the interruption. "I'd 'afta be able to read to do that, now, wouldn't I?" Then she shrugged, all sauce and undulating insolence as she tugged Giles's hand before her expression changed once more to one of a bona fide strumpet's business again and she wrapped her arm seductively around his middle.

"Come on big boy, I'll just 'ave to show you a good time somewhere else, won't I?" She pouted and giggled as they leaned together like a pair of drunkards and stumbled out of the alleyway toward the yard. "And if you can turn that ha'penny into a sixpence, I'll give you the time of your life."

Chapter Twenty-Three

As they hadn't paid the hackney to wait for them in case the driver got suspicious, the three of them had to walk almost to the Tower of London before they saw and hailed another. All the while Giles's emotions and nerves were all over the place.

To be fair, they had been for days thanks to the ticking clock Gervais had started, but that combined with a whole host of new feelings to heat his blood. The residual anger was now more from sexual frustration than jealousy—and he was big enough to call his initial reaction jealousy, and jealousy over Dalton to boot. Then there was still some genuine fear at the risks Diana was prepared to take to do her job and his powerlessness to stop her. Beneath all that, catching him off guard, there was also the unexpected thrill of the chase. Sneaking around the docks, spying, and succeeding in bringing villains to justice was a heady rush that made him as giddy as that fifty-year-old cognac had and just as reckless.

He wanted to pay the sixpence and kiss her. Drag her into his arms and taste her again. Explore those silk-clad legs properly as they hooked themselves around his. Make her green eyes sparkle with a very different sort of excitement . . .

Ruin them both before he was dragged away in irons.

That inevitability went some way to quashing his ardor.

"The Hays Mews behind Berkeley Square." The driver nodded at his clipped instruction as Giles helped Diana in and waited for Dalton to follow. Then because his unruly and—thanks to the rubbish heap he had crawled through—now very smelly servant had taken the center of one of the benches and spread out to massage what he presumed was the location of his stump, he had no option but to take the seat next to hers.

The carriage lurched forward, and she grinned as she sank back against the battered leather. "We've got him and what's even better is Coleridge doesn't even know it yet. I do so love being right, but unlike you, Giles, I never get to say I told you so to the people who most deserve it."

"Don't you?" As much as his body yearned and he wanted to remain mad at her for putting herself in danger, her triumphant smile was infectious and he was too elated to be angry at the risks she clearly took for her work. For the first time, he understood why she took them. He had never felt so alive. "I'd say having a few thousand people read your words and marvel at your cleverness must be beyond satisfying. As must seeing scoundrels like Mr. Coleridge getting their just deserts."

"There is that, I suppose."

"She has a nose for the truth, that's for sure. If anyone can find your mother, Your Grace, it'll be the Sentinel." Dalton winked then went back to massaging his leg.

"On the subject of your mother, Giles, the more I think about sending you alone back to Shropshire, the more unsettled I feel."

"It cannot be helped."

"But it can, Giles. If I come with you."

Hope bloomed eternal. Hope and something else. Something that transcended the ruthless bolt of futile lust her offer conjured, brought a lump to his throat, and made his heart swell with joy.

"I wouldn't ask you to do that."

"I know but I shan't sleep if I don't come, and I'd never forgive myself if the worst happens and I could have done something to prevent it. You have to admit, I do have a knack for uncovering the truth. Knowing where to find it seems to be instinctive to me, and surely that is a talent you could use in Shropshire?"

"Even though Hugh will definitely kill me if he finds out?" As much as he wanted her help and her presence in the darkest days of his life, he couldn't and wouldn't expect her sacrifice. "Or risk ruination if the world does? Your reputation and your career in tatters?"

"Even though." The ghost of a smile played on her lips. "Some risks are worth taking no matter what the consequences." Something odd swirled in her eyes before she glanced at her dirty hands, then rummaged in her pocket for a handkerchief to clean them with. "If we leave after my family departs for Hampshire, we have three uninterrupted weeks to dig into your background and nobody bar us will be the wiser. I'll have to think of a good excuse for Charlie, of course, because he won't be happy that I am deserting him again, but he'll forgive me because I am his best bloodhound. Can I whet his appetite by telling him that I believe the infamous Gervais Sinclair has sneaked back into the country?"

He smiled. "The infamous Gervais Sinclair has sneaked back into the country."

"Good—because something he said to you jars with what Olivia told me, so I want to set Charlie on it as a contingency."

"We have a contingency? That is reassuring when we barely have a plan. Care to share it?"

"Gervais seems to think that it is safe to be here in England again because all the witnesses to his crime are gone? But from my research Lady Caroline Derbyshire disappeared into the ether after the abduction and nobody has heard hide nor hair of her since. So how does he know she is dead when he is the last person who would be entrusted with her whereabouts?"

"Perhaps he has a connection still or as it's been thirty years and nobody has seen her, it is not an unreasonable assumption to make. The duke might well have been the last credible witness."

"Not if Olivia is correct and Lady Caroline took Holy Orders in Kent it isn't." She huffed at the absurdity of that theory before he could pour scorn on it. "As I said, it's a contingency if Gervais looks likely to beat us to the truth. That is still our first plan. We find it and we destroy it."

"Even though that is breaking the law?"

"Even though."

She spent the rest of their short journey to Berkeley Square outlining her plan of attack. When the hackney finally came to a stop she pulled her dark shawl over her head and tried to stop him from getting out and assisting her.

"This isn't the docks, Giles." She laughed at his frown and pointed to Hugh's gate. "This is Mayfair and that is home. I am perfectly safe from all threats of opium smugglers and ruffians with pistols."

"Yet I will see you to the door, harridan, because that is what a gentleman does, and *even though* I am unlikely to remain a gentleman much longer and will probably shortly swap my ducal ermine for Newgate's shackles, the manners are too ingrained to ignore—*even though* I am dressed like a guttersnipe and smell like the ponging Fleet."

She rolled her eyes but for once did not argue as he helped her out, even handed him the key so he could unlock the gate. "Do you really think you could go to jail?"

He shrugged. "I have no idea what the legal ramifications of my exposure will be."

"Have you taken legal counsel to find out?"

"What? And risk immediate arrest when my solicitor has to turn me in?"

She shook her head as if he were daft. "Any good lawyer works within the guiding principles of oath and honor set down in common law. Basically, in a nutshell, if you are his client and you confess anything to him, that information and any legal advice he gives you on the back of it are privileged. No court in the land can make him tell them because he has sworn an oath and his first duty must always be to you."

"And how do you know that?"

"Any journalist worth their salt has to know the law because we skirt around the edges of it often enough. I thought you admired Mr. Cribbage. Saw him as an ally to your cause."

"I do but . . ."

She touched his arm as they approached the terrace. "Talk to him first thing, Giles. Find out exactly where you stand before we leave for Shropshire. You never know, seeing as his family have served the Dukes of Harpenden for decades, he might know something pertinent that will help us. Trust him as you trust me."

"Says the woman who doesn't trust anyone." But he already

knew he would do as she commanded. He was starting to believe he would follow Diana to the ends of the earth if she asked him, as well as fling himself in front of a speeding bullet.

"I shall see you tomorrow, Giles. All packed and ready for our next adventure. Hopefully this one doesn't involve any midnight crouching in the shadows."

"I rather like crouching in the shadows with you. It's always entertaining."

"It is, isn't it?" She grinned as she turned to leave and he caught her hand.

"Diana, I . . ." There was so much he wanted to say and do and none of it appropriate for a man in his precarious legal position. So instead he settled for bringing her fingers to his lips and pressing a soft, lingering kiss on the back of them. "Until tomorrow, my Goddess of the Hunt and Hornet-Kicking Hunter of the Truth. I suspect I shall count the hours." Just as he always did.

She smiled as if she understood all he had left unsaid and so did he, so caught up in the poignancy of the moment that neither of them noticed they were being watched.

Chapter Twenty-Four

"Well, isn't this exciting?" Vee pressed her nose to the carriage window as the outskirts of London gave way to the countryside beyond. "Half of me is thrilled that we are all off on the most daring adventure while the other half still feels dreadful for lying to the others."

And lie Vee had.

Through her angelic, conniving teeth.

And with such convincing aplomb it forced Diana to reevaluate every aspect of her baby sister. For a young lady who gave off the impression that butter wouldn't melt in her mouth, she had certainly convinced everyone of her illness this morning, coughing and sniffing for all she was worth, while her face had burned scarlet with fever. But while Diana panicked at the unforeseen scuppering of her plans and Olivia and Minerva had been on the cusp of canceling their family trip to Hampshire, she had burned some more—but like a righteous martyr.

Of course they all still had to go to Hugh's estate without her.

It was the right and proper thing to do. Olivia had made plans to host a New Year's party for all his tenants and they would be devastated if that did not go ahead. Especially when they deserved it so, and in all likelihood, all Vee had caught was their maid's nasty sniffle, which would likely be over in a day or two just as it had for Tabetha. So there was every chance she would still be well enough to travel up to join them once it had passed. Besides—and she had stared at Diana with such fake gratitude as she clutched her hand on the top of her bedsheets—Diana would be here to look after her and she would send an express if Vee's fever worsened. Wouldn't she?

Cornered, Diana had nodded, but as Olivia and Jeremiah, Minerva and Hugh, as well as Payne, their trusty butler, all left in the carriage with great reluctance, and before she could pen a hasty note to Giles regarding the unexpected change of plan, poor sick Vee had rallied.

Instantly.

Then all hell had broken loose.

Her sister had seen her in the garden with Giles from her bedchamber window. Seen the way he had kissed her hand and her apparent expression of heartfelt adoration, cracked open her window and heard that they were heading to Shropshire as soon as the coast was clear, put two and two together, and completely got the wrong end of the stick.

Now Vee was intent on saving Diana from original sin. Of sacrificing her precious virtue before any holy vows had been taken. And while she heartily approved of the new romantic developments in their relationship and firmly believed they were meant for each other, a gentleman did not purchase anything from the bakery if the baker was giving away the apple tarts for free.

Therefore, and Vee had wagged her schoolmistress's finger in

Diana's face, she had no choice but to chaperone the pair of them. To save them both from their palpable lust while they courted in the proper way. And by proper, that would be in full view of Mayfair and not two hundred miles away alone in his romantic estate in Shropshire.

Diana was still unsure if the conniving she-devil believed all the lies she had constructed to explain the need to go to Shropshire without giving Giles or herself away. Giles certainly had no clue what Vee knew or what she didn't, so sat opposite them tight-lipped, shooting Diana baffled looks that she couldn't answer properly until they stopped at the first inn to change the horses and she could snatch a private moment.

If she could snatch a private moment, because Vee had appointed herself Diana's shadow, glued to *her* person in case *his* person got too close and the valuable *apple tarts* were given away gratis.

"If you had asked me what was going on before all your theatrics, I could have spared you the effort of lying."

Diana hoped her bemused glance at Giles looked as convincing as Vee's imaginary sniffle had. "Then I would have happily confided that Giles was in a fix and desperately needed some help finding enough evidence to prove his former steward's fraud." Subtly she nudged his foot with hers. "You suspect foul play, don't you, Giles? And need someone with a keen eye for detail in the reams of disorganized paperwork he left you in the hope that you can find enough evidence to get him arrested."

He nodded, still not trusting himself to speak, and did so with such a lack of conviction that Vee's eyes narrowed.

"Being a gentleman, he only asked for my advice." Diana tried to fill the tense void with more of her fabricated backstory. "That is why he asked me to meet him in the garden late last night. Isn't it, Giles? You sent a note. To ask my advice. Nothing more." She tried to communicate more with a pointed stare. "But being headstrong and stubborn, and knowing the idiot didn't have the skills to find the truth"—she gave Vee her isn't-he-useless eye roll—"I offered to accompany him. Obviously he argued vociferously against it, didn't you, Giles?" She nudged his foot again.

"Obviously." He attempted a smile.

"But you know me, I am headstrong . . ."

"So you keep saying." Vee was frowning now. All trace of the naive eighteen-year-old evaporating under her suspicious schoolteacher's glare.

"Because it is true." Diana aimed for blasé, even managed a wry smile as she wafted her hand in the air. "I am well aware of that failing. Once I get an idea about something I am like a dog with a bone. I've always been the same, haven't I, Vee?"

Giles's eyes were begging her to shut up, but while she knew they were right, she plowed on regardless. Spewing all her hasty lies aloud for a second time when the first had been bad enough, cringing that they sounded so much worse this time than they had in the panicked heat of the moment.

"So you see, Vee, you were quite mistaken that Giles and I were headed north for a tryst and you really are reading far too much in that silly mistletoe kiss to think we harbor feelings toward each other. As if I would swoon over anyone . . ." He winced at the hollow tinkle of her laughter. "And especially Giles. Anyone with eyes could see . . ." The toe of his boot pressed down on hers hard, but she had started, and seeing as Vee's eyes had now narrowed to slits, it seemed prudent to finish. She could still fix this. She had to. "Well, to be frank, anyone with eyes can see there is no more a frisson between me and him than there is . . ." As she floundered for a metaphor, Giles slapped his palm to his forehead.

"For the love of God stop, woman, before you dig us both into a bigger hole!" He sighed and turned to Vee. "The truth is I am in huge trouble, Miss Vee. *Huge* trouble. And because I need all the help I can get, I shall throw myself at your mercy and pray that you take pity on me."

Then, while her baby sister gaped in shock, he confessed everything from start to finish. The only thing he omitted from the sordid tale was Diana's role as the Sentinel. A noble omission she was determined to thank him for if she ever managed to snatch a moment with him again. Her romantic sister might have forgiven an attempted tryst and hidden it from the others to encourage a proper, chaperoned courtship, but she would bellow foul from the rooftops if she knew how dangerous her job at the newspaper really was.

"So, in short, I am not really the legal duke, and while I now know that my wise old solicitor thinks it unlikely I risk criminal charges for what was ultimately my father's crime"—he glanced back at Diana, allowing her to see his relief that her sound advice was accurate—"he also confirmed that if Gervais can find proof of my illegitimacy that corroborates whatever is written in that letter, then I will be stripped of both my title and my lands. Worse, if he is correct, and no witnesses survive who can make valid testimony about his abduction of Lady Caroline Derbyshire, then the warrant against him will also be dismissed and there will be no legal impediments impinging on his custodianship of Harpenden. He shall be free to do with it as he sees fit."

"Free to destroy it, you mean, with his reckless spending and hedonism!" Vee's outrage was now all loyalty to their friend rather than the shocking, panicked lies Diana had vomited to protect him. "Diana and Dalton are right. We must do everything in our power to stop him. We need to find all the evidence of your illegitimacy and we must destroy it. It's the only way to stop Gervais and protect the tenants on your estate." For all her youthful naïveté, the youngest Merriwell was probably the smartest of them all.

The "we" had touched him, Diana could see, and his voice was choked when he took her sister's hand.

"If *we* do that, then we will be breaking the law, Vee. We would be perverting the course of justice by trying to find a way to suppress evidence to perpetrate a fraud—and for that we could all go to jail. Even if Diana wasn't headstrong and stubborn"—his eyes flicked to hers briefly but shimmered with an emotion so intense, it made her breath hitch—"she is a grown woman, long past the age of majority, and she offered her help in full possession of all the facts. Insisted, in fact." He smiled at Vee. "You, on the other hand, did not and you are still underage and legally the ward of Minerva and Hugh. You are here solely to protect your sister, and while that intention is admirable, you have also unwittingly put yourself in grave danger. If I give you my word not to lay a finger on her—ever—will you allow me to send you back home with Dalton so I am reassured you are well out of harm's way? All I would ask is that you hold your tongue about where we are until somebody directly asks about it."

Vee digested this for a moment before her blue eyes hardened behind her spectacles. "You expect me to cower in silence then feed you to the wolves the moment they bay at my door?"

"To save yourself from being tainted by *my* scandal, yes, I do."

"Then you are an idiot, Giles Sinclair, because that is not how families work." Vee leaned across the benches to poke his shoulder with an outraged finger. "When I adopted you as my brother alongside Hugh, I did so on the full understanding that it came with certain caveats. One of those irrevocable caveats is that the Merriwell siblings always stand together against the world, no matter what."

"Then I am afraid I am going to have to put my foot down, Vee, and insist that you go home." Giles hammered on the roof and shouted to Dalton and the driver above to pull over, and determined dark eyes locked with two magnified steely blue ones. Both parties folded their arms. "I will not take you to Shropshire and that is that."

"Then I will find my own way there and you shall have to forcibly evict me from your estate. And"—her sister's chin lifted in defiance as she prodded Giles again—"I shall summon Minerva before I risk the footpads and dangers of the long road to Shropshire all alone, and then you shall have all three of us to contend with!"

"That is blackmail!" Giles glared at Diana, expecting her support. Vee did, too. She knew both of them too well to expect either to back down, so as the carriage slowed, Diana made a decision that she hoped she wouldn't live to regret.

"If the worst happens, we shall tell the authorities that Vee knew nothing and was merely present as a chaperone—but frankly, Giles, as you said yourself, you do need all the help you can get."

Chapter Twenty-Five

They made it to Shropshire close to midnight after three days of punishing travel where they stopped only to either change the horses or collapse at an inn for the night. Despite being in on the secret, Vee was still determined to be their chaperone, so Giles hadn't had a moment alone with Diana since he left her in Hugh's garden. Even tonight, with them all wilting from the exhaustion of thirteen full hours on the road, Vee had stood guard while the servants organized their rooms in case he got ideas. An irony that was not lost on him, because he had no shortage of ideas where the vexing second Merriwell was concerned. The ideas came thick and fast and with little encouragement. But he did not need a chaperone to stop him acting on them when the hopeless truth was incentive enough.

After complaining that he had arrived unannounced and with guests, Mrs. Townsend insisted on accompanying him to his bed-chamber. "We had a bit of an incident, Your Grace."

"If it is anything to do with another falling-out between you and Dalton, I do not want to know."

"I wouldn't trouble you with something so trivial, Your Grace. We had an intruder in the small hours of last night."

"In the house?" Giles's heart sank. He had expected Gervais would inevitably turn up here like a bad, prying penny, but it unsettled him to know that he had beaten him here.

"Thankfully just the grounds, but they attempted to get inside the house. Smashed a windowpane in the estate office." Which meant that Gervais wanted to search the household accounts for the answers, too. "Fortunately, my room sits above it and I am a light sleeper. I raised the hue and cry and they fled but I have ensured someone is on watch ever since in case they return."

An eventuality Giles did not doubt for a moment.

"Then let us hope that is that, Mrs. Townsend, and we have seen the last of them." A forlorn hope Giles did not believe for one second now that Gervais was close, but he would spare her from the burden of the truth for now. The fewer people he embroiled in the *Dirty Secret* until it became common knowledge, the better.

The housekeeper left him in his bedchamber with a roaring fire, a steaming washbowl, freshly turned-down sheets, and a plate of shortbread once the rest of the household retired for the second time. He ignored all to pace, and when he could stand pacing no longer he decided to check the security of the estate office, as he wouldn't put it past his uncle to try again tonight.

As he approached the steward's office, he heard the movement first before he saw a flash of light beneath the door as if someone had just lit a lamp, so he crept the last few yards to listen at the wood. There was a shuffle of feet. The sound of something being moved, so before he thought better of it, Giles burst in like a bull charging a gate. Hoping the element of surprise might be all that was needed to send his tenacious intruder packing again. Except it wasn't Gervais he scared witless with his entrance, it was Diana, and she reacted by throwing the account book she was clutching at his head.

He ducked a split second before the weighty leather tome hit the doorframe and they both slumped in relief. Hers was short-lived.

"Idiot! You frightened the life out of me!"

In case she threw another book at him, Giles raised both palms in surrender. "I thought I was being burgled." He pointed to the nailed wooden panel boarding the window. "Gervais tried to get in last night."

"He's here?"

"Who else would try to break into this office? There is nothing of any value here—apart from information. But it is interesting that it was this office he wanted to get into." He gestured to the neat walls of ledgers and files of paperwork on the shelves surrounding them. Ledgers and paperwork that he had meticulously gone through, cleaned up, and organized since her last visit to this office two months ago. He picked up the book at his feet and scanned the date, then smiled when he saw it was the one for the year of his birth. "I take it you couldn't sleep, either?"

She shrugged, sheepish. "How could I sleep when the answers have to be hidden in here somewhere? All we need is one loose thread, Giles, and then perhaps we can unravel the mystery. With any luck before that awful Gervais." She glanced at the broken window and shuddered. "Knowing he is here makes the clock tick faster, but rest assured, I am always at my best under pressure. The Sentinel thrives on a deadline." She smiled; one of the wry, honest, just-for-him smiles that he adored so much. "Thank you for keeping that secret from Vee. I've wanted to say that for days but . . ."

"Your sister is watching us like a hawk to make sure we act within the bounds of propriety."

Diana pulled a face. "She has it in her head that you and I . . ."

"I know."

"My baby sister has always had an overly romantic view of the world and, thanks to Olivia, is laboring under the misapprehension that we are the perfect pairing regardless of all our many differences. I've tried to tell her that she is barking up the wrong tree and that oil and water do not mix but—"

"Are we really oil and water, Diana? Because from where I stand I think I have more in common with you than I do with anyone."

She batted that observation away like a fly. "We do but we come from different worlds. I am a forger's daughter from Clerkenwell and you are a duke from Mayfair."

He shook his head. "I am a duke's bastard from God knows where. But even if I weren't, do you really think the title makes a difference to the man who carries it? That that alone puts us worlds apart?"

She averted her gaze to pull some ledgers from the shelf behind her. "It makes no difference as I am not cut out to be your duchess."

"I do not recall asking you to be."

Diana's spine stiffened as she realized the gravitas of what she had said, and she tried to cover it by selecting more books to add to the pile she was making on the desk. "I wasn't suggesting for one moment that you did, it was merely a flippant reaction to my sister's and Olivia's silly ideas. As if you and I could tolerate each other for eternity."

It was a statement rather than a question but she couldn't meet his eye, and that in turn made him hope that she was lying.

"But if I could ask . . ." He had no idea why he felt compelled to be honest but couldn't seem to stop. "If the chaotic mess of my life were miraculously gone and my ruination and scandal didn't loom on the horizon like the Grim Reaper . . . if I were in a position to ask anybody to spend eternity with me, it would be you, Diana."

She stilled but did not turn around. Did not speak, either, although he had no clue what he expected her to say. How exactly did one answer a proposal that wasn't a proposal? What was the point of pushing for something that was as unfair as it was untenable? Even if she felt the same, he couldn't in all good conscience have her, and his conscience was already burdened enough without taking on another load of crushing guilt. Never mind that he wouldn't be able to live with himself if he ruined her life out of his own selfishness. His situation was precarious, his feelings for her futile, and if by fluke they succeeded in their illegal quest and he kept Harpenden and the title, he would rather die than make her live his lie, too.

The net was closing in.

The wolves were baying at his door.

It was late and he was tired. Petrified and overwhelmed. Every nerve he possessed was frayed and his emotions veered all over the place. This wasn't the time for misjudged soul baring or inappropriate declarations.

"I think I am in love with you, Diana." When he acknowledged that thought he hadn't intended to speak it aloud, but it echoed in the silence. Then hung there while she stood as still as a statue. Facing the wall of ledgers rather than allowing him to see her eyes. Hugging one to her chest like a shield as if warding off an enemy rather than lowering her guard to a man who wanted to be so much more than her friend even though he realized that was impossible.

When the silence stretched to a breaking point and he could not bear it any longer, Giles edged toward her. "Say something. Anything . . ." He caught her elbow, gently forced her to face him, his heart in his mouth, choking him. Two green eyes shimmered with a maelstrom of emotions he could not read. "If I could ask, when all this is over, whatever the outcome, would you consider me?" She blinked like a startled deer and took a step back.

In case she bolted he closed the distance. Took her hand. Her fingers flexed in his but did not pull away.

"What is going on!"

They jumped apart at Vee's voice, but while Giles still reeled from the truth of his unexpected declaration and had no more words to explain anything, Diana became no-nonsense and slapped the ledger she had used to guard her heart hard upon the desk.

"Clearly we both couldn't sleep. Hardly a surprise when we have so much to do and so little time to do it with Gervais hot on our heels." She pointed to the boarded window. "He tried to break in last night."

It was the perfect deflection. Vee's eyes widened as she tightened her dressing gown. "Gervais followed us here?"

"No, sister dearest—he beat us here and might have already made significant headway on his own investigation, which puts us on the back foot." Diana grabbed a file of paperwork from the shelf. "Seeing as we are all here, we might as well make some effort to catch up. Vee, you take 1795, Giles do 1794, and I'll rummage through this." She tipped the contents of the file on the desk and, without so much as a questioning glance his way, yanked out the chair.

Despite the strong coffee coursing through her veins, Diana was still struggling to focus on the mountain of yellowed bills and receipts. It had nothing whatsoever to do with tiredness and everything to do with Giles's astounding news an hour ago.

He loved her.

He.

Loved.

Her.

And she had no earthly idea how to feel about that or rationalize what she did. She certainly felt something, and it wasn't quite the horror she had expected at such a declaration. Not that she had ever expected one. Since her father's treachery and that incident in the alleyway, she had done everything she possibly could to repel male attention. Closed herself off from the possibility of marriage and all the silly, girlish dreams associated with it.

It wasn't fear of men exactly, or fear of a repetition of what had happened that fateful night, because she understood most men weren't like that. Thanks to Giles, she also understood that her body was quite capable of responding to the physical if the touch came from a man she desired. And she did desire Giles. Always had. There was no getting away from that. It was more fear of the power of men and the way they wielded that power over women.

That was visceral, forged over a lifetime of powerlessness that she had only just left behind. There was, without a shadow of a doubt, a great deal of panic matted amongst that fear. Panic that her first reaction to Giles's confession was elation. Relief, happiness, and excitement had merged into something complicated and internal that had made her foolish heart swell irrespective of all her rational—or perhaps irrational—fears. Enough that if she were ever tempted to relinquish the tight control she held over her own destiny, if she were to consent to an eternity with someone, that someone would be Giles.

But to be that vulnerable with someone, to someone else's whims and edicts, terrified her.

Was it a justified terror?

That was the quandary filling her mind now. Was she mapping her past experiences on her present and denying herself something she now wanted? Giles wasn't anything like Alfred Merriwell. Nor was he like that brute in the alleyway or any of the legions of opportunists who had tried their luck at manipulating her in the past.

He was decent and funny, clever and kind. And he claimed to love her.

That was enormous.

Significant.

Terrifying.

Because if she allowed herself to love him back, trust him back, and he disappointed her, too, then what? Experience warned her it was best not to risk it even though her gut instinct—her reliably and usually irrefutable gut instinct—suspected he might be worth the risk.

Was that the root cause of her wariness? Did she no longer trust her own gut? Or was she too scared to trust it? Unfortunately,

Diana knew herself well enough to acknowledge that this might well be the case. Could she learn to trust Giles when life had taught her not to trust anything? And, more important, did she want to?

She risked peeking over at him and instantly felt bad. He seemed so lost and lonely, leafing through the ledger in his lap like a man who no longer cared about their quest. He was hurting, and she blamed her bad reaction for that. He had been quiet and withdrawn ever since Vee had interrupted them, preferring to stare at the columns in front of him than glance her way. She should have said something, anything like he had begged, even though she still couldn't think of a single thing to say and had no clue what the answer was.

"Have you found anything?" Vee pulled her out of her reverie. "Only you have been staring at that same piece of paper for the last ten minutes with a frown on your face."

"I am not sure." It was a convenient lie while she focused on the receipt properly for the first time in that ten minutes, then she frowned again. "Who died in March 1796, Giles? Your grandfather?"

She hated witnessing the effort it took him to compose his handsome features into an expression of nonchalance before he looked up. "No. He died several years before I was born."

"And your grandmother?"

"When I was around twelve, I think. We never met, or we didn't that I can recall." He couldn't hold her gaze and went back to the ledger. "She and the duke were quite estranged from my earliest memories. I assume that was because of the way she felt he had dealt with Gervais."

"Well, whoever they are they must have been important to warrant a headstone this expensive. And the bill is in your father's name, so he must have ordered it." Diana squinted at the faded ink and spidery handwriting to try to decipher more. "Carved limestone . . . Inscription . . . St. Llyr . . . Llanyre—with two *L*'s."

"It sounds Welsh to me," said Vee, unaware that the mention of Wales brought both Giles and Diana up short. "Lots of Welsh places start with two *L*'s. The two *L*'s are pronounced *Thlann* like Llandudno and that really long one that I cannot for the life of me spell from memory but that sounds like *Thlann vyre pooth gwin gith gogg-erra kweern drobbooth lan tuss-ill-yo goggo gauk* if you say it phonetically." She beamed at her own genius.

"That was marvelous." Giles forgot to be miserable for a moment to be impressed at Vee's pronunciation. "How on earth do you know how to say that?"

"I read, and because I cannot stand not understanding something, I went out of my way to learn." She shrugged, slightly smug and unrepentant in her cleverness. "I adore the Welsh habit of using two of the same consonants to make sounds that make no sense in English. Two *D*'s, for example are a 'th' and, conversely two *F*'s sound like one *F* here, whereas one *F* in the Welsh dialect is pronounced Vee—just like me." She grinned then shrieked, knocking her chair over as she stood. "There is someone outside!" She waggled her finger at the window. "I just saw a shadow."

As her baby sister had always had sensitive nerves, Diana rolled her eyes at her childish hysterics. "You are just being paranoid because of the attempted break-in. It's probably just a bush waving in the wind."

"Assuming bushes are man-shaped and carry lamps!" Vee rushed to the window with Giles, then the pair of them charged out of the room in the direction of the back door.

Convinced that they were both overreacting, Diana stayed put, then exploded from her chair, too, when she saw a dim light moving about outside.

By the time she reached the kitchen porch, Giles and Vee had plunged into the darkness after the intruder whose lamp was now nowhere to be seen. The only light came from the stars, which punched eerie holes in the night sky and cast the garden in menacing shadows.

"He went this way!"

Diana ran in the direction of her sister's shout, but it was Giles she caught up with first. "Where is Vee?"

He shrugged, putting a finger to his lips while scanning the darkness for any sign or sound.

They both stiffened as a twig snapped close by, then Diana almost had an apoplexy when a bloodcurdling scream rent the air a split second before her sister flew through it.

Arms flailing and nightdress billowing like a ghostly apparition, Vee hit something solid with a thud before she plunged into some shrubbery.

Giles got to the scene first and stared, because the youngest, and usually the most sedate Merriwell had turned into a raging banshee. One who had used naught but all four of her limbs to pin a wide-eyed and petrified young man faceup on the ground.

"Who are you and what do you want!" Spectacles askew and murder in her eyes, she bellowed in his face before Giles stepped in and unpeeled her. Then he hauled the stripling up by his lapels.

"Cousin Galahad. Fancy seeing you here." He made a great show of dusting the boy off as if digging intruders out of his rosebushes at two in the morning were a daily occurrence. "Miss Diana

Merriwell, Miss Venus Merriwell, allow me to introduce Galahad Sinclair, the idiot son of my evil uncle Gervais."

"I'm not an idiot!" The belligerent's drawled vowels and soft-ened consonants were unmistakably American, but the accent was different from Jeremiah's. The young man glared at Vee affronted while he yanked the thorny twigs from his body, as if she were somehow more in the wrong than he was. "And what sort of a stupid name is Venus?"

"About as stupid a name as Galahad is!"

"My sister asked you a question." Diana assumed her best girl-from-the-rough-end-of-Clerkenwell street-fighting stance. "What are you doing trespassing on this land?"

"The same thing as you, I reckon. Trying to find clues to the identity of *his* harlot mother." Galahad Sinclair jerked his thumb at Giles, whose dark eyes had narrowed at the insult.

In case his rigid control over his temper snapped and he took tonight's disappointments out on the young whippersnapper cov-ered in mud and leaves before him, she touched Giles's arm. The muscles were tense beneath. "You were right. Your cousin is an idiot. I am sure his charming father will be delighted to learn his son just confirmed that they have no evidence whatsoever to back up their ridiculous claims."

She turned back to the boy, who now looked a little more pan-icked but covered it well. "How old are you?"

Galahad Sinclair stood straighter in the hope that his excep-tional height would make up for the lack of years on his face. "Old enough."

"One and twenty?" A brief, surprised flicker of his eyelids con-firmed her guess wasn't wide of the mark. "Tell me, young Galahad, is it your ambition to follow in your foul father's footsteps and see the inside of a jail cell before your first quarter century? Because trespassing is indeed a crime on this side of the Atlantic, and so is attempted burglary."

"I'll admit to the first but know nothing about the second." He knew. His shuffling feet told her so.

"Of course you'll admit to the first!" Vee snarled in his face, the sprig of leaves caught in the hinge of her spectacles ruining the menacing effect she was aiming for. "Because I caught you red-handed, you snake!" She jabbed his chest hard and Galahad's eyes narrowed, but other than that he did not move a muscle in re-taliation. A detail that Diana could not help but admire. He might not be the sharpest chisel in the toolbox, but he was a proud blunt instrument.

"Where is your feckless father?" Diana glanced out across the black lawn. "Because believe me, he is not much of a father if he would abandon his son to us while he hides in the undergrowth like a coward."

Giles had described this boy as the image of his sire, and there was no denying Galahad Sinclair was destined to be an exceed-ingly handsome fellow if he managed not to get himself hanged before he fully matured, but he had said the eyes were different. If Gervais Sinclair's were as cold as ice as Olivia claimed, then these were molten.

"He's likely got his gun pointed right at you, so you'd best let me go before somebody gets hurt." The lad folded his arms, a cocky expression on his face, but Diana knew bravado when she saw it. Or at least she hoped she did. She had perpetually worn it at Galahad's age to mask the fear and shame that came alongside being an impoverished criminal's daughter who wanted to be something but was never given the chance.

She also knew the likes of Gervais Sinclair because she had grown up with a different version of him. It took a lot of strength to fight back to a parent like that when doing as you were told and keeping your head down was easier. It had taken her seventeen years to find the courage to break those shackles and forge ahead alone with her sisters into an even more uncertain future. But if she had had no siblings to walk shoulder to shoulder beside her, that rebellion might well have taken longer.

"He isn't here, is he, Galahad? He sent a boy to do a man's job to save his own sorry skin, didn't he? And he'll raise merry hell once he realizes you failed." Those proud, expressive eyes twitched again. "I shudder to think how he'll react when he realizes you tipped us off that he was here. Makes his job so much harder when he cannot sneak inside to find something to corroborate his letter. All his claims are based on hearsay, aren't they? One person's word written in a single vitriolic letter that is so flimsy you need tangible proof before you can use it?"

Young Galahad's eyes couldn't hold her gaze, so Diana knew she had read the situation right. As they blinked she saw the fear there and realized he was scared—but now more of his father than of them. She knew that awful feeling, too.

"Go!" She pointed in the direction of the gates. "Get off your cousin's property and don't come back or I will personally find and tell Gervais what a blithering idiot you have been." Galahad nodded, relief replacing the fire in his stare, went to run, only to be thwarted by Vee who caught him by the collar and almost strangled him as she yanked him back.

"We cannot let him go! He's a filthy trespasser. A crook who wants to steal from Giles! I say we call the constable or lock him in the dungeon!" Vee looked to Giles to back her up even though there was no dungeon. Instead, he simply looked to her. Trusted Diana with the decision because he knew how to trust. How had he managed that when the wounds of his childhood were as deep as hers?

"No, Vee." She touched her sister's outraged shoulder and sighed. "He is the helpless son of a crook and we know how that feels better than anyone, don't we?" Their gazes locked in unspoken understanding as they both remembered their past.

Vee's fingers loosened their grip and Galahad pulled away. In case anyone changed their mind again, he dashed down the driveway toward the gates then skidded to a stop to glance back at them bemused. Diana smiled. She did not need to hear his thanks to know how grateful he was for that one small act of compassion. Because people from her world rarely ever experienced it.

Chapter Twenty-Six

As much as Giles wanted to curl up in a ball and die somewhere quietly in a corner from the gushing new wound in his aching, bludgeoned heart, he knew he had to face her. The sun had been up for hours but he had avoided breakfast, using the excuse of checking on the progress of estate repairs to ride aimlessly while he left Diana and her sister to solve his mystery.

If all his mortified procrastinating had achieved anything, it had highlighted two irrefutable facts. The first was what he had said could not be unsaid no matter how much he was tempted to make excuses for it, and the second was he really did not want to talk about it again.

Ever.

He took a moment to compose himself outside the estate office then breezed in. "Have you found anything useful?"

There was no sign of the woman he had been avoiding but Vee smiled from behind the mountain of account books piled on the desk. "I suppose that depends on your definition of *useful*. I have learned a great deal about estate management and the names of every Harpenden employee over the last half century, though nothing so far about your predicament. But my sister is in the grip of a theory." She pointed to the Welsh stonemason's receipt that Diana had found the night before and had pinned to the middle of the only empty square of wall. He wandered to it to read it for himself. "She is convinced that is significant."

"Because it comes from Wales?" Over a decade after the duke's rebellious, outraged winter there.

Vee shook her golden head. "Because there is no mention of it in the ledgers—not here and not in London, either. She has a ridiculously good memory for such details and she's right. When everything else is meticulously cross-referenced in one of the estate books, that omission is an anomaly. So now she and Dalton are on a mission to prove it."

"They've left the estate?" He had spent hours out in the cold avoiding her when he could have managed to do that here in the warm.

"Apparently, they had to, to consult the parish records. I doubt my tenacious sister will rest until she finds out who that headstone was made for." She smiled as he stared at the pile of papers in the middle of the floor. Diana's spot. She liked to sit amongst it all cross-legged. "Have the pair of you argued?"

"Why do you ask?"

"There was an atmosphere last night and you have been keen to stay out of each other's way today. You left at dawn as if your breeches were on fire." She pointed to the ceiling. "My room overlooks the stables, so I saw you gallop off with a face like thunder, and when I asked Diana the same question she got that pinched look that she gets when she doesn't want to say anything before she remembered to roll her eyes and tell me I was imagining things."

"We exchanged a few cross words, that is all." He'd said them. She'd been cross with them.

"Can I give you some advice, Giles?"

"Don't I have enough of that from Dalton?"

She smiled in blatant pity. "Diana is a complicated soul and as suspicious as she is stubborn. If she gets an idea in her head, a team of elephants won't dislodge it until she is ready to let it go. That receipt is a case in point. She has a suspicion and until she has either proved or disproved it, it will linger unresolved. Or fester. She is much the same with people—all people and not just men. Though men especially and that is hardly a surprise when you consider the one we grew up with. After he left, that distrustful aspect of her character grew, and probably out of necessity. Three young girls alone are ripe for exploitation, and while Minerva stepped up to be a mother to me, Diana took on the role of protector when she was only seventeen, and had to remain that for five long, difficult years. So long that the inclination has become ingrained, and it takes her forever to trust someone. Look at Hugh. He's been married to Minerva a whole year, been nothing but lovely to all of us, yet Diana is only just warming to him. Still not ready to believe he is as decent as he is."

"And your point is?" He sat on the corner of the desk, curious as to whether she had more of an understanding of her prickly sister's mind than he did. Heaven knew a little insight couldn't hurt after he had made such a splendid hash of things with his unwelcome declaration. What the blazes had he been thinking to speak his feelings aloud?

"My point is, Diana needs the time and sufficient evidence to prove her suspicions are unfounded before she will let go of them.

People have to work hard to earn her trust—and I am sure you *almost* have it but . . ."

"But?"

"That now places you in the most precarious position of all as far as Diana is concerned. Because now, instead of doubting you, she is doubting herself."

Giles blew out a frustrated breath. "I have never done a single thing to make the harridan doubt me. If anything, I have always been brutally honest with your sister."

Too honest.

"And therein lies the rub. In Diana's suspicious mind that makes you too good to be true, and that in turn makes her all the more resistant to your charms. If you are going to win her over and get past all the barricades and obstacles she has built around her heart, you need to persevere. Rome wasn't built in a day. Strike while the iron is hot. Be the fly in her ointment. The stick in her spokes. Diana is a hard nut to crack, so find excuses to be alone with her."

He laughed at that ludicrous suggestion. "Even if I was inclined to do that—" This was madness. Pure folly. As pointless as a circle and as useful as a teapot made of chocolate. "How exactly would I do that with you, our self-appointed, idiom-quoting, and equally suspicious chaperone, watching us like a hawk?"

"I *was* your chaperone when I assumed Diana was ready to succumb to your charms. Now that I realize she has battened down the hatches and convinced herself she is immune to them, I have decided to revert to matchmaking."

"Do all the Merriwells blow hot and cold with such unpredictable frequency?"

"All I am saying is that I am inclined to turn more of a blind eye until the tide turns if you're tempted to grasp the bull by the horns." She giggled at her shameless but apt use of more idioms. "The more you prove to her that you are the man of her jaded dreams, the more chance you have of becoming him."

He shook his head. "I am not the man of her dreams, Vee. In my position, I cannot be the man of any woman's dreams. My situation likely makes me more the stuff of nightmares and I wouldn't saddle my current burdens on my worst enemy."

"You think Diana cares if you are a duke or not? Knowing my sister, you are more appealing without the title than with it. She has a healthy disregard for society—or perhaps she fears it. Either way, she has done a good job of remaining quite detached from it. You might have noticed she does that a lot, too—detaches. It is almost as if she believes that if she tries not to care about something, then she won't. That way, when it is taken away, she has convinced herself already that it won't matter."

Vee's kind eyes suddenly looked older and wiser than her years. "She will argue the toss until she is blue in the face if she cares the slightest bit to make you think that she doesn't, but if she really cares and she fears her arguments lack enough conviction and might give away the real her, she is silent. That, my dear Giles, is when you know that you have her. Why do you think we all give her such a hard time over you? Because several months ago she ran out of convincing arguments—even for herself. And her silence is deafening."

An optimistic theory his stupid heart liked the sound of, but Giles was nothing if not a realist. "She really isn't, Vee. I know this because I might have slipped up last night and plighted my troth." Saying it aloud ripped another hole in his heart, and he pulled a mortified face. "Suffice to say, she wasn't interested, and I cannot blame her. If I were in her shoes, I wouldn't want me, either, and I certainly was in no position to ask. I am kicking myself that I did."

"Did she tell you that she did not want you or was she silent?" Vee smiled kindly. "Because I will bet every book I own that it was the latter. When I arrived she looked uncertain, and Diana would usually rather die than allow that vulnerable emotion show. Despite her hard exterior, she has a big heart. It might well be wrapped in thorns and guarded by dragons, but she is still here, Giles. For all her lofty claims about barely tolerating you, she moved heaven and earth and lied through her teeth to be by your side in your hour of need and she is out there right now"—she cocked her head toward the window—"hunting for the truth on your behalf. And be in no doubt: If she finds it, she will break every law of the land to keep you safe from it and to hell with the consequences. If that isn't categorical proof that she more than cares for you, then I do not know what is."

That gave him food for thought. Or false hope. Or a selfish justification for ruining an innocent and decent woman's life all over again when she had only just repaired the damage wreaked by her awful father. "Forcing Diana into a corner wouldn't be fair."

"All's fair in love and . . ."

"Nobody died in this parish in February 1796 and was buried in Wales." Dalton burst through the door with his customary lack of manners, acknowledging Giles with a tip of his chin while he shrugged out of his greatcoat. "In fact, nobody has died in the parish and been buried in Wales ever. At least not that we could find—and Miss Diana dragged me to every church within ten miles, including the little Quaker place up in the hills. So now she's got the bit between her teeth." He rolled his good eye. "God help us."

"I heard that." Diana strode in, all windswept from her ride and still in the tight habit that did wondrous things for her figure. As she noticed him, her step faltered for a second before she masked it with indifference and Vee nudged his leg. "However, I will not be deterred from my quest. How far is it to Llanyre?"

"*Thlann-near* is about two hours' ride to the southwest." Vee grinned at her sister as she corrected her poor attempt at the proper Welsh pronunciation. "I consulted a map because I knew you would ask. If we leave now, we should arrive by one." She nudged his leg again, but unsubtly this time. "I say we strike while the iron is hot. What say you, Giles?"

Staying close to her sister was proving impossible because Vee either galloped on ahead with Dalton or hung back, confirming all Diana's suspicions that the traitor was doing it on purpose to leave her alone with Giles.

An unusually subdued Giles who was lost in his own thoughts.

She hated the silence. Hated more that hers had caused it.

"We have made good time." As they crossed a bridge, she pointed to a sign. "Only five miles left. I hope we find something so that I can tell you that I told you so. My gut tells me the Welsh connection is significant, and my gut is never wrong."

He said nothing for a moment then turned to stare at her. "I am sorry about what I said yesterday. It was a moment of madness that I have regretted since."

She covered the unexpected slice of disappointment with a sunny smile. "That *is* a relief."

"I am sure it is." His gaze was cold. Wounded. Desolate.

"It was a fraught situation and emotions were running high.

You have so much going on, Giles, I doubt you know which way is up, so I forgive you for your moment of madness and I am glad we can put it behind us." Of late they seemed to put a lot behind them. So much that it felt as though they were towing boulders through a bog.

"You see, that's the darndest thing . . ." His dark eyes seemed to bore into her soul. "I have spent every second since pondering what I feel and why I feel it, and the situation and the state of my mind have nothing to do with it. They have amplified things certainly. Perhaps even hastened things, but to quote you, the roots sprouted long before the shoots. I know I shouldn't have said anything—I should have taken the unfortunate truth to my grave—and Lord only knows I have no expectations, but this is a fraught situation. My emotions are running high. I am exhausted and so sick of all the lies I have to tell that it turns out I do not have the capacity to lie to you—even though I know that I should."

"What are you saying?" Part of her wanted to hear it. Needed to hear it. Yearned with every fiber of her being to have to face her own truth. The other part, the suspicious, jaded, terrified part, wanted to stick her fingers in her ears and run screaming into the hills.

His smile was so hopeless she could not bear it. "That even though circumstances and my own conscience dictate that I can never have you, the cruelest irony of all is that despite the futility of it, I love you with all my heart, Diana. I have since you first took my breath away, and I shall love you until the last breath leaves my body."

And with that he kicked his own mount into a gallop and left her dumbstruck on the road.

Chapter Twenty-Seven

"Remind me again what we are looking for?" Dalton surveyed the graveyard of St. Llyr's. It was a question Giles was glad the reprobate had asked because he was buggered if he knew, either.

Not that he understood much of anything anymore. Somewhere between the duke's death and this impromptu trip to Wales he had been sucked into a whirlpool that spun faster and faster and sucked him deeper and deeper every day. As he had no energy left to fight it and had no clue where it was taking him, he had apparently decided to live moment to moment, doing and saying whatever popped into his addled head.

"Any link to Harpenden that we can find—no matter how tenuous." Diana had already begun the search and was busy brushing away a tuft of overgrown grass from a headstone to read the inscription. She had taken his second ill-considered and futile declaration with the same stony silence as the first. To be fair, he hadn't expected anything else when the words had tumbled from his mouth. He only knew, in that strange moment, it had been imperative to say them. He was buggered if he knew why, unless he was caving under the pressure and going mad. Lord only knew he had enough incentive.

"So a needle in a haystack." Dalton rolled his eye, then asked the second question that was on the tip of Giles's tongue. "Anybody here speak Welsh? Because from what I can see, almost every gravestone is written in it."

"A detail that might well work in our favor, as the English will stick out like a sore thumb." Diana offered Dalton her most withering look, as if she were the only one present with a brain, careful not to so much glance in Giles's direction despite his position next to his butler. "The numbers are the same, though, so just hunt for 1796."

"Or 1795." She might be keen to ignore him and the emotions simmering between them, but Giles did not have the energy to. "A grave needs to settle for at least six months before you can set a headstone into it."

The brief flick of her eyes his way followed by the begrudging nod told him that she hadn't thought of that, so he patted himself on the back for not being entirely useless in the fearsome Sentinel's revered presence.

Beside him, Vee gasped. "Good heavens . . . why on earth did that not occur to us before? When is your birthday, Giles?"

"The duke always said it was the third of September, but then he also said that the duchess was my mother, so I wouldn't take that date as gospel."

The youngest Merriwell's lips moved as she did a quick sum in her head. "That fits! You came into the world at the beginning of September 1795, and the receipt for the headstone was for the end of February six months later. That cannot be a coincidence."

Knowing that Diana did not believe in coincidences, he surveyed the haphazard stones all around him. "You think my mother is here?" That prospect unsettled him some more because he hadn't realized until that second how much he had hoped she was still alive. "You think she died having me?" That possibility made him queasy as the whirlpool sucked him deeper.

As if she read his mind Diana decided to cease ignoring him long enough to smile in sympathy. "Women have babies knowing the risks, Giles. I doubt she blamed you for it."

"Easy for you to say when you didn't kill her." In case she was right his fingers went to the dented pocket watch hanging from his waistcoat, seeking reassurance from the stranger inside it who already felt so dear.

"I know." Her lovely green eyes clouded. "This was never going to be easy and I did warn you that you might not like what we found. But this is still just a theory, Giles, and could well be a wild goose chase, exactly as you said. Your mother might still be around for you to meet."

Grief swamped him as the truth seemed to bleed from the watch. "She isn't."

"Why don't we split up?" Sensing a potential thaw in relations, the matchmaking Vee surveyed the area. "Dalton and I can take that half of the churchyard and leave you and Diana to this side." She shot him a look that said she was trying to help him *strike while the iron was hot.* "We'll get through it all quicker that way." Then she yanked the butler away.

Alone again, the awkward silence settled like fog and he was content to leave it. He was too wounded. Too disappointed in her even though he had no right to be. He had said his bit, bared his soul, and now she needed to digest it—or denounce it. Whichever route she chose, the end result would be the same. With all his skeletons rattling for all they were worth and on the cusp of bursting out of the cupboard and running roughshod over everything, he had no future with Diana.

A sentiment she clearly shared, as in tacit agreement, for the next half an hour she searched one corner of their allotted section and he searched the other. Neither said a word, but when she did he knew by the quiet timbre of her tone that Diana had been right.

"Giles." She was kneeling beside an overgrown grave. "Look."

On leaden feet he walked toward her and stared at the stone. He did not understand the Welsh inscription, but the name screamed regardless.

Ffion St Clair
Hwyl fawr Cariad
1763—1795

"St Clair? And the date fits. Too coincidental?" She watched him stare at the letters.

"You don't believe in coincidences." Now, neither did he.

He bent to touch the ground and felt his mother. The connection was instantaneous. It overwhelmed him. Giles had no clue any tears had fallen until Diana pressed a handkerchief into his hand and wrapped her arm around his shoulders. He leaned his head against hers, needing her strength while he absorbed it all, and as if she knew he needed this time she simply held him close. When he was done she held his hand, led him inside the church, and left him to compose himself while she went to inform the others of her discovery.

"By God's Almighty grace I have been blessed to be rector here for forty years." The Reverend Griffiths was a kindly man with an unfortunate profusion of crinkly white hair, which sprouted from both his head and ears. They quivered as he led Diana and Giles down the aisle toward the vestry. "I pride myself on never forgetting one of my parishioners, so who is it that you seek?"

"My husband's mother—Ffion St Clair." Diana threaded her arm through Giles's then winced as she realized she was lying while standing in the aisle of a church. He clearly thought the same thing, too, as the wretch glanced heavenward and mimed being smited by the Almighty for the falsehood while the vicar's back was to them. "We believe she might have died giving birth to him."

"Ah yes. I remember Ffion well. A lovely woman with the kindest heart." He held open the door to the vestry and smiled as Giles passed through. "A sad loss to this parish. I see her in you. You have her eyes." Beneath her fingers, his muscles tightened and her heart broke for him.

"I think he has, too." She squeezed his arm, wishing she could spare him all the pain of today. "All he has of her is a small portrait." She nudged Giles to get it out and he dutifully snapped the watch open to show vicar the enamel. "Is this the same Ffion who is buried in the cemetery?"

"Ahh . . . yes, it is." The Reverend Griffiths caressed the tiny face with his fingertip. "That smile is sadly missed—as is her food."

Because she sensed he needed it, she slid her hand out of the cradle of his elbow to grasp his tight. "She was a cook?"

The vicar shook his head and, by default, his ear hairs. "A baker. Made the finest Welsh cakes you ever tasted and had such a delicate touch with biscuits they melted in your mouth. She owned the bakery in Llandrindod, and such was her reputation people traveled from miles around to sample her wares. As I recall, her shortbread in particular was exemplary." He pulled a loop of heavy keys from his belt and used them to open a robust metal chest.

"Well, that explains where my sweet tooth and lifelong love of biscuits comes from." Giles was still a tad overwhelmed, she could tell, despite his determination to cover it with a façade of flippancy. His fingers gripped hers like a vise. "I always wondered."

The vicar rummaged in the chest and produced a rectangular leather book, which he laid carefully on the table. "These are the burial records. We have to keep them under lock and key nowadays, though goodness only knows why around here. As I am sure you imagine, nothing much happens here in Llanyre. Ours is a small community and always has been. Most are born here and die here."

"Was she born here?"

The reverend shook his head. "Your mother was an exception to that rule as she hailed from Presteigne, if memory serves, closer to the border, but we adopted her as our own. Everyone hereabouts turned out for her funeral. Despite her lack of family, she was much loved." The vicar found the pertinent page and twisted the book to face them. Sadly, the record told them little more than the headstone.

"She died on September twenty-second." Giles traced the entry, his dark eyes bereft because this confirmed his worst fears about her cause of death.

"She did, God rest her soul, but not without a fight." The reverend sighed and touched Giles's shoulder. "She had been gravely ill the year before with pneumonia. It almost killed her, and that had taken its toll. When the childbed fever hit, she had few reserves left, so do not blame yourself for what happened. She had waited so long for a child. Called you her miracle. Adored you from the moment she set eyes upon you. Thankfully, she lived long enough to see you baptized, and that gave her some comfort."

"I was christened? Here?"

"You were indeed, sir, and by me." The vicar returned to the chest to pull out another volume and place it atop the first while he found the correct page.

Diana and Giles stared at it in shock.

September 5 1795 Giles Dafydd son of Ffion and Gerald St Clair of Llanyre

Gerald St Clair.

Too coincidental by any stretch of the imagination.

"You knew my father?"

"Not as well as I knew his wife." Both squeezed the other's fingers at this revelation. Both clearly wondering if the alleged marriage, like the coincidental surname, was a sham to hide his illegitimacy. "His business took him away often, and unlike your mother he always preferred to keep himself to himself." Of course he did because he was living a lie. Diana did not need to look at Giles to know he was thinking the same.

The vicar seemed compelled to fill their stunned silence. "As I recall, Mr. St Clair rented Holly Cottage on the outskirts of the village several years before you were born and seemed to like it here but he left the parish devastated, never to return after your mother's sad demise." The Reverend Griffiths offered Giles a pained smile. "There is no denying you are the image of him. You have his height, his coloring, and the same shaped face." The vicar gestured to Giles's dimpled Sinclair chin. "Mr. St Clair was a handsome fellow, too. How is he?"

"Also dead. He . . ."

In case Giles elaborated with any more of the truth than was necessary, Diana intervened. "He passed while my husband was still a small child, hence he knows so little of his family history." He flicked her an amused glance, then the wretch's eyes wandered heavenward again.

"I am sorry. I shall say a prayer for him at evensong."

"You should probably say a prayer for all of us. Especially my *wife*."

Diana pinched his arm to let Giles know this wasn't the time or place for his teasing. "Did Mr. St Clair organize the headstone on her grave?"

"He did, though I do not think he ever found the strength to visit it, the poor man, for she was his everything. Her death hit him hard. He was inconsolable with grief." It was Giles's turn to pinch her arm now. More out of disbelief at hearing about this version of his father than at her question. "So inconsolable he almost left without you, Mr. St Clair. Had the midwife not chased after his carriage and handed you to him, I daresay you might still be living here now."

"Perhaps he blamed me for her death?" By the pained acceptance in his eyes, Giles did not need an answer to that question. He also did not need to hear a stranger try to console him with empty platitudes and reassurances when he had lived his entire childhood and beyond with the consequences.

"There is an inscription." Diana cringed at her poor attempt at Welsh in her rushed attempt to save him. "*Hwyl fawr cariad*—what does it mean?"

"In English I suppose the closest translation is 'Farewell, my love.'" The Reverend Griffiths touched Giles's shoulder in comfort. "A more devoted couple I never did see than your parents. Theirs was a genuine union of love. A rare commodity indeed, as I am sure you can appreciate." The vicar smiled at Diana. "How long have you lovebirds been married?"

"It feels like five minutes." Giles offered her a suitably soppy grin.

"Another successful St Clair love match, too, I can see." The Reverend Griffiths offered Giles one of those man-to-man looks. "Tell me, how long did it take you to propose to your lovely lady?"

"I didn't propose. She did . . . didn't you, *cariad*?"

Diana narrowed her eyes then smiled for the older man's benefit. "My husband is teasing, Reverend. Of course I didn't propose. To be honest, I barely tolerated him to begin with—but he grew on me. Like fungus."

"And now I am the victorious *champignon* of her heart."

The vicar laughed. "You are just like your mother, Mr. St Clair. She liked a good joke, too. Ffion had a great sense of fun and adored the ridiculous." Another thing Giles had inherited. "So different in character from your father, and she teased him mercilessly as a result. But they say opposites attract and they were as opposite as any couple I ever knew—yet they worked and made each other happy from the day they arrived to the day he held her hand as she died."

"How many years did they live here?"

The Reverend Griffiths pondered her question. "It's so long ago I really couldn't say for sure. Eight years. Maybe nine." A clock chimed on the mantelpiece and he smiled with regret. "I wish I had the time to reminisce with you longer but sadly I have this evening's service to prepare for. Unless you can stay for it and we can chat after?"

They both shook their heads. "We have a long journey back."
Then grinned at each other for saying exactly the same thing at the
same time.

While Giles thanked the vicar for his time and his recollec-
tions, Diana stared at the damning record once more. A record that
confirmed not only Giles's parentage but also his father's blatant in-
fidelity. Or perhaps even bigamy if the vicar's assumptions and the
register were correct and Gerald Sinclair had purposefully taken
the abbreviated spelling of his ancestral name to marry another
wife while his duchess still lived.

The deeper she dug into Giles's past, the more rattling skeletons she unearthed. Lies heaped upon more lies and poor Giles
was the victim. Perhaps Ffion had been, too. Both parents had
taken the truth to their graves. But as always, a trace remained,
and this trace was explosive. Enough to strip Giles of his title if
Gervais ever found it.

Which of course he would if she left it to find!

In the absence of any better plan, she acted on impulse while
silently praying that the Almighty would forgive her for her ump-
teenth shocking lie in his house in as many minutes.

"Oh my goodness . . . I feel faint." She squeezed Giles's arm
to let him know she really didn't, and to his credit he still caught
her with convincing aplomb. She clutched at his lapels, channeled
Vee, and acted for all she was worth as she croaked, "My head is
spinning . . . I feel so parched . . ."

Playing along, Giles pulled out a chair and while he maneu-
vered her limp body into it he turned to the blinking vicar. "Might
I trouble you for some water, Reverend?"

"I shall fetch some from the font!"

As he hurried out, and conscious that time really was of the essence and before Giles lunged to stop her, Diana grabbed the book and swiftly tore out the page.

"What are you doing?"

"Saving you and every tenant who depends on you." She slammed the register closed and had barely stuffed the damning evidence down her bodice and resumed her feigned faint when the vicar returned.

"Thank you so much." She grabbed what she assumed was the same christening cup that had anointed baby Giles's head and gulped the contents down, relieved that despite his shock at her actions her fake husband still had the wherewithal to be *helpful* and deposit both the parish record books back into their chest before he fanned her face with his hand for a few minutes while her touch of the vapors subsided.

They managed to walk out at a sedate pace arm in arm, quickening it only to cross the graveyard, then giggling like naughty children, they made a mad dash down the lane.

Chapter Twenty-Eight

Giles could not explain quite how he felt beyond relieved. It made no difference that that came on the back of technical wrongdoing, or that he had found and lost Ffion in the same day. The burden on his shoulders was a little lighter, his future seemed a smidgen brighter, and Diana's actions gave him hope that she cared about him a great deal just as Vee had said. Not that he was in any position to do anything about it, but it was nice to know, all the same.

His buoyed mood was clearly infectious because the three of them had enjoyed a splendid dinner and at Vee's instigation were now doing something fun to round their night off despite it being almost one in the morning.

"It's a play!"

"We have already established that!" Diana glared at him in exasperation while Vee reenacted her charade for the fourth time. "Thrice! It's a play. Two words."

"And the first word is *the*," added Giles, grinning around a mouthful of shortbread just to vex her. For a woman whose acute investigative skills set ne'er-do-wells quaking in their boots, she had neither the talent nor the patience for a game even a child could master.

Vee nodded, rolling her eyes at them both as if they were the thickest dunces in a schoolroom, then held up two fingers.

"Second word," muttered Diana through gritted teeth while he sniggered on the sofa beside her because they knew exactly what was coming. Then chuckled some more when she nudged him. "Will you stop distracting me while I am trying to concentrate!"

Vee didn't disappoint and for the fourth time started to stomp around like a madwoman waving her arms in the air, wiggling her fingers for all she was worth, then pretending to recoil from something above. And just as she had four times previously, while a frustrated Diana dropped her head in her hands and groaned, she suddenly paused what she was doing, mimed an exaggerated belly laugh, and began to run around like a headless chicken being stung by a thousand wasps.

"*And* . . . your time is up." Dalton had been given the task of timing each round.

"Lord give me strength." Diana sounded like a broken woman. "How on earth is this fun? Put me out of my misery, Vee. What the devil was all that arm-waving nonsense about?"

"Obviously it is *The Tempest*!" Vee shook her head as she huffed, and began to act it out again as she explained while Giles stifled a laugh. He had worked out it was *The Tempest* on the first mime but had enjoyed Diana's furrowed brow and foot stamping far too much to have spoiled his splendid entertainment prematurely.

"This is the howling wind and the pouring rain." Vee stomped in a tight circle waving her wiggling fingers. "This is the thunder and lightning." She recoiled, covering her eyes with her arms.

"And this"—she replicated her exaggerated silent belly laugh—
"signifies that it is one of Shakespeare's comedies rather than his
tragedies."

"Forget about tragedy, that shocking mime was a Shakespear-
ean travesty." Diana scowled first at Vee and then at him as they
both collapsed in a fit of giggles. "I loathe parlor games."

"Only because you are useless at them." Vee wandered to the
biscuit plate then rolled her eyes at him. "You have eaten them all
again, Giles, haven't you?"

"I couldn't help myself, Miss Vee. Biscuits are in my blood.
We are definitely going to need some more." As he shrugged, unrepentant and quietly pleased that he finally had such a tangible
link to at least one of his parents, Dalton stood with undisguised
belligerence.

"I suppose you'll be expecting me to fetch them?"

"I shall help you and I shall heat some hot milk for us to dunk
them in." Vee herded the scowling butler to the door grinning in
her unsubtle matchmaking way. "I am sure I can trust the pair of
you alone for a minute."

The second she was gone the atmosphere in the room changed,
although this time it did not feel quite so chilly. That might have
something to do with Diana's heated blush, which had begun
blooming the second her sister exited the room.

"It's been quite a day." She couldn't quite look at him. "A day
for revelations."

"In more ways than one." Giles hadn't meant it how it sounded
and wished he could claw the sentence back and reword it so that
it did not sound so loaded when he saw her pained reaction. "That
wasn't a dig at you, by the way, at what I stupidly said to you. More a

comment on the other revelations concerning my parents than it was about . . ." His voice trailed off and he shrugged his awkwardness. "Perhaps I should apologize again for dragging that up, and then we can finally put all that behind us where it belongs?" Although he did not fool himself it wouldn't always be there. Lingering like a bad smell and spoiling everything they had had right up to the point he decided to pour out his heart.

"About that . . ." He might have known something would come along to spoil his good humor. "I am not sure we can put it all behind us. Things have been different since that—" She flapped her hand, her cheeks positively glowing crimson.

"Kiss?" Someone had to say it. Be the bigger person and try to fix the mess he had made from the foolhardy moment he had instigated. "Do you have any bright ideas how we can get past it? Because I really do want us to get back to being the unlikely friends and unconvincing enemies that we've always been, Diana. I cannot imagine not having your prickly presence in my life and I would hate it if you tried to avoid me."

She sat a little straighter and stared at the door rather than at him as if keeping watch. She chewed her lip. Blew out a shaky breath. Wrung her hands in her lap for all they were worth then swallowed. "Perhaps we shouldn't try to get past it."

What did that mean? "You want to cut your losses and run?" The very thought made him anxious. "Wash your hands of me forever?"

"Not exactly." She was staring at her busy fingers now as if her life depended on it.

"Then what exactly?"

"I was thinking that . . . well . . . perhaps instead of putting it all behind us we should . . . um . . ." This was a Diana he did not recognize. The forthright, reckless, indomitable, outspoken harridan he knew and loved seemed to have left the drawing room and been replaced by hesitant, vulnerable incarnation who was having a great deal of trouble speaking. Her eyes darted briefly to his and she screwed them shut, but not before he witnessed the battle going on in those emotive emerald irises.

"You are making me worried." An understatement. His heart was beating so fast he was in fear of it smashing his ribs to smithereens.

"Not as much as I am worrying myself, I can assure you."

"Try opening your eyes and breathing, then spit it out." She nodded at his advice. Inhaled. Opened her eyes. Then stared at him like a startled deer. "You were thinking that instead of putting it behind us we should . . . ?"

She stared for a few seconds more.

Blinked.

Blinked again.

"I was thinking that instead of putting it behind us we should . . ." She paused and Giles gripped her elbow, fully committed to shaking the words out of her if he had to, to put him out of his misery. "I was thinking that perhaps we should put it in front of us instead?"

It was his turn to blink. "What does that even mean?"

She pulled an uncertain face and flapped her hands between them. "That we acknowledge it . . . Don't ignore it. That we give it a go."

"Give *us* a go?" He couldn't have heard that correctly.

Her answering monologue was a rapid stream of thoughts that

he struggled to keep up with, but which filled his aching heart with joy.

"I know I've always been vehemently against the idea of a man or of losing my independence, but people change, don't they, and let's face it, you are not my father. Or that horrid brute in the alleyway. You are not even technically a duke anymore, for pity's sake. And if Minerva and Olivia are convinced that having a man in your life isn't such a bad thing and they are both equally as stubborn, then maybe I am doing myself a disservice by denying myself what my stupid heart and even stupider body seem to want. Especially since it heard Lady Sewell in the pergola and that has now given it all sorts of inappropriate ideas that go way beyond kissing. But wanting you doesn't automatically render me a helpless chattel, now, does it? Let's face it, we both know that you can issue orders like Wellington at Waterloo and I am still going to ignore you. I am the most headstrong person I know. Only a blithering idiot or a masochist would try to control me or change me and I have long been of the opinion that you are neither. Besides, giving it a go is more dipping a toe in the water than an actual commitment and toe-dipping isn't legally binding and both parties are still free to step away if it's all a big mistake. Obviously, I'd want to ease into things with a long courtship and . . ." She finally paused to take in some air, so before she started up again as her manic eyes suggested she was about to, he placed his fingers over her lips.

"*You* want to give *us* a go?" She nodded because his fingers were still over her mouth. "Even though I still have skeletons rattling here, there, and everywhere and I could still have the dukedom stripped from me at any minute?" He released his fingers to hear her verdict but kept them close in case she began to vomit more superfluous words.

She nodded again. "Even though." She smiled and cupped his cheek. "I cannot imagine not having the constant bane of you in my life, and with some intense training you might even make a decent assistant for the Sentinel one day. But I would hire you as an apprentice assistant."

"A harridan's apprentice . . ." He pretended to ponder it even though he could barely speak he was so choked with emotion. "What are the wages like?"

"Dreadful." Her lovely eyes were misted with tears. "You'd likely need another job to keep a roof over our heads."

Our heads. He liked that. Liked it a great deal. "That's all right, you can pay me in sarcasm and pithy retorts." Giles couldn't stop touching her. Her hands. Her face. The delicate arch of her eyebrow. "Besides, even if Harpenden goes, I still have plenty of money. I've been speculating for years and it turns out I am pretty good at it so I hope you don't mind living in Tavistock Square."

She laughed as she smoothed her hands over his shoulders. "Bloomsbury is so much more convenient for Fleet Street than Mayfair, but you would have to get rid of all that Egyptian nonsense in your ballroom. I will tolerate your rattling skeletons but am not living with a sarcophagus."

"It's empty."

"It's an ostentation and one you only purchased to inflame your father." Her eyes clouded. "I know that losing Harpenden would be devastating to you, Giles, but I cannot deny you being a baker's son rather than a duke is a great weight off my mind. I mean, look at me? I am a forger's daughter from Clerkenwell and not at all duchess material. Furthermore—"

He groaned and smothered the rest of that sentence with a kiss so decadent he sincerely hoped she would forget there was ever a furthermore. She wanted him—*Dirty Secret*, rattling skeletons, and all—so nothing else really mattered.

She smiled against his lips as he hauled her into his lap and they collapsed laughing backward on the sofa, then froze when they heard Vee's incensed growl from the hallway.

"You have some nerve turning up here again, Galahad Sinclair!"

Chapter Twenty-Nine

"I see this place hasn't changed a bit." Without waiting to be invited, Gervais oozed over the threshold of Harpenden Hall like he owned the place; something about his smug, covetous stare raised all Giles's hackles.

"What do you want?"

"You know what I want, nephew." He gestured to the walls around him like a king greeting his subjects. "I want what I am due."

"You are due another stint in jail." Diana stared at his uncle as if he were something stuck to her shoe. "Hopefully they will throw away the key this time."

"What a charming young lady you have found yourself, Giles. Works for *The Tribune*, doesn't she? Or at least that's where we've seen her fancy carriage drop her off whenever she's not sneaking around with you. Tell me, was she the one who tore your baptismal record out of the parish register?"

"I have no idea what you are talking about." Giles forced calmness even though every panicked sinew of his being wanted to adopt a combative stance.

"Oh, I think you do, *Mr. St Clair*. You and your lovely lady *wife* told the Reverend Griffiths that you were a poor orphan in search of his mother."

"We followed you." Galahad stepped up beside his father, his expression defiant, and Giles kicked himself for his own short-sighted stupidity.

Of course they had followed him.

They had followed him and he had led them to the truth. Thanks to his own preoccupation with Diana, it never occurred to him to cover their tracks.

Galahad cocked one golden eyebrow, his smug expression a mirror image of his father's. "Did you honestly think we wouldn't talk to the good reverend, too, cousin? He was very helpful. Especially when he realized you had spun him a pack of lies in the presence of the Lord before you defaced his register." He jerked his head toward Diana. "I told him that he'd been hoodwinked, as your *wife* doesn't strike me as the usual fainting type, but I figure even she might swoon when she realizes the penalty for that serious crime."

"Fourteen years transportation." Gervais was delighted to be the one to break the news. "And the best bit is you shot yourselves in the foot. Because it turns out there are strict rules and regulations about the keeping of parish records for just this sort of deceitful eventuality. Who knew so many impostors try to steal another's rightful inheritance that it is the law every parish has to file a duplicate Bishop's Transcript with the diocese?" He beamed as if this was the most wonderful thing he had ever learned in his life. "I certainly didn't until the betrayed but diligent Reverend Griffiths informed me of that convenient fact over tea after evensong."

He picked up a silver candlestick. Squinted at the hallmark. "I have advised him to press charges for the theft. I also advised him of your whereabouts and confess, the prospect of seeing you dragged away in manacles was worth the effort of the long ride back to Shropshire in the cold and the dark."

Bold as brass, Gervais wandered past him to inspect some of the other treasures on the wall. No doubt making an inventory of all he could sell. "Of course, a man with your connections, even tainted by scandal, is unlikely to be transported. So do not despair, nephew. A good lawyer will argue a lesser sentence, so I wouldn't worry. But I doubt Miss Merriwell will be so fortunate."

He turned and pinned her with a stare so malevolent it chilled Giles to the bone. "You are a forger's daughter, are you not, Miss Merriwell?" She stood tall and unflinching as he walked slowly toward her like a lion stalking his prey. "And a wanted forger's daughter at that. Unlike stealing the truth from a parish record, counterfeiting coin is a capital offense. Juries tend not to be quite so forgiving of someone with such a background and they will want somebody to pay for my nephew's crime. I hear life can be difficult for a woman all alone in the Antipodes. Especially such a pretty one." He reached out to touch her cheek and Giles gripped his wrist in his fist.

"Touch her and I will kill you with my bare hands!"

Something flickered in his uncle's cold, flat eyes, until he shrugged free and moved out of arm's reach. "The dregs of society have never been to my taste but clearly you follow your father in that. He always had his eye on poor little orphaned Ffion Jones, even as a boy. I should have known she was the one. Should have realized he had gone after her when I certainly wouldn't have. But if you will pardon the pun, it appears he had to have his cake and eat it when he could have had all the dessert he wanted and never taste the same one twice. But no. It seems his long-standing love of Welsh cake was his Achilles' heel and now that you've discovered it, all this is mine."

"Get out of my house." At Giles's acid-dripped words, Dalton raised his pistol and made a great show of pulling back the hammer.

"You heard His Grace. Get out or I'll shoot you both where you stand."

While Galahad's eyes widened at the threat, Gervais simply smiled. "I will be back with the proof and the constable and the law on my side. Then we shall see whose house this is."

Giles waited until the front door was firmly closed and bolted before he allowed the panic to take hold.

His fear wasn't for himself but for Diana because he knew Gervais might be right. This was a man's world and a rich man's world at that. A woman who dared to compete in it would be frowned upon by a jury made up of such men. A wanted forger's daughter would be frowned upon more. If they discovered what Diana actually did for *The Tribune* and made an argument about the ironic double standard of the most feared Truth Seeker and unmasker of villains on Fleet Street willfully breaking the law when it suited her to do so, she would be done for. Mr. Cribbage could likely save him from the worst, but they would likely punish Diana, and he wasn't prepared to risk pitting his solicitor's superior trial skills against a jury in what was effectively a game of chance.

He glanced at her pacing the hallway. Deep in thought. Her clever mind searching for another way to save him rather than seeing the danger to herself that now loomed larger and cast a shadow darker than his piffling *Dirty Secret* ever had.

"We're missing something. I can feel it!" She tapped her head as she frowned at him but continued to pace. "Something is niggling. Something is not right."

What wasn't right was her being punished when all she had ever done was try to help. For him—because Diana only ever kicked hornets to rescue someone else with no thought or care for herself.

"I am going to turn myself in." That was the only thing he could do to save her. "Turn myself in before Gervais has a chance. Confess I stole the page but only as proof of my illegitimacy and pretend I am as shocked to learn the truth of my father's deception as everyone will be. If I am completely transparent and don't try to fight it, there will be no need for any trial."

"No, Giles. Not yet. Bureaucracy is notoriously slow, and it will likely take days before Gervais has his proof. There's more to find. Another rattling skeleton. I feel it in my gut."

"It's over, Diana." It all was. He drank in the sight of her. All shimmering, righteous indignation, intelligence, and beauty. Lord, how he loved her. Loved how she thought. Moved. Fought. Kissed. "I need you and Vee to pack."

"What? No!" Her hands went to her hips.

"Dalton, be ready to leave with the ladies at dawn. Take them to Hugh in Hampshire. I want you to all be as far away from Harpenden as it is humanly possible before I surrender to the court in Shrewsbury tomorrow."

Her finger prodded him in the chest. "If you think I am going to abandon you and scurry off like a rat leaving a sinking ship, then think again, Giles Sinclair! I want to help!" She prodded him again. "Don't you see that I am the only one who can?"

He wasn't going to argue the toss over basic common sense, especially when even the fearsome Sentinel couldn't save him now. "If I have to wrestle you into the carriage myself, Diana, and padlock you in it, you and Vee are going home tomorrow." Before she could formulate a single word of argument he raised his flattened palm to stay her. "My decision is made and I will not be swayed."

It was all well and good that she was on a mission to save the world, but somebody had to save Diana from herself.

Loyal, stoic self-sacrifice might well be the most honorable and noble thing for Giles to do but it still grated on Diana's last nerve. That he expected her to meekly obey—to climb into his carriage in a few hours and abandon him to his fate—beggared belief.

That he expected her to stand by and do nothing when there had to be something she could do to save him was beyond the pale. That she had spent the last hour trying and failing to come up with a plan was neither here nor there. Losing one battle did not mean they had lost the war and retreating to his bedchamber to prevent her from telling him so was unreasonable in the extreme. And as for the ridiculous *My decision is made and I will not be swayed . . .*

Grrrrr!

The more she thought about that stupid, pigheaded, typically male edict, the angrier she became. Hence she was now striding toward his bedchamber, furious and determined to give him a thorough piece of her mind!

She raised her fist to knock then hesitated from banging a hole in the wood when she realized that announcing her presence would only give him another excuse to send her away. In his blinkered, pious state he'd probably lock his door before he stuffed a couple of handkerchiefs in his stubborn ears to drown out her bellowed arguments. So instead, she grabbed the handle and barged in unannounced.

Giles shot up from the mattress stunned but his eyes were too focused as he blinked at her to have just been roused from sleep. Given the undisturbed state of covers, he had been lying upon them like a corpse staring at the ceiling while he contemplated his fate. All stoic and noble and self-sacrificing and beyond annoying.

"You should be plotting your next move, not wallowing in a pit of self-pitying martyrdom!" She shook a quaking finger at him as he jumped to his feet, trying not to notice that those feet were bare and that the only thing he had on apart from his breeches was an untucked and billowing linen shirt that was wide open at the neck. The last thing she needed when she wanted to remain righteously indignant at the wretch was a rumpled, crumpled, and much too physically appealing Giles.

"Get out, Diana. I have nothing to say beyond what I have already. My decision is made—"

"And you will not be swayed. Yes, I heard that nonsense loud and clear but have decided to ignore it because it was ridiculous! In fact you are ridiculous to even think for a moment I would cut and run when the hornets start to buzz. Hornets are my stock in trade and I haven't been stung by one yet!"

He started toward her with murder in his dark eyes and in case he manhandled her out onto the landing, she turned the key in the lock then dropped it between her breasts. The metal was cold as it slithered beneath her nightgown to rest against the barrier of her belted robe at her waist.

His eyes narrowed as his hands went to his hips and he loomed over her. "If you think that is a deterrent, harridan, think again."

"If you think your empty threats intimidate me, idiot, you can think again, too. We both know that you would rather die than hurt me." She put her own hands on her hips and glared up at him, defiant. "We are in this together whether you like it or not, Giles Sinclair, and trust me, I am twice as difficult as you are and quadruple as resourceful. I did what I did on the full understanding of the consequences and there is not an icicle's chance in hell that I will not confess to the authorities that I stole the page in the parish register if it saves your pigheaded bacon, so unless you want to wave my prison ship to the Antipodes goodbye from Tilbury Docks, you will hear me out!"

He folded his arms. "Say what you came to say and go." Although his belligerent stance made it plain he was in no mood to listen. Aware that hers was no better, Diana forced her shoulders to relax and exhaled.

"Why don't we sit?"

"Why don't we not."

She could waste precious time with the petty argument he seemed determined to have or she could take an unfamiliar leaf out of Vee's book and try to be the peacemaker. Instead of reacting as she usually would in the face of such idiocy, she glanced around the candlelit room for a suitable place to park her bottom. As the only place was the bed, she sat there. "I would have thought the duke's bedchamber would be the most impressive in the house. This room is tiny."

As she had hoped, the unexpected change of subject disarmed him enough to answer even though he still did so resolutely upright, his stance as unyielding as his pigheadedness. "The duke's bedchamber is impressive." He jerked his head toward the door, unwittingly informing her that even after all these months he couldn't bring himself to sleep in it. The emotional wounds inflicted by his father were just too deep.

"Is this your old room? The one you slept in as a boy?" There was a casual air of easiness about the place that was all Giles. The real Giles and not the superficial façade he presented to the world. The furnishings built more for comfort than to impress and nothing like his ostentatious Egyptian-themed ballroom back in Tavistock Square. His penchant for luxury was evident in the soft blanket and crisp sheets beneath her fingertips. The sumptuous feather mattress and pillows were the sort you would sink into. The artworks on the walls were bold, striking, and filled with color, like the man who owned them. The eclectic pile of reading material on the nightstand was a window into his soul—a witty novel filled with social satire, a weighty tome on modern farming techniques, a history of the feuding Plantagenet kings. On the rug next to the nightstand an illustrated encyclopedia of the flora and fauna of Shropshire sat on a pile of well-read *London Tribune*s; the fragment of the headline visible announced it as the edition where she had first exposed the Camden Canal swindle. There because he was proud of her.

Cared about her.

Loved her with all his stupid, misguided, noble heart.

His gaze followed hers to the newspaper and he winced. "Say what you came to say, Diana. Please."

"Give me some time to do some more digging into your parents' relationship and on Gervais. The Derbyshire abduction cannot possibly be his only crime. Olivia told me there was an incident with a maid that your grandmother covered up, and a hundred more rumors of goodness knows what. There will be more rattling skeletons in his cupboard, I know it. I'll find something else and once I do, we can use that as leverage. I'll wager everything I have that he'll run away to save his own skin again."

"*If* you can find something in time? And even *if* you do, it will only be a temporary deterrent until the next time he comes back or Galahad does and demands what he is due. No matter what we might think of them, the law is on their side. They both have a stronger legal claim to Harpenden than I ever had."

"I still think it is worth a punt."

He laughed without humor, his dark eyes bleak. "The only thing that separates the good gamblers and the bad is their ability to know when to walk away. I was dealt a bad hand, played it as best I could, and bluffed for all I was worth, but Gervais found the ace and once he plays it this game is done."

"So you are just going to give up?"

He shrugged. "Giving up suggests I have a card up my sleeve when I don't. I never did. I always knew the duke's lie would eventually run its course. What I did not know was how long the sands of time would grant me before I had to surrender to the truth. Depending on your point of view, the best and worst possible circumstance was always that the dukedom died with me because before I met you it was inconceivable that I would ever consider passing that burden on." He reached for her hand but withdrew it at the last moment. "Now that I know my noble piety only stretches so far, and as much as it terrifies me to relinquish the fate of my tenants to Gervais, I cannot deny that a part of me is also relieved because I am so sick of all the lies. The pretense is exhausting."

"But . . ." She sighed, frustrated, and tried to think. There had to be something she could do. Something she had missed. As if he read her thoughts he shook his head.

"There is no but, Diana. That is the trouble with a hornet's nest. When it gets kicked, there are buzzing hornets everywhere. But these hornets are mine, just as the sting in the tail is also mine to contend with. I dragged you into this but I will not drag you down with me. I will turn myself in tomorrow, plead no prior knowledge to the deception, and pray for leniency. That is the only card I have left."

"I want to help you."

"No, Diana. You want to rescue me because that is what you do. But you really can't. Nobody can. If anything, if your part in any of this becomes public, if the authorities learn that we tried to circumvent justice being done, then I risk losing my freedom on top of everything else. Much better that I was on a quest to find the truth and once I did I surrendered to it. Or you'll be the one waving my prison ship goodbye at Tilbury."

He was right as he so often was, drat him. Any whiff that he had tried to perpetuate his father's lie would damn him in the eyes of the law and the public. Everyone enjoyed seeing a cheat brought to justice, and the higher the fall from grace the better. "You do not have to do that alone. I could . . ."

He pressed a finger to her lips, his smile sad. "Yes, I do." Giles did not need to repeat that he loved her because she saw it shimmering in his eyes. Felt the length and the breadth of it to the depths of her soul. "You have worked hard to get where you are and will not be the one to destroy all that because you feel a misguided sense of loyalty to me. I thought, in a moment of madness, I could ignore my conscience because I wanted there to be an us so badly it was worth it. Now I realize I love you too much to ruin your life with my scandal. That wouldn't be fair, so I have to do what is right."

"You think this is right?" She shook her head in denial. "I don't want to be free of you. I want to be with you, idiot."

"Maybe, once the dust is settled—"

"You are without a shadow of a doubt the most irritating man I have ever met. Once the dust is settled! The *dust*. Is *settled*! How dare you!" She was all done with tact and diplomacy. "Who decided you get to dictate the terms? I do not answer to you, Giles Sinclair! You made me fall in love with you—"

"You love me?" That admission made him smile as if he couldn't quite believe it.

She was too infuriated to pause and wagged her finger at him instead. "You made me throw all my plans of blessed spinsterhood out of the window, made me yearn for an eternity stuck with a vexing, flippant, annoying rogue like you, and now you rescind the offer and try to send me away?"

He was still smiling with awe and wonder. And stubborn regret. "Hopefully not forever. Just until I know you are safe from all Gervais's twisted machinations. He can do his worst to me, but I would rather die than give him any opportunity to hurt you. And he will hurt you. Be in no doubt of that. I saw it in his eyes and so did you." She had but Diana never cowed to bullies or threats. "He knew too much about you not to use it to get his twisted revenge."

"But we are missing something. I know it. I still have so many unanswered questions. Turn yourself in if you have to, but let me stay here so I can keep digging on your behalf."

He sighed. "Time has run out, Diana. I have to do this next part alone and I will find it all that much easier if I know you and your family are safe from harm. I need you to go, but if I could beg one final favor before we part company . . ." He did reach for her hand this time, not to hold but to caress reverently on the mattress for a moment before he tugged his away. "I would ask that the Sentinel writes the truth for me and that it goes to the presses the day you return to London whether the story has broken or not. Gervais can say what he wants about me and the duke—but I don't want him to paint my mother a harlot."

"I'll write it." She gave in to the urge to touch his face, brushing her fingers through his hair. "But I shall give it to Vee to deliver because I am not leaving you."

"But, Diana—" It was her turn to press her finger to his outraged lips.

"Giles, when have I ever listened to any of your sensible advice? I shall do what I think is for the best no matter what you have to say on the subject. Would you desert me if the tables were turned?" Of course he wouldn't. He was by her side irrespective of how ridiculous he thought her idea or how many times he gloated that he had told her so. He was steadfast and resolute. As reliable as he was vexing. An exceptional man in every sense.

"But the tables aren't turned and I cannot, in all good conscience—" She silenced him with a kiss then prodded him in his distracting, noble chest.

"I am afraid my decision is made—and I will not be swayed.

I love you and that is that. If it all goes to hell in a handcart, you can be assured that I know that you told me so and we shall honeymoon in Botany Bay together."

She watched a complicated array of emotions play across his handsome face. Emotions that started with joy that she returned his affections, relief that she wouldn't leave him alone, and then ran the gamut through gratefulness to guilt. Before the guilt got a foothold and he dug his heels in she kissed him again and kept on kissing him until he groaned against her mouth and kissed her back. "This discussion isn't done, Diana."

"It is for now, Giles." She looped her arms around his stubborn neck. "So shut up and kiss me."

Chapter Thirty

He tried to be noble—bless him.

Tried to be a gentleman. But Diana wouldn't let him. Each time he pulled away to end their kiss, she nibbled his ear or nuzzled his neck until his lips found his way back to hers where they belonged. His glaring lack of willpower where she was concerned empowered her to be bolder as the seconds ticked to minutes and then time became irrelevant.

He did not resist when she pushed him back on the mattress and allowed his hands to smooth over her curves when hers explored his chest over the soft linen. When her fingers dipped beneath the hem of his shirt to touch skin, he sighed against her mouth, his eyelids fluttered closed as she lifted the fabric from his body to allow her lips and tongue to follow the same path as her fingertips.

She marveled in the flat, hard planes of his abdomen, tracing the dark dusting of hair that arrowed through his navel upward with her eyes first, and then her palms, to the muscles of his chest. Reveling in the way his nipples puckered as her breath whispered over them; the strangled groan that rolled deep in his chest when her lips tasted them. Humbled by his trust as he lay passive beneath her curiosity. Intrigued by the impressive bulge in his straining breeches that seemed to grow bigger with every caress.

Needing more, Diana kissed him deeply. As their tongues tangled he dragged her body to lie atop his, his big hands splayed across her bottom, moaning his appreciation when she straddled his hips and their bodies touched as intimately as they could through the barrier of clothes.

Sensing he would do nothing without her express permission, she reached for his hand and guided it to the belt of her robe, then rolled, dragging him with her to give him the space to undo the knot.

He took his time untying it. Some of that, she realized, was to prolong the sweet agony, but the rest was due to his own nerves. His own clumsy fingers.

Because she overwhelmed him so.

The significance of what they were doing swirled alongside the desire in his eyes. The candlelit turning the few flecks in his irises molten when the belt finally gave and she wriggled her arms out of the sleeves and smiled up at him from the pillow.

In case he needed another blatant invitation, she pulled him down for another kiss, moaning her encouragement as his palms smoothed down her hip, down her thigh, and dipped beneath her nightgown to brush against the bare flesh of her leg. Then upward, with aching slowness, setting every nerve ending ablaze with nothing more than the single finger he traced over her skin.

Like a soft summer breeze he skimmed the curls at the apex of her thighs. Barely a touch but her body's reaction was intense. Her womb clenched with need. Nerves she had no idea she possessed throbbed, and her hips arched in protest as his fingers wandered to her stomach.

As if the wretch knew he was torturing her, his mouth found a different lazy trail to follow along her jaw, down her neck. It lingered far too long on her collarbone and she felt his smile against her breast before he kissed her aching nipple through the thin muslin.

Diana did not recognize the earthy, wanton sound which emanated from her throat. Never realized that she could make such a noise, until the hand that had ceased its exploration of her midriff slid beneath the fabric to cup her other breast and elicited an earthier, desperate, and scandalous response. One that caused her hips to grind shamelessly against his and the most feminine part of her body beg for them to be joined.

Her greedy fingers went to his waistband and fumbled with the buttons, and when they refused to comply with the speed she demanded, she brazenly learned the shape of him over his breeches while his mouth finally found her bare breast and she writhed against his sheets because she could barely stand the exquisite pain.

Then all at once she was writhing alone. Every fiber of her being mourning the solid weight of him above her. His touch. His kiss. His passion.

As her eyes refocused from their haze of lust, he was stood beside the bed. Both hands fisted. Every muscle tense. His breath sawing in and out as if he was fighting for control. He raked a shaking hand through his rumpled hair and tore his gaze from the exposed bottom half of her body as if he could not trust himself to look. "This is dangerous . . . *you* are dangerous." He turned his back to her. "For the love of God, cover yourself up, woman, and go to your own room before we both do something you'll regret."

You'll regret.

Not *he* would regret. That significant distinction delighted her.

He unraveled a fist and stared at the key, then marched toward the door to save them both. His hand was unsteady as he wrestled with the lock. Only when he had cracked the door ajar did he risk turning around. "You need to go. Grab some sleep before you leave at dawn."

When she didn't move he closed his eyes. "Please, Diana. I am begging you. If you love me, go."

She took her own sweet time standing then undulated toward him, feeling more powerful and more beautiful than she ever had in her life. Who knew she had it in her to be a seductress? To want to be seduced? It was a heady and thrilling revelation she fully intended to bask in.

As he risked looking at her again, convinced she was finally going to comply with one of his idiotic demands, she stopped dead barely a foot from him. "I do love you. With all my heart. That is why I will never go." Then smiled as she slipped the nightgown from her shoulders and wiggled until it fell in a puddle at her feet.

His Adam's apple bobbed and he swallowed.

Licked his lips.

"I don't want to ruin you."

"That's a shame, because I fully intend to ruin you, Giles."

His gaze raked her body as she walked naked to the door and clicked it closed. Stared helplessly at her outstretched hand for several moments until he took it and she led him back to the bed. Then hauled her into his arms and tumbled them both to the mattress.

This time when he kissed her he did not hold back; nor did she want him to. They were long past that point. She wanted him so much she feared she might die from the wanting if he didn't put her out of her misery soon.

But of course, the wretch did like to eke every bit of entertainment out of her desperation and insisted on kissing her everywhere. And gracious, did he worship every inch. He laved her breasts and teased her nipples until she growled her impatience, then still took his own sweet time working his way down her stomach. Kissing her navel. Her hip. The sensitive flesh at the crest of her thighs and then . . .

"Ohhhh . . ." She shuddered as his tongue did something languid and sinful between her legs. "Oh, Giles . . ." It was too delicious to rebel against. Too addictive to be missish about, so Diana sank back into the downy mattress and simply enjoyed it until it all got too overwhelming, and her wits began to desert her.

"At least I finally know where *right there* is." Every nerve ending she possessed clearly stemmed from that one tiny spot and instinctively she tensed against it. Fought it as she hovered on some invisible, unfamiliar precipice. "I've wondered about that since we overheard Lady Sewell and her fake Russian count in the pergola."

His deep chuckle against her body made her sigh with pleasure and grip the sheet. "Will you stop distracting me while I am trying to concentrate."

"I'm sorry . . . carry on . . . I was convinced I was made without all those accoutrements, that is all . . . I've always been so indifferent to that side of things . . . At least I thought I was but . . ." As if he sensed her panic he paused long enough to stare all along her nakedness and into her soul.

"Are you aware that when you are unsettled by something you either are as silent as the grave or babble like a brook?"

She was stark naked with a man between her legs! Of course she was unsettled. Albeit in a deliciously thrilling way. "And your point is?"

"No point. Merely an observation although I adore the juxtaposition." His gaze raked her body. "I also adore this view." His eyes flicked to her most private place. "Now, kindly stop distracting me and try to trust me. Just this once let me be in charge." His heated, knowing smile was reassuring. "I am so convinced you'll enjoy it, I am prepared to wager you might even swoon."

"I disapprove of swoon . . . ohhhh . . . *ohhhh* . . ." Any further conversation became impossible as he did things to her she had never known existed. Such sublime and seductive things that her hips strained beneath his lips and her body craved release.

She no longer felt any embarrassment to be so intimately bared. No longer cared that she was boneless. Shameless. Desperate for him.

Every kiss brought her closer. Every caress took her higher. As she moaned her pleasure she watched Giles. His dark eyes locked with hers while he loved her, swirling with so much desire it was visceral. She felt his adoration everywhere, because it shimmered off him in waves. She had never felt so feminine. So sensual. So powerful despite relinquishing all control. Never trusted another as much as she did him in that moment.

Then something wonderful happened to her body as she accepted that. Rejoiced in that inconceivable new truth. It tumbled over the edge and it pulsed and fizzed and melted into a deep, warm puddle of exquisite sensations that seemed to go on and on as she fell.

When they finally began to subside he was smiling down at her, his face inches from hers as his fingers played with her hair. His erection pressed against her womanhood, insistent but not the least bit threatening. The new intimacy between them as thrilling as it was destiny. "You should probably know that there's another *right there.*"

"I had a feeling that there might be." She slid her hands around his waist, filled them with his bottom. Reveling in the weight of him. The glory of him. "Show me."

"I would love to. I burn to but I need to tell you that I can't marry you yet, Diana. Not while everything is such a . . ."

"I do not recall asking you to." But he would when the time was right and that was enough for her. "In fact, I was the one who insisted on a long courtship, remember? However, I have decided I am not so keen on a chaste courtship, so I do insist you introduce me to the other *right there* and that you do so right away."

And he did. Edging slowly inside her with such considered and gentle tenderness that he took her breath away. Only this time, as the passion built and she lost her wits again, when Diana found herself once more on that unfamiliar precipice, he was right by her side as he always was. Telling her how much he loved her as he held her hand. And when she told him she loved him back, and would until her dying breath, they dived off the edge together.

Chapter Thirty-One

"I don't want to talk about my skeletons anymore. I am sick to the back teeth of them. I want to know about yours."

They hadn't slept. Giles hadn't wanted to waste a second on sleep when he was still resolute that she was leaving after breakfast.

He hadn't broached the subject yet. Hadn't wanted to spoil the precious, perfect last moments they had, even though time was very definitely running out and his delectable, passionate Hornet-Kicker wasn't likely to leave without a fight. "Start with the brute in the alleyway." Now that he was calm and had the wherewithal to recall all the jumbled things she had babbled before she plucked up the courage to tell him that she loved him. "Do I need to kill him the moment I return to town?"

She sighed, clearly weighing up whether or not to risk baring all of her soul, so he traced the tip of her naked breast to remind her that she had bared everything else and so had he.

"I had just turned seventeen and things at home were dire. My father was in a great deal of trouble. Of course, none of us knew quite what or who he was involved with but some dodgy characters kept hammering on our door. Every time someone came, he hid and told one of us to get rid of them. One of the most insistent was a debt collector. A greasy, meaty, leering fellow."

Unconsciously she shuddered and pulled the covers up, her lithe body suddenly tense beneath his fingers. "If I was the unfortunate one to open the door, he would demand the money but then lean and whisper that he would forget the debt if I paid it in kind."

Giles could tell by her expression that it wasn't her work the lecher had wanted as payment but he held his tongue and masked his fury, sensing she needed to trust him with the truth in her own way. "One night, my father came to visit me at work. I worked in a tavern for a while back then, amongst so many other things to make ends meet. It was an awful job. It wasn't so much the work I loathed but the customers, who would often try to take advantage so you had to be on your guard. Constantly. Not that my useless father cared. So long as he got my wages he never cared what dangers I put myself in. He had never visited me there before. Never visited me anywhere before as we never got on and only ever argued, so I should have listened to my instinct that he was up to no good. But I didn't. I agreed to take the shilling he gave me to the pawnshop to pay one of his stupid debts. Except when I got there, the shop was closed and the moneylender was awaiting me in the shadows."

"Your father sent you into a trap." Giles decided there and then that if Alfred Merriwell ever turned up again he would flay the flesh from his despicable bones and feed it to the dogs. He'd even buy a pack of dogs to feed it to.

She nodded. "He grabbed me. Dragged me farther into the alley and tried to force himself on me. Told me not to struggle and do what I had been sent to do—as had been agreed. Thankfully, all the randy patrons back at the tavern had forced me to learn a trick or two, and as he bent double clutching his bruised jewels I ran for my life. When I tackled my father about it he denied it, obviously."

"Obviously."

"But I knew he had turned a corner and realized he had gone from being a feckless, good-for-nothing drain on our resources to a real danger to the three of us, so I started digging into his business. Then used the truth of his crimes as blackmail. Threatened to spill all to Bow Street or one of the crooks he had double-crossed if he ever dared put one of us at risk again. Must have done such a good job of scaring him that he left us within days and . . . well . . . you know the rest."

"You rescued your sisters." Because of course she had. "And thus the roots of the suspicious, rescuing Sentinel were born."

She smiled at his perceptiveness. "My sisters don't know any of that. I never told either of them about the incident in the alleyway or my hand in pushing out our father."

"Why?"

She shrugged. "At the time Vee wore more rose-tinted spectacles than she does now and would never have believed him capable. I also felt guilty for landing Minerva with the burden of parenthood and plunging us into abject poverty." Then she sighed. "And, I suppose, I did not trust either of them to realize that even three dirt-poor young girls all alone in a world full of predators were better off without him."

"Thank you for entrusting me with it." He kissed the tip of her nose and when that wasn't anywhere near enough hauled her back into his arms one last time before he had to tell her she was most definitely going home until his mess was over. "Have I mentioned that I love you, harridan?"

She laughed against his lips. "Talk is cheap, and actions speak louder than words. I dare you to make me swoon again."

"A dare, is it? Then I accept, and gladly, because Giles Sinclair never shies away from a challenge." He burrowed under the bedcovers in search of her sensitive breast while she giggled and he groaned when someone rapped on the door.

"Bugger off, Dalton! I said after breakfast!"

"It's me. Vee. I know it's early, Giles, but I have had an epiphany and when I couldn't sleep I found Ffion in the ledgers and I am convinced it is significant, but I cannot find Diana anywhere." Before he remembered he had unlocked the damn thing in his pitiful attempt to be gentlemanly, the door swung open and the youngest Merriwell squeaked in horror at the sight of them entwined together in his tangled sheets.

"Oh my goodness! Oh my goodness!" She gaped in shock, squeezed her eyes closed, then spun around. "You've ruined my sister!"

"If it's any consolation she's ruined me right back." Giles winced at a mortified Diana. "And you did tell me to be the fly in her ointment."

Diana thumped him and buried her head under the covers while poor Vee buried hers in her hands. "I think your definition of a fly in the ointment differs significantly from mine."

"Why don't we meet you downstairs in the estate office? Give your sister and me time to put some clothes on." The covered lump beside him groaned.

"Yes, why don't I do that." Vee did not need to be asked twice and broke into an actual run in her haste to get away.

"Well, that was awkward."

Diana erupted from the blankets like a volcano. "You had to unlock the door, didn't you!"

He smiled sheepishly. "In my defense, I was trying to be noble at the time. Then you seduced me with the whole disappearing nightgown trick and I confess I forgot about the door."

She rolled her eyes, more embarrassed than peeved, and began to scramble around the room for her discarded clothes and it seemed rude not to watch such a splendid sight. Once her disappearing night-gown was back on and her robe knotted, she gathered up his clothes and threw them at him. "No smart remarks when we get downstairs. Leave me to handle Vee. At least in the short term." She smiled as she patted her burning cheeks. "Although you should probably polish your pistols in case she has already summoned the cavalry."

"I've never owned a pistol. I told you, Giles Sinclair is a lover not a fighter. A very thorough and diligent lover, too, as I hope you would agree."

Her green eyes smoldered for a moment at the memory. "You could always borrow Dalton's." And with that she left to face the firing squad first.

"I suppose you want an explanation?" Diana edged into the estate office where Vee was bashing about with ledgers, cringing from head to foot.

"There is no 'suppose' about it, Diana!" Another ledger slammed onto the pile, releasing a puff of ancient dust from the pages. "Seeing as you have apparently decided to ignore all my warnings and give all your apple tarts away gratis!" Her sister stomped to another shelf to destroy, refusing to look at her.

"I love him." Vee's fingers paused on the spine of a ledger. "I wish I didn't, I'm not quite sure how I allowed myself, but there it is. It seems I am not so immune to the opposite sex as I always believed. He claims to love me, too."

"He does." Vee sighed and turned, a wistful smile on her blushing face. "That is obvious and has been the entire time we've known him, but trust you to doubt it."

"I don't." Even though her suspicious head cautioned her against such folly. "Or at least I don't want to."

"Old habits die hard." Vee gestured to the table and they sat, smiling as they both patted their blushing cheeks. "You've always been a tough nut to crack. Harder than both me and Minerva when we all had the same upbringing."

"I am not entirely sure that we did."

Her little sister frowned then nodded. "That is a fair comment. You both shielded me from the worst of it."

"Perhaps too much, as you thought our father walked on water." If they had to have an awkward conversation, it might as well be painfully awkward. She and Vee had always clashed a little. They had always been as different as chalk and cheese.

Vee digested that for a moment before shaking her head. "I *wanted* him to walk on water, Diana. But deep down I always knew that he didn't. That he was a wastrel with no morals and even fewer principles. The way he left you and Minerva to cope with everything always bothered me, and if I willed him back it was to relieve that burden. I foolishly thought that if I wished it hard enough, mined through all his flaws to the good that I prayed lurked beneath them somewhere, I could redeem him into becoming the father I always dreamed of."

"That is where we differ. Where we have always differed. I always wanted him gone."

"I know that, too." Vee reached across the table to take her hand. "And it turns out your way was better for all of us although I didn't see it at the time and resented you for it. Blamed you for it." At Diana's frown she shrugged. "I know about the man in the alleyway and the threats you made to Papa afterward." She smiled without humor. "The walls were thin in Clerkenwell, and I have always been a light sleeper."

"You knew I sent him away." That certainly explained why she and Vee had always butted heads.

Her sister's ragged laughter surprised her. "Even then I knew he just needed an excuse to justify leaving. I tried not to believe he was that mercenary, tried to give him the benefit of the doubt because that is what I do—or what I did because I was young and immature and so desperate for us to be a family that it was easier to ignore the truth than acknowledge it and grow up. For years I tried to convince myself that I had misheard that altercation despite remembering it verbatim. When that didn't work, I convinced myself that his denial that night was sincere and that you only refused to hear it because you and he had never got on. But then I also saw how bad you felt for Minerva and me afterward, how hard you worked to support us all, and I knew, deep down and despite all my childish and desperate denial, that you acted in our best interests. Unlike him, you have always acted in our best interests. For a long time now I've wanted to thank you for it. For being brave enough to stand up to him and to save us. Our father was a hideous man—a lying, cheating, shameful excuse of one—but I have also long been of the opinion that you shouldn't use that as an excuse to guard your heart against all men. You deserve to be happy, Diana. And despite my mortification at catching you both . . ." She flapped her hand blushing furiously. "I am also delighted that you have found the man of your dreams. Giles is a good one."

Diana couldn't help smiling. "He is exceptional."

"He is. And I cannot wait to be your bridesmaid!" Vee giggled. "At the moment, I am always the bridesmaid and never the bride."

Diana winced. "About that . . ."

Chapter Thirty-Two

"It was something Gervais said." A bright-red Vee couldn't meet his eyes as she deposited another ledger on the pile. "About your father's love of Welsh cake and his particular weakness for Ffion Jones." She kept glaring at Diana, though, as the sisters had clearly had words. So many they had been sequestered in the estate office for an hour while he paced in purgatory outside. "And I knew I had seen the name somewhere in one of the staff lists. But here's the thing . . ."

She tapped the entry, accidentally glanced at him, and then clearly wished she were dead. Or he was. "Diana asked me to search back a decade, but the first mention of Ffion goes back farther. She started working at Harpenden Hall as a kitchen maid in 1777, straight from the orphanage in Presteigne when she was apparently only fourteen and was dismissed at the age of twenty-one. Gervais did say your father had always wanted poor little orphaned Ffion Jones—even as a boy."

"He did." It was obvious the find had piqued Diana's inquisitive, suspicious mind as she went to fetch her own pile of copious notes to rifle through them. "You might be onto something, Vee . . ." She quickly scanned several pages then slapped one with the back of her hand. "It fits!"

"What fits?" As per usual he was struggling to keep up. Although in his defense Giles hadn't slept a wink thanks to his splendiferous roll around his mattress with the most vexing Merriwell. He was still basking in the afterglow and so undone by the miraculous knowledge that she loved him that he could barely focus on anything else.

Diana loved him.

She.

Loved.

Him.

That was just . . .

"All the dates fit!" She spread her notes out on the desktop above the ledgers. "The duke was born in 1764, which would have made him just thirteen when Ffion began to work here. He would have been twenty when your grandfather dismissed her!"

"And?"

"And that coincides with his outraged winter in Wales. He hadn't reached his majority when he came back and still 'married the bride the old man picked out in the end.'" She slapped her notes again. "I'll lay money he went after Ffion."

It all made sense, he supposed, but he still couldn't see the significance. "So he had a fling with the kitchen maid and rekindled it later."

"But what if the affair never ended?"

"So he kept a mistress? Half the married gentlemen of the *ton* keep a mistress." At Vee's glare Giles pulled a face. "I am not suggesting that I will, for my heart is pure and my intentions honorable and your sister has thoroughly ruined me for all other women—but it is hardly a surprise the duke did when he loathed his duchess. I fail to see how this changes anything. I am still his by-blow whichever way you look at it."

"You've got visitors apparently." Dalton limped in without knocking with his customary insolence and still shrugging on his coat. "And they've brought luggage according to that gorgon Townsend, who is now in the full throes of a conniption because they apparently need both breakfast and rooms and you neglected, once again, to tell her that you had invited company."

"If I haven't invited anyone, who the blazes are they?"

Dalton shrugged as if that important detail hadn't crossed his mind. "All I know is I had my bacon ripped out of my hands and was told to fetch you."

"Who calls at bloody seven in the morning?"

His surly butler shrugged again. "Ours is not to reason why, ours is but to do. All I know is I've been sent to fetch you and then carry up all their bleedin' luggage because it's the footman's day off."

"Forget the luggage and ready the carriage for the ladies." As bizarre as it was that the authorities would have brought luggage, Giles wasn't prepared to take the chance. The luggage might well be Gervais's, with the scoundrel standing by outside to see his nephew dragged away in irons before he took possession of the house.

As if she read his mind, Diana's hands went straight to her hips. "We've been over this and I am not leaving."

"And if she isn't going, neither am I." Vee folded her arms, the defiant tilt of her chin a mirror image of her sister's. "Somebody needs to protect Diana's virtue."

"First." He jabbed his finger in the direction of Diana. "Yes, you are and that is that, and second." He stabbed it toward Vee. "I am afraid that horse has bolted." He was about to instruct them to stay put while he investigated, when they barged past with Dalton in tow.

"It had better not be Gervais!" Diana was on the warpath, her fists clenched and ready to swing.

"Or that cocky idiot Galahad!" Vee wrestled a pike from a suit of armor without breaking her stride while Dalton locked his mangled hand around his pistol and Giles had to sprint to keep up. Like Amazons they burst through the drawing room door ready to do battle on his behalf and stopped dead.

Because it was neither the authorities nor his evil uncle who awaited him. It was blasted Mr. and Mrs. Regis and their stuttering daughter Dahlia who stared at the weapons wide-eyed while her teacup clattered into its saucer.

Giles wrestled in front and gave the others a warning glare before he forced a smile. "Mr. Regis. Mrs. and Miss Regis." As Vee tried and failed to hide the six-foot Tudor pike behind her back, he tried to make a joke out of it. "My apologies for the unorthodox welcome but we had an intruder the other evening and it is better to be safe than sorry. What an unexpected and *early* surprise."

"The early bird catches the worm, Your Grace, and as we overnighted a mere fifteen miles away at an inn that failed to meet our high expectations, we thought you would not mind us encroaching on your hospitality for breakfast as well."

"As well as what?"

"Our weekend visit. You did invite us, after all. At our convenience as I recall."

It was on the tip of Giles's tongue to tell Mr. Regis that he had invited himself before he told him in the strongest possible terms that now was not the least bit convenient—but before he spoke, his upstart of a butler stepped forward.

"Miss Dahlia." Beside him, Dalton sighed the name like a benediction. "How lovely to see you again."

Giles blinked at him in shock, then was stunned to see Dahlia smiling soppily back. "Hello, Dalton. How are you?" Miraculously, she managed to say that without a single stuttered *um* or *er* or frantic glance to her father.

"All the better for seeing you, Miss Dahlia." It might well be Giles's imagination—or his distinct lack of sleep—but there seemed to be a frisson in the air. Clearly Diana sensed it, too, as when their eyes met, she cocked one dark brow in question. "And good day to you, too, Mr. Regis. Mrs. Regis." Dalton bowed his head politely, his only eye never leaving Dahlia's smiling face—and it was actually a rather pretty face when she smiled. "Allow me to show you to your rooms." He swept his arm toward the door and glared at Giles as if this unwelcome visit was a fait accompli simply because the insubordinate rascal had decreed it. "You have a good hour to freshen up before breakfast is served."

As they all followed him, Giles called him back to hiss in his ear. "They cannot stay!"

"I am merely getting them out of the way while we formulate a plan, Your Grace, seeing as we currently don't appear to have one."

"Or we could simply tell them to leave, which is what I am going to do while you ready the carriage as instructed. Because I can assure you that I do have a plan."

"We've been through this, Giles." Of course Diana had the ears of a bat and took umbrage at that whispered exchange, so he closed his eyes and prayed for strength before he put his manly foot down.

"Diana—I am afraid my decision is made and—"

"Finish that sentence and I guarantee they will be your last words on earth." Two furious green eyes narrowed inches from his face.

"Like I said, I'll get the Regises and their lovely daughter out of the way." Dalton limped to where Dahlia and her family eavesdropped with undisguised interest and ushered them out of the door just as Mrs. Townsend stormed back through it with a face like thunder.

"You have another unannounced guest, Your Grace!" Her lips were so pursed, she looked ready to blow on a bugle. "A Mr. Cribbage. I have left *him* in the hallway as I am running out of places to put them all."

"My solicitor is here? In Shropshire?" That couldn't be good. He flicked a worried glance toward Diana as they both set off in his direction with Vee hot on their heels while Mrs. Townsend scurried behind.

"Am I expected to provide him with a room and breakfast also at such short notice? Because Your Grace might have taken the trouble to inform me." He ignored his housekeeper to rush toward his lawyer.

"What has happened?"

Mr. Cribbage stared pointedly at their audience. "I have news, Your Grace. Information I felt too delicate to entrust to the post."

Mr. Cribbage stared warily at Diana and Vee as they followed Giles into the drawing room.

"It is all right—the Misses Merriwell know everything. Warts and all." Giles gestured for the man to sit. "To be honest with you, Mr. Cribbage, I am rather relieved to see you. Events have taken a bit of a dark turn." Without any preamble, he brought his solicitor up to speed before Dalton arrived with some tea. "So before I and my loyal accomplices are arrested, I have decided to turn myself in this afternoon. Pip Gervais to the post and pray for leniency."

Mr. Cribbage had silently frowned through most of the convoluted tale, and his bushy gray brows were now entirely knitted into one. "If you do not mind me saying, I feel that might be a tad hasty, Your Grace."

"That is exactly what I said." Diana perched on the arm of his chair to wrap a reassuring arm about his shoulders before she realized that that was a rather proprietorial and wifely thing to do. "I suspect there is more to find."

"And I suspect there is the slimmest chance His Grace might well be legitimate after all."

"I think I am going to need more biscuits." Giles slumped back in the chair. Shocked but too overwhelmed by all the twists and turns to allow himself to believe it while the solicitor pulled out a tatty notebook.

"My father had rather a fractious professional relationship with your grandfather in much the same way as I had with yours. His legal advice was often ignored. From what I discovered in our firm's archive, your grandfather was even more unreasonable than your father. So unreasonable, in fact, that my father took to documenting all their conversations for his own protection, as the duke had a tendency to think he was above the law."

He pulled his pince-nez out of his pocket and clipped them to his nose. "Most are, as I am sure you can imagine, mundane matters pertaining to the estate, but while hunting for any mention of Gervais, I stumbled across this from March 1784." Mr. Cribbage cleared his throat to read. "*His Grace came to the office quite agitated without an appointment desirous of information regarding the laws of annulment after an elopement. I informed His Grace that such things are never easy to obtain, especially if both parties freely entered the union—no matter how disadvantageous the match. However, if, as His Grace intimated, the marriage was clandestine because it occurred over the border and one of the parties was under the legal age of majority, a petition could be raised citing that the marriage took place without parental consent and request that it be rendered null and void as a result.*"

Diana squeezed Giles's limp hand. "That coincides with the duke's outraged winter in Wales." He nodded but still seemed too stunned to speak, so she did. "What happened next, Mr. Cribbage?"

"Nothing. Not another mention in the notes, nor could I find a record of any such petition being raised or an annulment granted to anyone from your grandfather's close acquaintance. But a few months hence there are a flurry of notes about your father's upcoming marriage settlement to the woman we all believed was your mother. From what I can make out, it all happened very fast and at your grandfather's instigation."

"So if we assume he did marry Ffion in the early part of that same year . . ."

Mr. Cribbage nodded as he saw the significance dawn in her

face. "Then he was still married to Ffion when he married the duchess, and still married to her when they had His Grace eleven years later."

"The duke was a bigamist?" Giles, bless him, was struggling to take it all in.

Mr. Cribbage threw up his hands. "He *might* have been a bigamist. We'd need to find evidence of the initial marriage to prove it—but if we can, we also prove you are the legal heir. A clandestine marriage can only be challenged if both parties are alive. It cannot be voided now that they are both dead."

"A needle in a haystack then!" Giles shot out of his chair to pace.

"At least we know it is over the border." That was enough of a dangling thread for Diana to tug on. "Most over-the-border marriages occur at Gretna Green, surely?"

"Assuming it's the Scottish border and not the Welsh one twenty miles away."

Mr. Cribbage grinned at Vee, impressed. "You are very astute, young lady, and you are quite correct. Simply because a marriage is classed as clandestine doesn't necessarily mean it happened in Scotland. There are many other ways to get the deed done. If Ffion was born in Wales, was of age, and was known to the parish, the banns could have been read there well away from the Duke of Harpenden's notice and therefore have been uncontested—even if His Grace's father was still below the age of majority. At twenty, it was perfectly legal for him to marry."

"But young enough to have had the marriage contested, and perhaps naive enough to believe it was void if that was what his overbearing father told him." Mr. Cribbage seemed as excited by it all as Diana.

"Ffion grew up an orphan in Presteigne, so that strikes me as a good starting point as any. If we draw a blank there, we head to Gretna."

"And hope we find our needle before Gervais gets his slimy hands on it." Giles was still pacing.

"If you want my opinion—"

"I really don't, Dalton!"

Dalton rolled his eye and carried on regardless. "Seeing as we already know Gervais has a talent for following you, I could high-tail it to Gretna Green this morning with the carriage as if you are all in it while you all race to Presteigne after. If what you seek is there, the quest is done. If it isn't I'll still have first claim on the truth in Scotland before that grog-snarfing scallywag Gervais is any the wiser."

"That is actually not a bad idea, Giles." Diana caught his hand and smiled. "Why don't I have some horses saddled?"

"Your Grace, I am at my wit's end!" The door crashed against the wall as Mrs. Townsend slammed through it again. "If you had planned a house party, it is beyond the pale that you neglected to tell me! Were I the son of God, and able to perform miracles, I could conjure a banquet out of five loaves and some fishes, but I only have a quarter of a side of bacon and the butcher's shop is closed today so I am at a loss how to feed the five thousand!"

Giles blinked at her and threw up his hands, looking ready to explode himself. "I have no idea what you are talking about, woman!"

Mrs. Townsend pointed a quaking finger to the hallway and looked ready to burst into tears at any moment. "You have more visitors. Four of them, and I have no earthly clue what I am supposed to do with them."

"I swear this place is busier than Piccadilly Circus!" Giles started toward the door then froze when a livid Hugh strode through it.

Chapter Thirty-Three

"You lying, duplicitous snake!" Hugh grabbed him by the lapels. "You gave me your word you had no designs on Diana, and all the while you were plotting your seduction!"

"I really wasn't plotting anything of the sort, old boy."

"He really wasn't, Hugh." Diana rushed to intervene but was blocked by the twin juggernauts of Minerva and Olivia, who were equally as incandescent with rage. "I insisted on coming to help him because Giles is in trouble. Huge trouble. Isn't he, Vee?"

The youngest Merriwell's gaze darted between both her sisters, her loyalties clearly split. "He is in trouble. That's the truth."

"Really?" Hugh pushed him away then shook a letter in the air before he shoved it at him. "Then how do you explain this?"

Giles winced as he scanned Vee's neat handwriting, informing whoever found the letter not to panic that she and Diana were not at home, because she had thwarted their plans to run away together to Shropshire and had accompanied them to act as their chaperone instead.

"Why would Diana need a chaperone if you had no intentions toward her—*honorable or otherwise*." Hugh spat Giles's reassurances back at him with such venom his eyes bulged while a stony Jeremiah loomed behind him, his jaw clenched so tight it was a wonder he still had any teeth. "What the bloody hell is running away together the second my back is turned if it is not dishonorable? And what sort of an effective chaperone is an eighteen-year-old girl around a practiced seducer like you?"

"Not a particularly effective one, as it turned out." Vee pulled a face as Diana glared. "Well, that is the truth, too, isn't it? Especially after I caught the pair of you this morning?"

"And where did you catch them?" Minerva had a maniacal glint in her eyes. One that stated quite clearly that Giles's days were numbered. It was so ferocious that Vee caved instantly under the intense pressure.

"In his bedchamber. In the altogether." She covered her face with her hands as if she was picturing it all over again, only the glowing tips of her ears visible as she hammered in the final nail. "He ruined her but says that he won't marry her."

"Yet!" screamed Diana, clarifying. "He is being noble and trying to protect me from the scandal."

"Noble?" Jeremiah's growl dripped menace. "If you ask me, he made you the scandal, Diana." He took several intimidating steps forward, his fingers flexing as if he was pre-warming them before he wrapped them around Giles's neck. "And now I am going to pummel him!"

Hugh stopped his stepfather's determined advance with his gloved palm. "You can have what's left of the Judas after I've finished with him." He turned back to Giles, his face contorted as he peeled off the glove and tossed it to the floor. "Choose your weapon!"

Giles stared at the crumpled leather, which had landed with the first two fingers poking upright as if even the glove were horrified by what he had done. "I know this all looks bad—"

"Bad! *Bad!* You've ruined my sister and refuse to do the right thing!" Minerva grabbed him by the lapels and shook.

"I haven't refused. I adore the harridan. I've loved her since the moment she lambasted me with her first pithy set-down and really cannot wait to spend all eternity shackled to the prickly minx. She feels the same." He smiled at her and she smiled back. "Don't you?"

"He's my fungus."

Giles grinned and blew her a kiss as everyone else frowned, touched by such a gushing public declaration from a woman who liked to pretend she had no heart but actually had the biggest one he knew. "And I am the fly in her ointment."

"Please never say that again." Vee winced as she covered her face.

"So propose to the girl!" Olivia screamed this.

"I will—eventually—you have my word."

"Your word is worthless!" Hugh jabbed his chest with his index finger. "As this debauched situation confirms!"

Diana broke free and rushed to his side. "To be fair to Giles, he was a perfect gentleman until I convinced him not to be."

"She was very persuasive." That comment earned him a jab in the ribs from her.

"And it was also me who stipulated a long courtship." She threaded her arm through his, selfless and loyal to the last.

"At least long enough that all the skeletons currently rattling in my cupboard are out of it. Which hopefully won't be that long."

"Long! *Long!*" His friend's eyes bulged again. "That isn't good enough, damn it, and I demand satisfaction!"

"Look . . . so long as the constable doesn't arrive beforehand to drag me away and send me to Botany Bay, I promise you'll be first in line to shoot me, so would you mind letting me ride to Presteigne first to find out once and for all whether I am the fraudulent, bastard son of a duke or a bigamist's legitimate heir?" Giles spread his palms, imploring. "Only this whole estate depends on me, old boy, the sands of time are running out, and I have to find all the answers before my evil uncle Gervais destroys it and steals my ducal ermine. And most especially before he exacts all the pent-up and petulant revenge he harbored for my father and grandfather on the love of my life instead."

"Diana's in trouble, too?" Straightaway they all stiffened as their loyalty to her overrode everything else.

"Only by proxy." He shot her an exasperated look. "And only if she refuses to listen to reason and confesses like she has threatened."

"To what?"

As Hugh's expression turned from incensed to baffled, Giles shrugged. "It is a very long and convoluted story, which I can explain on the way if you want to come?" He swung the dented pocket watch he now always wore in the air between them like a pendulum. "Only the clock is ticking, and Diana and I really need to go."

"So do I," said Vee, rushing to stand beside them. "We've worked too hard and gone too far to fall at the last furlong and we cannot let Gervais win."

It was late afternoon by the time their two carriages trundled back to Harpenden Hall. Diana and Giles had been forced to travel in separate ones to Presteigne, not so much for propriety's sake, but more that between them they could bring all the others up to speed. However, once they had searched parish records and discovered that the page that should have listed all the marriages from the winter of 1784 had been torn out, she had been allowed to return in his to console him. Albeit under the beady, furious gazes of Hugh and Minerva.

She had tried to buoy him with the irrefutable facts that now leaned heavily in his favor. First, the rector of St. Andrews bore witness to the fact that the page had been there before he had entrusted the register to a gentleman only hours before they arrived. From his detailed description of his faded blond hair and unusual pale-blue eyes, that gentleman was without a doubt Gervais. Second, if the page had been removed by Gervais then its contents were dangerous to his blatantly unlawful quest to claim Harpenden. And third, there were still the Bishop's Transcripts, which Mr. Cribbage was racing to the diocese to consult, even though the lawyer wasn't convinced they were quite as reliable a contingency as Gervais had made out. So all was not lost. She firmly believed that. Giles, on the other hand, was less convinced as he alighted the carriage with his shoulders slumped.

"All I know for certain is that the duke always resented me because he obviously blamed me for killing the love of his life."

Although that wasn't his fault, she knew that was probably the truth, too. "What you need is a nice plate of biscuits and some sleep." Sensing that they needed some space, their chaperones hung back as they walked toward the house. "Then you will see the wood for the trees and the light at the end of the tunnel. We are going to win this, Giles. I promise."

There was no humor in his halfhearted smile. There were

shadows under his dark eyes. His distracting broad shoulders were slumped, and his gait was heavy. "I just want it over, Diana."

"I know, and it will be. Soon."

"My nerves are so frayed that . . ." He saw Mr. and Mrs. Regis waiting for him at the front door with Mrs. Townsend and groaned. "What the blazes are they still doing here? I told Dalton to send them packing before we left."

"Did you all enjoy your excursion, Your Grace?" Mr. Regis's smile was tight at the sight of them arm in arm, then grew tighter still at everyone else spilling out of the carriages and headed their way. "Where is my daughter?"

"How should I know?" Poor Giles had lost the ability to feign politeness.

"But she left with you. Hours ago."

"As you can plainly see, she did not." He gestured behind him but did not stop walking. "And in case you are too thick-skinned to see it, now is not a good time for you to be here, either, so kindly pack your bags and go. And please do not come back. I am sure your daughter is a lovely young woman and I feel dreadful that my father let her down by dying but she is not for me, no matter how many times you try to thrust her under my nose." Giles turned to Mrs. Townsend, who was doing her best to blend into the shrubbery. "Locate Miss Dahlia and then dispatch the lot of them, please. Then bring me biscuits. All the biscuits."

Diana smiled at them all. "It has been a fraught morning. Mrs. Townsend, could you have some tea brought to the drawing room as soon as you have assisted these lovely people with their packing."

"We will not be leaving without our daughter!" Mr. Regis

bristled with indignation. "I demand to know what you have done with her!"

"Have you checked her room?" Giles was on the cusp of exploding. "Perhaps she has locked herself in there to escape you. I know I would have if I were her!"

"Allow me," said the housekeeper, clearly eager to escape. Then she promptly scurried up the stairs to do just that while Giles stalked to the drawing room and flung himself on the sofa.

They all filed in behind him and sat in awkward silence until Mrs. Townsend returned with her eyes wide. "I am afraid Miss Regis is gone."

"Of course she is gone," said her father. "She left in her riding habit beaming from ear to ear."

"By gone . . ." Mrs. Townsend shuffled from foot to foot. "I mean completely gone. The wardrobe is empty and all her clothes are missing . . . but I did find this." She held out the letter to Giles, only to have it snatched from her fingers by Mr. Regis.

He scanned it then turned purple and lunged at Giles as if he was going to strangle him. While Jeremiah and Hugh restrained him, Olivia picked up the missive, read it, pulled a face. "Miss Dahlia has gone to Gretna Green with Dalton, where they apparently intend to kill two birds with one stone. They have been in love for months—or so it says here—and are tired of keeping it a secret."

Unexpected news that seemed to cheer Giles up. "I knew he had a paramour and thought I sensed a frisson between them. But Dalton and Dahlia . . . who knew?"

"Oh my poor girl!" Mrs. Regis flapped in a panic. "She's been lured away by a pirate!"

"Not according to this." Olivia handed the woman the letter and wrapped a comforting arm around her shoulder. "They forged their alliance after the duke died—when Mr. Regis kept calling at Giles's house—then met in secret daily after, where one thing led to another and because the perfect opportunity presented itself and because they may soon be blessed by the patter of tiny feet, she has decided to take matters into her own hands."

"Good for Dahlia," said Giles, not helping at all. "Although what she sees in Dalton is a mystery, to be sure." Then he frowned. "Although I am not sure the world is ready for more Daltons when I have always thought one was bad enough. But at least I know why he was so determined to go to Gretna Green. Something makes sense, anyway."

"Your Grace, you have another visitor." A footman poked his head around the door and Giles nodded.

"Of course I do."

"A Mr. Galahad Sinclair."

Chapter Thirty-Four

A very different Galahad Sinclair was awaiting them in the Great Room than the one they had seen before. This one looked older. Stood with more confidence. Smiled as Giles, Diana, and Vee burst in furious. Before the youngest Merriwell launched at him, he raised his palms in surrender.

"I come in peace, Miss Venus, so put away your claws." Then he turned to Giles. "And I come bearing gifts, cousin." He held out a satchel.

Wary, Giles took it and peeked inside then retrieved a piece of paper not quite believing what he was seeing. "This is the page from the parish register." As Diana and Vee huddled close to read it, he spotted the entry he so desperately needed to see.

Gerald George Gregory Sinclair of the parish of Mayfair and Ffion Jones of this parish Married in this church by Banns on this twenty-eighth day of February in the year one thousand seven hundred and eighty-four.

"I don't understand." Because Giles didn't. This single sheet of paper exonerated him but labeled Gervais as the pretender. The duke had even used his real name. No ambiguous St Clair like they had found in Llanyre, or Saint Clair like his ancient Norman ancestors, but *Sinclair*. Loud and proud.

"My father thinks we burned it, so he's celebrating with a whore back at the inn because he thinks there is no copy—to either this or the birth record you already have."

"Why does he think that?"

"Because that is what I told him when I returned from the bishop. It never occurred to him to check that there actually had been a huge fire at the diocese fifteen years ago that destroyed everything." Galahad shrugged, taking in all the portraits on the walls. "But he also assumed I was too stupid to switch that page before I tossed it on the fire and that I am on his side when I'm not." He stared at Giles levelly. "I never was."

"Now I really don't understand." But by the glint in her canny eyes Diana was already beginning to make sense of it.

"He duped Gervais."

The young man nodded. "I thought you knew. I didn't realize till that night I let you find me that you were clueless about my involvement, and I didn't dare risk telling you at that point because neither of us had anything and I needed her to find it." He flicked his gaze to Diana. "Once you found Ffion, he remembered who she was and where she came from, so we got there at dawn and found the missing piece of the puzzle before you did. Prior to that, all we really had was the letter."

Galahad flicked his head at the satchel again. "That's in there, too, but it's redundant now. The embittered words of another one of my father's many women who also happened to be the lady's maid of the duchess. Words that claim she overheard her telling you that you were the duke's bastard and the real son of a harlot."

"Agatha." Giles shook his head stunned. "The duke dismissed her the same day the duchess died. I've always wondered what happened to her."

"From what I've been able to gather they corresponded all the time while the duchess was alive. Him promising her they'd be together as soon as he could find a way to get her across the ocean just so that he could keep a pair of spying eyes in your father's house. When she was turfed out of that house, my guess is he had no further use for her. I have no idea what made him reach out to her again. He doesn't confide in me about anything—unless he is roaring drunk and I can keep him lucid long enough to pry it out of him. He especially doesn't discuss his women—he's too busy trying to convince me he loved my mother even though he made her life a living hell. When he was home, that is. Which as I am sure you can imagine wasn't often once he'd spent all her money."

"Was?"

Galahad offered Vee a tight smile. "She died. Last year. And my dear old absent pappy came home to pick over the carcass of what was left. Then that letter arrived and here we are. Only he expected to have plenty of time to gather his evidence, and I thought I had plenty of time to beat him to it and destroy it, so your father's death threw a stick in the spokes, I don't mind telling you. But we got there in the end and justice prevailed."

"Justice or revenge? Or perhaps you want something else, Galahad?" Suspicious to her core, Diana stared at the young man with narrowed eyes.

"If I was about to blackmail my cousin or extort money out of him for the truth, I'd have to be an idiot to have given him it all up front—and in front of a pair of witnesses, too. I'd also have been an idiot to have written to my long-lost uncle Gerald before we came, tipping him off about what my father knew." Which finally explained what had sent the duke into a panic. "Or to break that window or snoop around your garden with a lantern or drip you all that information along the way. But contrary to what you all might think . . ." Galahad made a point of staring at Vee. "I am no idiot though it's served me well to act as one."

He smiled, his emotive eyes dancing. "And I should imagine that you of all people know that sometimes justice and revenge are the same sides of the coin, Miss Diana. I confess I've never really thought of any benefit to this beyond being the one to tell my feckless father just how much I hate him before I cut him out of my life altogether. This is a day I've waited for, for as long as I can remember, and good should always triumph over evil, don't you think?"

"What are your plans once you've delivered the news?" Like Giles, Diana was starting to like his new relation.

Galahad shrugged at her question. "I confess I never thought that far ahead but I'm a resourceful fellow, so something will come up." He inclined his head as he smiled, clearly chuffed to bits that his plan had succeeded. "So I shall wish you a good day, Miss Diana . . . Miss Venus." His eyes lingered on the youngest Merriwell before he held out his hand to Giles. "It was a pleasure to meet you, Your Grace. When one has been as starved of family as I have, it's nice to finally meet some." Giles knew how that felt.

"At least we share a grandmother." Galahad pointed to the line of portraits and shook his head. "But as I suspected, none of these illustrious relatives are mine, any more than they are my father's. Not that that stopped him trying to take what wasn't his—and not that that ever stopped him."

"Why do you say that?"

"Didn't you ever wonder why our grandfather had no time for Gervais? Why he and our grandmother were estranged? Why you Sinclairs all seem to have the same coloring and features yet my father doesn't?" Galahad stared up at the group portrait and the golden cherub so at odds with every other face on the wall. "He was more of a bastard than anyone and knew it, too. Because his mother often told him the twenty-fifth Duke of Harpenden killed his real daddy in a duel." The young man laughed. "It took a whole bottle of cognac to prize that juicy detail out of him. A waste of money now that I see it plain as day on these walls."

As Galahad turned to leave, Giles caught his arm. "Stay for some tea. Meet the rest of the family."

"Family?" For the first time his cousin looked baffled. "I thought we were two of the only three Sinclairs left?"

He recognized the hint of longing in the young man's eyes. The buried need to belong somewhere, hidden beneath all the pride that masked the ache of being alone. Uncared for. Unloved. Lost. Lonely. Giles knew how that felt, too, and was glad he didn't anymore.

"Well, they are my adopted family, really. At least they are until I can convince this harridan to marry me." He grabbed Diana's hand as he led his cousin to the door. "And all a pain in the backside just like her. Can you believe she intends to insist on a long courtship? It is as if she has no respect for my dukedom at all."

"That is because I much preferred him as a baker's son and

have no desire to be a duchess." Diana threw open the door only to find Olivia listening at the keyhole, with Hugh, Minerva, and Jeremiah suddenly pretending they hadn't been even though they were stood right behind.

Olivia, of course, was entirely unrepentant. "You probably should have thought about that before you allowed him to see you in the altogether, dear." She skewered Giles with her glare. "Now that I take it that there are no outstanding impediments preventing you from doing the right thing, I shall expect you to do it with all haste."

He squeezed Diana's hand. "I'm game if you are."

As the woman of his dreams blinked, Olivia was outraged. "With a proper proposal, Giles Sinclair." She pointed to the floor. "Done in the proper way. At least pay some lip service to the expectations of propriety!"

It wasn't exactly the circumstances he had envisioned for a proposal, but then again he had never envisioned being able to propose, and there was a sense of irony about the occasion that appealed to his sense of the ridiculous. So he took her hand and was in the process of going down on bended knee when another fist hammered on his door. Giles threw up his hands in despair.

"I don't know anybody else, so who the bloody hell is it this time?"

Mrs. Townsend, who had thus far done a very good job of blending into the paneling, scurried to open it.

"I have an urgent message for Miss Diana Merriwell." The courier guarded the missive to his chest when his housekeeper tried to take it. "It is for her eyes only."

Dark brows furrowed, Diana tugged her fingers from his to

take it, then grinned as she read the contents. "I was right! I knew I would be. My gut is never wrong."

"What is it?"

She looked positively sinful as she undulated toward him like the cat who had got the cream. "Lady Caroline Derbyshire—or rather Sister Caroline—is alive and well and living in a nunnery in Kent. She is also happy to bear witness that a certain Gervais Guillaume Sinclair abducted her and tried to force her into a marriage in order to get his grubby hands on her dowry. I asked Charlie to check and he came up trumps." She handed the letter to Galahad. "My gift to you, as I think you will enjoy giving him that bad news most of all."

"Thank you—unless you want to come, too? Make it our first family outing." Galahad grinned at her and then at the strangers who were eyeing him with interest. "After you've been proposed to, of course. Consider it an engagement present."

All eyes swiveled to them and he saw the panic in her lovely eyes, and knew exactly why it was there.

"Diana Merriwell." Giles dropped to his knees and stared deep into her eyes. "My Goddess of the Hunt, Hunter of the Truth, and Fearsome Kicker of Hornets—for some inexplicable reason I love you, and much to your chagrin, you love me, too. I know that scares you, and heaven only knows I don't deserve you, but we both know that there is nobody else we would each like to spend eternity with and, quite frankly, nobody else who could stand us enough to want to. So marry me. Today . . . tomorrow . . . in twenty years if you feel I deserve to be tortured for that long. I do not care so long as you say yes." He stood and tugged her into his arms so she could see his very soul. "Don't overthink it, as we both know that your suspicious brain will only tie you in knots again. Trust your gut—you just said yourself that it is never wrong."

He had her there and she knew it. "Grossly unfair, Giles Sinclair."

"Alliteration and rhyme and all off the top of your head." He kissed away the wrinkle between her furrowed brows. "Have I mentioned that I also adore your way with words?"

She offered him a begrudging smile but still couldn't bring herself to say yes. "I hope you don't expect me to ever behave like a duchess. Or behave at all, for that matter. Or curb my opinions or censor my tone. And I will not comply with any orders under any circumstances—even if you are right—because I shall always do what I think is best regardless."

She was looking down her nose defiant, so he kissed it. "All I expect is you, Diana—why on earth would I want to change all the prickly, rebellious things I fell in love with?" He kissed her lips this time and smiled against them. "And I should like it noted that in return you have my solemn pledge to always be insufferable, to vex you, to tease you, distract you, and delight in telling you that I told you so—for as long as we both shall live. How does that sound?"

"Much to my complete disgust, all rather . . . tolerable."

He kissed her properly and she melted against him. "And the long courtship?"

"There will be no more funny business until you have put a ring on my sister-in-law's finger!" Hugh slapped his glove in his palm, intending to be menacing, but it had the opposite effect and they both giggled.

"Unnecessary." Diana's mouth brushed his again as if she

couldn't get enough of it and did not care who saw it. "Especially if we follow Dalton to Gretna Green."

"I like the sound of a clandestine marriage." It felt fitting and right. "We could honeymoon in Scotland. Take a tour of the Highlands . . ."

"We could." She smiled a little sheepishly as she straightened his lapels. "Or we could honeymoon in Bloomsbury. Only I overheard something peculiar at Lady Bulphan's about a magistrate and it's been niggling ever since . . ."

"Does the Sentinel ever sleep?"

They winced at his slip, as five outraged voices screamed in unison.

"Diana is the Sentinel!"

"You had to kick that hornet's nest, didn't you?" She shook her head and glared at him as if he were a half-wit. "And we had just smoothed things over, too."

"In my defense, I am a little overwhelmed. It's not every day a chap becomes engaged to the woman of his dreams."

Her expression softened, and despite all the uproar, wagging fingers, and angry hornets everywhere, he saw the love shining in her clever eyes. "What do you propose we do now, idiot?"

"I haven't a clue, harridan." He sighed then cuddled her close while the others all railed at them from every quarter. "But I do know we are going to need more biscuits."

Acknowledgments

Obviously, the person I owe the most thanks to for this second installment of my Merriwell Sisters trilogy is my husband. You see, I wrote this book during the height of the pandemic, when London was completely locked down for the second time in that drab, cold time between New Year's and spring. It made writing it a rather unique experience as I hardly saw anyone while I worked on it.

As my kids are both adults who have long since flown the Heath coop, the long-suffering Mr. H and I lived in a weird bubble with just our dog Trevor, and the only escape from that was the long nightly walks the three of us took together around a country park near where I live. So it is my husband who had to listen to my daily ramblings about what I had written and where I thought the story was going, and because neither of us had anything better to talk about, *Never Rescue a Rogue* rather took on a life of its own. The main protagonists, Diana Merriwell and Giles Sinclair, became almost like family to us—except they were the only family doing anything exciting—and we would lament their continued resistance to the obvious attraction they had for each other as if they were real people who needed their heads knocking together.

It was, with hindsight and despite the misery of the global pandemic, a unique way of working, as usually I never discuss my plots with anyone. I didn't before this book, and I have lapsed back into the solitary habit of mulling my writing in my head again, so I see *Rogue* as a sort of collaboration even though I rejected absolutely every single one of my non-writing husband's useless, cringeworthy, or downright implausible suggestions! But he helped me see the wood for the trees and made me laugh as we walked the dog, so I shall be forever grateful for that.

I would also like to thank my friend and assistant Amy Fisher, who took it upon herself to help me launch the first book—*Never Fall for Your Fiancée*—into the world and has stuck with me since. She also helps run my Facebook group—Virginia Heath's Headstrong Hellions—and despite the thousands of miles between London and Kansas City, we have constantly laughed, lamented, and put the world to rights over coffee (or in this Brit's case, tea) thanks to the wonder that is video conferencing. You have been a godsend, Amy, and I absolutely adore you!

Obviously, there are so many others who deserve acknowledgment here, too, but special thanks go to my marvelous agent, Kevan Lyon, who always has my back, and Jennie Conway, who edited this book and bought this series for St. Martin's Press. I would also like to thank the Romantic Novelist Association, and most especially my colleagues on the board who are all as passionate about romantic fiction as I am and work tirelessly for that organization, which supports, champions, and nurtures its writers here in the UK.

Finally, I must give a shout-out to my regular writing retreat buddies, as every time we go away to "focus on our craft," I laugh so much I cry. Liam Livings, Lucy Morris, Alison French, and Kelly Stock—thank you for being the best friends, the best support network, and the best tonic a girl could ask for. I love our little escapes and hope they continue to infinity and beyond.

When VIRGINIA HEATH was a little girl, it took her ages to fall asleep, so she made up stories in her head to help pass the time while she was staring at the ceiling. As she got older, the stories became more complicated, sometimes taking weeks to get to the happy ending. Then one day, she decided to embrace the insomnia and start writing them down. Now her Regency rom-coms (including the Wild Warriners and Talk of the Beau Monde series) are published in many languages across the globe. Twenty-four books and three Romantic Novel of the Year Award nominations later, it still takes her forever to fall asleep.